"I thoroughly enjoyed the Christian background an[...]
of this book. It also answers some major questions t[...]
life. I can't wait for the next two books!"

Karina Ragazzo, Age 16

"The Miller brothers have nailed it. This book takes you to wild and magical lands reminiscent of the places where Tolkien and C.S. Lewis wandered in their books. I thoroughly enjoyed reading about the many exotic locations and intriguing characters of Hunter Brown's first adventure, and through it all I found myself examining my own commitment to *the Author* as well. This book makes you question if there is a greater purpose being fulfilled in every happening of your life—all part of the story He is writing for us. Well done! I look forward to more of the Codebearers' adventures to come in this exciting and creative work."

Susan Peterson, Retired Educator

"Hunter Brown makes you think! He is an ordinary high school boy who gets thrown into some high-action adventure. In the middle of all this come profound questions about life and death, good and evil, freedom and allegiance—questions that are worth asking in a story that is worth reading."

Katy Cooley, School Teacher

"When reading this book, I got lost in the story and felt as if I wasn't just reading anymore but was actually there, watching what was happening. The story seemed alive and very exciting. But be warned, it is hard to put down. My mom had to call me 3 times before I could gather up enough willpower to put the book down. Awesome book! I enjoyed it VERY much! I highly recommend it for kids and adults. It has a great message and lots of interesting vocabulary! You should definitely read this book."

Jonathan Carter, Age 12

"This book is a page-turner! This is not my normal choice of genre, but I couldn't put it down! The characters are captivating and the story intriguing. It left me wanting more!"

Amy Wood, Pastor's Wife and Mother of Two

"*Hunter Brown and the Secret of the Shadow* was thrilling. You can't put it down. It's action-packed and a great adventure. I am eager for the next book."

Jessica Hughes, Age 16

"Well done! The Miller brothers are very gifted and conscientious writers. Even though *Hunter Brown and the Secret of the Shadow* is a work of youth fiction, it is based on a well-informed and incisive understanding of the faith. The book offered me not only keen biblical insights, but also a rare reading pleasure I haven't had for years."

Chaplain Major John F. Tillery, Maxwell AFB, AL

"In this book, along with all the pageantry, terror, dragons, evil tyrants, lurking demons, and spellbinding anxiety, is the story of a young man who made bad choices and found redemption. This book is engaging for all ages and creates opportunities for discussion about high moral standards and making good choices."

Arthur Kelly, Christian Education Coordinator

"It is not easy to find a work of fiction aimed at young teens that uses as its theme the importance of good character and courageous choices. *Hunter Brown and the Secret of the Shadow* is a rare find that presents us with colorful, original characters that grow in strength and virtue as they face down a formidable enemy. Fast-paced adventure, vivid settings and suspenseful twists are the background for learning about faith, self-knowledge and the value of friendship. Thank you, Miller Brothers, for fiction that will both entertain and enrich our young people."

Susanne Greenman, Middle School Paraeducator, 17 years

"Hunter Brown is an awesome story! I really liked the plot and how the story was written. It's one of the best books I've read in a long time! Hunter is a cool character and he makes some good decisions. I think Hunter Brown is a book that a lot of kids will like!"

Mary Cooley, Age 11

"Hunter Brown was an awesome book. It had lots of details like mysterious characters and great drawings. They are awesome. I love the picture of the Scrill and lots of other pictures. Www.codebearers.com is the coolest Web site ever. I am a member of Codebearers. I can't wait till I can play lots of games and challenges with my friends. I like everything about *Hunter Brown and the Secret of the Shadow*!!!!!!!!!!!!!!!"

Daniel Fogle, Age 10

Dear Friend,

If you have found this book, please read it with the utmost urgency. It details the sequence of events that led to my unexpected death. What you are about to read is true. But I must warn you, there are forces at work that do not want you to read it. Beware.

H.B.

THE CODEBEARERS SERIES™

HUNTER BROWN

and the Secret of the Shadow

THE MILLER BROTHERS

Warner Press

CONNECT • EQUIP • INSPIRE

Dedicated to

The Author

The Codebearers Series™ I: *Hunter Brown and the Secret of the Shadow*

Published by Warner Press Inc, Anderson, IN 46012
Warner Press and "WP" logo is a trademark of Warner Press, Inc

ISBN-13: 978-1-59317-328-9

Editors: Karen Rhodes, Robin Fogle, Arthur Kelly
Creative Director: Curtis D. Corzine
Layout: Kevin Spear

Library of Congress Cataloging-in-Publication Data

Miller, Christopher, 1976-
    Hunter Brown and the secret of the Shadow / The Miller Brothers [Christopher and Allan Miller]. — 1st ed.
        p. cm. -- (The Codebearers series)
    Summary: When a mysterious book comes into their possession, strange things begin to happen to ninth-graders Hunter, Stretch, and Stubbs, from a strange janitor and a supernatural book to a disappearing bookstore.
    ISBN 978-1-59317-328-9 (pbk.)
    [1. Magic—Fiction. 2. Friendship—Fiction. 3. Space and time—Fiction. 4. Adventure and adventurers—Fiction.] I. Miller, Allan, 1978- II. Title.
    PZ7.M61255Hu 2008
    [Fic]—dc22
                            2008019044

Printed in Canada
2008 – First Edition

www.warnerpress.org

www.codebearers.com
The Codebearers Series™
Lumination Studios

ACKNOWLEDGEMENTS:

The Miller Brothers would like to give thanks for the personal and professional
assistance the following people provided during the writing of this book:
Mom and Dad for being ready to listen, read, and encourage all along the way.
To our secret agents in Hawaii, Alaska and Ocean Shores—you know who you are.
Peon-man and our "favorite aunt Barb" for staying up late on our behalf.
Our super-editors Karen and Robin for making us look good.
Regina, Curt and the rest of the gang at Warner Press
who dared to take a chance on us and have treated us so well.
And Ryan,
thanks for challenging
us to take a closer
look at the Author's
inscription on every
part of our lives
...and may the three of us enjoy watching the ripples of that
conversation grow for years to come.

CHRISTOPHER OFFERS SPECIAL THANKS TO:

Angela, my joy. You endured more evenings alone for the sake of a silly book than
any wife should be expected to (exactly why, I may never know). The love and
support you shared this year is immeasurable—I am forever grateful. To Keegan,
your enthusiasm in seeing Daddy's latest pictures made me smile. And Truitt, who
one day will be old enough to read this book, you are a treasure. Last but not least, to
Allan for following me on this hare-brained idea to write a novel—well done my
"red" friend.

ALLAN OFFERS SPECIAL THANKS TO:

My Sarah—no man could ask for a lovelier wife. Though you might deny it, you have
more to do with the creation of this book than anyone will ever know. Your love,
support, and prayers allowed me to put my heart into it, and in doing so, yours as
well—for my heart is forever yours. My sons T & H—one of my greatest treasures is
getting to share my stories and art with you. I love your excitement, fan art, story
ideas and all the questions. But most of all, I love you. My big brother Chris—dreams
are great, but so much better when they are shared. Keep dreaming big with me...
just give me time to catch up every once in a while.

CONTENTS

CAST OF CHARACTERS

Author (awe-thore) – the mysterious, unseen writer of worlds

Aviad (ah-vee-awd) – a powerful man who is believed to be the son of the Author

Belac (bell-ak) – a swamp troll

Ephriam (ef-ree-am) – a Codebearer captain from the Shard of Abeosis

Evan (eh-vin) – a messenger from beyond the Veil

Faldyn (fal-din) – a suspicious Codebearer captain from the Shard of Perga

Gabby (gab-bee) – an elder member of the Codebearer resistance

Gerwyn (ger-win) – an elder member of the Codebearer resistance

Hope (hope) – a member of the resistance

Hunter (hunt-er) – main character, high school student

Kane (cane) – one of the Gorewings

Leo (lee-oh) – the newest Codebearer captain from the Shard of Tepi

Petrov (pet-rov) – captain from the Shard of Obduront; the current commander of the Codebearers

Rathclaw (wrath-claw) – one of the Gorewings

Samryee (sam-ree) – a Codebearer captain from the Shard of Sinos

Saris (sar-ice) – a narcoleptic Codebearer captain from the Shard of Torpor

Sceleris (s-lair-is) – commander of all evil forces

Strangler (strang-ler) – one of the Gorewings

Stretch (stretch) – one of Hunter's best friends from school

Stubbs (stubs) – another of Hunter's best friends from school

Tyra (tear-ah) – a Codebearer captain from the Shard of Sophmalan, and the only woman captain

Venator (ven-ah-tore) – a skull-masked enemy who haunts Hunter's dreams

Zeeb (zeeb) – a peg-legged goblin who serves as Venator's chief aide

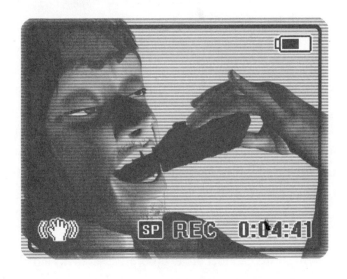

Chapter 1

The Worst Last Day Ever

It was the last day of school and I was running for my life. My friends and I had just pulled off one of the best pranks ever. It's not like we were *trying* to get in trouble, or anything, it's just that we were determined to get even with the school bully before summer break. After all, Cranton had gone out of his way more than once to make my life miserable this year so it wasn't as if he didn't deserve it. Besides, the last day of school was the perfect time for payback.

Stretch and I had planned the whole thing out weeks in advance. We called it *Project: Fireball*, an elaborate scheme that required hijacking a bag of brownies from my sister's bake sale and modifying them with a bottle of *Stu's Unreasonably Wicked Hot Sauce*. All we needed was a decoy. Kitty Swanson, the most popular girl in the whole school, had been Cranton's crush for the entire year and was the perfect candidate. The objective was simple enough: inject the brownies with hot sauce and leave them in a bag on Cranton's "reserved" cafeteria table, along with a note from Kitty in the girliest handwriting we could manage.

Stretch and I watched with anticipation, recording every moment of our latest attempt to humiliate Cranton on my video camera. If everything went as planned we would be posting the footage on our Web site for the whole world to see. It would be the thirteenth and final installment of our online video series. Our subscriber list had grown considerably over the school year as we devised and recorded some of the greatest pranks ever achieved by a student at Destiny Hills High School.

Stubbs, the third member of our enterprise, sat to my left cleaning out his pudding cup with his index finger, completely unaware of the events that were about to unfold. It was better that he didn't know. He was terrified of Cranton and had labeled him an "untouchable" as far as pranks go, and for good reason. Cranton was the self-proclaimed leader of the so-called Cobras, a gang of high school thugs who loved picking on their weaker classmates. Nope, it didn't take a genius to know that Cranton was trouble, but the way we figured, what Stubbs didn't know couldn't hurt him. Adjusting the focus, I held back a smile as Cranton eagerly read the forged note we had planted:

> Cranton,
> I'll miss you this summer.
> Kitty ☺

He looked inside the bag and turned to raise an eyebrow at Kitty, seated at a nearby table. Feeling his uncomfortable gaze over her shoulder she turned to see who it was. Her face contorted in disgust as she quickly looked away.

"Oh man, did you get that on tape?" Stretch half-whispered trying to keep from laughing.

"Yeah, yeah...I got it. That was priceless." I could no longer contain the broad smile that now crept across my face as I anticipated Cranton's next move. Keeping my eye trained on the small LCD screen, I adjusted the zoom so that Cranton's face nearly filled the screen.

"What's going on?" Stubbs asked, suddenly aware of our intense preoccupation. "What are you guys...?"

"Shhh, just watch," Stretch interrupted in a hushed tone, gesturing toward Cranton's table.

At last, the moment had arrived.

Biting into one of the tainted brownies, Cranton's face lit up with a goofy smile. At first he appeared unfazed and even began preparing for a second bite. Then, without warning his confidence faded, his eyebrows lowered and his chewing slowed. There was a brief pause for a moment as the effects of the hot sauce began to kick in. Suddenly, Cranton half-spat, half-puked the searing sweets all over the table and guzzled down the remainder of his soda pop in an attempt to ease the pain, spilling some of it down his face and neck in the process. The students around him erupted in a mixture of confused laughter and disgust.

Cranton's eyes furiously searched the room and met with mine through the viewfinder. His expression hardened and in that moment I realized that somehow he knew. A sudden burst of adrenaline rushed through my veins. It was time to run!

So that's how it started. The three of us were being hunted down like fugitives by Cranton and his gang and since there weren't many new places to hide on school property we had to get... well...creative.

Slipping around the corner of the gym I spotted a dumpster and we quickly dove in, letting the lid shut tightly behind us. Within moments we heard the footsteps of our angry victim and his Cobra crew as they sped past, hollering and cussing as they ran. Our plan had worked for now, or so it seemed. All we had left to do was wait in silence until the school bell announced the end of lunch. By then, we figured it would be too late for Cranton to do anything before school let out for the summer.

"That was close." I panted nervously, trying to catch my breath. "Did you see the look on his face when he realized that those brownies were filled with hot sauce?" I couldn't help but chuckle.

Stretch was the first to respond. "I have to admit it was one of your more brilliant plans and he totally deserved it too after giving me that atomic-wedgie yesterday. It still hurts to sit down in class."

Stretch had been an easy target for Cranton all year. He stood out because of his long lanky legs, freckled face and bright red frizzy hair, but his looks were only half of the problem. Stretch was what you might call a "mathlete" (a nice way of saying math geek), which was okay with me because it was one of the only classes in school I was any good at, thanks to his tutoring. He was also one of the most pliable people I knew. You could get him to go along with just about anything, which was great to have in a friend, but it also made teasing him a pretty easy task.

Stubbs was a different story. I could tell he wasn't pleased.

"You guys are both nuts! You could have gotten us killed." Yup, he was furious. "Do me a favor, next time you decide to prank an untouchable, leave me out."

He had a point. He hadn't asked to be included in our little prank; he was simply guilty by association. Stubbs was nearly a year younger than me and at four-foot-four inches was considerably short for his age too, especially standing next to Stretch. His real name was Clarence but we called him Stubbs because he was the most stubborn person we knew. If you ever suggested an idea that didn't fit within his carefully constructed comfort zone, you could be sure he'd let you know about it and wouldn't change his mind. We often wondered if he was actually allergic to anything that posed a challenge. Even the mere mention of something adventuresome would spark an asthma attack that could only be calmed by his trusty yellow inhaler, which he made sure to carry with him everywhere. Fortunately, his family was pretty well-off and that made hanging out with him a bit more fun.

Five minutes later we heard the school bell ring. Lunch was over and we were going to be late to class if we didn't hurry. Pushing up on the dumpster lid we discovered we were in a heap of trouble. The lid wouldn't budge—it was latched shut. We were stuck.

"You've got to be kidding me." Stubbs wasn't getting any happier. "First you get me in trouble with Cranton, and now I'm locked in a dumpster. Great! Way to go, Hunter." Breathing heavily, he fumbled for his inhaler and took a quick puff of medication before continuing the tirade. "I hope your little prank was worth it."

I tried to keep calm; after all, I was pretty much the unofficial leader of the group. "We're going to get out of here, don't worry. Let's just make as much noise as we possibly can and someone is bound to hear us."

For the next several minutes we pounded on the dumpster and screamed as loud as we could, but it was no use. Our ears were ringing from the racket, but we had not managed to catch anyone's attention. The situation was hopeless.

"Oh man," Stretch whined, "I have to pee! How much longer do you think we'll be in here?"

"If no one finds us we could easily be locked in here for days," Stubbs blurted out.

"Days! I can't be stuck in here that long. I've got a chess match tomorrow; I'm challenging the Grand Master. It's a big deal!"

Stretch was starting to freak out. His eyes darted between Stubbs and me, searching for a little sympathy and finding none. A chess match was the least of our worries at this point.

I had long since given up trying to understand Stretch's fascination with the game. I mean, the guy was obsessed with it. He even carried around a chess piece in his pocket that he called his "lucky knight." It was the piece he'd used to win his first competition. Chess, to me, was boring. He had complained every year that our school district didn't have its own chess club so his parents drove him to the neighboring school district to compete. We had encouraged him to start his own club but he lacked the drive to do anything on his own.

Suddenly it dawned on me. "Wait a minute. Stubbs, do you have your cell phone?" By ninth grade all the lucky kids carried cell phones. Stubbs went beyond lucky. Not only did he have a cell phone, but he had the new Z-Phone, the envy of everyone at school. His parents had given it to him for his fourteenth birthday. The Z-Phone was the hottest device on the market. He could send a text message to someone in class who could bail us out of this mess.

"Oh yeah, I almost forgot." He flipped it open and frantically started to type a message to a classmate. He was just about to send the message when the phone chirped and the screen went blank. "That's funny, the screen won't light up. Oh no!"

"What?" Stretch asked.

"My battery's dead; I must have forgotten to plug it in last night after I finished downloading those new ring tones you told me about."

Stretch and I groaned at the news and the string of bad luck we had just run into. What had we done to deserve this?

The dumpster was considerably dark. Our only light source was coming from a few small holes near the top of the back wall, and what little glow remained from the Albert Einstein face on Stretch's glow-in-the-dark shirt. (The guy had no fashion sense.) We were dirty, stinky and incredibly late for class. Things couldn't have gotten worse. Our teacher, Ms. White, would probably write us up for detention and our parents would find out about the whole thing.

Then, a miracle.

"Hang on, I think I hear someone coming," I said. Sure enough we could hear the crackling of footsteps on gravel not far from where we hid. Banging on the sides of the dumpster we screamed frantically for help. At this point we didn't care if it was Cranton who found us, getting beat up would be far better than our current situation.

Click. Ka-chunk. Creeeeeeek.

My heart thumped faster as the lid began to open. The figure of our rescuer was temporarily silhouetted by a sudden burst of painful daylight.

"What have we here?" The man's voice was deep, raspy and authoritative, the type of guy you didn't say *no* to. Forcing my aching, teary eyes open I squinted to catch a glimpse of the stranger who had just saved us from the city dump. As my eyes adjusted to the light, I met the silvery gaze of one of the toughest looking old guys I had ever seen. His face was tan, weathered and rough, his bright-white hair pulled back into a ponytail. He wore a short scraggly beard and the stern look of a gunslinger who was sizing up his opponent. He was dressed in a dark blue jumpsuit and white T-shirt that barely covered his escaping chest hair. *He must be the janitor on duty,* I thought to myself.

"So now, what are you boys up to?" he inquired, while holding up the dumpster lid with one hand. "Thought you could skip class now, did ya?"

"No sir...we got stuck in here playing hide-n-seek," I lied. He narrowed his eyes and watched us intently as we clambered out of the dumpster and breathed in the fresh air. The janitor raised a brow, "So it wouldn't have anything to do with your little lunchroom fiasco, would it?"

We were busted!

"How did you…?" I started to ask.

"Oh don't be so modest, Hunter. It's all over school. They're calling you...what was it again? Ah yes! Hunter the PrankMaster." For a moment I felt a sense of pride. I was famous, maybe even cool. Then he added, "I'm sure the principal will be equally impressed."

The good feeling was gone.

"Oh!" I said lamely.

"Hey, Hunter, how come you're getting all the credit?" Stretch was feeling left out. "It was my idea too, you know!"

Stubbs was the last to get out, rolling over the edge of the dumpster and toppling to the ground. "Just for the record, I had nothing to do with it. These guys planned everything and drug me into it."

"You're not really going to tell the principal, are you?" Stretch pleaded with the man, who almost smiled in return, enjoying our predicament far too much.

"You know, since it's the last day of school, I might be able to help you out, but I think it's only fair that you do a small favor for me."

"What exactly did you have in mind?" I winced, half expecting the three of us to be scrubbing the boys' bathroom after school.

"Well for starters, the boys' bathroom is a mess and needs to be thoroughly cleaned before they close school for the summer. So, you three can help..." he paused for effect, a hint of a smile crossing his lips, "by running an errand for me this afternoon."

Whew!

Stretch accepted the deal before my better judgment raised a question. "Anything, anything! Just don't tell Principal Pickler!"

The man grinned at the desperation in his voice.

"Good. I won't tell a soul. Listen closely. An important item is on hold at a bookshop downtown," the man said as he scribbled on the back of a business card. "Give the owner this card; he'll be expecting you."

I took the card and examined it quickly. The front was bright white and completely blank except for a curious glossy logo that could only be seen when angled in the light just right. The logo was composed of a symbol that looked something like a *W* in the center of the card, surrounded by a circle. Turning the card over I found the address marked out in large sloppy penmanship.

1421 LATHROP AVE

"If you hurry, you should be able to pick it up and be back here in a half-hour before school is out. Meet me in the boys' bathroom. Got it?"

We nodded in agreement.

It was an odd request to say the least, but with newfound freedom we headed out to retrieve this "item of importance" for our custodial savior. Little did I know this seemingly innocent errand would forever change the course of my life.

We made our way to the address written on the back of the card. The small, used-book store was only a few blocks from school but I had never noticed it before. That was no surprise as I rarely ever read books. A sign in the window advertised *Book Repair Services*, though I couldn't imagine why anyone would want to repair a book. Heaving open the heavy wooden door we were greeted by several mangy cats and the smell of old books and garlic.

"Pewww!" Stretch winced. "It smells worse than the dumpster in here."

Five wooden shelves ran the length of the floor, slightly askew from the aging floorboards that gave the room a crooked feeling. The aisles between the shelves were narrow, uncluttered and drew our eyes to the far back of the bookshop, where an oversized oak counter sat unoccupied. The front of the counter was scattered with flyers advertising local events that had long since passed, and an antique cash register that only a select few would still have been able to operate. A silver bell was conveniently placed near the edge of the counter with a handwritten note taped to it that read, *Ring for Service*.

Ding. Ding. Ding. We rang the bell.

"I'll be right with you," a small voice called out from behind the counter. An odd-looking man with short legs, wispy hair and magnified spectacles on an oversized nose shuffled out with a pile of books stacked much too high. "Just finishing inventory. These books don't take care of themselves you know. Whoa!" A black cat ran out from behind the counter with a yowl as the ancient store owner tumbled to the ground, sending the once neatly sorted pile of books flying in every direction.

"Oh bother," he sighed as he lifted himself from the floor. "I suppose I'll have to start all over now, won't I?" Book by book he restacked the pile as we waited. When the last book was gathered, he turned to a clipboard and began humming and flipping casually through the sheets of paper that were attached to it. A full minute passed before I began to wonder if he had forgotten about us altogether.

"Ah hem!" I cleared my throat in an effort to catch his attention.

"Yes, how can I help you gentlemen?" he simply replied without even looking up from his work.

"We were told to give you this." I passed the card across the counter, capturing his full attention at last. "There's something here we're supposed to pick up."

"Well now, let's see what we have here." He turned the card over in his hands and then looked back at us, squinting down over the counter through his magnified spectacles as if examining a bug. "This was all you were given?" the man asked, though I wasn't entirely sure it was really a question.

"Yes," I replied. "The man who gave it to us said you would be expecting us."

The man's face brightened. "Indeed I was, and you're precisely on time too," he said, pointing to a strange grandfather clock-like contraption that was unlike anything I had ever seen. A series of abstract symbols circled its face and a single arm moved quickly to the second symbol from the top.

"Just one moment then—I know *exactly* what you need." He disappeared again behind the oak desk, leaving us alone for the moment.

"Don't look now," Stubbs whispered, "but I think we're being surrounded." Turning around we found ourselves encircled by nearly twenty cats, eyeing us with uncanny intelligence.

"This place gives me the creeps," Stubbs shuddered, "and I'm... *achoo!*" he sneezed forcefully, "allergic to cats. Let's get out of here."

"Let's just finish our errand and get back before..." the book keeper popped back up before I could finish.

"Here it is," he said presenting what appeared to be a large book wrapped tightly in cloth and tied shut with twine. "The invoice shows it's paid in full, so unless you need anything else..."

"No!" I answered abruptly, hoisting the heavy book off the counter. "We'll just let ourselves out." With that I turned to go.

"Wait!" the man hollered. "You'll need this as well." His age-worn hand held a golden key that was meant to accompany the package. "Keep it with you at all times. Leaving it could lead to grave consequences, I'm afraid." Without thinking, I snatched the key from his grip and buried it in my coat pocket, much to the dismay of the old man. "You're welcome." And with that he disappeared into the back room for the last time.

"Oh…uh, thanks," I called back awkwardly, now keenly aware of how rude I had been.

Clutching the book beneath my arm I tiptoed around the cats and out the front door with Stretch and Stubbs. Now all we had to do was get the book to the janitor before school was out and we would be home free for the summer.

Back at school we headed straight for the boys' bathroom where we were to meet the janitor, but there was no sign of him. Judging from the smell of things it hadn't been cleaned either.

Leaving the bathroom, we set out in search of the janitor and were just about to give up when we rounded a corner and plowed straight into Principal Pickler. Teetering on her high heels, the startled principal toppled to the ground amidst a snowfall of office paper.

"What are you three doing out of class?" she fumed.

"We were running an errand across town to..." I started to answer but didn't get far.

"Stop right there!" Pickler cut me off, raising her hand sternly. "What did you just say? Leaving the premises during school hours is strictly prohibited for students!" she scolded as she gathered her papers together. "Who sent you?"

I tried to explain. "The janitor sent us to get this; he said it was important!" I handed her the package, which she unwrapped to reveal an antique book with a latch and keyhole. It must have been unlocked because it opened easily and she flipped through the pages quickly. From where I stood I could tell that every page in the book was blank, an empty journal—there was nothing of importance in it at all.

Pickler was getting annoyed. "Hogwash! Our janitor is gone today...he phoned in sick last night. Besides, even if he were here, he would most certainly not be authorized to give kids permission to wander off school property. You're going to have to come with me."

Seated quietly outside Pickler's office we waited for the verdict while she discussed the situation with our teacher.

"I hope you're proud of yourself, Hunter," griped Stubbs. "Do you even realize that I had a perfect attendance record until today? Now I might as well have a big black *Tardy* written on my forehead for the rest of my life!"

"Do they really keep track of stuff like that?" Stretch wondered aloud.

"Oh yeah," Stubbs insisted, "the office records everything. I doubt I'll even make it into a good college. I'll probably end up living in a van."

I tried to calm him down. "Hey, it's not my fault. Besides, once they realize we're telling the truth your record will be cleared, trust me."

Stubbs disagreed, "You expect them to believe us? They probably think we're lying about all of this. As far as they're concerned we're just ninth-grade losers who tried to skip class on the last day of school and got busted."

He was right, of course, they wouldn't believe us. It didn't help that the janitor had mysteriously disappeared, our description of him didn't match any other member on staff, and what was worse, we didn't even know his name. We had nothing.

Ms. White and Ms. Pickler came out of the office. "As unlikely as your story is, we have to take it seriously. Frankly, we're concerned about a person posing as school custodian, wandering around our facilities. Did anyone else see this man?"

My mind was racing. "The invoice!" I shouted, leaping from my chair and surprising myself in the process. "The bookstore owner said the package was paid in full. If we go back and explain the situation maybe we could look at the invoice and find the janitor's name." At the very least I figured the owner could vouch for us being there this afternoon, to prove we hadn't lied about where we went.

My enthusiasm must have worked because somehow we managed to convince Pickler to follow us to the bookstore. That's when things took a very weird turn. The shop was gone. Disappeared. Vanished into thin air. It was as if someone had taken the stores on either side of it and pinched them together over the top of where the bookstore once was.

No bookshop. No book keeper. No invoice.

"No way," Stubbs was in shock, "we were just here! I swear! The bookstore was right there between the TV repair shop and…and the hardware store. I promise."

Ms. Pickler came unglued. "Oh I get it. This is another one of your pranks, isn't it, Hunter?"

"No, ma'am, I…" the question was apparently rhetorical as she showed no intention of listening to my plea of innocence.

"I can't believe I trusted you guys. This is the lamest excuse for an excuse I have ever heard." I tried to cut in, but she was just getting warmed up. "Well, you've clearly wasted my time and now I'm going to waste yours. Congratulations, boys. You've just earned yourselves detention! When we get back, I'm calling your parents and you're going to spend the rest of your afternoon cleaning the boys' bathrooms!"

The summer was off to a terrible start.

CHAPTER 2

THE BOOK IS OPENED

Grounded! A weekend is a long time to be alone with your thoughts, especially when you don't deserve to be grounded in the first place. No one believed me and I really couldn't blame them. To be honest, I was beginning to doubt it myself. Sitting alone in my room I replayed the events of the day that had led to my unfortunate punishment.

If only we hadn't gone on that stupid errand! I stewed. *I'd be going out with my friends this weekend instead of being cooped up here.*

The bedroom door shot open; it was my sister Emily. "Hunter," she growled from the doorway, "Mom said to clean up your room and put this away while you're at it." She dropped my backpack on the floor with an unexpectedly loud *THUD!* "What do you carry in that thing anyway…bricks?" She shot a disgusted look my way and waltzed down the hall to her room.

Walking over to my bag, I was amazed to find the ancient book squeezed tightly inside. "How did that get there?" I wondered aloud. I didn't remember Stretch or Stubbs sneaking it back from Pickler after she had confiscated it. Maybe she had given it to Mom when they had their little meeting after school.

I pulled the book out of the bag. It was heavier then I remembered. "What on earth is so important about an empty book anyway?" I wondered, placing it on my desk. For the first time I examined it up close. The book was bound in soft brown leather and engraved with intricate markings etched in gold. The corners of the book were rounded and well-worn, bearing the evidence of age. Centered on the top third of the cover was a strange symbol that looked identical to the glossy logo on the card the janitor had given me. Although now seeing it in raised-gold, I could tell it was not a *W*, as I had thought before, but more like three intersecting *Vs* surrounded by a circle.

I tried to open the book but was disappointed to find that the latch wouldn't release. "Must have locked when Pickler closed it," I mumbled to myself.

Flipping the book over on my desk I was fascinated to find the intricate markings continued to the back as well. On the back was a series of consecutively nested circles. A gold medallion embossed with the image of a tree was the centerpiece of the design. Embedded in the trunk of the tree was a red gemstone that commanded my attention. As I gazed at the peculiar stone an amazing thing began to happen around the outermost ring. A dozen symbols began to etch themselves into the cover of the book, perfectly positioned around the medallion like the numbers of a clock.

How in the world? I thought.

With nervous hands I ran my fingertips over the embossed grooves of the symbols, proving they were indeed as real as they looked. It wasn't clear what they were supposed to represent, a foreign language or some kind of code perhaps.

Only a single mark appeared in the inner circle, a simple arrow pointing outward from the medallion a quarter of the way between the first and second symbols. Before I had time to inspect them further the characters sank back into the cover, fading from sight. Clearly, this was no ordinary book.

"Magic?" I whispered in wonder.

Growing up, I had always wanted to be a magician. For my tenth birthday Dad had even bought me a *Magic for Beginners* kit with *32 tricks to stun and amaze your friends*. I learned to master most of them, but they were cheap gimmicks in comparison with what I was now seeing. No, this was something much more—this was *real* magic.

Now nothing mattered to me more than finding out what was inside the mysterious, locked book. If there was magic to be learned I wanted to know it. I suddenly remembered the key the book keeper had given me—still tucked away safely in my jacket pocket. Kicking through the huge pile of clothes on my floor, I tried to recall where I had placed it. Eventually, I unearthed the lost jacket and retrieved the key. It was cold and also bore the inscription of three interlocking *Vs* on its handle, an obvious connection to the mysterious symbol on the front of the book.

Placing the key in the latch, I felt a sharp tug as it pulled itself into place. *Twing*. I released my hold. A harmonic hum began to reverberate throughout the room and seemed to be originating from the key. Gathering my courage I took hold of it once more. This time the shaft and handle felt warm to the touch as I slowly turned the key. *Click*.

The markings on the cover instantly glowed to life, as golden light streamed through the channels and engravings of the book. The latch fell open on its own and I stepped back in surprise.

With trembling hands I stood, my eyes transfixed on the amazing book. Then a most dreadful, yet oddly familiar voice whispered over my shoulder, *"Do not open it!"* I turned around; there was no one there. *"Destroy the book,"* came the voice yet again from behind my back.

"Who said that!" I demanded. There was no answer. The drone from the key grew steadily louder, pulsating through my chest and calming my fears. The tone was like that of a distant choir and caused me to turn once more to look at the book.

"Stay away," the voice whispered again. This time I recognized the voice as my own, except colder and divided as if there were more than one of me speaking at a time. I shuddered. I didn't particularly like being told what to do, even if it was by my own voice.

"I can't destroy it," I reasoned out loud. "This book could be valuable, maybe even worth millions. Besides, I haven't even looked inside yet." I took a step toward my desk, then another. The closer I got, the more I longed to know what was hidden inside the book. Finally, I was close enough to touch it. Taking hold of the cover I lifted it open.

An explosion of light burst from the pages and lit up the room as if someone had just drawn open the curtains. I shaded my face from the brilliant pages and waited for my eyes to adjust. When I could see once more I discovered words slowly appearing on the pages, as if they had been written with invisible ink and were reappearing for the first time.

So it wasn't an empty book after all, I thought. I read the text. It began:

Born into darkness,
deceived by the Lie,
a door has been opened,
through which you must die.
The world you now know
will soon be no more.
Your fading is certain;
your death will be sure.

The riddle was strange, to say the least, but there was something about it that seemed as if it was written directly to me.

Your fading is certain;
your death will be sure.

The final line made me uneasy. Invisible cold eyes seemed to be staring over my shoulder. I had the growing feeling that I was being watched and turned around to ensure the room was empty. Satisfied that I was still alone, I turned to the next page and began to read a fascinating story about a legendary Author and his mysterious book.

In the time before times, the Author put his pen upon the pages of a book. The ancient words he wrote outside of time became the manuscript of a story unimaginably complex and complete. This story was the Author's greatest achievement and he was pleased. Then as the last stroke of the last word on the last page was written, something extraordinary happened. The words the Author had so beautifully crafted came to life in a wonderful way, made possible only by the greatest of powers, used in the most perfect of ways. It was the first story.

In the center of the world was a beautiful garden where there stood a special tree that was older than the story itself. How it came to grow in the garden of this world, no one knew for sure. Unlike other trees, it did not draw its life from the earth; but rather, this tree was the source of life to the world in which it existed.

A sacred stone was set into the trunk of the tree that contained the Author's secrets, coveted by all who lived there. The stone also carried with it the power to change the fate of the world forever.

For this reason the stone was not to be touched except by the Author alone, for the power that flowed from it was far too deadly for any written being to withstand. Only the Author himself could bear to hold such knowledge.

The story continued, but I paused as something caught my eye. The text appeared to be written by hand, and yet there was something completely unnatural about it. Looking closely I discovered a most amazing thing—I could see through the words. As if looking through tiny windowpanes into another world, I could see beyond the book into another place. Instinctively, I placed my hand on the text to find out how it was accomplished. As my fingers brushed the text, the book took hold of my hand like a magnet, pulling my palm firmly against the page. A surge of warmth raced up my arm and my body went numb. I was unable to move and watched helplessly as the room began to spin around me. The effect was subtle at first, starting slowly but with ever-increasing speed, until at last the bedroom disappeared in a stunning blur of light.

Moments later the light faded and the spinning subsided, leaving me in a bewildered state of dizziness. When at last I gathered my senses, I found myself in the midst of a beautiful world. A rich and fragrant garden aroma filled the air, and I took in a long deep breath that satisfied me in a way I had never felt before. I was unable to move on my own, floating in the air like a ghostly spectator watching a story unfold all around me.

The garden was full of lush plants and trees that were much larger than any I had ever seen. I was heading toward a giant tree standing in the center of a grove of smaller ones. Golden branches burst from the thick trunk. They were covered with iridescent leaves that sparkled like gems. Veins of light, much like those on the book, flowed downward from the tree's limbs into the ground, bringing energy and life to the world around them. But what commanded my attention most of all was a large scarlet stone embedded in the base of the tree. The stone seemed to be alive with a glowing red energy that swirled like fluid. I wanted desperately to touch it.

No sooner had the thought crossed my mind, than a brilliant being stepped out from behind the tree. The figure was beautiful beyond description, draped in a white robe and bathed in light, though its face remained hidden beneath a cloaked hood. The radiant being raised a hand toward me and beckoned me to come touch the stone. Before I could respond, a sharp chill shot through my chest as a second figure, robed in black, emerged from behind me, passing through my body as if I was only a ghost. The very idea of having been passed through caused my stomach to turn. I felt as if someone had robbed me of my personal space and walked away with it. Trying to escape the feeling, I turned my attention back to the tree.

From what I could tell, the figure that had just emerged was only a boy, not much older than me. He obeyed the spirit's command with a slow steady pace, confidently approaching the one who had summoned him. The boy paused for a moment as he arrived at the base of the tree. The brilliant being pointed to the stone once more, reassuring the boy of his calling. Then with purposeful resolve the boy stepped forward and pried the gemstone from its place.

Immediately the radiance of the shining figure dimmed, revealing a pair of villainous eyes that had once been concealed by its deceptive light. With a menacing laugh, the now darkened being vanished altogether—its purpose fulfilled.

The boy thief was left alone, holding the treasured stone in his hands. Warm and inviting at first, something went terribly wrong. A black cloud began to form within the gemstone, swirling around like trapped smoke. The red glow grew suddenly brighter and hotter in the hands of the boy. The thief's confidence faded and he tried desperately to throw the stone away, but could not—the stone had scorched itself into his hand. Falling to his knees he let out a tortured scream that echoed through the sky. He held the stone at a distance, shielding his face from the light with his free arm, in hopes of protecting himself from the intensity of its power. Unfortunately, his suffering had only just begun.

As the stone smoldered in the grip of the thief, I noticed the world around me begin to change. Storm clouds gathered overhead with unnatural speed. I looked to the tree as a single leaf began to melt, dripping off its limb, creating an inky puddle below. A black plague spread through the branches and soon the entire tree was stained with ugliness. Sinking down into the earth, the vile poison saturated the land. Everything began to die and take on wretched form.

Unable to turn my gaze from the horrible fate the boy was suffering, I watched as a phantom serpent emerged from the stone. Its eyes burned hot as fire but its scarlet body was ghostly and transparent. In addition to fangs, three horns curled forward from its head, two on either side of its jaws and one on top. The serpent coiled itself around the boy's arm, searing a trail of red markings as it went. As it wound its way to the boy's neck, the snake opened its jaws and sank its fangs into his skin, releasing poison into his blood.

With a loud crack the stone severed in two, and in a sudden flash of light, the serpent was gone. The ground began to rumble and shake. The boy in black, released from his torment, struggled weakly to stand up amidst the tremors. Still clutching the two pieces of stone tightly in his hand, he turned toward me and my heart began to pound with fear. Though his face was still shielded behind one arm, I could see his eyes. They were black, hollow and hauntingly evil.

Abandoned by the deceitful spirit, the boy ran quickly away from the once magnificent tree, back down the path and disappeared through my chest. I wanted to turn and chase him but the book had other plans—pulling me upward into the sky as if some invisible force had snatched me by my stomach and carried me away.

Faster and faster I went. I couldn't tell if I was rising or falling, my skull throbbing from the force. My stomach turned, I wanted to heave, but my body remained numb and unresponsive. A stunning display of pink lightning flashed around me as I spun through a tunnel of inky darkness. I must have been moving at an incredible rate, but the wind in my face was surprisingly soft and warm. My limbs flailed helplessly, suspended in the void, and the terrible thought occurred to me that I had no control over anything.

As quickly as I had been pulled away, I found myself tossed onto the floor of a new place. Slowly, I stood and pulled myself together.

"That's a relief," I muttered, grateful to find I could once again move on my own.

Glancing around, I was surprised to find myself in the halls of my own school. *Was I back home?* Perhaps, but something was wrong. Everything was dark except a light shining from behind the door of the principal's office, which swung open as I approached. Inside, Pickler sat in her executive chair reading my report card.

"Hello, Hunter," she lowered the card to greet me. Her eyes were as black as night, just like the boy's eyes in the garden.

I shuddered. Stepping back, I collided with Stubbs and Stretch, blocking my exit. They too had darkened eyes.

"Hey guys, uh, what's going on?" I asked nervously.

They didn't answer, staring back in silence, arms crossed, daring me to try and get past them.

"Leaving so soon?" Pickler mocked. She stood and took me firmly by the ear. "Your detention has only begun!"

"Ouch!" My ear began to throb under the pressure of her nails. "Detention?" I questioned. "What do you…?"

A loud rumble, like that of an earthquake, began to rattle the room. With a sudden gust of wind the roof of the building was torn completely off, exposing us to a horrific storm that was raging outside. Debris and paper blew everywhere. Pickler tightened her grip on my ear and yanked me down to the ground. Outside, the sky was heavy with clouds, spinning out of control from hurricane-force winds.

Blackness enveloped the room as if something or someone were overshadowing us. Looking up, I saw what I thought I'd never see again—the flaming eyes of the phantom snake from the stone. The creature had grown considerably since the last time I'd seen it—a hundred times larger, easily twice the size of the school. The serpent lowered its ghostly red head to our room and opened its jaws to reveal a jagged row of massive fangs and a forked tongue.

Pickler released me and looked up in sheer terror as the snake lunged downward, gripping her in its mouth and swallowing her whole with one terrible bite.

"Oh!" I groaned in disgust at the sight. As much as I disliked Pickler, this was no way for her to die. I turned to the guys.

"We need to get out of here…now!" I shouted over the humming wind and storm above.

"No, Hunter!" Stubbs frowned. "We can't! This is how it ends!" With that he too was quickly swallowed up by the serpent. Now I was left alone with Stretch, who was sobbing uncontrollably.

"C'mon, Stretch!" I yelled, dashing out from under the desk and through the door, expecting him to follow. He didn't budge as I passed him. Once I was safely in the hallway, I turned to call him one last time.

Stretch just stared back at me with his hollow eyes and called out, "Good-bye, Hunter!" Then he disappeared into the monster's mouth.

Tears welled up in my eyes. I raced through the school to the front doors and shot down the steps as fast as my legs could carry me. All I could think about now was getting home. As I ran through town I noticed everyone had the same black eyes and hollow gaze.

The phantom serpent's burning gaze followed me as I turned down Main Street and headed for my house. With a hiss of satisfaction, the serpent wove its way across town, gaining on me quickly and swallowing up anyone unfortunate enough to fall in its path. Somehow I managed to make it home, arriving just in time to see my mother and sister dart inside the house.

"Mom! Mom!" I yelled out, knowing she couldn't hear me over the noise of the storm raging overhead. I bounded over to the door, which was securely locked. Try as I might I could not get their attention. I was just about to give up when the door cracked open, stopped only by the chain lock.

I could hear my sister's voice, "Hunter...Hunter...is that you?"

"Yes, let me in, quick." I glanced over my shoulder and saw the monster bearing down on me. "Hurry, Emily, there's no time!"

Emily shut the door and fumbled with the chain but it was already too late. The dreaded scarlet snake rose up behind me and the last thing I saw before it swallowed me up was my sister's face, her eyes black and hollow, her jaw dropped open in disbelief.

"Hunter, Hunter..." her piercing voice echoed through the darkness.

I awoke with a start, seated at my desk, my face planted in a puddle of saliva beside the book.

"Hunter, wake up! What do you think you're doing?" My sister had barged into my room. My heart was still racing with fear, my brow sweaty and cold. The book was open but the pages had turned to the end of the book and were once again empty.

"I don't know. I...I must have fallen asleep," I sighed, relieved it had been only a dream. My left ear was not as convinced; it was still throbbing as if Principal Pickler had actually pinched it. Sitting up, I wiped a string of drool off my face and looked up at my sister.

"Nice, Hunter," she scolded. "You were supposed to clean this place up an hour ago. Come down for dinner! Mom's going to be upset."

Emily quickly spun around and headed downstairs. Getting up to follow, I realized the golden key was clutched tightly in my hand. Tucking the key away in my desk drawer, I closed the book and headed downstairs.

Dinner was always a bit of a fiasco in my family. Ever since Dad had left, Mom had started making an effort to have dinner together as a family. That might have been a good idea, but Mom really didn't know how to cook. She tried her best but we were often dining on over-cooked meat and under-cooked rolls. Tonight was the rare exception—Mom had ordered pizza. I would have preferred to choke down Mom's home cooking if it meant not having to listen to a half-hour of my sister's conversation.

Emily was perfect at everything; she was top of her class, captain of the soccer team and even managed to teach swim lessons twice a week. Having a perfect sister was a drag, it made me look...well... pathetic. For starters, I couldn't remember the last time I achieved any grade above a C; when it came to sports, I was a certified klutz and I had never learned how to swim. The only thing we shared in common now was our last name.

"So, how was your last day of school, Emily?" Mom started the usual small talk.

"Great. Mr. Schmidt gave me a brochure about a program at the college I could apply for. He thought I might want to take a few advanced classes over the summer," she touted in a cheery tone reserved for her friends and for Mom.

Mom was pleased. "That's a great idea; what classes?"

"I'm not sure yet; I was considering..." the conversation droned on, but my mind drifted back to the book and the vision. If what I saw was only a dream, it was the most vivid dream I ever had. Every detail was still fresh in my mind as if it actually happened. My attention rushed back to the dinner table when I heard my name.

"So, Hunter, I heard you got in trouble at school again." My sister was teasing me in her own subtle way. "What did you do this time?"

"I'd rather not talk about it," I muttered, stuffing my face with another slice of pizza. I let the grease from the cheese drip down my chin just to gross her out.

"Ewww, you're such a dweeb!" She held her napkin to her mouth as if she was going to vomit.

"Hunter, stop bugging your sister," Mom scolded. "Oh wait, that reminds me, Em…" She redirected the conversation. "I'm going to need you to stay home with Hunter tonight while I head over to Grandma's for a bit. She's not feeling well."

"But Mom, I was going to Jessie's house for movie night, remember?"

"Oh that's right." She looked over at me as if I was an inconvenience yet again. "Hunter, do you think you can manage to keep out of trouble for one night while I visit Grandma for a few hours?"

"Yeah, Mom, I'll be fine."

"Remember, you're still grounded. No video games, no Internet and definitely no friends over," she reminded me.

"Okay, okay, I know."

"Fine then, clean up the dishes and go upstairs and read a book or something. I'll be back in a few hours."

I cleared the table and headed back to my room. The book seemed to stare at me from the top of my desk, daring me to open it once more. I tried my best to ignore it.

I had the house to myself; so, despite my mother's wishes I took the liberty to play a few video games on the Internet. After all, it's not like I *deserved* to be grounded.

An hour later I decided to take a shower and get ready for bed. Maybe a little sleep would do me good. When the hot water ran out I dried off and brushed my teeth. Raising my arm to the mirror I wiped the steam away, expecting to see the usual bushy blond hair and oversized ears that reminded me of my father. What I saw instead made my stomach lurch and the blood drain from my face in horror. Something was wrong with my reflection.

My own face glared back at me, but my eyes were inky black and my lips were curved in a wickedly satisfied smile. I lost my breath; my chest felt heavy, as if a great stone was pressing against it. Something moved from behind me. I turned but no one was there.

Out of the silence I heard a whisper. *Find him...*

Nearly tripping over the bathroom scale, I spun around once more expecting to find the intruder, but the room was empty. I ran out of the bathroom, away from the mirror and my own haunting reflection. I kept telling myself it was all in my head, but I could do nothing to calm my nerves.

I tried my best to fall asleep but every time I closed my eyes, I saw visions of my darkened face—the emptiness was unforgettable. It consumed my mind, but try as I might, I could not prevent the visions from captivating my every thought.

Then it hit me. Maybe there was more to the story in the book. If there was, I didn't want to read it alone. I needed a witness, someone who could confirm what I saw.

Without thinking, I grabbed the book and tossed it into my bag. Being grounded would have to wait for another day; right now I needed to meet with the guys to prove to myself that I wasn't going insane.

I logged on to the computer and fired off a text message to Stubbs's cell that read:

```
MEET @ 12B
BOOK IS MAGIC
BRING STRETCH
```

Against Mom's orders, I slipped out of the house, grabbed my skateboard and tore off as fast as I could. I was so focused on getting to the studio I didn't even notice I was being followed.

CHAPTER 3

THE MESSENGER

The city of Destiny was a small metropolis. The downtown district was nestled along the waterfront and boasted a few buildings that were too small to be called skyscrapers, but big enough to feel important. We lived on the outskirts of the city in an area known as Destiny Hills. We had lots of rain in the winter, but in the summer it was the perfect place to live, well…almost. Our neighborhood wasn't what you would call the safest, but with only one parent to pay the rent, our house was all Mom could afford.

The street lamps over King Street were dimly lit, flickering a sickening hue of orange over the road. Skating six blocks down and two blocks over to McKinley Avenue, I crossed the intersection and slipped into the alleyway behind Skeeter's Bar and Grill. Uncle Jim owned the building and the restaurant. During spring break he had allowed us to renovate the vacant apartment above the restaurant into a make-shift video production studio.

I liked Uncle Jim. Ever since my father left us, my uncle had made a considerable effort to get to know my friends and me better. Of course, his interest was most likely Mom's doing. She had started worrying about the lack of a father figure in my life and shortly thereafter, Uncle Jim and I had met and struck an agreement. I could use apartment 12B as a video studio, if we promised to paint the apartment over the summer and run some errands for him now and then. I was excited about the offer, especially since he included some used video equipment in the deal, and Mom was relieved that I was staying out of trouble. That's how Studio12B was born.

When I arrived at the alley entrance the lights were already on upstairs. I hid my skateboard behind a stack of empty boxes and leaped up the staircase, skipping every other step. The door was securely locked as expected. My knocking four times, pausing for two beats then knocking twice more prompted a voice from inside to ask a question.

"What's the password?" Stretch tried his best to make his voice sound deep and mysterious but I detected a hint of a smile.

"Snakeheads," I said boldly, a subtle stab at Cranton's gang.

"No, that was last week," came the reply with a chuckle.

"Oh right, I forgot!"

Every Friday we changed the password, a scheme we had developed on the off-chance that someone we didn't know might try to gain access to the studio. Of course, no one had ever been interested in breaking into our place, but somehow just having a secret password that changed every week seemed cool, so we adopted the policy and did our best to enforce it.

"Let's see." I paused for a while. We had talked about the new password only yesterday but at the moment I couldn't remember it. Last week was *S* and this week would be something that started with *T*. "Tomahawk?" I half asked, half said.

"No that was Stubbs's idea." Stretch was enjoying this. "We decided on using mine instead."

"You mean *you* decided," Stubbs groaned from behind the door, still bitter about having his password rejected once again. We were already twenty letters into the alphabet and he had only named three passwords to-date.

"C'mon guys, it's me, Hunter; just let me in already."

"Hey, rules are rules. You gotta know the password or you can't get in." They were taking this *way* too seriously.

"Fine!" This was frustrating. "Uh, Titanic... Twinkies... No wait... Time warp! That's it, time warp!" With the correct answer the door swung open at last, granting me access to my own studio and the meeting I had invited them to.

Stubbs looked up as I entered and set my backpack down in the chair beside him. He looked a bit put-out at having been called to our studio so late. It was only ten-thirty, but Stubbs was an "early-to-bed" kind of guy and this wasn't fitting into his plan.

"So what's going on? How do you know the book is magic?" He cut right to the point.

Feeling safer in the apartment, I recapped everything that had happened that evening. Stretch and Stubbs leaned forward with interest as I told them of the glowing book, the mysterious symbols, the humming key and the strange voices. Their eyes widened when I told them how I entered the book—about the garden, the tree and the boy. I explained that I had seen them as well, with darkened faces, being consumed by a monstrous snake. They looked understandably frightened, but when I told them about the bathroom mirror incident, their jaws dropped to the floor.

"Okay, I'm officially freaked out now," Stretch was worried. "What are we going to do? I don't want to be snake chow."

Stubbs wasn't easily convinced, "Oh come on! Are you suggesting the book is predicting some bizarre future where we all turn into black-eyed zombies and get eaten? 'Cause if you think I'm going to fall for that then you're crazy."

"I don't know what to think, Stubbs, I'm just telling you exactly what I saw."

"Still that doesn't mean what you saw will actually come true, does it?"

"Well no, I guess not." It hadn't occurred to me that the guys would question what I had seen.

"And you said yourself you thought it was a dream, right?" Stubbs was really starting to annoy me.

"Then how do you explain what happened to my reflection in the mirror, or how the bookshop vanished earlier today?" I challenged. "There's something strange going on here and you know it!"

He opened his mouth as if to speak, then stopped. I was right and he knew it. This was no dream.

Stubbs tried to reason, "Okay, what we know for a fact is that this book has caused us nothing but trouble ever since we got it, right?"

"You can say that again," Stretch pointed out, "I haven't had such a weird day in my life."

"So, maybe the book is cursed," Stubbs offered enthusiastically.

"I don't believe in curses," I said.

"Oh yeah? I saw this documentary on TV once where some kids found a cursed idol and it kept haunting them and ruining their lives until they burned it." He seemed pleased with his reasoning and concluded with confidence, "I think we should destroy the book."

"Destroy the book?" I burst out. "Aren't you curious about what gives the book its power? If we get rid of it, we'll never know what this was all about." I looked up at the guys again; they were listening. "Have you ever considered that maybe we're *supposed* to have the book? That maybe it's trying to warn us of something?"

"So, what are you suggesting we do?" Stubbs snapped.

As crazy as I sounded to myself, I needed my friends to see for themselves what was in the book. "I think we should read it together and see if we can find out where the book came from."

"Oh no! Are you nuts?" Stubbs breathed in through his inhaler. "That is the worst idea you've had yet. The last thing I want is to end up like you. You can't even look at yourself in the mirror anymore."

He was right, I was afraid of my own reflection. Gazing into the mirror earlier this evening had revealed something evil hidden in me.

"Here." Stubbs tossed me a hand mirror we had kept in the apartment for writing secret messages. The idea was to write our messages backwards and decipher them by reading them in the mirror. I had learned this clever trick while writing a research paper on Leonardo DaVinci earlier that year. Now, with mirror in hand, I began to tremble at what secrets it might reveal about me.

"Well, what are you waiting for? Go ahead, look at it!" Stretch's voice wavered in anticipation. My hand shook as I held the mirror up to my face, eyes tightly shut. "What do you see?" he gulped.

I slowly opened one eye, then another. The blackness wasn't there—it had disappeared.

"It's gone...I mean, my reflection is normal again. I don't understand. I saw the blackness in the mirror only an hour ago." Nothing was making sense anymore.

"Maybe you imagined…" Stretch started.

"I didn't imagine anything, okay?" I was starting to lose my patience.

"Guys, arguing won't get us anywhere," Stubbs tried to calm things down. "One thing seems clear, the longer we stay away from that book, the more normal everything seems to be."

Stubbs was right. The book had already caused problems at school, at home, and now my own friends were at odds. The silly thing was, I didn't even like books. I'd rather wait for a movie to come out any day than spend my time reading. But this book was different; it was real and it had something to do with me. My own fear of the book seemed to keep me connected to it. I couldn't shake the feeling that there was something more to be learned and I was determined to find out what it was.

"Can't you guys just trust me on this?" I was starting to lose faith in my own friends.

Stubbs was calm for the first time this evening. "It's not that I don't trust you, Hunter. I believe you; every bit of it. What I don't trust is that book."

"So what are you saying?" I asked.

"I'm saying you can do what you want, but I'm going home. I'm in enough trouble as it is, and the last thing I need right now is to get involved in another situation with that cursed book." Without further discussion, Stubbs gathered his things and walked out the door. We stood there, watching him ride off on his bike into the night.

"Well, it looks like it's just you and me again, Stretch." I didn't give him time to consider his options. He was more likely to go along that way. "Grab that blank tape over there, will you?"

"What for?" Stretch questioned.

"To record what happens. We'll need proof we're not crazy when we come back."

"Come back?" Stretch's voice wobbled a bit as he handed me the video tape. I loaded it into the camera. "Back from where?"

"From...uh..." I stumbled for words. I didn't know what to say. Then a deep voice from the studio doorway answered for me.

"From beyond the Veil..." Turning in surprise, I saw a tall figure enter the room. We had forgotten to close and lock the door. As the figure stepped forward, we instantly recognized him as the "janitor" from school. Now he was dressed strangely, in a dark grey hooded cloak that added to the mystery of his presence.

"What are you doing here?" Stretch growled. "You were supposed to meet us back at school. You ditched us! Because of you we got detention!"

"Yes, I'm sorry about that but I'm afraid it couldn't be avoided. Trust me!" He spoke with urgency as he gently closed the door behind him, making sure we were alone.

"Trust you! Why should we trust you?" I challenged. Even though he had saved us from the dumpster we had plenty of reasons *not* to trust him, the least of which was posing as a custodian. Then again, he had never actually claimed to be a janitor; we had just assumed he was.

"Who are you anyway?" I asked.

"My name is Evan, a messenger sent here to help you." He leaned forward slightly and raised his eyebrows. "I believe you're being hunted."

"Hunted? Who's after me?"

"The Shadow. They are coming for you, Hunter. You have something that belongs to them." He spoke as if I knew what he was talking about.

"I don't understand; what do I have that anyone could possibly want?"

"More than you know," his voice was steady and calm. "Tell me, Hunter, have you read the book?"

"A little."

"What did you read?"

I strained to recall the riddle that had first appeared on the opening pages of the book.

"Something about darkness, a lie, and a door through which I must die," I replied and shuddered.

"And then?" he wanted to hear more.

For the second time that evening, I recounted my entrance into the book and what I had seen.

"When you returned," he inquired eagerly, "what did you see when you looked in the mirror? What did it reveal?"

A terrible feeling grew in my chest. "That I..." I paused for a moment glancing over at Stretch who was looking as nervous as ever, "that I'm being watched."

An uncomfortable silence passed.

Evan spoke evenly, allowing his next words to sink in. "Listen closely. The book has connected to you, Hunter. You have been given the opportunity to see how things really are. The Shadow are aware that you have been called and they will do anything to keep you from leaving. More than anything, they want you to forget what the book has shown you."

I lowered my gaze, uncertain of what to say. Nothing made sense but at the same time I knew it had to be true. After all, I had seen it, and "seeing is believing"—or so I thought.

"These Shadow you keep talking about. Who are they?" I questioned.

"Parasites," he answered, "an alliance of dark spirits from another realm who are living among you. They have been here since the dawn of time, using man as their host to survive. The world as you see it is an alteration, an illusion they have manipulated your mind into believing. Everything you see is hidden by this facade. Those of us in the Resistance know it simply as the Veil."

"You mean these creatures are living inside Hunter, playing with his mind?" Stretch asked, his expression as bitter as if someone had just served him a pile of spinach.

"Actually," he turned to Stretch and added, "in both of you."

Stretch's expression worsened. "Gross!"

"But why us?" I questioned.

"Oh, it's not just you. Everyone in Destiny is living under the effects of the Veil. They believe life is good, and they are in control, but the reality is just the opposite. The truth is, this world is fading and the Shadow are in complete control over your lives." Evan turned and looked directly at me, "Your father knew all too well the workings of the Shadow, which is why he left. He was looking for answers too."

The sudden mention of my father had a strange effect on me. All at once I shared something in common with the man who had abandoned my family. He had disappeared three years ago this summer. Emily and I had heard heated arguments between our parents nearly every night leading up to his departure. Our parents were at odds over something, though we were never told exactly what it was.

"You know my father?" I asked, hoping for some information of his whereabouts, maybe even some way of getting in touch with him.

"Yes, I knew him once. I first met your father at a gathering of the Resistance. He had just discovered the secret of the Shadow and realized something was terribly wrong. At the time he didn't understand why the Shadow existed or how they were connected to our own world. Your father and I had a difference of opinion over the matter and parted ways. I lost touch; I'm afraid I don't know where he is now."

"That makes two of us," I mumbled.

"Listen boys," he reassured us, "the important thing to remember is that this world is not what it seems; *you* are not what you seem. Everything you see is a lie—as long as you stay here you cannot trust your vision. This book is an exit that takes you beyond the Veil to a place where everything is real. It is a link to the truth. To a realm that is connected to our own so deeply you can see it at work even now if you try." At this he looked around as if sensing something we could not.

Stretch's eyes followed his gaze around the room and he squirmed at the thought of invisible beings in this world.

"How do we get rid of them?" Stretch asked, still sickened at the thought of being infected.

"Once you are infected, the effects are irreversible. There is nothing you can do to get rid of them," he said with finality. Then he stepped forward, bent down and put his hand on our shoulders. "But there is someone who can. Someone who has helped others—someone who has helped me." Until that moment I had felt as if I was already lost. His smile seemed to reassure us that we had some hope.

"Who can help us?" I asked.

Evan looked around as if someone was listening in, lowered his voice and spoke in a hushed tone, "His name is Aviad." The lights in the studio flickered off for a moment and then back on, as if the mere mention of the name carried a power of its own. Evan looked up, "They're here. There isn't time to explain everything now. Quickly, follow me and do exactly as I say."

With that he threw open the door and ran down the stairs. We grabbed up our things and hurried after him to the edge of the alley. He pulled himself tightly against the wall—we did the same. Peeking around the corner he motioned for us to follow again.

We made our way across town, ducking behind parked cars and dodging down blind alleys. In a curious game of hide-and-seek we tried to lose the invisible beings hot on our trail. Evan was moving faster than we expected. It took every ounce of effort to keep up with him.

"Where are we going?" Stretch broke the silence with his question.

"Somewhere safe," Evan shot back, not breaking his stride. A few blocks later we arrived in an alley across the street from a small church. Crouching in the darkness we stopped to catch our breath.

"You sure move fast for an old guy," Stretch wheezed.

Evan grinned, apparently amused at the thought of being called old.

"Where are we?" I asked.

"That church is one of the safe-houses the Shadow seldom enter. Inside we can use the book undetected." His eyes scanned the scene, making sure we were safe and finally alone. Then something caught his eye. Evan held up his hand and pointed across the street.

"See that?" he asked. We shook our heads. "There, by the gate in front of the church. Look for the negative light." I focused intently on the wrought iron archway that separated the sidewalk from the churchyard. At first nothing was there, and then as I stared more intently I could barely see the illusion of movement. Sucking the light out of the air ever so slightly was a vague shape pacing back and forth in front of the entrance.

"Dispirits," Evan spat in disgust, looking concerned, "two of them. Someone must have tipped them off."

"Wh-what is that? What does that mean?" Stretch quivered.

"It means this isn't going to be as easy as I hoped." He looked us over for a moment. "I'm going to see what they want. Stay here. No matter what happens you must promise to stay hidden and protect the book." We nodded silently, not knowing what we were in for.

Evan stood up, pulling his hood over his head and stepped boldly out of the safety of the alley into the street. I watched as the hazy movement in front of the building froze. The Dispirits had noticed the cloaked stranger approaching them.

"Show yourselves!" Evan commanded, and all at once, the beings formerly cloaked in darkness appeared out of their invisible hiding places. They were skinny bug-like creatures, each with six arms, oversized antennas, and two very long legs on which they hobbled in an awkward upright position. At the end of each arm was a gruesomely clawed hand. Their faces were mostly frog-like, with bulging eyes and wide lips, but the long sharp teeth that protruded up from their bottom jaw made it obvious they were dangerous. Stretch grabbed the camera and started recording the scene. It would make great footage for our studio Web site.

As the Dispirits hobbled toward Evan, one of them opened its mouth and hissed. "Where issss the book?" Its voice was long and drawn out.

"It is safe; you cannot have it," Evan announced with authority.

The Dispirit chuckled, wiggled its antennas and sniffed the air. "You lie, Shhhhining One. It issss near, issssn't it?"

Evan didn't respond. He just stood there firmly, unafraid.

"The boy issss already ourssss. Leave him alone and we will let you be." As they spoke, black fog began to come out of their mouths. Evan stepped back to avoid the mist. The two Dispirits began circling Evan as if ready to pounce. One of them licked its eye with a long elastic-like tongue.

"The boy is no longer your concern," Evan replied. "He has been called by a higher authority."

"There issss no authority but our own," spat one of the creatures. "You cannot ssssave him, he issss already dead. Your misssssion is foolishhhh. He will die like the otherssss you tried to sss-save. You shhhhhould not have come alone."

Evan removed his hood and took what appeared to be the hilt of a sword from his side. "I never travel alone!"

With the hilt of the sword tightly clutched in his hand, Evan spun around and slashed through the air. The creatures leaped out of the way as, with a flash of white light, an invisible blade scorched the ground where they once stood.

"Whoa! How cool is that?" Stretch smiled as we watched the action from the shadowed safety of the alley.

Evan attacked again, this time removing one of the second Dispirit's arms. The creature backed away in pain, dripping black, tar-like blood on the pavement.

The first Dispirit leaped high into the air above Evan, claws bared in a deadly downward attack. Evan swung around quickly and sliced through the middle of the beast with his invisible sword. Immediately, the Dispirit who was just inches above him disappeared in a wispy cloud of inky blackness, which flew away into the night sky. The remaining injured creature gathered itself and lunged over the top of Evan, coming down several feet behind him. "Futile!" it shouted, as its long tongue shot out immediately from its mouth and struck the back of Evan's neck.

"Ahhhh!" Evan fell to his knees in pain, grabbing the back of his neck. A red welt appeared, stinging from the touch of the Dispirit's poisonous tongue.

"Hopelessss!" The creature lashed out again before Evan had a chance to retaliate, this time the tongue scarring the hand that held his sword. Instinctively, Evan dropped his weapon from the searing pain, realizing too late that he had just made himself vulnerable. The creature quickly grabbed the sword with its tongue and threw it away. The sword landed under a black car parked in front of the alley, just a few feet from where we were hidden. Quietly, I crawled over to the car and reached for the hilt. It was just out of reach, my arms were too short.

"Stretch," I whispered loudly, motioning for him to come over. "I can't reach it!" Stretch followed my lead and made his way to the vehicle. He handed me the camera and lay down on the ground in an attempt to reach the sword.

I lifted the camera up from behind the car to see how Evan was doing. The creature continued lashing out with its tongue at Evan, who was doing his best to dodge the attacks. With each failed lashing the creature yelled out words of discouragement.

"Failure! Defeated! Foolissssh!"

"I've got it!" Stretch grabbed the sword and pulled it out from under the car. He passed his hand safely above the hilt, feeling for a blade that did not appear to exist. "Awesome."

"Not now, Stretch," I said grabbing the sword and giving back the camera. "We need to get the sword to Evan!" While the Dispirit's back was turned to me, I took the opportunity to sneak up the sidewalk to the next parked car. Evan was another fifty feet away and saw me approaching with the sword. He moved so the creature continued to turn its back toward me. Stealing the opportunity, I darted quickly up the sidewalk and behind a delivery van that was parked near where Evan and the Dispirit stood.

"You havvvve been beaten, Shhhhining One," the Dispirit hissed with excitement. "Now tell me where the boy issss, or he will die."

"You cannot take him, he is wanted by another," I heard Evan say weakly.

"Then you will ssssuffer!" the creature hissed.

I lay down and looked under the van. From where I lay, I could see Evan's legs just past the creature. *Here goes nothing.* I slid the sword under the van and out the other side. Evan saw it and dove under the creature's legs, rolling out the other side with blade in hand. I jumped out from behind the van in time to watch the creature disappear into a black mist as Evan ran it through with his mysterious sword. Once again the dark cloud swirled in the wind and flew up into the night sky.

"Thanks, that was a little too close," Evan said, feeling the back of his neck with his hand. He took the sword and laid it on his scar, which healed almost immediately.

"Where did you get that?" I asked in amazement, eyeing the sword.

"Later. Right now we have to move quickly; more are on their way. Do you have the book?"

"Here it is!" Stretch called out as he ran back to where we had been standing, carrying my backpack with him.

"Good, there's been a change in plans. You'll have to leave the Veil on your own. Do you remember how to use the book?" Evan asked hurriedly.

"I think so. I just touched the words and it pulled me into the story. But I didn't have much control over where I went, I mean—I was just watching things," I recalled.

"That is because your connection with the book was weak. The book was simply showing you glimpses of another world. This time will be different. With the knowledge I have given you, the book will become an exit from the Veil and…" Evan stopped abruptly, holding his finger to his lips. A slow hissing murmur began to grow steadily louder.

"What—what is it?" I whispered.

Stretch's face went white. He pointed a quivering finger over my shoulder. Turning around I saw hundreds of eyes appear on the walls of the alleyway as a fresh horde of Dispirits took form, clambering over each other.

They had found us.

CHAPTER 4

A SLIMY EXIT

Run, boys! Find Aviad!" Evan called out, bearing his sword once more, ready to defend us at any cost.

"But how?" I asked.

"The Resistance will help you. Now go!" With that Evan spun his sword around and dove into the growing horde of wall-climbers. A dozen of the creatures were sent to the sky with the first white flash of his invisible blade. We watched in stunned amazement at his skill with the sword until one of the creatures dropped to the ground and ran toward us with ferocious speed. Before it could reach us a blur of silver light flew past us and collided into the creature, sending it flying to the ground. The Dispirit lay there, stunned for a moment, and then dissipated into an inky cloud of blackness and floated away.

What was that? I wondered.

There was no time to find out. Seizing the moment we ran across the street to the church, in hopes of finding safety. We rushed up the concrete steps that led to the building's main entrance and pulled heavily on the doors. They didn't budge. We shook them with fury but it was no use, they wouldn't open.

"It's no good, they're locked. Quick, this way!" I led us down the stairs and around to the back of the church in hopes of finding another entrance. No luck. The doors in the back were locked as well. It looked as if we were going to have to use the book in the open.

"Do you think they saw us?" Stretch wondered.

"Don't know, and I don't want to find out. Here, I've got the book!" I gasped for breath. "The key should be in the back pocket of my bag." I turned my back toward Stretch so he could reach my backpack and search for the key.

"Key—right!" he responded, rummaging through my things. "Oh man, I can't find it. It's too dark!"

Thwapp!

A loud noise came from somewhere in the darkness, the sound of a giant bug-like creature, landing nearby. We froze.

"It's them," Stretch whispered.

I pulled off my backpack and dug for the key only to find it wasn't where I had left it. "Crud!" I whispered. My mind wandered, retracing my steps, trying to remember where I could have misplaced it. *It had to be here.* I checked my jacket pockets again and came up short. *Where could it have gone?* I retraced my steps aloud.

"I swear I put the key in my pack with the book. No, wait! I left it at home in my desk drawer," I recalled. It was a mistake I already regretted.

Thwapp! Thwapp!

Two more Dispirits landed nearby. A black fog began to settle in over the graveyard that sprawled out behind the church. Then the voices began.

"You can't hide foreverrrr." The voices sounded close, too close, as if their voices were inside our minds. I gave Stretch a worried look and tucked the book inside my jacket. He looked as scared as I was.

"What now?" Stretch was in need of direction and so was I. Without the key the book would not work and we would be sitting ducks.

"I dunno. Let me think!"

The creature spoke again, "Give ussss the book and you can goooo free!"

Stretch was scared, "Th-th-that sounds reasonable. We give them the book, they leave us alone, no one gets hurt."

"Are you crazy? Evan risked his life to protect us and the book, we're not giving it to them," I started to remind Stretch, but the voices interrupted.

"Evannnn isn't herrrre," hissed the voices. Suddenly, I felt very alone. Maybe Stretch was right. I began to doubt that we could actually escape. Every hopeful thought I had faded into despair. There was no escape from the Dispirits. My mind flooded with dark, depressing thoughts. I could think of nothing but failure and I would easily have given up the book then and there if a familiar sound hadn't shaken me from my daze.

Hummmmmm.

I had heard this sound before. The same pitch had originated from the key in my room, with traces of a chorus hidden in its tone. The sound seemed to be coming from somewhere across the graveyard. Maybe in all of the commotion I had dropped it along the way. My mind cleared and immediately focused on retrieving the key.

"We can't stay here," I determined, grabbing my bag and tearing out into the graveyard. Stretch, not wanting to be left alone, kept close behind. We ran through the mist in a frantic search for the musical key. We were getting close, I could tell. One misplaced step later and the ground seemed to disappear, sending the two of us tumbling into darkness.

Our fall was slightly cushioned as we landed on damp, freshly dug soil. The contents of my unzipped backpack spilled on the ground around us, camcorder and all. Uncle Jim would not be happy if the camera was ruined.

"Stretch, you okay?" I called out.

"Yeah, I think so. Where are we?" Stretch pondered aloud.

Overhead, a rectangular opening framed the sky above, allowing a small amount of starlight to spill into the bottom of the hole.

"Take a wild guess. A six-foot hole in the middle of a graveyard," I said, searching the ground for the tiny flashlight I had kept in my pack.

Stretch gasped, "You mean, we're in a...a...?"

Before he could finish I flicked on my flashlight, revealing the smooth walls of dirt and roots around us and confirming his deepest fears.

"A grave!" Stretch complained.

"Shh. Do you hear that?" I said, noticing the humming had grown considerably stronger.

"Hear what?" Stretch replied, apparently oblivious to the sound.

"That humming. It's the key; it's got to be here in the grave somewhere." I spun the flashlight around and tried to pinpoint the source of the sound.

"You're hearing things," Stretch muttered, picking up the camcorder and brushing it off. He pressed record and pointed the camera at me. The red light blinked on the front of the camera, a hopeful sign that I hadn't damaged it beyond repair. "Probably hit your head when we fell in."

I ignored the comment; what I was hearing wasn't in my head. The sound seemed to originate from my end of the grave, just below the surface of the ground. Holding the tiny flashlight with my teeth I began digging wildly with both hands, flinging dirt between my legs. Only a few inches down I hit something hard.

"Here, hold this!" I said, handing the flashlight to Stretch, who held the camcorder with one hand and took the flashlight in the other. With increased motivation I dug quickly around the edges of what appeared to be a small jewelry box and freed it from its burial place. The humming subsided as I held it up. The simple leather-wrapped black box was about seven inches long and two inches deep, with a three-digit, tumbler-ring combination on the front.

"Whoa, how did you know that was there?" Stretch was impressed.

"I didn't. I think it was calling me." Whatever magic was involved was working for us at the moment, not against us. It was an encouraging sign.

"Well, hurry up and open it; there are giant bugs out there looking for us, remember?" Stretch spoke with anxiety.

Unfortunately, the box was locked. Examining the combination lock, I found that seven numbers were etched on each tumbler ring, and each of the rings offered a different set of numbers in no particular order. It would take a miracle to unlock the combination before the Dispirits found us. *So much for magic being on our side.*

"No good," I fumed, "it's a dead end. We'll never open it before the Dispirits find us. There must be hundreds of combinations here."

"Three-hundred and forty-three to be exact," Stretch offered confidently, still recording my every move. To say he was a math whiz would be an understatement. He was so quick with numbers I often wondered if he was part robot, with a calculator built into his brain. The talent he possessed was both amazing and annoying at the same time.

"How do you do that?" I asked.

"What? It's easy. You just take the number of symbols on the first dial, multiply it by the number of symbols on the second dial, and then multiply that number by the number of symbols on the third dial. See, seven times seven, times seven is three-hundred forty-three."

I just shook my head. Robo-Stretch was at it again.

"Hang on, there's something written on the bottom of the box," he pointed out.

I flipped the box over to find a peculiar riddle carved into its base.

SEVEN IN TURN BY EACH OF THE THREE,
TEN MUST CONCLUDE TO UNLOCK A KEY.

"Another riddle, huh? So, what does it mean?" Stretch wondered, finally shutting off the camcorder and setting it down on my backpack.

"Seven in turn by each of the three," I repeated aloud. "That must refer to the number of symbols on each of the dials. There are seven symbols on three dials." The conclusion seemed logical.

"Okay, I'll go with that but what about the next line? Ten must conclude to unlock a key."

We sat in the dark for precious seconds, pondering the box's cryptic riddle while the beasts that sought to kill us wandered above us somewhere in the night. I started thinking out loud.

"If a key is really locked inside that would answer the second half of the line. So, maybe the first part means the number ten has to conclude the last two numbers of the sequence."

Before the words left my mouth I began rotating the last two dials in hopes of finding the numbers we needed. Since there were only seven random numbers on each dial I was relieved to find that the last two could make the number ten. It seemed to be working; now all that was left to do was try the first dial in all seven selections. Unfortunately, none of the seven sequences worked. Logic had failed me once again.

"Come on, we don't have time for this," I fumed, incredibly frustrated.

"Wait a second," Stretch's face lit up. I listened intently to my mathematically gifted friend. "*Ten must conclude* could also mean that the numbers have to add up to ten."

"Okay, but that still leaves a lot of combinations."

"Not as many as you might expect, but I don't think we'll need to try them all anyway. We already know the answer. Read the first line again."

"Seven in turn by each of the three," I repeated.

"Exactly, so if we take seven to the power of three we have seven times seven, times seven…"

"Three-hundred and forty-three!" I finished excitedly, remembering Stretch's calculation from only moments before.

"Which adds up to ten!" Stretch smiled, obviously proud of himself. "I know, I'm a genius. You can thank me later."

My fingers turned the dials in eager anticipation. When the last number was in place, a slight click announced we had gotten it right. I opened the box.

Inside, set in a velvet form shaped perfectly to fit, was a golden key identical to the one I had used earlier that evening. A simple handwritten note was tied to the handle that read:

FOUND KEY IN YOUR DESK. USE IT NOW.

The mysterious note's meaning was clear. It was time for us to leave.

Thwapp! Thwapp! Thwapp!

The sound of three more Dispirits landing near the grave reminded us we were not alone. "They've got us cornered. Those... those *things* are going to find us." Stretch didn't like our situation but it wouldn't matter.

"No they won't. We won't be here long enough!" I answered, putting the key into the book's latch and turning it. The book lit up as before and I threw it open, the pages shining like a beacon into the night sky. If the Dispirits didn't yet know where we were, they would now. I read the opening page out loud for Stretch to hear:

Born into darkness,
deceived by the Lie,
a door has been opened
through which you must die.
The world you now know

will soon be no more.
Your fading is certain;
your death will be sure.

"You ready?" I asked hurriedly.

"I dunno," Stretch wavered. "Have you ever had that feeling that no matter what you choose you're going to regret it?"

Yeah, I knew the feeling well. I got the same feeling before Ms. White's pop quizzes. Even though they were multiple choice there was no way to guess the right answer. It was a test you were intended to fail.

"The odds of us coming back from wherever this portal takes us are slim-to-none!" Stretch calculated.

"Yeah, well the odds of creatures as ugly as those Dispirits existing was slim-to-none this morning too!" I countered. "Besides it's our only way out. Are you with me?"

At first Stretch didn't look sure, then he resigned himself to what he felt was the lesser of two fears. "Oh man, I'm going to regret this," he winced as he reached out his hand and closed his eyes.

"See you on the other side!" I said taking his hand in mine.

A terrifying hiss interrupted our escape as one of the Dispirits shot its ugly head over the edge of the gravesite. The sound of our voices screaming in unison echoed through the graveyard and miles beyond. Feasting on our fears, the creature began slashing wildly at us with its gruesome claws, licking its lips and crumbling the walls of the grave with every stroke.

"The booooook!" the Dispirit screamed, catching glimpse of the prize at last. We dropped to the ground in horror as the Dispirit lunged forward to steal the book away.

Somehow, in the midst of the commotion, my hand brushed the words of a page. A sudden flash of blinding light erupted from the book, suspending the Dispirit's attack in midair. For a moment we remained frozen in time, aware of our surroundings but unable to move. It was as if time itself had been stopped by the power of the book.

Nothing else happened; the world did not spin as it had in my room. Instead, we remained motionless statues in the mouth of the grave with the Dispirit's claws bared only inches away.

Then, something changed.

The effect was subtle at first, merely a slight tugging at my feet as if gravity had gradually begun to increase. Next, the ground beneath us grew softer and wetter, giving way beneath the soles of our shoes. The weight of my body seemed to increase and I began sinking down into the mud.

The murky mire inched its way up our bodies like quicksand, threatening to bury both of us alive. The grave was swallowing us up.

The last thing I remember seeing before the ground finally took me under was Stretch's frozen face, eyes squeezed tightly shut, mouth open in a silent scream.

Beneath the surface of the earth everything went black. I wasn't breathing, but oddly enough I felt no need. The darkness lasted for quite some time, though how long exactly I cannot say. Gravity was pulling stronger, continuing to draw me somewhere.

After endless minutes of traveling through the muddy ground, the numbness subsided and my feet broke free, dangling above what seemed to be an opening below. I hung there for a moment, suspended between two worlds. Then, with a sudden lurch in my stomach, I slid out of the earth above me and fell into the nothingness below. My free-fall slowed almost immediately to a soft floating halt. My arms and legs were released from their frozen state and I regained ownership of my movements once more.

At first, there was nothing to see—emptiness seemed to surround me. Weightless in the cold wet blackness I caught a glimpse of shimmering lights high above me. The glistening beams appeared to be moving in a rhythmic dance, repeating their pattern of motion and captivating my attention.

Floating upward, I began to inspect the flickering shapes overhead. As I moved higher, a severe pain grew in my chest as the sudden desire to breathe returned. All at once it hit me; I was under water.

Having never learned to swim, my mind flooded with fears from the past. I remembered the one and only time I tried swimming in the murky waters of Lake Liwa. I would have died that summer if the camp lifeguard hadn't heard my scream for help and rescued me.

Now here I was, trapped underwater in an unfamiliar place. My body went into shock and I began kicking the best I could, trying desperately to reach the surface for a breath. I needed air and I needed it now.

As I struggled, I saw another figure floating above me. Thinking it was Stretch I reached out in hopes that he could help me swim. Instead, the body spun limply around and the horrific face of a dead man stared back at me. I held back my urge to scream and tried once more to make my way to the surface. More and more bodies floated around me, appearing out of the gloomy darkness.

At last, I broke the surface and gasped for breath. I struggled to keep my head above water, but after a few moments I sank back into the blackness. Try as I might, I couldn't stay afloat. I broke out of the water once more and screamed, "Help!" before sinking under the waves a second time.

On the way down I swallowed a mouthful of water and knew I wouldn't be coming back to the surface on my own. As I fell toward the lake floor, I collided with another body. I pushed it away, shocked to find a chain attached to its back, tethering it to the lake floor.

An arm fell over my shoulder. I turned and found myself surrounded by the limbs and bodies of other helpless victims trapped in their watery grave. Using my last ounce of energy I struggled to fight them off.

My vision began to fade, but before I could pass out, another hand grabbed me firmly by the arm. I tried to resist at first but it wasn't any use—my body would no longer respond to my mind's commands. Then I realized I was being pulled to the surface. I was being saved.

With the help of my rescuer, I reached the water's surface quickly and was pulled into a small wooden boat. The shadowy figure dropped me onto my back and pressed heavily on my chest. I rolled to my side, coughing up a large amount of black water from my lungs and gasping for air. I was breathing again.

Half conscious, I turned over and gazed up into the face of the one who had saved me.

"Welcome, Hunter," she said softly.

Her hooded silhouette was lit only by the reflection of a pale sunset off the surface of the water. My vision blurred and everything faded away.

CHAPTER 5

A NIGHT OF QUESTIONS

I lost all sense of time, at first only aware of the sound of voices whispering and the crackling of a campfire somewhere nearby.

"You think he's the one?" a deep voice asked in a hushed tone.

The reply came from a young girl. "He's here, isn't he? That means he has a chance."

"What if he doesn't make it?"

"That's out of our hands."

A nauseating odor swept through the air causing me to stir. Something was burning.

"He's waking up," the man said.

My eyes fluttered open to find a girl about my age gazing down in concern. *Was this the one who had saved me?* Her face was tan, her eyes gentle brown, and she wore a hooded cloak that was pulled up over her head. She was pretty, too pretty, and it made me nervous. As she placed her hand gently on my forehead, my heart quickened. The warmth of her touch sent a shiver down my spine. I was freezing and my stomach had turned suddenly sour.

"You're very cold. How do you feel?" she asked.

I hesitated—too nervous to say anything. Every time I tried to talk to a new girl I had the same problem. In my mind I wanted to sound cool and confident, but when it came down to actually speaking, I stumbled, the king of bad first impressions. I sat there, unable to respond, my face flushing with each passing second. She looked at me funny. *Come on, Hunter, say something...anything.* This was taking way too long.

"I feel w-weird," I finally answered. *Genius!* After two minutes of awkward silence, that was the best I could come up with? *Bad first impression: check! What a dork!*

"That's to be expected; the transition between realms can be disorienting. You'll feel better soon enough."

I glanced around, taking in my new surroundings. I was lying outside on a fur pelt of some kind, covered in a pile of woven blankets. The campsite was situated beside a great black lake at the edge of a thick forest of timber giants. The air was fresh and clear with the scent of pine needles floating on a gentle breeze. The sun had already set, lingering just below the horizon, leaving a layer of reddish-orange haze behind.

A massive man with broad shoulders and ruddy skin was hunched over a campfire tending a pot of bubbling stew, the apparent source of the stench that had awakened me. He wore a fur cape draped over silvery battle armor, outlined in places by a soft orange glow that seemed to emanate from within the armor. Centered on his breastplate was the glowing mark of the interlocking *Vs*; the hilt of a sword hung at his side.

"W-w-where am I?" I mustered enough courage to ask.

The man responded in a booming voice, "You, my soggy friend, are on the Shard of Inire in the glorious realm of Solandria." As he spoke, he stood proudly and banged his fist against his armor, signaling his loyalty to the country. He appeared even more intimidating now that he was standing and I didn't know whether to be afraid, or comforted by his company. Of course, I had never heard of the Shard of Inire, or a land called Solandria, but thought it best not to insult him by saying so.

"I'm Hope, by the way," the girl offered, "and this is Captain Samryee, my protector."

"But you can just call me Sam!" he interjected. "Least that's what my friends call me."

Friends! The mention of the word made me painfully aware that something was wrong. Stretch was missing.

"Where's Stretch?" I asked.

The two of them looked at me blankly.

"Y-you know, my friend! He came through the book with me."

"You were alone," Hope replied slowly.

"But he was with me when we entered the book. He's gotta be here!" Stretch was a far better swimmer than I was and could have easily made it to shore on his own. If he had made it, chances were he was still nearby, maybe even looking for me. "We have to find him," I said, sitting up. "We can't leave him out there alone."

"Wait, Hunt..." Hope started to say.

I started to stand but was shocked to find my shirt and pants were missing and quickly pulled the blankets up over my chest in embarrassment.

"Whoa! Hey, where are my clothes?"

Hope fought back a smile. My face flushed red again. *Awkward moment number two!*

"Sorry about that, I should have warned you. Sam took your clothes and laid them out to dry while you were still recovering," she explained. "They'll be ready soon."

I scanned the campsite and spotted my clothes spread out on a stump near the fire, next to the remainder of my belongings—the book and my backpack, which was pretty much empty. That's when I remembered Stretch had left the camcorder behind in the gravesite. *Uncle Jim is going to kill me,* I thought, thoroughly worried about what might have happened to it. I wanted to gather my things and head out to find Stretch right away.

Sam spoke up. "Trust me, lad. It'll do no good heading out t'night. Leaving the Veil is a journey ya have to make alone. Even if your friend did make the exit, he could be anywhere in Solandria. That book has a will of its own, you know."

Great, I wish Evan would have told us that before we left.

Sam continued, "Besides, these woods is full of Shadow. They'll be looking for ya. Long as we stay together we're safe enough."

It was difficult to accept but I had to trust them. This was their realm, their rules—I was merely a visitor.

"I'm sorry, Hunter," Hope tried to comfort me, "but Sam's right, we need to stay together. We can't risk losing you. We'll meet up with the others in the morning and send out a search party to look for him. If he *is* here, we'll find him. I promise."

"Others?" I asked. "What others?"

"Why, the Resistance of course," the man's face beamed. "They'll want to meet you straight away, seeing as we've been expecting you."

"How did you know I'd be coming?"

Sam and Hope exchanged glances, unsure of how to respond. Hope was the first to offer an explanation.

"Evan told us about you. He said he was going to try and reach you before...well, before it was too late."

"Too late for what?"

She lowered her voice, "Solandria is not what it once was; it is a world at war. Sceleris and his Shadow warriors rule the majority of the land here, intent on annihilating every last remnant of those who resist his rule. But there are rumors that Aviad has returned and he intends to set things right. Evan received word that Aviad wanted to meet you, which is why he went to Destiny to find you."

"But why me?"

"We're not sure but Aviad has never been wrong before."

With that Hope stood and moved toward the fire, serving up a hefty bowl of the stew. She had pulled back her hood, letting her wavy brown hair fall forward across her face. Beneath the cloak she wore a white blouse trimmed with gold edging that hung loosely over her leather-wrapped leggings. She turned back around and approached me again, carrying the bowl gracefully so as not to spill it. My nervousness had passed, for the moment.

"Here, try some of this. It will help with the nausea," she offered, kneeling beside me again.

The smoldering concoction made the cafeteria food at school look appetizing, but I was starving and decided to try it in spite of my better judgment. She raised the spoon of soup to my mouth and I took a sip. It tasted even worse than it looked—bitter, oily and stringy.

"What is that stuff?" I coughed. "It's awful!"

Sam chuckled, "Serpent stew! Me mum's own recipe. It'll put hair on your chest, to be sure, but there ain't nothin' like it for nourishment and you'll be needin' every bit of it for our journey tomorrow. We've got a long hike ahead of us if we're gonna make it back by noon." He grinned broadly as if a half-day's hike were something to look forward to.

"Sam's right," Hope said. "Eat up, you'll be glad you did."

Somehow I managed to force down the remainder of the bowl of soup. Fortunately my mother's home cooking had trained me well. I had learned to grin and bear it. As I finished, Hope tossed my dry clothes into my lap.

"You better put these on before bed. We may need to break camp in a hurry tonight if the Shadow come snooping around." Hope turned her back while I quickly slipped my pants and shirt on.

I looked out into the blackened woods and wondered if any were watching us right now. The reality of the situation began to settle in my mind. I was in a strange land with no clue how to get back home. I was being hunted by horrific creatures that until recently, I didn't know even existed, in search of a man I had never met. To top things off, my best friend was missing somewhere, alone, at the beginning of a quest neither of us had fully understood.

My concern must have shown on my face because Sam quickly added, "Ah, don't worry none, Hunter. I've fought many a Shadow in me time. They're as afraid of me as you are of them, I'll wager. They won't be getting close to ya tonight—I'll make good and sure of that." He grinned and tapped the hilt of his sword. It glistened in the firelight and I marveled at the magnificent weapon.

"Hey, Evan had a sword like that," I said, recognizing the weapon.

"Yes, it's a Veritas Sword," he said as he unlatched the hilt from his belt, holding it up in the light for me to see. "The weapon of choice fer a Codebearer, crafted by the Author hisself. This here blade was designed ta pierce the heart and soul of any that dare to cross its edge. Over time the blade develops a bond with its bearer. The stronger the bond, the more powerful the blade becomes."

"How does it work?" I wondered.

"Its power comes from the Code of Life—the truths the world exists on. The blade at rest remains invisible and is useless." He passed his hand over the cross-guard to prove the absence of the blade. "But in the heat of battle, the will of the sword burns ta life and the blade becomes sharper than any known ta man." Without warning he took the weapon in both hands and brought it down with a savage chop onto a large piece of firewood. An arc of light trailed behind as he split the wood cleanly in two. "Ya see, Hunter," he smiled, "the Veritas Sword is the only weapon a Codebearer can use ta truly defeat the Shadow. It was fashioned by the Author and carries the Code of Life in its blade. If there's one thing the Shadow can't survive, it's the truths of the Code."

"Codebearer?" I asked.

"Aye! Those of us whose minds have been freed from the Shadow's lies and the darkness inside," Sam said, pointing at his chest. "We Codebearers are entrusted ta be keepers of the Code. It's an honor I'm proud ta bear."

The book had mentioned something about the Code of Life and I figured that was what Sam was referring to. I made a mental note to read the book again later. He pulled a short log closer to my make-shift bed and sat on it, settling in for what appeared to be a lengthy explanation.

"Tell me, Hunter, how much do ya know about the one called the Author?"

"Not much really. I mean, I read a little about him in the book, but I didn't really get that far. From what I read, he created a pretty amazing story."

"Not just *a* story," Sam replied, "*The* story!"

I was confused. "What do you mean?"

"Let me put it this way," he said pointing out toward the forest behind me, "those trees over there, where did they come from?"

I glanced over my shoulder. A breeze was blowing and the trees swayed to the rhythm of the wind. They were tall and majestic, much like the great redwoods of my own world. Assuming life worked in a similar way here as it did back home, the answer to Sam's question was fairly obvious.

"A seed."

"And where did the seed get its life ta create such a tree?"

"From the soil?" I guessed, not thinking too much of it.

Sam continued, "So then, where'd the soil come from?"

My head was spinning, "Huh?"

"What I mean, Hunter, is that everything owes its beginnin' ta something else. If ya go fer 'nough back you'll have ta decide what created the very first thing. Either it was created by nothin', which is impossible, or there must have been somethin' that had no beginnin'. Somethin' outside of nature—a supernatural bein' who was always there."

He stopped to make sure I was following and then continued with his explanation.

"This is the first truth of the Code: Nothing comes from nothing. So, everything we see, think, feel and experience owes its existence to this One Thing—the Author of all things."

"I never really thought about it before," I replied.

"Ah, ya see, the Shadow have done a good job of closin' the minds of men ta the truths of the Code. That's where the Resistance comes in. Our job as Codebearers is ta make sure knowledge of the Code doesn't fade away. We are a small group, ta be sure, but without us truth would disappear and life inside the Veil would be a whole lot worse than it is even now."

"So the Author in the book is the Author of Solandria?"

"Not just Solandria, but every realm. He created them fer a purpose, Hunter. Think about it, where once there was nothin', now every livin' thing works t'gether ta survive. Why, every detail, down ta the very cells inside yer body, is a result of the Author's handiwork."

"Sam, you're confusing the boy. He's had enough for one day, don't you think?" Hope chimed in.

"I s'pose you're right," he said with a wink as he picked up his seat and moved back toward the fire.

"He can lecture for days, if you let him," she said with a smile. "Sam used to be a teacher in the Veil lands, where you came from."

"Has he ever gone back?" I said looking over at the man, trying to imagine what it must have been like to be in one of his classes.

"Sure, from what I'm told being in Solandria is like being in a parallel world. You can travel between the two whenever the Author calls you. Sam has a life in the Veil lands just like you do, Hunter. Except, not necessarily in the same time period as you."

"You mean Sam could have lived in the Veil during an entirely different time than me?"

She simply nodded in return and offered no further explanation. I boosted my courage and decided to learn more about who she was.

"So what about you, Hope? What did you used to be?" I asked, sounding less nervous than before.

"Me? Oh, I've always lived here," she answered.

"You mean you've never been to the Veil lands?" I asked, feeling somewhat awkward referring to my home by the new name.

"No, not yet."

"Will you go someday?"

"That's not for me to decide."

I didn't know what to say, so I kept quiet.

"You better get some sleep," she insisted. "Daybreak will come soon enough and there will be plenty of time for talking tomorrow."

The conversation stopped there. Hope rolled out a fur bed for herself and crawled under the covers. Sam threw another log on the fire and pulled his cloak tightly around his face.

I lay down on the makeshift bed, gazing up at the cloudless night. The stars were fantastic, making me feel so small and insignificant in the midst of a universe so much bigger than I.

I closed my eyes and Sam's words echoed in my thoughts. *Nothing comes from nothing. Everything we see, think, feel and experience owes its existence to this One Thing—the Author of all things.* If what he said was true, something was out there beyond the stars intending for life to exist. The wonder of it all was amazing. If someone wanted me to exist that meant there was a purpose for my life. For the first time in a long time, I felt wanted.

Opening my eyes again, I wondered how many stars there were. Stretch would have had a calculated guess for the occasion if he were here.

Poor Stretch, I thought, *I wonder what he's doing right now.* Here he was, lost and alone in a strange world, and it was my fault. I had brought him into this mess; I should have been left alone. What if the Shadow had found him first? Or worse, what if he had drowned in the lake? Even if he had managed to swim to shore, he wouldn't know how to build a fire and would most likely catch pneumonia.

The possibilities were endless and the guilt of the *what ifs* weighed heavily on my heart and kept me from sleeping.

I thought of home, of my mom, of Stretch and then at last, my mind became too tired to worry anymore and gave in to a deep satisfying sleep that seemed to last for days.

Chapter 6
Ambushed

Dreams are weird things. They rarely make sense, and when they do, it's nearly impossible to figure out what they mean anyway. So what's the point in having them?

Now, in my experience there are three kinds of dreams. In the first category, you have good dreams. The kind where you win a brand new bike, your dog Lucky comes back home after being gone for three years, and you get to fly in a hot air balloon with your favorite rock star. Cool.

Then you have the second group, a category I like to call totally bizarre dreams. You know, where things go ridiculously wacky and you end up arriving late to school only to find you forgot to put your pants on and your teacher is a talking bunny. Don't laugh, it could happen. Remember, check for pants everyday!

Finally, there is a third category of dreams: dark, disturbing and heart-pounding nightmares—the kind where you're chased by ugly beasts from another dimension and you can't seem to shake them no matter how hard you run. Sound familiar? Welcome to my life.

As I slept by the fire, my mind drifted into this third category—nightmares. I'm sure the fact that the last twenty-four hours of my life had taken such a disturbing turn had more than a little to do with it. But unlike most dreams, this one I wouldn't easily forget.

A lone figure stood high atop a rocky ledge, surveying the canyon trail a thousand feet below. He was young, only a boy, but the staff in his hand made him so much more. Cloaked in black, he stood alone, his face covered by a ghostly white skull-like mask. In contrast, his eyes were dark, emotionless beads of black. The boy stood, boldly unafraid, silhouetted by the angry sky. The clouds swirled unnaturally and cast an eerie green glow on the rocky terrain below. A storm was coming.

"Fools," he sneered, looking down at a small gathering of warriors crossing the trail. "They have no clue who they are dealing with, no idea what I am capable of." The gem atop his staff glowed red from within.

"Master," a short peg-legged goblin limped up to the boy's side. His squat features placed him well below the size of a three-year-old child, but he was kneeling, which made him the perfect size to punt should you be so inclined. He had no neck, only a head that fed directly into his round torso. The goblin's oversized yellow eyes were expressive and bright as they stared up at his master with eager expectations.

"What is it, Zeeb?" his boy-master growled back, his sharp voice declaring he didn't like interruptions.

"Sir, they are nearly in position. Shall I sound the attack?"

Unmoved, the boy peered over the edge of the canyon once more and watched the army of twelve marching steadily forward along its winding path.

"No!" he shot back, "I'll handle this myself."

Leaping out over the chasm, he fell down toward the canyon floor at breakneck speed, guided by an unseen power. Amazingly, he landed on his feet only twenty paces in front of the advancing warriors, perfectly blocking their progress through the tightly carved canyon. A small wisp of dust rose to the air from the impact of his landing and he looked up from his stance, staff pointed directly at the men.

Immediately the warriors drew their invisible swords and prepared for the worst. "We come on authority of the Author, you must let us pass," the captain said boldly. A green glow from the mark on his golden breastplate flashed brighter as he spoke.

"Then by all means, go ahead and try," the boy challenged in defiance. If they wanted to pass, they would have to pass through him.

The warriors did not move; instead, they stood their ground, carefully watching the surrounding walls as well as their backs. They had been outsmarted and they knew it.

"No?" he scoffed. "Not a single one of you is willing to test me?" He shot a passing glance over the group. "But surely, even if the Author is not with you the odds most certainly are; twelve grown men against one puny boy. What are you waiting for?"

"Step aside, Venator," the captain demanded, recognizing his foe.

The skull-faced boy turned quickly toward the captain. "Make me," he replied, raising his staff. A red burst of light shot out, igniting the ground in a fiery blaze around the group. They had been tricked. Some of the warriors backed away in fear, but the captain did not; he stood his ground amidst the flames and smoke.

"Your illusions do not fool me," he yelled over the flames. "We are here on the Author's business. Leave us now before I am forced to take drastic measures." He lifted his Veritas Sword high for the boy to see, but something was wrong. The choking smoke from the ring of fire had done its job; one by one the men began to fall—poisoned by the effects of the potion.

"Cover your faces, men!" he shouted. The pungent smokescreen rose into the air, erasing the boy from view. They had to get out somehow, quickly. "Forward now," came the orders from the captain. Six men ran out, leaving the remaining six paralyzed on the ground.

As quickly as it started the fire faded away. Only a small group was left standing—those who had been quick enough to cover their faces and run forward. The captain searched for the masked figure that had caused the fire, but he had disappeared, his mocking voice echoing off the canyon walls.

"Well done, captain—leaving your own men behind—how clever. You haven't changed a bit; you are still one of us, one of the Shadow."

The captain did not allow his enemy's words to hold him back; nothing could be done for his men, at least not now. They were in the Author's hands. No longer was his priority to save his own, but to contain the problem by capturing the masked enemy.

"Show yourself, coward!" the captain raged.

A sinister laugh reverberated through the air. Under the circumstances, it was impossible to tell where it came from.

"I do not take orders from a traitor," the cold voice replied. "But if you must have something to fight, I will give you what you want."

Thump. Thump. Thump.

The ground shook with the thunderous steps of a creature approaching from behind the curtain of mist. The valiant soldiers turned and raised their swords in anticipation of the coming beast.

"Hold your ground men, this will not be easy," commanded the captain.

Thump. Thump. Thump.

The footsteps grew louder, the beast ever closer but still hidden. The cracking of gravel beneath the powerful steps could now be heard.

Five warriors stood strong, one shook in fear. He was young and inexperienced in battle.

"W-w-what is it?" the sixth warrior asked.

"Nothing we cannot handle," came the reply. "The Author does not test us beyond what we are able. Remember that well."

The sixth warrior looked down at the frozen bodies of his friends, collapsed on the ground, and wondered if the Author was really with them.

"You mean like them?" he spoke out of fear. The captain ignored him.

Thump. Thump. Thump.

"Steady men! Here it comes."

An eerie silence fell over the canyon. Nothing moved, not even the wind. Whatever was hidden behind the veil of smoke had come to a sudden stop, taunting them with anticipation of what would come next. One minute. Two minutes. Still nothing.

"Is...is it gone?" the sixth soldier shook.

He looked to the captain for answers. The captain did not flinch, staring forward at the threat, staying his position.

"Don't drop your guard," he said with authority.

The men obeyed, holding firm—all of them except the sixth, whose fears were running wild.

"I can't take it anymore!" he screamed, turning to run.

"William, no!" called the captain, but it was too late. As the young warrior fled, a horrible beast leaped out from the mist and clobbered the boy with its thick head, sending him flying through the air and into the cavern wall with a hard, loud crack! His limp body slid to the ground, injured and unable to move. A slight moan escaped his lips before he passed out from the pain.

The creature spun quickly around to face the remaining warriors, eyes glowing green with evil intentions. Its forearms were thick and sturdy like the trunks of large trees. In contrast, its slender tail and hind legs were thin and weak in appearance.

"Shhkreeeeeeee," the creature wailed, opening its jaws in a hideous roar that was amplified by the canyon walls; the noise was deafening. Its gaping mouth revealed several layers of teeth hidden inside, beyond the larger fangs that hung from its upper jaw.

"It's a Scrill!" shouted one of the men.

"Spread out and surround it," barked the captain. "Aim for its middle!"

The men did as they were told. The Scrill lunged at a warrior who was caught off guard and only managed to swing weakly at the beast before being thrown to the side like William. Two of the warriors seized the opportunity and attacked the backside of the beast, the weaker half of the creature.

"Watch out!" a third yelled, as the creature raised itself into a handstand and flipped itself over onto its strong forearms. The two now-vulnerable attacking warriors swung helplessly at the Scrill's strong forearms, but only managed to nick them. One soldier was quickly hurled to the left by its swinging head; the other grabbed by the monster's mouth and thrown to the opposite side.

The captain now stood face to face with the beast, only ten paces from the ugly head. Two warriors remained alert, one on either side of the creature. "Quickly, we must all three attack at once. Now!" He raised his sword in a brave assault, the other two following his lead. The captain tried to distract the creature, running straight for its head, while the other two bore down on its back.

The Scrill didn't fall for it, leaping high into the air to avoid the attack and bouncing off a canyon wall before falling back to the floor. The Scrill's mammoth front legs landed squarely on top of one of the remaining warriors with an awful crunch and it slammed the other warrior to the side with a strong kick from its rear legs.

The captain alone was left and took advantage of his only remaining opportunity to run away. He knew he was beaten and fighting was futile without more men. But it was too late even for running. The Scrill chased down the captain in no time at all, backing him up against the rock wall. The captain dropped to the ground and raised his sword weakly in fear of what would come next.

"Shhkreeeeeee!" the creature yelled, opening its ugly mouth and lowering its head for the kill. To my surprise, the captain did not strike the beast. Instead, he simply closed his eyes in anticipation of the inevitable, but it never came.

The Scrill's treat was postponed by the awkward pattering and clicking of peg-legged footsteps announcing someone's arrival. The goblin Zeeb approached from beneath the creature's legs.

"Well done, my pet," he said soothingly, attaching an iron chain to the collar on the Scrill's neck. "I'll bleed this one myself!" he said, pulling a dagger from his belt.

"Hold your blade, Zeeb," came the orders from out of the dark. The boy with the staff stepped forward, his white skull-mask appearing first from the shadows.

"But, Master Venator, he wears the mark of the enemy. We must…" the goblin pleaded for blood.

"It matters not," the boy interrupted. "This one is special. I have another plan for our brave Captain Faldyn and I want him alive."

The goblin hesitantly stepped back, out of respect for his master's command, and shot an angry gaze toward the captain. The captain returned the gaze, his brows furrowed in challenge.

"Your anger serves me well, Faldyn. Nothing has changed; you are still one of the Shadow."

The man ignored his enemy's words. "Get to the point, Venator. What do you want from me?"

"I have a message for the Codebearers," Venator said, pulling a scroll from his sleeve and holding it out to the captain. "Go and tell them what happened here today. Tell them that I am coming for the boy."

The captain took the scroll willingly, obviously defeated by his failure to save his men. Venator turned to go, stepping over one of the captain's fallen men on his way.

"Wait," Faldyn called out, "What will you do with the others?"

"Zeeb!" Venator shouted his command in response to Faldyn's question, "Gather the wounded and take them to Dolor, the Shard of Suffering. Thanks to Captain Faldyn, they will soon learn the penalty for betraying the Shadow and Sceleris, our Sovereign."

"And the dead?" Zeeb asked feebly.

"Leave them lie; their bones will be a reminder to all who pass this way that I am lord of this land!"

Venator raised his staff once more and disappeared. The sky poured rain on the captain and the fallen men.

"Get up," Zeeb glared, kicking the captain. "Get up, now!"

As my dream came to an end I heard Zeeb yelling, "Get up, get up, get uuuuuuuuuuup!"

"Get up, Hunter! It's time!" Sam commanded, shaking me from the dream. I sat up in a hurry, drool running down my cheek, completely unfamiliar with my surroundings.

"You best pack your things, we'll be leaving shortly now," he reminded me. Dawn had barely broken, and already he was hovering over me like a nagging mother who didn't want me to miss the bus.

I glanced around the campsite, half forgetting where I was. Sam was already dousing the flames of the fire, sending a white plume of smoke and the aroma of burning wood into the air. Hope was nowhere to be seen.

What a strange dream, I thought to myself. I had never dreamed about warriors and battles. Talking bunny teachers, yes! Epic battles, no! To top it all off, the whole thing was so vivid and clear that somehow it felt as if it had actually happened. Rubbing the sleep from my eyes, I tried to shake the feeling that I had somehow awakened from one dream only to find myself in the next.

Grudgingly, I willed myself out of bed and made my way over to gather my things. A thin layer of mist covered the surface of the lake, adding to the chill of the morning air. It looked so peaceful today but I knew better. I knew about the bodies hidden below.

Staring out over the lake, I wondered how soon I might find a way back to Destiny. Hope had said you could travel between the worlds, but how long before I would be shown how? I could only imagine what my family was thinking by now. Mom undoubtedly had feared the worst and was up all night calling the cops, searching for me. The thought of Mom worrying made me sick to my stomach. Of course, no one would find me now, not here. I didn't even really know where "here" was. There wasn't anything I could do to send word, not until I learned how to travel between the worlds.

On the other hand, maybe my disappearance would give my sister, Emily, a reason to regret the way she always treated me. I smiled selfishly at the thought.

I picked up my things and began placing them, one by one into my backpack. A deck of cards, a pile of old homework, still unfinished, a pencil, a few blank video tapes (useless without the camera) and the amazing book that had brought me here.

Hope startled me from behind. She was holding a bow over her shoulder but there was no quiver for the arrows, which I found somewhat odd. After all, what good is an unarmed weapon? "Ready for a hike?" she asked.

"Oh yeah," I blurted out in response. "I usually try to run ten or twelve miles every morning, you know. It helps me keep in shape," I lied, trying to impress her. *Lame again.*

"I don't know," she added, "we keep a quick pace. You sure you can keep up?"

"Yeah easy."

"Good, cause we're already waiting on you."

Evidently I was the only one still getting ready. "Oh right, sorry. I'll just finish packing my things here."

She smiled and turned to go. I slapped my forehead for sounding so stupid and jammed the remainder of my things into my bag, along with the book. Sam had loaded most of the items from camp on his shoulders and was already plodding out into the woods. Our journey had officially begun.

The trail we took was narrow, overgrown and intersected with many other larger pathways that seemed much easier to travel. I wondered why we were avoiding the main roads, but assumed there must be a reason. The vegetation of the woodland floor grew thick and large at times, slowing our progress when it grew over our pathway. Sam was out front leading the way, clearing the trail as he went. Hope followed behind me, obviously amused at my attempts to dodge the branches Sam was flinging behind him as we passed.

We didn't talk for fear the Shadow were nearby. According to Hope this was their territory and the woods were crawling with them. With each step I felt watched, as if someone or something was lurking behind every tree, ready to attack us at any minute. It wasn't long before we encountered our first patrol of Shadow guards. Ducking in the bushes, we watched them march up the broad muddy path in front of us.

"Four Dispirits, two Gorewings," Sam whispered to Hope. She nodded in return, pulling back her empty bow in preparation for a fight. Amazingly, as the bowstring reached the apex of its tension a gleaming arrow of light appeared out of nowhere, arming the previously harmless weapon. It was impressive to be sure, but my attention quickly returned to the approaching threat.

The towering brutes Sam had referred to as Gorewings made the Dispirits look weak by comparison. Dressed in black armor from head to tail, these new Shadow warriors were massive beasts who walked upright on thick muscular legs. Each warrior wore armor with a red, double-*S* mark painted on it.

Broad and strong, their upper bodies were easily twice as wide as that of the largest man. Their skin was rough and battle-scarred. Their leathery wings were folded behind their backs as they walked.

As they neared our place in the road, I ventured another look at their terrible faces. Large ears and jagged teeth gave them a bat-like appearance. Two long horns curved backward out of the top of their heads. Their eyes were bright yellow and pure evil.

The patrol marched right past us without hesitation, grumbling amongst themselves about how to divide the reward when they found the boy. I could only assume that by "the boy" they meant Stretch or me. I swallowed hard at the thought of being confronted by one of the brutes that had just passed by. Once the coast was clear we continued the journey and I tried my best to forget what we had just seen.

The next few hours passed quickly. By midmorning I was exhausted and wanted desperately to rest, but my pride wouldn't let me. I had to prove to Hope I wasn't a wimp. *Oh man, why couldn't they have ridden horses or something?* Still, we pressed on, not slowing the pace.

The sun had nearly reached its peak in the sky when Sam came to a sudden stop, firmly raising his hand. Hope pulled back her bowstring in response, igniting another arrow in the weapon. The sounds of the forest were louder now that we had stopped moving. Sam had obviously sensed something but I saw and heard nothing. For a moment, all was quiet. A lone crow cawed overhead, adding to the suspense. Then, all at once there was a rustling in the bushes and over a dozen skillfully camou-flaged warriors, covered in shrubs and leaves, popped up. They had spears and swords drawn, pointed directly at us. We were surrounded; it was an ambush.

Somebody, please tell me this is only a dream.

Chapter 7

The Feast of Unitus

"It's me—Sam," Sam shouted, dropping his things to the ground. "We found the boy!"

"Fall back, men." A slim man with auburn hair and hazel eyes raised his arm to call off the attack. He wore silver armor, similar in design to Sam's, only his had blue glowing markings and he wore a long navy cape.

Sam frowned at the man. "What is the meaning of this, Ephriam? We journey for seven days in search of the boy and what thanks do we get when we return? You send out a welcoming committee to give me a heart attack."

"Sorry, old friend," he flashed a smile, "I couldn't resist seeing if your senses were as sharp as ever."

"Yeah, well if you had *half* a sense, you would have thought twice about it. I was about to leave your men flat on their backs."

"No doubt about it," Ephriam replied with a chuckle.

The two embraced fondly in laughter.

"Good to see you again, Sam!"

"And you as well. How long has it been this time?"

"Six months tomorrow, if I'm not mistaken. The scouts said you were on your way, and I wanted to be the first to greet you. Let us get your things; we'll walk the last mile together." Ephriam raised a hand and whistled. The men moved quickly to carry what we had brought.

"Well now, you must be Hunter, the one everybody's talking about," he continued, extending his hand. "Captain Ephriam at your service. I am honored to make your acquaintance."

"Hello," I said weakly, shaking his hand. I felt out of place in the midst of the reunion of old friends.

Ephriam leaned over and half-whispered in my ear, loud enough for everyone to hear. "Tell me, Hunter. Has Sam been feeding you well, or is he still forcing that horrid stew of his mother's on his guests?"

I shot a glance over at Sam. "Well he…" I started.

"Don't say it! The look on you face says it all. *Tisk, tisk* Sam, you should be ashamed of yourself, torturing our guests like that."

Sam rolled his eyes. "You're just jealous I didn't make enough for you too!" He groaned rubbing his nose.

"It matters not! The Feast of Unitus is already being prepared. The sooner we get there, the sooner we eat! Shall we?"

With that his men led the way down the narrow path. Until that moment, I hadn't realized how hungry I was. My stomach growled like a lion, threatening to eat me if I didn't throw it a peace offering soon.

As we continued through the forest, the tree covering began to thin ever so slightly, making more room for the thick underbrush to grow even thicker. Then, seemingly in the middle of nowhere, we came to a clearing where a secluded pair of trees wound tightly together, twisted in an ancient embrace. Ephriam stopped in his tracks and raised his Veritas Sword in front of him. With a loud shout he called out, "We come for Sanctuary!"

Amazingly, the twin trees responded to his voice, coming alive with movement and unwrapping themselves to reveal a crack of light between their trunks. When at last the twisting subsided, the trees had bent to form an archway beneath their tightly clasped branches. The opening they formed radiated with light and color. One by one the group stepped confidently toward the light and disappeared through the secret portal. When it was my turn at last, I hesitated to take the first step, still rubbing my eyes at what I had just seen.

Hope gave me a nudge from behind. "Well, what are you waiting for?"

Swallowing hard I stepped into the light as the others had done before me. Crossing the threshold I found myself instantly transported to a wide and serene grassy hillside beneath a spectacular blue sky. Nestled in the valley below, an immense city of white stone and majestic buildings spread out before us. The sight of it took my breath away, the white walls of the expansive city reached as far as the eye could see, well beyond the rolling green hills in the distance. The architecture was simple yet elegant, the buildings covered in lush green foliage and topped with pale green rooftops. The entire place seemed at one with nature, bursting with the natural beauty of the surrounding meadows and woodlands—a perfect paradise.

"What is this place?" I asked in wonder.

"The Shard of Sanctuary—a city of refuge, and my home," Hope answered. "You'll be safe here, the Shadow have never found it."

Two wide gates swung open to greet us as we approached the white walls that separated the farmlands from the fortified city. Inside, the streets felt wider and more open than I had expected, but they were still bustling with commotion; people were coming, going and chatting amongst themselves wherever they went. The majority of the people streamed towards a large temple structure near the center of the city.

As we approached the temple courtyard, a small crowd had gathered to welcome us and it felt like all eyes were on me. Everywhere I looked women were whispering and pointing, while men stood side by side, nodding as I passed.

Hope nudged me, "Looks like you have an admirer." Out of the corner of my eye I noticed a small boy running beside me. I looked down at him and smiled, which stopped him dead in his tracks. He turned suddenly shy and burst into tears, running back to hug his mother's legs.

"Sorry, I didn't mean to…" I started to apologize to the mother of the boy, but she turned away, cradling her son before I could catch her attention.

Hope laughed, "You make quite the first impression, don't you?"

"Yeah, I get that a lot!" I winced.

"Hunter!" a familiar voice interrupted the scene. I turned quickly to see someone approaching from across the courtyard.

"Evan, you made it!" I replied in surprise. He apparently had just arrived.

"Yes, I…" he paused, raising an eyebrow in mock concern. "Now wait a minute. What's that supposed to mean? Of course I made it."

"Well, it's just that the last time I saw you there were like…a hundred Dispirits piling on top of you."

His smile couldn't remain hidden for long, "Oh right—that! They did have pretty good odds there, didn't they? Funny thing about Dispirits though…"

I cocked my head in curiosity, as if to ask, *what?*

"They can only attack what they can *see*." Evan lingered on the last word and rippled his fingers in the air with a hint of mystery, seeming to suggest he had become invisible.

"You mean, you can…?"

"Ah! I can only do what the will of the Author allows—no more, no less. You'll learn soon enough that anything is possible when you come to grips with your own limitations."

I marveled at the prospect of being able to become invisible. Was it really possible? Evan left no time to ask for a demonstration, but quickly changed the subject.

"I'm glad to see you made it as well. Where's your friend?" he asked nonchalantly, glancing around the courtyard as he spoke, expecting to spot Stretch.

I felt guilty for having temporarily forgotten. If things went terribly wrong, I might never see Stretch again. Hope answered for me before I had a chance to speak.

"Sam is sending a search party back as we speak. If he made the exit he'll be found."

"I'm sorry," Evan's face turned solemn. "I should have known that the probability of you arriving together would be slim. Still, I have faith that he was called as well, and if that is the case we'll see him again soon."

"How can you be so sure?" I asked.

"Nothing in life happens by chance, Hunter. The Author always creates a way for us to meet him…to find him."

Nothing in life happens by chance? That seemed entirely strange to me. After all, I had been taught in school that the whole universe had been created by sheer chance, and that life itself was a result of a series of accidents that ended in the evolution of the human species. Until recently I had never really doubted it. It seemed highly unlikely that everything around us was part of some orchestrated plan. But, as I considered Evan's words, I remembered my own experience in the church graveyard, and the mysterious key I found buried in the ground. I decided to ask him about it.

"When Stretch and I were running from the Dispirits I heard a humming sound—it came from a box that was buried in a freshly dug grave. But Stretch couldn't hear it."

Evan gave me a puzzled look but listened intently.

"I dug up the box and inside we found the key I had left behind in my room, just in time to let us enter the book before the Dispirits caught us. Do you know anything about that?"

"No, not at all. What did the box look like?" he asked, his eyes wide with anticipation.

"It was just a black box about this long," I held up my fingers several inches apart, "and it had a three-digit combination lock on the front. A riddle was on the bottom that Stretch was able to decipher just in time for us to exit before one of the Dispirits grabbed us. I think we were meant to find it at just that moment."

Evan finished my thought, "And the fact that it required both of you to open it makes me certain that Stretch was supposed to come as well. That's a good sign indeed. Like I said, nothing happens by chance."

Hope cut the conversation short. "Sorry to interrupt but we better find a table before all the good seats are taken."

"Indeed!" Evan replied. "Find your places; we'll have time to talk later."

Evan's mention of food reminded me I was still starving, and suddenly I noticed several long rows of tables piled high with food. Everyone in the courtyard began finding a seat in preparation for the feast. There wasn't a single inch of space left on the tables, though the assortment of food was unlike anything I had ever seen.

"What's the occasion?" I asked Hope.

"The Feast of Unitus. Once a year, at the start of summer, each captain from the seven shards of the Resistance must come and give a statement of allegiance to our cause as a sign of unity."

Looks like I got here at the right time, I thought, looking over the spread.

"We'll sit over there." Hope pulled me nearer to the middle of the center table. Sam and Ephriam, who were still busy catching up and swapping stories, were seated across from us. On their right was an empty chair, which Evan ignored, taking the one next to it instead.

A bell rang loudly, turning everyone's attention to our table. A blonde-haired man with a well-trimmed goatee stood with his arms raised and the crowd quieted in anticipation.

"That's Petrov," Hope whispered. "He is the current Commander of the Resistance."

The man spoke with authority, his voice strong and loud.

"Friends, I am grateful to see so many familiar faces gathered here from all corners of the realm of Solandria. It is truly an honor to meet once more in this place of peace, to affirm our loyalty to the

Resistance and to the protection of the Code of Life." The crowd offered a round of applause.

"At this time I would like to formally recognize the captains who are here today." Each one stood in turn and acknowledged the crowd as Petrov called out their names to rousing applause. "On my left, Samryee from the Shard of Sinos, and Ephriam of Abeosis, and to my right, Tyra from the Shard of Sophmalan, Saris of Torpor..." The bearded man sitting beside Tyra did not stand as the others had; instead, he sat with arms folded, in a sound sleep.

"Saris!" Petrov said louder, trying to command the attention of the sleeping captain.

Tyra nudged the man with her elbow, startling him awake to the laughter of the crowd. He stood awkwardly, painfully embarrassed to be caught napping.

"So sorry to interrupt your nap, Saris," Petrov joked with a gleam in his eyes. "Shall I continue then?"

"By all means," the man offered, "my deepest apologies."

Petrov proceeded to name the remaining captains, "Leo of Tepi, myself from the Shard of Obduront, and of course Faldyn of Perga," he pointed at last to the empty chair, "who has yet to arrive, I'm afraid."

He waited for the applause to die down before continuing his announcements.

"We are equally honored to have in our presence a new face as well, a visitor from the Veil." At this announcement everyone turned to look at me. My face reddened in awkward embarrassment and I raised a hand in an uncomfortable acknowledgment of their stares. Petrov smiled warmly at me, "Welcome, Hunter. We're glad you made it."

"Thanks," was all I could manage to say.

The tables buzzed noisily with a hundred conversations about "the new guy."

"Now," Petrov raised his voice over the murmuring, "as we begin the feast let us raise our glasses in honor of the Author." Everyone quieted as they raised their goblets high in the air. I fumbled awkwardly for my own, nearly spilling it in the process and raising it several moments too late. "May the restoration be swift, and may he find us worthy keepers of the Code until the Kingdom is restored."

A hearty, "Hear! Hear!" rose from the crowd as everyone took their first drink. I followed their lead and took a sip of one of the sourest concoctions I had ever tasted. It was like sucking on a lemon, only much worse. My face puckered in immediate reaction to the tart beverage.

Hope giggled at my expression. "It's an acquired taste," she whispered, "you'll get used to it."

With the way the first sip tasted, I couldn't help but wonder why anyone had ever tried a second sip to find out.

Then in his loudest voice yet, Petrov shouted, "Let the feast begin!"

CHAPTER 8

A COMMISSION OF SORTS

I stuffed myself on the strange selection of food. For the most part it was really good, much better than Mom's or Sam's cooking for sure. Still, I was probably better off not knowing what I was eating. Most of it was unrecognizable but I figured as long as it tasted good I really didn't care what it was.

My only disappointment was in having to listen to the constant jabbering of the white-haired old lady sitting on my right. Her name was Gabby Goodsmith and she had nearly burst with excitement to find herself seated beside a "newcomer." She was nice enough and all, but spent considerably more time talking than eating.

"Why, aren't you just a blessing to us all," she said in a sweet voice. "It's so good to see young'uns your age finding their way out of the Veil. I mean, so many of them are so wrapped up in themselves now-a-days they don't have time to take a second look at what they're wasting their lives on. Take my grandson for example. We hardly see him anymore; he's so into his video games and what-have-you. He could sure use a friend like you. You'll have to meet him someday. I've tried more than once to tell him about the way things really are but he won't have anything to do with it, just treats me like a senile old lady. Can you imagine? No respect, I tell ya. That's the thing, you know, kids these days don't respect their elders as they should."

The one-sided conversation droned on and on, to no end. Her husband, Gerwyn, sat beside her in silent contentment, gumming his food slowly as she babbled on about the state of the Veil and how foolish her children were for ignoring the warnings of the book. Every so often she would end a thought by turning to her husband and saying, "Isn't that right, dear?" which gave her surprisingly enough time to snatch a quick bite from her plate as he looked up, smiled and nodded in agreement.

The feast was over now but Gabby showed no signs of slowing down. The table emptied with the exception of a few remaining groups scattered here and there. During one of Gabby's "isn't-that-right-dear" moments Hope was able to gracefully pull me away from the endless conversation.

"We really should be going, Hunter," she said.

"Thanks," I whispered after we were a safe distance away.

"Don't mention it."

"Where are we going?"

"To the Temple. The Commission of Captains will want to meet you."

We traveled across the courtyard to an elaborate structure built mostly of wood. The closer we came, the larger the temple seemed to grow. The intricate carving incorporated many detailed symbols and markings—the largest and most recognizable were the interlocking *Vs* hanging above the main entrance. The roof line was shaped like a gigantic A-frame that covered the central structure and extended far enough beyond it to create a covered walking path supported by thick square pillars on all sides.

We entered through the main doors and into a grand hallway at the front of the room, where the six captains were already seated around a large triangular table. Evan was there as well, telling a story with animated gestures and a wide grin. I could tell from the expressions on their faces it must have been a good one.

Commander Petrov was the first to greet us. "Ah, Hunter, you're just in time. Please, find a seat. Evan was just telling us how he found you locked in the dumpster." The room was still warm with laughter from the recent telling. My face grew suddenly red. I glanced nervously around. Hope disguised a smile behind her hand. *My string of bad impressions continues. Thanks, Evan.*

"Yeah, that wasn't one of my finest hours," I shrugged, choosing a seat next to Petrov.

"As a matter of fact I'm reminded of when I first met Petrov," Evan started.

"Oh, don't tell that again," the commander tried to stop him.

"And why shouldn't I? It's a great story."

"Yes, tell us!" said Leo, the youngest looking of the captains. "I don't believe I've heard this one."

"No? Well then, that's settled. I remember it well," Evan continued. "I had returned to the Veil in hopes of finding the young lad. You were about…what was it, Petrov, nine? ten?"

"I was fourteen and you know it," Petrov closed his eyes in embarrassment.

"Oh yes, that's right," Evan continued, pretending to have forgotten. "You see, he was rather small for his age."

Sam interjected with booming laughter, "Sure, but it didn't stop him from tryin' to drive his father's car, did it?"

"Hang on, now. I was just about to get to that part. You don't want to spoil the story for everyone do you?" Evan said with a wink.

I glanced over at Sam whose face still held a wide grin.

"Forgive me; it's just that this is one of my favorite stories about Petrov. Go on!" He motioned with his hand for Evan to continue.

"So, I was looking for the boy on his family's farm and just as I come walking down the driveway a car bursts out of the barn and heads straight at me. I could barely see the boy's head above the steering wheel. It was Petrov and he would have run me right over if it weren't for my quick thinking."

Petrov couldn't pass up an opportunity to clarify the situation and jumped in the conversation. "What he means to say is that he panicked and ran like a little girl. Didn't you end up on the roof of the car, Evan?"

A fresh round of chuckles began.

"True enough, but it was the only thing on the farm you couldn't hit." Evan didn't hesitate with his comeback, much to the delight of the rest of the group.

"So there I am on top of the car, hanging on for dear life as Petrov single-handedly destroys the farm. Crashing clear through the pigpen and into the pasture, he apparently didn't know how to stop the car. You should have seen those poor cows getting out of the way as fast as their legs could carry them. It's a wonder he didn't hit any of them, really."

"Oh this is good," Ephriam said, as we all tried to imagine Commander Petrov as a fourteen-year-old boy.

"Ah, but that's not all," Evan continued. "Before I could steady myself and reach in to help the boy, Petrov opened the door and jumped out on his own, rolling across the meadow, and managing to cover himself completely in cow manure."

This time the room exploded in laughter, even a little chuckle from Petrov.

Eventually the commotion died down and Petrov, his smile fading, took the opportunity to direct the conversation to more serious matters.

"So Hunter, on to more pressing matters! We have been looking for you for quite some time. You have questions I'm sure, and now is the time for some answers. But before we continue I have to ask, do you want to know the truth about who you are?"

The question was not one I was expecting. *Who was I?* Only a few days ago I had thought I was just your average kid with lower than average grades, and a slightly higher than average chance for getting into trouble. All of that had changed with the discovery of the book and the reality that the world I had known was not what it seemed. Whatever the truth, I had come too far to go back now. I wanted to know everything.

"Yes, I'm ready," I said, not really as sure as I sounded.

Petrov knelt to look me straight in the eyes, measuring my ability to understand what he was about to explain.

"I hope you are. We don't want to lose you to the Shadow." He walked back toward the table and placed his hands on the back of his chair. "Tell me, Hunter, how much do you know about the realm of Solandria?"

"Not much," I acknowledged.

He rolled out a map covered with a scattering of various-sized islands too numerous to count.

"Solandria is a shattered world comprised of a series of floating islands, or shards as we call them, in the midst of a great void. In case you are wondering, we are currently here, on the Shard of Sanctuary," he explained, pointing his finger to one of the smaller islands near the right edge of his map. "Solandria exists on the other side of the Veil, which is the only world you knew until now. The two realms are connected, linked if you will, like opposite sides of the same page. One cannot exist without the other."

"The book Evan helped you recover is very important. It offers glimpses of truth from the very hand of the Author himself. Do you have it with you?"

I nodded.

"Bring it here; I want to show you something."

Evan gave a nod of approval and I reached into my bag to remove the book. It seemed even heavier than before as I struggled to hoist it up to the table. Pulling the key from my pocket, I set it down beside the book. Petrov moved to my side and placed his hand on the cover.

"For many, the truths in this book are a burden that will become too heavy to bear. Some think them to be fairy tales or obsolete stories, but once you understand them and take them to heart, they will change you in ways you cannot possibly imagine."

"You mean the Code of Life!" I said bluntly, surprised by my own boldness.

"Very good," Petrov said, raising an eyebrow in shock, "you must have been listening to Sam!"

Sam beamed with pride. "What can I say? I'm a good teacher!"

"Indeed, the best," Petrov responded, matter-of-factly. "Yes, the Code of Life is the order of all things and the way by which we must live if we want to fulfill our purpose."

"This book," he continued, "is the Author's Writ, our only connection to the Author himself. It is the best place to start in order to understand who the Shadow are, why they are here and more importantly, what they want with you."

My heart raced when I remembered that I was wanted by the Shadow. I clasped my sweaty palms tightly beneath the table to keep them from trembling.

Petrov unlocked the book and spoke to it in a confident tone. "Tell us the origin of the Shadow!"

To my amazement, the book flipped open of its own accord, stopping about a third of the way through at a blank page. A few seconds later the handwritten text began to appear.

"Ah, here it is," Petrov exclaimed. "I think you'll find this selection to be very enlightening." He read the passage out loud in a commanding voice for all to hear.

> Keeper of the manuscripts,
> The Author's trusted Scribe,
> Betrayal grows in darkened spaces—
> toward the one who places—
> The light inside your eyes.

> Into a world 'twas not your own
> You entered uninvited
> To seek a knowledge yet unknown—
> a sacred stone—
> With secrets locked inside it.

A sudden flash, the gift of sight,
True knowledge you acquired
And shattered in that poisoned act—
The life that you desired.

A curse of death became your prize,
Your gain, a fatal loss.
You chose a wide but darkened path—
a way of wrath—
A broken bridge to cross.

Shadowed one, O fallen one,
Go gather all your kind.
You aimed to take the Author's place—
your death embraced—
With a throne that could not bind.

Banished to a world you broke,
Still blinded by your power.
The Author's will moves forward still—
your role fulfilled—
Until that final hour.

So now you live in hosts unknown
To rule what is not yours;
They follow you with veiled eyes
and silent cries—
Behind your prison doors.

Together you are bound as one
United by the curse.
Forever held between two worlds—
Until death finds the first.

Betrayer, do you know your name?
Do you see what you have done?
You will never be the same—
A Shadow you've become.

He closed the book and looked up at me, ignoring the obnoxious snoring of Saris who had fallen asleep during the reading.

"As Evan has surely explained already, the Shadow are an alliance of the most vile creatures imaginable. In the Veil they remain invisible to human eyes. Sometimes referred to as ghosts or Shrouded Ones, they carry out their devious intentions through the manipulation of the mind. They inhabit the hearts of men, using them as their hosts to carry out their wicked plans."

"But why?" I asked, "I mean, what is it they hope to accomplish?"

"What indeed?" he replied, "That, Hunter, is why I have shown you this passage. It details the intentions of their master—the first to be called a Shadow—the most despicably wicked being that has ever existed. Even the Shadow fear him, for he is a terrible master of darkness. His name is…Sceleris."

Sceleris. The mere mention of that name sent chills up my spine as though it carried an unspeakable curse. As Petrov continued, the mood in the room grew increasingly somber.

"All who join the cause of the Shadow have pledged their souls to serve Sceleris. He despises all that is good and claims to offer true freedom to those who oppose the Author's will. He hates the Author and anything to do with him, which is why he has committed himself to erasing all knowledge of the Author from our worlds."

Petrov paused a moment and I nodded eagerly, acknowledging that I was following his every word.

"According to the Author's Writ, Sceleris was once a powerful scribe. He was a trusted friend of the Author himself, even given a position of great honor as the keeper of the Author's manuscripts. As such, Sceleris would have seen the Author enter these books on many occasions. Perhaps he was even invited to visit them from time to time with the Author. Whatever the case may be, at some point, his desire to control a book of his own grew unbearably strong. Simply being the Author's scribe wasn't good enough anymore—Sceleris wanted to be an Author himself. So, without permission, he entered the unfinished pages of our world, hoping to steal the Bloodstone and alter the story to make it his own."

"What's the Bloodstone?" I questioned, recognizing its importance.

Sam replied first, "The Bloodstone is the sacred stone the passage was referrin' to," he stated plainly. "It's what holds the secret of the Code of Life."

"Yes," Petrov resumed the conversation. "Sceleris believed that possessing the Bloodstone would give him the power he needed to control our story, but he also knew the Author had placed a curse on anyone who took the stone. So, using his powers of persuasion he convinced another to take it for him. The stone was shattered, sparing the life of the one who took it, but spoiling the stone's power for good."

As they explained, I sat in stunned silence, recalling the imagery of the boy in the garden and the stone that had shattered. I had seen this all before, exactly as they were telling it now.

"Of course, Sceleris' plan did not succeed. The Author discovered his betrayal, and as punishment for his crimes he bound Sceleris to our world—written into the very story he had once longed to control. No longer would Sceleris be able to return to the Author's library in the realm beyond our own. His life-force was broken and Sceleris became a shadow of his former self. Only his spirit remained. He is now forever tied to our story—the spirit of evil at work in our world."

"Naturally, his hatred for the Author only grew as a result. And to this day he is alive and active, seeking revenge for what the Author has done."

"But, what happened to the Bloodstone?" I asked, curious to know what occurred after my vision of the garden thief had ended.

"That, I'm afraid, remains a mystery. We know that Sceleris is unable to command its power for himself because he is only a spirit. Instead, he has used others throughout history to accomplish what he cannot. The Bloodstone has been passed from generation to generation, finding its way into the hands of many Shadow warriors who have claimed its power as their own."

Under the gentle gaze of Evan I felt a sudden urge to come clean about what I had seen in my vision of the garden.

"I think I've seen the Bloodstone before," I said aloud, much to the shock of the other captains in the room. "When I read the first pages in the book I touched the words and the story took me into a garden where the Bloodstone was kept."

"What did you see?" Petrov asked curiously.

"A boy approached the tree and some kind of bright being called him there. The boy stole the Bloodstone and it shattered in his hand. That was all it showed me," I concluded.

A few of the captains exchanged looks and muttered to each other. What I had said apparently caused a stir. A sense of excitement was growing in the room but Petrov pretended not to notice, his emotions hard to read.

Evan quickly approached Petrov. "You see? It's as I said. He has the gift; his vision confirms it."

"So it would seem," came the response. Petrov narrowed his eyes and examined me again.

"Confirms what?" I asked, aware that I appeared to be the only one who didn't know what they were talking about. The room grew eerily quiet, all eyes on me. They knew something about me, something important.

"You have been given a gift. A vision such as this is rare. Indeed, we have not had one from the Veil speak such things before."

Petrov's words left the room silent.

While I never much cared for what others thought of me, being singled out like this was a bit unnerving. I might be a little more comfortable with the attention if I wasn't completely ignorant. The question had to be asked.

"What does the vision mean?"

"I don't know." Petrov paused briefly, giving weight to his words. "But what is clear is that Aviad called you here to accomplish something of great importance. The vision is evidence that you have been chosen. Even if we knew the vision's meaning, it would not be for us to say. Aviad will explain this to you, and we will do everything in our power to get you to him, when the time is right."

Aviad. The name rang with importance, but I knew so little of him. He was the one Evan had mentioned before, the one who could supposedly help free me from the Shadow.

"I don't mean to be rude, but who exactly is Aviad?" I asked. "I mean, why is he so important?"

Evan answered first. "That is a question with many answers. Some have called him a mighty warrior, some a sage, while still others have written him off as simply a fool. As Codebearers, however, we believe he is the son of the Author himself, the true ruler of the twin worlds of Solandria and the Veil."

Sam proudly added, "Ya see, Hunter, Aviad was the one who freed our ancestors from the Shadow's lies. He established the Resistance and taught them how to employ the Code of Life, how to use it, and more importantly, how not to."

A thousand new questions leaped to mind, ready to be asked, but a commotion from the back of the assembly stole the moment. An armor-clad man stumbled in, holding his side and limping his way to the front of the room.

"Commander, I bring an urgent message," the man announced, breathing heavily. "If you would permit, a word with you in private?"

The mood shifted from excitement to a nervous buzz surrounding the arrival of this tall warrior. I found something oddly familiar about him—black hair, dark green cape. He seemed injured and out of breath.

Though he calmly remained seated, Petrov's eyes betrayed a deep concern. "Captain Faldyn, the council would hear your message. What is it? What happened to you?"

The captain shook his head. "My men and I were on our way here, but there was...an ambush...agh!" He held his side in obvious pain "...an ambush prevented us. We fought to a man, but only I remain."

Shock rumbled through the room as the news struck. Petrov stood quickly to steady the swaying captain. "Faldyn, take my chair. You must sit, brother."

He fell into the seat and drank greedily from a cup Sam held for him. The liquid eventually seemed to ease his condition enough to speak again, though with a heavy spirit.

"I couldn't save my men, but let it be said, I would have fought to the death if not for the enemy's design for me to deliver this message." Faldyn slowly removed a snakeskin scroll from his belt, handing it to Petrov.

"All were lost?" Petrov's voice had lowered to a stunned whisper. He broke open the scroll and read it silently to himself. As he read the concern in his eyes overflowed to etch itself deeply in his brow.

Looking back at Captain Faldyn, Petrov resumed his commanding calm. "Who sends this threat?"

Faldyn did not answer immediately as he sifted through his memories. "Venator."

Upon hearing the name, I suddenly remembered my last dream. The boy from my dream was Venator and this man was the fallen captain. Every detail of Faldyn's report raced into perfect alignment with what I had already seen the night before while sleeping.

Faldyn continued, "His skills in the forbidden arts have grown, I'm afraid. He had a power the likes of which I have not encountered before!"

"He comes for the boy." Petrov's voice addressed the council after reading the message.

I didn't need to ask who "the boy" from the scroll was. The answer was clear by how quickly all eyes darted back to me. Short-lived as it was, Captain Faldyn's arrival had provided me a temporary escape from the spotlight. A chair clattered to the ground as Leo stood quickly to address the council.

"Commander, in light of this new information shouldn't we take measures to move the boy tonight? Hunter will not be safe until he has reached Aviad."

Petrov diffused the sudden outburst with a calming gesture before he answered. "No, that will not be necessary. We remain here until Aviad sends word of where Hunter should meet him, just as we were commanded. Remember, everything in his time and place."

Leo wasn't convinced. "But we risk the security of this hideout as long as he is here. You know as well as I do what danger the camp would be in if the Shadow found out. Surely we cannot afford to..."

His words were cut short as Petrov forcefully broke in, "I know full well the risks, Leo. The truth is we cannot afford to act on our own outside of Aviad's orders. No doubt the Shadow will enlist every resource they have to find us, but we must not respond in fear."

Fear. The way I figured it fear wasn't something you just ignore. Sure, you can downplay a misguided fear, like when those creaking and popping sounds at night start messing with your mind. You talk yourself down from the initial scare when you figure it's "just the house settling."

But then there's the fear like I was feeling now—the very real fear of knowing there were ugly, evil creatures hunting for me this very second. That would be one of the reasonable fears that you listen to and act on. I for one couldn't help but express my opinion.

"Um, excuse me, Commander. I was thinking that maybe getting a head start on this 'meeting Aviad' trip wouldn't be so bad. 'Cause, uh, sitting around here and waiting for the Shadow to find me isn't sounding so great."

Petrov respectfully gave a few seconds pause before answering with a hint of amusement in his voice.

"Who said anything about sitting around? You'll have your work cut out for you learning the art of war."

War? Was I hearing this right? They were crazy if they thought I was going to fight in a war. Dispirits were bad enough, but from what I had seen in the forest there were creatures far worse than that working for the Shadow and I didn't want to meet up with them.

"Whoa, you've got the wrong guy. I came here to get away from the Shadow, to find out how I could get rid of them, not to get involved in a war," I said.

"Listen to him," Tyra burst out, her eyelids flickering wildly as she spoke. "It's worse than I thought; we found the boy too soon. He's not ready. Why, he's so full of fear the Shadow will smell him a mile away."

With that the room erupted in arguments over whether or not I was indeed ready to go. Each captain was talking over the other in disagreement, except, of course, for Saris who was still soundly snoring in his chair. This went on for several moments.

"Silence!" Petrov shouted at last, putting an end to the commotion and startling Saris from his sleep with such a jolt that he fell off his chair. I would have laughed at the man if the tone of the room wasn't so tense. Petrov ignored Saris as he clambered back into his chair, wondering what he had missed.

"Aviad thinks he is ready to be here, and I am willing to trust his judgment. The boy stays with us. All we can do is wait."

Looking around at the warriors surrounding the table I couldn't help but feel a bit out of place. Evan must have sensed my insecurity and took hold of my shoulder, looking me straight in the eye.

"If I know Aviad, then you have much more to offer than you think. Who knows, you might even be the one who will turn the tide of this war."

The words he spoke weighed heavily on my heart. *Could it really be that I was part of a bigger plan to restore this world? Me? The goof-off who had barely passed gym class? What good could I possibly offer to help win the war?*

"But why me? I didn't ask for this. It's like I said before, you've got the wrong guy. I don't even know the first thing about fighting in a war."

Petrov raised his eyebrows. "I'm afraid there are circumstances in life we have no choice in. You can't run from the Shadow, Hunter. Like it or not, this war has come to you. You can decide either to fight, or try to avoid it and let the Shadow have their way with you." I was at a loss for words.

Looking me in the eye Petrov concluded, "You have been called for a purpose, Hunter. Aviad does not make mistakes. He will confirm his plan for you. So what do you say? Will you join the Resistance and learn the ways of the Code?"

All eyes were on me again. *What did I want?*

"I'd like to go back home for awhile and see my family first, if that's alright. You know, let them know I'm here and safe. Maybe if I had more time…"

Petrov spoke firmly, "Unfortunately, time is something you do not have. The Shadow already know you are in Solandria, which means your window of opportunity is closing quickly. Turn back now and they have already won. There is no promise of a second chance. You may never return."

Fear gripped me by the stomach and took control of my mind. Then, to make matters worse, that hideous voice spoke again in my mind. Cold and divided—the same one I had heard in my bedroom just before I opened the book.

Don't be a fool.

My head began to throb and I placed a hand to my temple to try and relieve the pressure.

They do not care for you. They will use you and leave you to die. Go back home and leave them to their own demise. This is not your war.

I closed my eyes and tried to weigh my thoughts. The idea that someone had chosen *me* was hard to believe, I had so little to offer. Still, my quest would not be complete without at least a visit to Aviad.

I swallowed hard. My fears began to subside slowly. My decision became clear. I would seek the truth.

"Okay, I'll give it a shot," I said at last, the words escaping before I could think twice. The weight of the decision had been lifted from my shoulders—I was committed. Evan released an audible sigh of relief. Sam grinned wide with pride. The others appeared mildly encouraged.

"Very well," Petrov nodded, his voice solemn with importance. "You'll start first thing in the morning! Sam will continue your training, I assume, as it seems he has already begun."

"With pleasure," Sam replied, "and you'll want to be sure ta get good and rested tonight for what I've got planned."

I could only imagine what that beast of a man had in mind when he thought of training. *Oh man, what was I getting myself into?*

"Then it's settled. We'll make arrangements for you to stay with the Goodsmiths. They have a spare room that is available if I'm not mistaken."

Oh no, not Gabby! I winced.

Hope cast a knowing smile my way that seemed to say, *I'm sorry!* The meeting quickly adjourned and the captains broke into conversations amongst themselves. Hope found her way back to my side.

"You did well," she offered.

"I'm glad you think so. I'm not so sure I'm ready. I mean, I still have so many questions."

"Questions are good, Hunter; they make us hungry for truth. Just be patient, the answers will come in time. Come on!" she nudged me. "I'll show you the way to the Goodsmith's cottage if you'd like."

"Do I have another choice?" I pleaded with a smile.

"Oh stop!" she laughed. "Gabby isn't all *that* bad. Besides, she probably tires out early at her age. She and Gerwyn will enjoy having you spend some time with them. You give them something to smile about."

"I suppose so," I thought aloud. Old people had never been my favorite. They were just so, so...boring. And they smelled funny too.

Together we wandered across the courtyard and into the woods beyond the fortress walls. A brisk walk down a winding path and over a cobblestone bridge brought us to the base of a rather large tree. A spiral staircase was wrapped around the trunk and led upward to a large two-story home nestled high in the roost of the great oak.

"Cool! That's their place?" I gawked.

"Yup, and you thought they weren't any fun," Hope teased, leading me up the stairway.

Gabby, glowing with an enthusiastic smile, answered the door and was more than willing to entertain me for the duration of my stay. She pulled me inside and had me sit on the couch, sneaking a cup of tea into my hand before I even knew it was there. It was going to be a long evening.

Chapter 9

The Revealing Room

Nothing is more annoying than being jolted awake by the sun in your eyes. I pulled the blankets over my head in hopes of ignoring the brilliant morning sunlight that streamed through the windows of my room, but it was no use. Morning had arrived. My room in the upper tower of the Goodsmith's home was spacious and comfortable, but I had found it difficult to sleep—kept awake by anxiety more than anything.

As my mind whizzed through the previous day's events, I came to the sudden and shocking realization that I was going to be late for my first day of training. I fumbled with my clothes and scurried downstairs to the welcome smell of a well-prepared breakfast.

"Don't you dare try and leave here today without a bite to eat now, you hear?" Gabby threatened. "You have a long day ahead of you, and you'll thank me later."

Not wanting to argue with the woman, I scarfed down something that tasted like ham, and some orangey-blue eggs. The meal was tasty but I didn't have enough time to fully enjoy it. I offered a quick thanks to Gabby and tore off down the winding stairway back to the fortress.

Hope was waiting at the gateway and led me to the training grounds—a place they called the Academy. The large circular building with a green domed roof was centered in a wide park-like courtyard. We passed by a group of children several years younger than me, paired together in fencing matches with wooden swords. Their instructor wandered from pair to pair, overseeing their progress and monitoring their techniques.

"'Bout time you showed up." Sam seemed to come out of nowhere. "I was beginnin' ta wonder if ya was changin' your mind. You look terrible, did ya sleep at all?"

"Not much," I replied.

"You will tonight, I guarantee it."

That didn't sound good. I cringed.

"Seein' as you're pretty wet behind the ears with all of this Codebearer learnin' I think it's best we find out what ya've got before we get ta yer trainin'."

Turning to one of the young boys in a nearby training circle Sam shouted, "Philan! Come here, lad, I'd like ya ta meet Hunter."

"Hey, you're the new guy at the feast last night! My dad told me you were someone pretty important." I liked the kid already. He was young, maybe nine at most, and a bit scrawny for his age but he obviously had a good head on his shoulders.

"That he may be, Philan, but it's my task ta prepare Hunter fer the journey that lies ahead of him. I was wondering if ya could do me a favor and line up with Hunter fer a quick fleet-foot test?"

Leaning over my way Sam explained, "It's just a simple race really, ta see how fast ya can get from this spot ta that stump over yonder. Ya up ta it?"

"Yeah, sure. But, uh," I lowered my voice, "shouldn't I be racing against someone a little closer to my age?"

"Philan's got speed enough fer measuring ya against right now. So then, if ya both will toe up ta the line…"

I didn't want to show up the poor kid too quickly. With a distance of a hundred feet or so to run, I figured I'd start our pace slow and then pull ahead in the last twenty feet. An admirable plan I thought. I caught Philan's eye and gave him a friendly nod.

Sam called out "On yer mark. Get set. Go!"

We were off, but only two strides into the race I'd seen enough to know that Philan wasn't your average kid when it came to running. I had not even gone halfway and he was already ten feet ahead of me. I couldn't lose to a nine-year-old! I abandoned my first plan and ran all-out to win this silly race. I was gaining…I was nearly on his heels…then without warning Philan disappeared. *What had just happened?* I turned my head to look for him.

About that same time I remembered my gym teacher's rule; you know, the one about keeping your eyes on the finish line and not getting distracted by watching other racers. Yeah, I'm pretty sure that would have helped keep me from tripping up and performing the world's biggest face-plant on the dirt track. Then again, my gym teacher had never raced a kid who could do what I just saw. What *had* I seen?

Jerking my head up from the dust cloud I'd created, I located Philan's figure ahead of me just in time to see it landing on the ground and skidding to a stop at the stump.

"Well done, Philan!" Sam called out before turning to me. He attempted to sound concerned while holding back a smile. "Ho, ho! You alright there, Hunter?"

"Yeah...never...better," I said bitterly between spitting out the lovely taste I'd acquired from the dirt. "What just happened?"

"Ya lost the race." Sam was missing my point.

"No, not that! I mean, how did he...?"

Sam finished my question for me. "How did Philan beat ya to the finish?"

I nodded.

"Because he believed he could, Hunter. Ya didn't think that one so young could beat ya, now did ya?"

I shook my head. He was reading my mind.

"One thing I've learned is that ya can't look down on others because of their youth. Some of the greatest feats are accomplished by some of our youngest. Seems they can come ta believin' easier than the older among us, which in the Author's eyes, makes them the greatest warriors of all."

I looked back at Philan and struggled to see how one so small could ever be considered a warrior. Still, what I had just witnessed during the race proved there was more to him than met the eye. I couldn't wait to learn how he had done it.

"I have hope for ya, Hunter, being as you've come here as young as ya have. Mark my words; one day these young'uns will be the ones who will lead the Codebearers in battle."

"Teacher Sam, do you need me for anything else?" Philan interrupted, joining us back at my face-planting fiasco.

"No. That'll do, thank you, lad."

"Good race." Philan offered a handshake. "Need a hand?"

Not only super-fast, he's super-mannered. "Yeah, sure kid... whoa!" Philan might not have had the size of Sam, but he nearly launched me into another face-plant, considering how quickly he pulled me up. The mud in my eye and losing the race were enough humiliation for the last five minutes. My ears were glowing red—I could feel them. Even so, I waved to Philan as he bounced his way back to his training group.

"Guess I've got a bit to learn, Sam," I muttered, rubbing my newly dislocated shoulder.

"Well then, we best be gettin' started. Follow me."

He led Hope and me into the Academy and through an empty stairwell at the end of a long hall. As we walked he began to review what I had learned so far.

"Since we don't have much time, I figure we'll be doin' good ta cover the basics. You'll recall we began our discussion 'bout the Code of Life back on the Shard of Inire. Do ya remember what the first truth was?"

The answer came suddenly to mind, as we descended the darkened stairs. "Nothing comes from nothing," I said somewhat proud of myself.

"Good, so then, what is it that all things come from? What one thing do we owe our existence to?"

"The Author!" I responded, hoping it was the answer he was looking for.

"Ah, but what does that mean?"

I wasn't quite sure what he wanted. Was it a trick question?

"Uh, that the Author created everything that exists?"

"Yes, but there's much more ta it than that; not only is he the Author of all things, but he created all things fer a purpose. He has a reason fer everythin' he made."

He stopped abruptly in his tracks and turned to face me, wagging his finger in my face. His sudden turn caught me by surprise and it was all I could do to stop myself before crashing into him.

"Don't be forgettin' this, Hunter. Nothin' escapes the Author's reach. He is in control of everythin'. This is *his* story, his world—he alone is the One who determines what can and cannot happen. He is the cornerstone of the Code of Life. Everythin' else I try and teach ya will flow out of yer belief in this truth."

The Author is in control. I made a mental note to commit it to memory, though I wasn't exactly sure how it could be true. After all, I was in control of my own life—wasn't I?

Down the winding stairwell the three of us continued without further conversation. By now we must have been several hundred feet below ground and yet we were still descending. The stairway seemed to continue forever, but after several more minutes of silence, we came at last to the foot of a massive wooden door.

"Ah, here we are, the Revealin' Room. It will be our trainin' ground fer the next few days. Shall we?" He winked and walked through the door without opening it as if it didn't exist, leaving Hope and me alone.

"Whoa! Cool, a magic door!" I said, striding headlong into it with confidence.

SMACK! I fell back in pain, holding my face in my hands.

"Ouch, that hurt!" Hope rushed to my side, trying to conceal her laughter unsuccessfully. "You alright?" she giggled.

"It's not funny; I think I broke my nose!" I spouted. *Not to mention my pride.*

"Sorry, it's just that you should have seen yourself," she said, helping me to my feet. I looked up at the door again—it just stood there, taunting me to try again. There were no handles so I approached it slowly this time, pressing my hand flatly against it and giving a firm push—it didn't move. I pushed harder, applying more pressure but it was thick and wouldn't give an inch.

"I don't get it, how did Sam do that? It won't budge!"

Hope rolled her eyes, "Of course not; it's not that kind of door. It's obviously a test of some kind," she said taking several steps back and glancing around.

"Look, down here." Hope drew my attention to a plaque that was embedded in the ground. She read it aloud.

ONLY THE HUMBLE OF HEART SHALL PASS

"Great. Why didn't I see that before?" I wondered.

"Maybe because you were *too cocky* to notice it?" she said. I fought back the burning desire to defend my actions, if only to keep from further proving her point, and sounding foolish.

"Fine," I conceded, rubbing my nose. "If you're so smart, what does it mean?" I asked, in a cynical tone that was usually reserved for my sister. My words found their mark. Hope shot a wounded look back at me, obviously shocked at my response. *What was I doing? I liked her! I didn't want to offend her.*

She looked really sad. *Time to bail water; the SS Hunter was going down fast.* I adjusted my tone, "Sorry, that was the nose talking," I added in a friendly voice, pointing at my sore nose. "What I meant to say was, do you have any ideas?" It wasn't the best recovery ever written but it seemed to work, as her smile quickly returned.

"The nose talking? Is that the best you could come up with?" She laughed.

"Yeah, I guess that did sound pretty dumb." We shared a laugh before turning once again to the riddle in the ground.

"Well, being humble means being teachable and open to change," she said. "It makes sense. After all, you're here to learn, right?"

"Yeah, so?" I wondered, not getting it.

"So, I think it means that if you have a truly teachable spirit, you can pass through the door." It sounded stupid but I didn't want to say so. Instead, I watched silently as she tested her theory, fully expecting to be sharing sore noses in a few minutes. She stood on the plaque and closed her eyes. A moment later she stepped forward and to my amazement walked through just as Sam had done.

"Great, just great!" I muttered alone beneath the mocking glare of the door. "First I get beat in a simple race by a nine-year-old, and now I'm shown up by a girl."

"Teachable, fine! I'll show you how teachable I can be!" Gathering my willpower and chanting under my breath I walked to the door.

"Teachable. Teachable. I'm teachable!"

SMACK!

"Aargh!" My frustration boiled over, and I kicked the door hard, stubbing my toe in the process. Anger raged through my veins and I expressed it in a string of choice words that would have grounded me for a month if my mother had heard them. When at last I had calmed down, I took a deep breath.

"Okay, Hunter," I reasoned with myself, "just let go. You obviously have a lot to learn. You're not here to impress anyone, just be willing to learn."

I stood on the plaque and looked down past my feet to the inscription. *Only the humble of heart shall pass.* A simple thought passed through my mind before I knew where it came from. *I can't do this alone. Give me a teachable spirit.*

I closed my eyes and stepped forward, this time fully expecting to be smacked in the face again. Several steps later I realized that something had changed. I opened my eyes to a bright yellow sky in the middle of a golden forest of autumn trees. Looking back over my shoulder I saw the wooden door still firmly in place behind me—I had passed through, but exactly to where I was not sure.

The stone-set pathway beneath my feet led to the base of a short flight of stairs, and on to a circular atrium spacious enough to accommodate a small gathering of people. The platform was covered by an open-air brass canopy that was supported by several marble archways all the way around. Sam and Hope stood waiting near the center of the platform beside a stone pedestal that looked something like a sundial.

"There you are, Hunter." Sam was the first to notice I had arrived. "Well done, lad. Took me a whole lot longer than that ta enter first time I tried. Always was a little stubborn, me mum would say. Anyhow, now that's behind us you'll be ready fer trainin'."

He motioned for me to step forward. A breeze blew through the atrium, bringing with it the crisp smell of fall.

"How did we get here?" I asked. "I mean, how is this possible? I thought we were deep underground."

"Still are," Sam replied. "This is just an illusion. The Revealin' Room can be anyplace we need it ta be ta complete yer trainin'. Here, I'll show ya what I mean."

As I approached the pedestal that stood beside Sam and Hope, I noticed it wasn't a sundial after all, but rather a mechanical interface made up of a rather complex sequence of nested dials. Sam adjusted the settings and pressed a button in the center of the device.

The golden forest that surrounded us faded into blackness, disappearing with a flash as if someone had just turned off a television. For a brief moment the atrium, stone pathway and door were the only items that remained in sight. Then as quickly as our previous environment disappeared, a new one flashed into form. We were on a high mountain peak in the middle of a soft snowfall. The snow-capped mountains surrounding us were hidden by powder-white clouds.

"Whoa, cool," I marveled, sticking my tongue out to catch the snow that fell from the sky. *Amazing, it even tastes like snow. Like virtual reality,* I thought, *only better.* Everything was so real. This place was unbelievable.

"Wish I had a room like this back home," I said, dazzled by the scenery. The horizon seemed a million miles away. "Sure would make being grounded a lot more fun."

"Pretty nifty, eh?" Sam boasted. "Here, I'll dial up another one."

Splatt! A snowball the size of my fist hit me in the back of the neck, sending a chill of frozen snow down my shirt. Hope had taken a cheap shot when I wasn't looking.

"Oh you're going to pay for that one," I muttered under my icy breath, collecting a snowball of my own. She ducked quickly behind Sam who was already working the dials to take us to another location. I hurried around to get a clear shot, launching my snowball just as Sam pressed the button on the dial. Hope flinched in anticipation of the snowball's impact. The environment disappeared and took the snowball with it, only inches before it met its target.

"Ha! Missed me," she bragged in the blackness between worlds.

"Hey, no fair!" I moaned. Hope made a silly face and I returned the gesture, cracking a smile that soon gave into full laughter.

The moment was cut short with the arrival of the new environment Sam had dialed up. We found ourselves placed in the lair of an enormous black dragon. The creature's glowing red eyes shot open, pupils dilating—its slumber interrupted. A low growl rumbled in its throat, expressing its displeasure to find us there.

"Oops!" Sam replied, "Didn't mean ta do that."

We froze in place, not daring to make a sound for fear of further angering the beast. The dragon leered at us; hunched like a tiger on the prowl it circled the atrium. Its tail swept slowly across the ground behind it, black smoke bellowing from its nostrils. When at last it had completed a circle the beast drew itself to full stature, towering over us. A trickle of wet drool dripped from its mouth, running down its jaw and falling to the floor beside me.

"Okay, Sam. We can go back now," I whimpered.

"Hold on, I gotta get this here dial ta spin."

A terrible screeching roar pierced my ears and echoed throughout the cavernous lair, causing all three of us to scream in terror.

"Ahhhhhhhhhhhhh," we yelled in unison.

Eyes wide with fear, Sam slammed his fist down on the button just as the dragon raised its ugly head and blew a fiercely hot flame into the atrium. I fell to the floor, eyes tightly shut, expecting the worst as the heat from the flames warmed the air around me. Everything went silent. Several moments later I peeked one eye open to find Sam and Hope hunched over me. We were alive.

"Sorry 'bout that, Hunter; I accidently took us ta the final exam." Sam apologized. "Quite a scare there, wasn't it? Ya okay?"

My heart was still pounding from the sheer terror of the experience as I gathered myself together and stood back up. Nothing was singed. Other than having the living daylights scared out of me, I seemed to be doing okay.

"Final exam? W-what do you mean by final exam?" I gulped.

"Oh, don't worry about that none. We won't be sendin' ya back there until you're good and ready. Besides, I ain't never lost a student yet." He spoke with false confidence and a smile that quickly faded. Then, pursing his lips and glancing upward in thought, he added,

"'Course, there was that one time with Bobby Bungle, but that was different. The guy was a knucklehead."

"What happened?" I questioned.

"Aaah! No use dwellin' on other people's failures. We've got some training ta do. This way, then."

With that, Sam lumbered down the atrium stairs, expecting me to follow him immediately, which I didn't. Instead, I hesitated, taking time to survey our new environment first.

We were in a large cylindrical study with a strange assortment of furniture placed haphazardly throughout. A magnificent red carpet covered most of the stone floor, and the walls, for the most part, were plastered with dull portraits, detailed maps and crammed bookshelves. Considering it safe to proceed, I started down the steps. My gaze quickly shifted above an ornate table across the room where a holographic map hovered in slow rotation. The image seemed to be projecting from a book that was flopped open on the table.

"Well, hurry up, lad. No time ta dilly-dally." Sam motioned hurriedly with his hand for me to join him. I took my place in a stiff, high-backed chair at the foot of a table. Hope sat to my left in a larger overstuffed chair that looked much more comfortable.

"Tell me, Hunter. Have you used the book lately?"

"Not much," I said, which was mostly true. As a matter of fact, so far I had managed to lug the thing around with me everywhere, but had not actually cracked it open since the day I first read it alone in my room.

He pulled the book that lay open on the table into his hands, snapping it shut and dousing the hologram in the process.

"The Author's Writ," he explained lifting the book from the table, "is more than just readin' material. It's a connection ta the Author himself. Don't be takin' this book fer granted, ya hear? If ya are goin' ta become a Codebearer, I suggest ya spend time committin' some of it to memory. It will do ya good in the heat of battle."

I nodded with renewed interest, wondering if my copy of the Writ was capable of projecting images as well.

He pointed to the symbol of interlocking *Vs* on the front of the book. "Now, we'll start at the beginnin'. This here is the Author's mark. It is used by those who follow his way."

"What do the *Vs* stand for?" I asked. I had wondered about that since the very first time I'd seen them.

"Ah yes, glad ya asked. *Via, Veritas, Vita*," he said boldly, tracing each *V* on the cover with his finger as he said it. "It comes from a phrase that means *the way of truth and life*! It's the Codebearer's mantra, ya could say, reminds us that the Author alone holds the answers ta life."

I nodded, taking in his words, anxious to learn what secrets were held within its pages.

"Now then," he cleared his throat in preparation for my lesson. "Tell me, Hunter, have ya ever been afraid?"

"Yeah," I shrugged. *What kind of question was that?*

"What do ya fear most?"

"Lots of things, I guess." That was true; there were so many things it was hard to know where to start. Before I had come to Solandria I was afraid of drowning, heights and birds. Now, my priorities of fear had changed to include being captured by the Shadow, having to fight in a war and in a funny way—I was afraid of success. As a matter of fact, I had always been a below-average kind of guy. So, once I learned to accept it, the only thing I felt I could truly succeed at was failure, and it seemed to be working out for me so far.

"A true Codebearer fears only one thing. Do ya know what that is?"

I hesitated to answer, growing tired of the question game. "Sceleris?" I guessed at last.

"No, someone much more powerful than that."

"The Author?" I answered with more than a hint of confusion.

"Exactly!" His response shocked me.

"But I thought the Author was good. Why should I be afraid of him?"

"He is good—ya can be sure of that. But don't take fer granted that he's immeasurably powerful. He's in control of every detail of our lives, and when we really understand that it leaves us no choice but ta tremble."

"I thought fear was a bad thing."

"Only when it's misplaced. Our fear of the Author offers an overwhelming sense of peace when it comes ta the trials we face. After all, what can happen outside his plan?"

Something didn't add up. "I don't get it. If the Author is in control of everything, then why do bad things still happen? Why couldn't he simply write them out of existence—or not write them in the first place?"

"There's only one possible answer ta that question, as far as I can figure. He has a purpose fer even the evil things that happen, Hunter; that's what I've been trying ta tell ya. We experience the Author's story every day. Some pages are full of hope, happiness and good things, while others are harder ta accept and full of difficulties and trials. Both pages come from the Author's hand and in the end, somehow, the story is better because of it. If ya can understand this truth, ya won't fear anything but the Author alone."

Try as I might I couldn't grasp what Sam was saying. He led me to several passages in the book that seemed to prove his point, but I couldn't bring myself to believe them. If the Author allowed evil into existence for a purpose then there was really no reason to resist it. And I really didn't like the thought that my life was controlled by anyone other than myself. I was the master of my life, wasn't I?

We debated the subject for several hours. The frustrating conversation only added to my confusion and seemed to offer no help in preparing me for the challenges that lay ahead.

Weary of the lecture, I began fidgeting in my chair. Sam noticed and looked up from his reading.

"What is it?" he asked.

"Well, I was wondering when we were going to get to the cool stuff. You know: how to fight the Shadow, how to run like that boy outside or disappear like Evan said he could do."

"I can't teach ya that."

"Why not?"

"Because it can't be taught. It can only be learned, and ya learn it first by takin' the words of the book ta heart. The Code of Life has a will of its own. It will change ya if you let it."

"But how is this supposed to help me? I don't understand it at all," I complained.

He pursed his lips to one side in thought. "Fair enough," he said, "let's put it ta the test. Follow me."

He led us back up to the atrium, turned the dials and pressed the button on the pedestal once again. In a flash, the room changed as it had before and brought us just outside the entrance of a cave. A low howl of wind escaped the mouth of the cave; it sounded like the groan of a dying animal. After what I had seen of the dragon, I wasn't so sure I was ready to explore this cave.

"What is this place?" I asked, a little unnerved at the look of it. Dark. Cold. Wet. Mysterious.

"A test. Ya go in alone. When yer finished, we'll be waitin'." With no further instruction, he handed me the book and gave me a gentle push toward the entrance. One lonely step at a time, I willed myself into the darkened mouth of the cave. I glanced back over my shoulder at Sam and Hope. She wore a concerned look on her face, one that seemed to imply she knew what I was in for.

"Trust the book," Sam called out, "and pay attention ta what ya see."

Then, as if by magic, the mouth of the cave began to close up behind me. Stones appeared out of nowhere, forming a solid rock wall between me and the world outside. I ran back to the wall, feeling for anyway out, but it was too late. There was no reversing what had just happened. I was trapped.

"Okay, Hunter," I assured myself. "It's only a test. You can do this."

CHAPTER 10

FEAR AND THE SWORD

A single torch hung on the wall beside me, casting a pulsing orange light over the scene. Pulling the torch down from its place, I carried it aloft into the dark unknown.

Creeping dread haunted my thoughts. Each step I took echoed off the walls and played tricks on my mind. *Footsteps! Is someone following me?* I thought to myself. A quick glance over my shoulder confirmed that I was still alone but did little to calm my anxiety. Winding through the tunnel, I made my way slowly to the back of the cave, brushing away thick cobwebs along the way.

Somewhere ahead a blue light gleamed, casting a soft glow on the cave walls in front of me. The passage floor was lined with clay pots and vessels of various shapes and sizes—many of them broken and covered in dust. I stepped carefully around them as

I passed, hoping not to make noise. Finally, the tunnel turned abruptly to the left and opened into a large spacious cavern.

No dragons. No dragons. Please, no dragons.

To my relief the room was empty, save for a short pillar directly across the room. It stood atop a short flight of steps, flanked on either side by stone statues of cloaked figures with their hands resting on carved swords. A beam of sparkling blue light shone down from somewhere far above, illuminating an item that was at rest on the pillar. From this distance it was impossible to tell what it highlighted, I would have to cross over to check it out.

A similar pair of stone statues was carved from the walls on either side of the passageway entrance, looking out over the cavern ahead of me—faceless figures draped in hooded cloaks, hands clasped in front of them. They were nearly mirror images of each other, with the exception of one missing feature—one was grasping a stone torch, and the other one was empty handed. The blue light above the pillar offered more than enough visibility to navigate the room, so I figured I could set my torch down for the moment.

Convenient, I thought, placing my torch in the empty grasp of the second statue. With a sudden slide and a loud *Ka-Chunk,* a stone wall fell behind me, blocking the path back to where the cave entrance used to be.

"Okay, okay, I get the point," I said aloud. "Now it's doubly evident that there's no turning back."

I stepped forward in hopes of examining the pillar across the room but with my first step the floor gave way beneath me, disappearing into a deep chasm. I collapsed awkwardly, dropping the book and twisting my ankle in the process. Spinning around I barely grasped the ledge in time as a larger section of the floor crumbled down into the bottomless pit below. Hanging precariously by my fingertips I glanced out over the void that threatened to swallow me alive. I winced at the thought of it, willing myself to hang tight.

"Er!" I grimaced as I tried to lift myself.

Was Sam trying to kill me? Ms. White's tests suddenly seemed tame in comparison to what I was now facing. With considerable effort, I pulled myself back up to safety and sat for a moment, trying to calm my racing heart.

Luckily, the book had fallen safely on solid ground. I gathered it up and examined the cavern floor carefully. It appeared to be cracking and weak, a false path hiding the terrible chasm beneath. The ground between where I stood and the pillar could not be trusted.

"How in the world," I thought out loud. "There must be another way to reach the other side, but how?" With no way to turn back, I looked around hoping to find a message of some kind, or an obvious way to pass, but nothing presented itself.

Suddenly, Sam's words came rushing to mind. *Trust the book,* he had said as the cave had shut behind me.

Of course, I reasoned, *the book must have a solution or a map of some kind to help me navigate.*

I set the book down on a rather large stone resting beneath the formerly torchless statue. Speaking loudly as the others had, I asked the book a question:

"How can I reach the other side?"

Surprisingly, it opened on its own and flipped quickly to a blank page. I watched in wonder as a cryptic message appeared as if it was only just being written.

You will walk by fire and not be burned.

The puzzling statement left me pondering its meaning for several minutes with no success.

"Well, that was no help," I finally concluded. Reaching toward the book I decided to turn the page myself in search of something else. The sound of stone grinding on stone stopped me cold. A sudden movement caught my eye—the arm of the statue began to move. I stepped back in shock.

The statue's hand holding my torch lowered until it settled just above a large jar. Then, as if on purpose, the torch slipped from the statue's grasp and dropped into the jar. Cautiously I walked over, casting an uneasy glance back at the statue on my way. The jar was carved of stone, not clay, as I had originally thought. Peering inside I found it was connected to a deep well that fell far below the level of the floor.

"Okay," I said to myself, "my torch is gone, now what!"

I stared absently into the dark hole of the jar. Then a flash of orange-red flames shot up the well and caused me to stumble back in surprise.

A tongue of fire raced around the circumference of the room along both sides—meeting together behind the pillar across the room. The fire continued out from the pillar, down the steps and zigzagged across the fragile ground in front of me, igniting a path of fire as it headed back to where I stood.

The flames sped toward me with such intensity I stumbled backward, pressing myself tightly against the stone door that locked me in the room. The flames stopped abruptly at the edge of the room, slightly to the left of where I had first stepped out.

"Whoa!" I looked out in amazement at the scene as I walked forward slowly. The flames burned hot and brightly as I approached. The book lay open just as I had left it—at the foot of the statue. Leaning over to pick it up, I read the words once again. *You will walk by fire and not be burned.*

Surely it didn't mean what I thought it meant? I couldn't be expected to actually walk in the fire, could I? I didn't even know if the floor could hold my weight, but there was only one way to find out. I picked up a decent-sized stone and tossed it out onto the flaming pathway—it landed with a solid thud and the ground did not collapse. I would have considered this an encouraging sign were it not for the raging fire that now occupied the space where I would have to walk.

"You gotta be kidding me," I shuddered, completely stunned at the impossibility of what I knew I must do to pass the test. I repeated Sam's words to myself, hoping the very sound of them might offer some encouragement.

"Trust the book! Trust the book." It wasn't going to get any easier.

I moved as close to the edge as my courage would allow, then a little further. My heart rate accelerated, my hands shook in fright and I raised my foot, preparing to step forward into the fiery path. I held my breath and took the first step.

The ground was firm and hot, but surprisingly, despite the intensity of the flames, I was not burning. The book was right. I released an enormous sigh of relief and laughed in amazement. I was going to make it.

With careful steps I made my way across the floor to the base of the stairway leading up to the pillar, beneath the uncomfortable gaze of the stone guardians.

As I climbed the stairs, the pillar's top came into view and I saw it—the hilt of a sword—a Veritas Sword. I reached into the light and grasped the leather-wrapped handle. Lifting it from the pillar, I ran my other hand over the cold metal, examining the simple design. The first thing I noticed was the Author's mark boldly engraved at the top of the golden hilt, set in the center of a circle where the invisible blade would appear. The crossbar moved outward from the circle, angling slightly upward from the shaft. The weight of the sword felt at home in my hands, almost as if it were made for me alone, perfectly balanced by a pommel at the base that made it easy to handle. The thought occurred to me that perhaps this was not just any sword; maybe this was *my* sword. A shiver shot up my spine.

Wide-eyed with wonder, I passed my hand over the top where the blade would be. Then, with a broad smile, I clasped it in both hands and began swinging it around in imaginary swordplay.

"Hunter the Codebearer," I shouted victoriously, "slashing through the Shadow's ranks with master skill, sending them to the void before they knew he was there." I continued my clumsy display of swordsmanship, pretending to slice the stone guardians through their middles. Then, it happened.

"Codebearer, you are NOT," a dark voice echoed throughout the room, interrupting my moment of triumph. Fear welled up inside me. I spun around in search of the unwelcome visitor, nobody was there. It was the same voice that had haunted me in my bedroom at home just before I opened the book. *"You belong to me. I will teach you the meaning of fear."* I didn't like the sound of that.

Clomp!

A loud noise from behind commanded my attention. I turned to look, sword lifted in defense. What I saw made my heart skip a beat. The stone guardians were missing. Not good.

Whoosh! Thud!

A stone sword crashed to the ground, just missing its target—me. The guardians hadn't disappeared; they were alive and apparently trying to kill me. A surge of adrenaline raced through my veins and I lurched out of the way, dashing across the stairs, trying to escape their reach. The stone warriors followed with determination, knowing full well there was nowhere for me to go.

Smash! The left-handed guardian swung his sword down hard, landing only a few inches to my right. Raising my new Veritas Sword in response, I swung it downward, hoping to inflict some damage to its arm. Nothing happened. The blade remained invisible and passed by the stone without so much as a scratch. My weapon seemed useless in comparison with the visible swords my attackers were wielding.

Swish-swish!

The guard returned with a low double slice, inflicting a sharp sting to my leg where the blade had grazed me. It was a light cut but I could feel warm blood trickling down my leg already. This was no illusion, it was real. I was in trouble.

By now the second guard had circled around behind me, his movement alerting me to his presence. I turned to face him just as he brought his sword up over his head to deliver a death blow. I rolled backward under the legs of the first guard, just as the right-handed one began lowering his sword in a powerful swipe that was meant to cut me in half. As luck would have it, the blade came down at the same time the first guard lowered his head to look between his legs, severing his neck in my stead and sending his head toppling down the stairs.

I couldn't have planned it better if I had tried.

While the first statue stumbled away in search of its head, the second paused in sudden realization of what had just happened. Then, with a fierce red glow where its eyes should have been, it came after me with the stride of a man who had a score to settle, closing the distance between us in no time at all. I dodged a series of attacks, narrowly escaping death with every blow. Try as I might, I couldn't get the Veritas Sword to work; it was of no value to me. If I didn't figure out something soon I'd be diced sushi for sure.

I ducked beneath another pass of the sword with ease, but did not expect what followed. A swift kick placed squarely to my chest, knocked the wind from my lungs and launched me down the stairs. *Ouch!* I landed hard on the floor.

Weakened and sore I looked up to see the guard approaching slowly, steadily and purposefully. It knew I was defeated and was no longer in a hurry. I tried to stand but the pain in my leg and my chest was unbearable. Instead, I scooted myself backward in a feeble attempt to delay the inevitable death that was approaching with each footstep of the guardian. He lifted his sword slowly in anticipation of victory.

The final moments of my trial seemed to move in slow motion. The red-eyed guard with sword raised high; the other still looking for its head; my hands reaching back to pull myself away; and the sudden sensation that the ground was giving out beneath me. In my effort to escape I had scooted back onto the crumbling floor. It cracked beneath my weight and I plummeted headlong into the blackened chasm below.

Down. Down. Down.

Far below I could see the platform of the Revealing Room take form, growing larger and larger the further I fell. I expected to make impact with a spectacular thud, proving to the world that I had failed once again. Death was coming. I held my breath in fear and tried my best not to cry. Instead, I let out a long helpless scream.

Remarkably, just before hitting the ground, my fall began to slow until it came to a complete stop midair. Suspended only inches above the platform by an invisible string, I dangled with feet sprawled and arms flailing. The platform was empty and the room completely black. All at once, the force that held me in place released its hold and I fell the remaining four inches to the ground.

Smack!

I landed flat on my face—which hurt, even from only four inches up. As soon as I could look up I discovered I was back in the study. Hope was nervously pacing the room and Sam sat quietly reading a book. The soft thump of my body announced my arrival.

"Hunter! You made it!" Hope shouted, running toward the platform.

Sam looked up casually from his reading, "Well, well…looks like ya chose the black pit exit, eh? Very popular choice," he chuckled.

"Chose? More like I was chased into it by some freaky statue dudes with swords!"

Sam rose from his chair to make his way over to the landing. I tried to stand but my body was sore and my left leg throbbed from the cut I had gotten.

Hope raced up the steps excitedly, "You got the Sword and—you're hurt!" Her enthusiasm faded into concern when she saw me favoring my leg.

"It's nothing really, just a…" I was about to say a scratch, but I looked down and realized it was much more than that. My left leg was covered in an inky black fluid that seemed to be flowing from my wound. The sight made me sick and lightheaded.

"Whoa, what's going on? What's wrong with me?" I shouted in horror, growing more and more nauseous by the second.

Sam raced up the stairs of the platform and brushed Hope

aside. "Here, I better have a look at that!" He widened the tear in my jeans with a stern tug and examined the broad wound. "That's a nasty little cut ya got there, lad. Hang tight, this'll probably hurt a bit." Pulling his Veritas Sword from his side he pressed it against the wound. A sharp burning sensation shot through my leg and into my thigh. My body screamed in protest from the pain.

"Ow!" I snapped, flinching from the touch. "That hurts!"

"Now, don't be such a baby. It'll be over soon enough," Sam replied, pressing harder.

I gritted my teeth and clinched my fists, fighting back the urge to push the sword away.

"Just a second more," he assured me. "There we are, good as new."

I was astonished. There was a slight scar where the wound had once been, but other than that it was completely healed.

"Thanks," I said, inspecting the scar.

Sam simply nodded.

"What was that stuff coming out of my leg?" I asked, appalled at what I had just seen.

"It's your blood, Hunter."

"Why was it black?"

"Your blood has always been that way. You're infected, remember? It's just that—well—you've never really seen it before now."

Black blood. The thought of it grossed me out even more and I shivered. Sam helped me to my feet and reached down to retrieve my fallen Veritas Sword.

"I see ya were able to return with yer sword. Well done, Hunter! So, did ya learn anythin'?"

I thought about it for a moment. "That I've still got a lot to learn," I replied at last. "And that I can trust the Author's word, even when it doesn't make sense, just like you said, Sam."

He gave me a hearty slap on the back, his face wearing a broad smile of encouragement.

"Aye. And I'll keep sayin' that ta my grave. But it's one thing ta say it; another thing entirely to give yer life ta it."

"You passed your first trial, Hunter," Hope beamed her approval. "You trusted the Author and got your sword. You should be proud."

"I guess. If you can call that passing," I grumbled. "I couldn't even get it to work when I needed it. I feel like a failure."

"With failure comes learnin'," Sam insisted. "Now, about those, how did ya put it, 'freaky statue dudes' that chased you?"

"Yeah, what about them?" I asked.

Sam pressed further. "Well, those statues don't just come alive on their own. What happened in there?"

"I don't know," I answered. "I recovered the sword and then there was a voice that…"

"A voice?" Sam questioned, looking a little stunned.

My pulse quickened from the memory. "Yeah, it was the same voice I heard back home. You know, the one in my room," I explained.

"What did it say?" he asked darkly.

"Uh, something about how I wasn't a Codebearer yet. And that it would teach me the true meaning of fear. That's when the statues attacked me."

Sam's face looked disturbed. There was something bothering him. He stared blankly at the ground, perplexed by what I had said.

"What is it?" I asked, breaking his concentration, hoping he would have some answer as to where the voice was coming from.

"Sorry, I'll have ta ask Petrov about this." He looked my way. "Fear's a funny thing. It's a force we must all reckon with. Yer fear seems ta belong ta someone other than the Author."

"Who?" I asked.

"I don't know. But in time you'll learn to close yer mind to every voice except that of the Author." He changed subjects, choosing not to expound further on the issue. "Well then! On ta our next lesson: swordsmanship. Gather yer things, Hunter. We've got work ta do."

With that he bounded down the stairs and disappeared through the thick wooden door. Hope smiled and tossed me my pack. I caught it midair, nearly collapsing under the weight of it. The book inside had grown considerably heavier. I played it off like it was no big deal, but silently wondered how Hope could handle it so easily, as if it weighed nothing at all. I hoisted the pack onto my shoulders and followed them down the platform, wondering what Sam had in store for me next.

THE TEMPERING STONE

One hundred ninety-eight stairs later we reached the Academy exit and stepped out into the blinding sunlight. My legs felt as if they were on fire, my muscles burning from the climb. After that experience I promised myself never to take another elevator ride for granted as long as I lived.

Hope, on the other hand, bounded off without so much as a whimper from the climb. She wanted to practice her archery, leaving the sword training to Sam and me. It left me wondering, was I really that weak?

The courtyard was full of young warriors in training. They were dressed in white jumpsuits layered with leather armor. From the looks of things, they were in the middle of their own swordsmanship lessons. The youngest students were lined up in rows. Each wore a blindfold and wielded a wooden version of the Veritas Sword. Their mentor, Captain Ephriam, was calling out challenges to which the kids would respond with various wobbly thrusts and jabs. I noticed the boy who had beaten me in the foot race was among the young Codebearers in training. He was swinging his wooden sword with fierce passion at his invisible foe.

The whole exercise made me smile, remembering an old family video of me swinging at a piñata during my sister's ninth birthday. Apparently all the adults thought each of my swing-and-misses was the cutest thing in the world. Even though I was just five then, I can still remember how frustrated I felt each time my uncle Jim intentionally lifted the piñata out of my reach. The whole episode ended with my last swing clobbering the video camera.

That part always brings a good laugh when we watch the tape. No one ever knew that I had hit the cameraman on purpose to make them all pay for my humiliation. It still kinda bothered me that I never told Dad I was sorry for breaking the camera lens and his pinky. But what's a humiliated five-year-old supposed to do?

The clashing of metal on metal directed my attention to an older, more advanced group of students who were paired up in sparring matches, with real Veritas Swords.

Though they were only practicing with deliberate, choreographed moves, I was still quite impressed by their displayed abilities. As I watched, these mock battles began to take on a dance-like quality—smooth, gliding light-trails of the swords punctuated by brilliant bursts as blade met blade.

"So, why doesn't my sword work like that?" I asked, pointing to the girl who had just finished a series of rather impressive attacks. With each move of the sword a bright white arc trailed behind, evidence of the blade's active presence.

"Hasn't been tempered yet. Couldn't hurt a fly in its untrained state, but that'll soon change," Sam replied. I followed him around the side of the Academy across a small field and up a grassy, rock-dusted knoll with a rather large white stone resting on top.

"Welcome to the Temperin' Grounds," Sam announced with energy. "Yer instructor waits." Sam motioned toward the stone as if he were expecting someone to appear any minute. I craned my neck around, looking for the supposed instructor, but no one was making his way toward us.

"Oh, I get it. I have an invisible instructor to train me on how to use an invisible sword, is that it?" I was actually giving this idea serious consideration, seeing how unconventional my lessons had been so far.

"Invisible instructor? Where did ya get an idea like that? No, no, no. Your instructor is as real as the stone in front of you." He cleared his throat and in a slightly softer tone added, "As a matter a fact, it is the stone."

Now, I didn't see *that* coming. Invisible knight, yes. Block of stone, no. By now, though, I had experienced enough to start rolling with it.

"Okay then, so how does Sir Stone teach me to use my sword?"

With half a smile Sam proceeded to walk around to the other side of the stone. He placed his fingertips on the great white rock. "This here 'Sir Stone,' as you call it, is goin' to help ya in temperin' your blade. Your connection ta the Veritas Sword is weak, but that's ta be expected for a lad so new ta the trainin'. But, with the help of this stone, yer blade can be strengthened, sharpened, made ready fer the day when it's called inta action."

In one swift motion Sam brandished his Veritas Sword without effort. He spun around, and with a flash of blue light, carved a deep gash into the stone as if he were only cutting a stick of butter at the dinner table.

I still couldn't get over how incredibly cool this weapon was! I imagined myself slicing through brick walls, severing tanks in two, and slashing the wheels clean off Cranton's new mountain bike to prevent him from chasing me after I pranked him yet again.

Noticing my apparent heroic expression, Sam sought to reel me in. "Now don't be foolin' yerself into thinkin' you'll be makin' much more than a scratch ta start with. This temperin' will take time."

As Sam strode back to my side, I noticed the surface of the rock begin rippling around the area of Sam's fresh cut. Then, right before my eyes the gash appeared to fill in with new rock—as if it healed itself. "Whoa! Did that just…?"

"Self-reset," Sam replied matter-of-factly. "The Author outdid himself when he created those." I ran my finger over the place Sam had slashed only moments ago. The equivalent of a rock-like scar remained, but other than that it had healed perfectly.

"Amazing," I gawked.

"Imagine the alternative. Why we'd have ta bring in new rocks for students every day!" Sam moved on without hesitation. Apparently, understanding how a rock can be self-healing wasn't on the lesson outline. "Right then, let's see ya have a go at it."

My thoughts scrambled to refocus on the task at hand. *Attack the stone.* Lifting the hilt of the sword like a bat, I swung at the rock like a fastball with more than a little mustard on it.

WHOOSH!

Strike one. I whiffed it.

Just as it had in the cave, my sword passed by the intended target without making a connection. It remained invisible and undetected. I grimaced in embarrassment.

Sam spoke reassuringly, "That was fine. Now strike again."

Shaking off my disappointment, I tightened my grip on the sword handle. "You can do this, Hunter," I whispered to myself. "It's all in your head. See the blade. Be the blade."

It seemed fitting to do a couple of methodical up and down motions to find my target in the center of the stone. Once I finished employing my new "technique," I closed my eyes and took in a deep, cleansing breath. I imagined myself standing confidently, sword raised high overhead, then coming down in a strong arc that pierced the rock with such force it split in two.

I opened my eyes, determined to achieve what I had seen myself do. Drawing on all my strength I raised the sword high overhead and lunged toward the stone, yelling at the top of my lungs, "AAAAAAH…"

Oomph!

The sword stubbornly froze in midair above my head. Were it not for my extreme grip on the hilt, my momentum would have carried me face-first into the stone. As it was, the unexpected hang time lasted but a second and I was barely able to catch myself before colliding with the stone "instructor."

I threw my sword to the ground in frustration. I could feel my ears glowing red. "See what I mean? The sword hates me!" I demanded hotly. "What was that?"

Sam picked up the sword and spoke calmly, "*That* would be *you* trying ta command the Veritas Sword ta do what you want. As ya can see, ya can't do that, Hunter."

"Now you tell me," I muttered.

"This sword is yers, but it's not yers ta own. The blade gets its power from the livin' Code itself. Yer responsibility is ta dwell on the Code, and let the sword do the rest."

"What's that supposed to mean?" I shot back. *More mumbo-jumbo about the Code and how it's supposed to make everything work. That was no help at all.*

"Well, it means that…"

A new voice called out from the base of the hill and our lesson came to an abrupt halt.

"Captain Samryee," the short man said, "pardon my interruption but you were expected at a briefing that started thirty minutes ago."

Sam turned to me with a guilty expression. "Whoops! Where's the time? Ah, sorry 'bout the short lesson, Hunter, but I'm gonna have ta leave you alone for a bit while I…"

"It's okay, Sam. Go on. I'll be fine," I said, surprisingly calm.

"Ya sure?"

I gave the reassuring nod he was looking for and took my Veritas Sword from his hand.

"Well, I'll be back soon enough ta continue our lesson. Until then, keep swingin'!" He swung his fist in the air with enthusiasm and stomped down the hill behind the messenger. I watched them disappear down the knoll and around a bank of trees.

"Keep swinging?" I questioned aloud. So far that hadn't returned any results. Oh, right. And don't do anything to upset the sword—it's got an attitude.

"I'll never get it," I sighed, taking a few hapless swings at the stone without really even trying.

Of course, cutting into a solid block of stone with an invisible sword would be easy enough if this was a video game. There would be something like a "power boost gem" to ignite the blade, or maybe something that offered magical energy for cutting through stone. Better yet, I could look up cheat codes on the Internet to unlock a new weapon—that was usually my style. Unfortunately, this was no video game. The stone was real and my blade, unreal.

I took another look at the hilt, turning it over in my hands. Maybe there was a button to push or a secret lever. I tried gripping it different ways, hoping to find something, anything that would unlock the secret of this weapon.

"Hi, Hunter," a young voice interrupted my investigation. The boy who had beat me in the race earlier this morning had brought a couple friends with him as well.

"Oh, hey there, Phil," I said.

"Actually, it's Philan," he corrected, "and this is Alice and Ollie." Philan's friends were obviously eager to meet me. Alice, a girl with white hair, silver eyes and a broad smile, was the first to step forward. She shook my hand in an enthusiastic grip and spoke with a heavy lisp.

"Wow, ith tho nithe to meet you. Philan thays you're thomeone pretty thpecial, but you theem pretty normal to me. Don't you think tho, Ollie?"

Ollie bobbed his head in agreement and smiled shyly.

I wasn't exactly sure whether to take it as a compliment or not, so I just smiled and continued letting her shake my hand for far too long.

"Ollie doethn't talk much, tho I just talk for him all the time," Alice continued.

Philan climbed to the top of the white stone while Alice finished her greeting. "So, how many cuts have you made today?" His question caught me off guard. If there was one thing Philan didn't lack, it was boldness.

"Well, I haven't..." My mind scrambled to find some answer that wouldn't make me appear to be a total loser in front of his friends.

If I was honest, this wasn't possible—so I lied. "I haven't cut all fifty that I set out to but I'm getting close." There, it wasn't a complete lie, just not the truth.

"Oh wow!" Alice gawked. "You muth be pretty good."

Ollie's eyes grew wide as he undoubtedly entertained visions of me cutting the Tempering Stone down to size in quick, easy strokes.

Philan looked at his feet and sighed, "Man, I still haven't even made a scratch."

Philan's honesty put my charade to shame. He bounced right back, "But I keep swinging away like they tell me to. Want to see my blisters?"

I had to lean backward quickly to avoid the two grubby hands he thrust in my face. Judging from the calloused skin he had been working at it for some time.

"Whoa! Hey, yeah—those are some pretty nasty ones you've got there, kid."

"Uh-huh. But I found it gets easier when I say the Code out loud."

"Code?" I blurted out eagerly, realizing too late that I had just blown my cover as an expert swordsman.

"Yeah," Philan replied slowly, casting a suspicious glance at me. "You know, the Code of Life."

"Oh right, that Code," I replied smugly. "I thought you meant like a secret code of some kind. Ha! Imagine having to say a secret code to unlock the blade. Wouldn't that be funny?" I forced a laugh until Philan cracked a smile and joined me. Alice didn't look too sure.

"So then," Philan asked, cocking an eyebrow, "what part are you working on?"

The truth was I had no idea how the Code worked with my sword, but I had to think up something quick in order to avoid exposing my previous lie. My mind raced back to the phrase I had read earlier in the cave.

"Uh, I'm currently working with, 'You will walk by fire and not be burned,'" I said, hoping that it was indeed part of the Code.

My three admirers looked more than a little confused.

"Huh, I've never used that one with the thword before," Alice said.

"Yeah, it's kind of advanced stuff," I bluffed. "You know, new techniques—strictly on a need-to-know basis and all that."

The kids soaked up my every word. Somehow I got the impression they actually believed me, though why they thought I was someone worth looking up to I'll never know. Having admirers felt kind of cool, but I couldn't help but feel a bit uncomfortable with the idea of anyone following my example. Philan had a lot going for him without me screwing his life up. If one of us needed to follow the other, I'd think it should be *me* following *him*.

"Cool. Maybe I'll try that next," Philan said in wonder.

"Sure, kid. Knock yourself out!"

Jumping down from the stone Philan turned to leave, "Well, we better get back to our training."

"Good luck on reaching your fifty, Hunter!" Alice called back as she followed Philan away. Ollie waved. And with that they were racing back toward wherever their tempering stones awaited them.

"You too!" I called after them. "I mean, you too on getting one... cut." I let my voice trail off weakly.

Way to go, Hunter. Real smooth. I thought about the way I'd acted and was disgusted with my weak charade. *How about even getting one scratch yourself, buddy?* I had been wasting enough time already trying to find a way to make the Veritas Sword work. Now, at least I had an idea of what to do. If there was something to this whole Code of Life thing, then there was only one way to find out if it really worked.

I scanned the area around me, making sure I was alone. Since I had no idea what exactly I was supposed to be doing, I couldn't help but feel a tad self-conscious. Straightening my grip on the sword I lifted it once more above my head. "Okay, here goes nothing."

In my best *open-sesame* password tone, I recited the only passage I could remember, "You will walk by fire and not be burned."

Bringing the sword down swiftly, I felt nothing.

"Urgh!" I grumbled. To say I was annoyed would be an understatement; however, my determination to get something right won out over my urge to see just how far I could hurl the Veritas Sword handle this time.

Maybe you say it as you strike. It was worth a try. I reset my attack stance, then brought my sword down as I raced through the words, "Youwillwalkbyfireandnotbeburned."

Another *Whoosh!*

Another "Urgh!"

I was beginning to believe that anything I tried to do with this sword was destined to fail. *Maybe that's it. You can't do this, Hunter.* My thoughts rang through loud and clear. Normally, I might have brushed it off as a negative voice telling me to give up, but as I pondered these words they did not discourage me. The truth of their meaning grabbed me and I realized all at once what had been eluding me all afternoon.

"Of course! It's just like the door to the Revealing Room or the pathway across the crumbling cave floor. I had to learn to rely on the Author to complete them." The light had turned on. So, *that* must be the secret—to rely on the Author.

With newfound intensity I once again brought my sword level with my eyes. Closing them in reverence, I offered up silent words of submission to the Author of this world. This time, as I spoke the words I didn't just say them, but I felt their very meaning somehow spring to life:

"You will walk by fire and not be burned." The very promise that these words carried seemed to surge through the Veritas Sword as I repeated my blind swing at the stone.

Whoosh!

I opened my eyes, expecting nothing to have happened and was completely shocked to find that something had! A fiery blue flame was emitting from the handle like a supernatural torch.

"Well done, lad!" The flame retreated as my startled jump nearly sent me rolling down the hill. Sam was back.

"Sam! Don't do that to me!" My heart was still racing with fright, though not so much from Sam as it was from what had just happened with my sword.

Sam was beaming with pride, "I see ya already discovered the sword's illuminatin' properties. I hadn't planned ta cover that with ya until tomorrow's lessons. I didn't expect ya to get past scratchin' the stone today."

"Oh, the stone? Yeah, well…" I had a momentary urge to bend the truth in my favor once more, but something nudged me away. "Actually, I never figured that part out. This whole flame thing was kind of an accident really."

"The Author's not in the business of making accidents. Ya learned what ya learned fer a reason. Of that ya can be sure."

I wasn't so sure I could repeat the trick, especially in battle, but I appreciated his encouraging words.

Sam continued, "We'll pick up on the temperin' stone trainin' again tomorrow." Sam scooped up my backpack and handed it to me, "Oh, I almost forgot ta tell ya. The Patrol Guard think they may be on the trail of your friend…uh Slim…or whatever his name was."

My face lit up, "Stretch!"

"Oh yeah, Stretch…that's it."

"This is great news! I can't believe you found him. When will he be here?" I asked eagerly. I could really use a friend right about now.

"Well, uh…about that…they haven't exactly found him yet. They came across this and they think it might belong to him. Ya recognize it?"

Sam opened his hand and held out a white chess piece. I recognized it at once. It was a knight—undeniably Stretch's lucky knight. My excitement faded when I considered what it meant. Stretch never went anywhere without it. Something had happened to him.

"Now there, don't go hangin' yer head like that. I'm sure it isn't as bad as it looks. He probably just dropped it. Anyway, we're doublin' our efforts ta find him now that we have somethin' ta go on. He can't be far now, it's only a matter of time before he turns up, I'm sure."

His words did little to comfort me. What if I was responsible for my friend's death? How would I ever live with myself? Sam let a few moments pass before trying to change the subject.

"Well, it'll be dinner soon and Mrs. Goodsmith insisted I return ya on time," he said, lumbering down the hill and motioning for me to follow. I did, but I couldn't stop thinking about Stretch.

"Sam, don't you think it might help if I go out with the Patrol? I mean, if Stretch sees me with you guys..."

Sam squelched my enthusiasm, "Yeah, then the Shadow could just as easily see ya too. No, Hunter, we can't take that risk. But don't worry, I've ordered the men ta leave food and provisions for him ta find. We'll do everythin' we can ta bring him ta safety. Other than that we'll have ta trust the Author is taking care of what we can't right now."

For the next two and a half days I awoke each morning wondering if that would be the day we found Stretch or received word from Aviad that it was time for me to come. Even though the answer would ultimately be *no* on both accounts, I had little time to worry between all of my training under Sam.

Every morning started with readings and lectures from the Code of Life. After each session the book continued to get heavier. A test would follow in the Revealing Room, followed by swordsmanship lessons in the upper grounds. Surprisingly enough, as I learned more passages from the Code of Life, I was able to finally not just scratch my Tempering Stone, but put a few good hacks into it as well.

Beyond practicing my use of the sword for light I also was given a crash course on its healing abilities. The sparring proved much more difficult than I'd first thought it would. More often than not I was picking myself up after one of the other student's basic moves knocked me clear to the ground. Even so, for as much work and humility as the training required, I was beginning to find that I actually enjoyed the challenges and daily regimen.

It wasn't until the end of the third day that Sam broke our routine.

"I thought ya might like a little surprise," he said. I wasn't sure how to interpret the mischievous look in his eyes.

What was I in for now?

Leading me behind the Academy, Sam strode up to a six-foot-tall, cloth-draped item. He paused to give a sort of mini-speech.

"Hunter, I've been real proud of how far ya've come along in so short a time. And if I've learned one thing in life, it's that ya've got ta stop every now and again ta appreciate where you've been." The way Sam's speech was going I wasn't sure if I should be expecting the concealed object to be an oversized trophy.

Taking a fistful of the cloth, Sam yanked the sheet away to reveal a stone knight. Not just any stone knight, *the* stone knight, the one that attacked me in the cave on my first day of training. Unlike our first meeting, however, I wasn't afraid. Granted, it may have had something to do with the setting. Above ground in the sunlight was much less intimidating than in the Revealing Room's darkened cave. Still, I felt different.

Sam chuckled, "Ya don't seem quite as afraid as ya did that first day. I guess that proves my point: Ya've come a long way, Hunter." As if he was reading my thoughts, Sam added, "Go ahead; take a swing at him again now that ya know how ta use your sword properly." I couldn't hold back the grin that spread across my face.

This was going to be good. Mimicking the fluid motion of my swordsmanship teacher, I quickly drew my Veritas Sword from my belt and slashed out with the words as I spun, "By his fear, a man declares his master!"

Chluck!

A momentary white light arced across the statue's shoulders. Completing my spin, I came to a stop and locked eyes with my stoic adversary. For a moment nothing happened, then the statue's head slid forward and dropped to the ground. Sam and I laughed hysterically.

"Well, well," a gripping and authoritative voice called out from over my shoulder. "I see the rumors are true. You have taken well to your training and in only three days too. Very impressive."

Petrov approached the three of us with an urgent stride. A pair of guards followed a short distance behind him, adding a sense of importance to his visit.

With the quickness of a boy caught playing with his dad's favorite golf clubs, Sam attempted to scoop up the fallen head, put it back in place and assume a casual stance. "Oh, hello Commander. Ya think three days is impressive? Just wait till we've gotten a full week under his belt."

"Impressive indeed." Petrov's praise brought a satisfied smile to Sam's face. Then, nodding to the stone knight he added, "Even though your unconventional use of Academy training equipment does violate a few policies."

Accidentally bumping his hand against the statue, Sam caused the severed head to topple once again. All he could do now was smile and shrug sheepishly, "Nothin' a little glue won't fix."

Petrov rolled his eyes, "Even so, as effective as your training has been I'm afraid it has come to an end." The finality of those words caught both Sam and me by surprise. Petrov explained, "We received word from Aviad today, delivered by eagle. It's for you, Hunter."

He drew aside his cloak and removed something from his belt. The small scroll was sealed with a wax imprint of the triple *V*. With timid hands I took the scroll and cracked it open, glancing back at Sam before reading it.

"Well, go on, boy. What does it say?" Sam urged me.

I turned my eyes back to the scroll and read it.

Hunter,

*We must meet as soon as possible. There are things
you need to know, important things I can only
reveal in person. Please come immediately. Petrov has
been given the location of my refuge. I look forward
to our meeting.*

Aviad

"Well then, that'll put your trainin' on hold for now, won't it?" Sam responded, a hint of regret in his voice that our time had come to an end.

"But…but, I'm learning so much," I stuttered. "There are things I still want to…"

"I know and I'm sorry, but it will have to wait," Petrov commanded. "The request has been sent and it is not our place to question the timing of it. You leave first thing in the morning."

I cast a worried look at Sam who nodded in return.

"He's right, Hunter. This is the most important meeting of yer life. You can't miss it."

"Do you think I'm ready?"

"It doesn't matter what I think. Ya've been called." He looked down at his feet and added, "Aviad knows what he's doin', I'm sure of it."

That made one of us.

Walking home that evening was bittersweet. Plenty of times over the last few days I had wanted desperately to be anywhere besides the Academy, but now that I knew I would not be returning I felt a growing sadness. The Code of Life was finally starting to make sense, at least parts of it were.

There was no better place to learn than here at the Academy.

Look at the bright side, Hunter, I told myself. *At least you won't have to pass the Final Exam.*

When Gabby heard the news of my invitation, she immediately set to work preparing a nice meal for me as a sending off party. I had grown to like the woman. She was fun, in her own odd sort of way—eager to help, as much as to talk. Hope, Evan and Sam joined us for the celebration. Gabby's husband, Gerwyn, was his usual silent self except for the moment when he raised his glass unexpectedly and said in a rather gentle voice, "May you find joy on whatever path the Author leads you."

"Thanks," I said raising my glass with him. Joy seemed an odd thing to take on my daring journey. Strength, courage, luck; in my opinion, those would have served me better—joy just seemed less essential. Still, I knew the old man meant well so I drank to joy.

Sleep came easily that night, almost before my head hit the pillow. My mind was weary from a full day of training and I was ready for some rest. Little did I know as I drifted off, another vision was about to disturb my sleep.

THE DRAGON PROBE

The vision led me deep inside a rugged mountain fortress. The doors of a cavernous chamber burst open when Zeeb, the peg-legged goblin, stumbled down the serpentine staircase surrounding the room. One misstep and the goblin knew he could easily slip off the narrow staircase and find himself skewered on the jagged, spear-like rock formations that riddled the chamber floor. Reaching the final step, Zeeb released a snort of relief and skittered across the stone floor, his uneven steps echoing off the empty walls of the cylindrical room. He hurried toward a giant cauldron that burned with emerald fire. The fire's gleam flickered out from the center of the otherwise darkened room, casting eerie movements off the jagged spires and onto the walls.

Venator, the boy-magician, was gazing into the pool of flames, searching intently for something of importance. He was so focused on his thoughts he didn't even notice the goblin entering the room.

Passing around the far side of the fire pool, the goblin knelt and cleared his throat to interrupt his master's trance.

"Ah hem! Excuse me, Master," he intruded nervously.

Venator's eyes shot to the side, rudely disturbed by the interruption. "I hope for your sake the news is good, Zeeb!" he scowled at the limping aide.

"It is!" he replied. "Very good, indeed."

"Well then, get on with it," Venator demanded coldly as he walked away from the cauldron.

"We received word from the prison guard," Zeeb said as he followed his master around the room, taking four hurried steps to each of his master's long strides. "One of the fallen warriors finally agreed to give us the location of the Codebearers' hideout in exchange for his freedom. I have the coordinates here."

"Excellent! I'll send a probe to see if his confession is true. Ready the troops for battle and await my word," Venator replied, picking up his staff and returning his attention to the fiery pit. He had heard enough and dismissed the goblin with a wave of his hand, but Zeeb remained, looking up with concern. Apparently, there was more.

"What is it?" Venator sneered.

"I was wondering if you had any news from the source," Zeeb continued. "Do we have time to attack before they send the boy to meet Aviad?"

A soft rumble shook the chamber. Small pieces of rock fell from the ceiling as the tremor rattled Venator's lair. It only lasted a moment, but it was enough to strike fear into both of their hearts.

Venator spun around with fury, "How dare you mention that name in this place!" The goblin fell to the ground beneath his master's rage. "You know well the penalty for speaking it!"

Venator gripped his staff tightly. A red fire burned to life within the gem of the staff, growing steadily brighter. A phantom serpent emerged from the light and made its way toward the goblin.

"Please, my lord! I beg you..." Zeeb pleaded, eyeing the snake, "I was only trying to..."

Venator was not moved, allowing the ghostly snake to wrap itself around his servant's neck and choke the breath from him. Suddenly, Venator snapped his fingers and the snake retracted instantly back into the staff. The goblin fell to his knees gasping for air.

"You have become careless, my friend," he said at last. "Sceleris would not be pleased. Let this be a warning to you. *Never* make the same mistake again."

"Yes, my lord!" Zeeb responded between breaths, rubbing his neck.

"Good. The boy is being moved sometime tomorrow. Exactly when and where the meeting will take place, I have not been told. It is all the more reason for us to act quickly; he is weakening by the minute. The traitors have fed him many lies and we must find him and help him see the truth before it is too late."

Venator stormed past the goblin, heading back toward the cauldron. As he approached, the flames rose to create an image, though I could not tell what it was.

"After all," Venator concluded, "more than one soul hangs in the balance."

"What are your orders then, sir?" Zeeb asked, awaiting the command.

"Send word to the legions. Tell them the time to act is now. We must crush the Resistance while they are still gathered. No longer will they defile our land with their presence."

"Yes, my master." Zeeb bowed and hobbled quickly away to spread the word.

Venator remained beside the fire pool, gazing into the swirling smoke. He picked up a single burning coal from the fire and held it up. Though it glowed hot in his hands it did not appear to burn him. As the ember faded the room went suddenly black.

Heart pounding, I sat straight up in bed, my brow soaked with sweat. It was still dark outside and I found myself alone in the Goodsmith's guest room. There was no use ignoring it anymore, there was something happening to my dreams, and I needed to tell someone.

Glancing out the window I could tell from the bluish tint near the horizon that morning was well on its way. Sam was undoubtedly awake and preparing for the day already, getting dressed to defend the realm from Sceleris' grasp if necessary. Me? I was usually the one defending myself against the alarm clock with my snooze button. Needless to say, I wasn't normally your "early-to-rise" kind of guy, but today I decided to make an exception. Besides, I was already awake, thanks to the dream.

I hurriedly threw on some clothes, hoisted my pack onto my back and flung open the door. To my surprise Gabby stood in the doorway with her hand poised as if to knock.

"Oh! I'm sorry, dear. I heard you moving around and was coming to see if everything is alright."

"I'm fine, just getting an early start that's all." I chose not to tell her about my dream; it would only encourage her to talk more.

She cocked her head curiously at the pack on my shoulders. "It's a bit early to be heading off, isn't it? I thought you wouldn't be leaving till after breakfast. You know I never like to send a young man away without a proper meal."

"Oh, I'll be back for breakfast. I just want to, you know, take a walk or something."

"Just like my Gerwyn," she smiled. "Always up early to participate in the morning rounds—they've always been his favorite. You go on now and be sure to come back for your morning meal, you hear? It will probably be the last good thing you'll be eating for days!"

As I made my way down the stairs and out the front door Gabby called out, "If you see Gerwyn, tell him not to linger. He'll be wanted back home before too long."

The coolness of the predawn morning air sent a chill down my spine. It was the kind of temperature that puts an extra zip in your step, urging you to hurry to a warmer destination. I had decided to head toward the Academy grounds, the most logical place to find Sam or at least someone who would know where to find him.

Before striking out, I gripped my Veritas Sword and held it in front of me. "Even the darkness is light to him," I spoke boldly. Just as before a light blue glow emitted from the sword, lighting my way.

As I hurried through the chill I rehearsed the details of my latest dream so as not to forget any of it. As I remembered the dream, the gentle glow of my sword seemed to fade beneath the flood of my thoughts.

My focus was interrupted when a sudden blaze of green light streaked across the sky, lighting up the forest as it plummeted to earth.

Boom!

The object struck with such force I could feel the path tremble under my feet. *What was that, a meteorite?* It seemed to have landed not too far off, just near the perimeter of camp. No one was around so, drawn by intrigue, I stepped off the path to work my way toward it.

My plan was to get close enough for a quick peek and then alert the guards if there was any danger. If it was a meteorite then I'd finally have something to one-up Stubbs's story about how his dad bought him a piece of moon rock. Heck, I had a sword that could cut through anything. Getting souvenirs off a sky-fallen rock would be a breeze.

As I neared the crash site, I noticed several trees were on fire surrounding the scene of the collision and a peculiar, almost sulfuric smell soured the air. Undeterred, I pulled my shirt over my nose and moved ahead. Dark smoke billowed and swirled to the surface of a large crater, which hid the fallen object below. A greenish glow and crackling sound radiated out of the hole as evidence that something was burning within.

Crack!

A brilliant light like a lightning strike erupted from the center of the crater. The flash sent me tumbling backward in shock; I froze with fear. Something was emerging.

The smoke pool began to twist and rise, molding a massive form like modeling clay. If I hadn't been so scared out of my wits I might have enjoyed the amazing, almost beautiful sight. Long neck, broad shoulders, giant fiery green wings—it was near impossible to make out any other details through the thickening haze, but I had a pretty good idea this was not going to end well.

I was about to get up and run for help when two sharp red eyes cut through the smoke with their light and fixed themselves on me, stopping me cold. The smoke that had formed the beast dripped off like water to the forest floor and revealed the cracked lava-like skin beneath. The invading visitor was exposed at last—a dragon! I wanted to scream but couldn't find my voice.

The dragon was dressed in battle armor and lowered its head to my level, far too close for comfort. I closed my eyes in anticipation of the inevitable fiery blast that would come. The foul, warm breath from the dragon's nostrils blew my hair out of my eyes as it hovered just inches away. Still, nothing happened.

What was it waiting for?

A low soft rumble rolled from deep inside the dragon's throat. *Here it comes*, I thought. But the soft rumble never turned into the ferocious growl I had expected. Oddly enough, it sounded kind of friendly. Almost like it was *purring?* Reluctantly, I opened one eye.

If I had been asked to make a list of the top one hundred things I would never see in my lifetime, this surely wouldn't have made the list. Not because I expected to see what I saw, but because it was entirely unimaginable. To my surprise, the dragon was more or less bowing to me. Either that or it was waiting for me to make the first move before it snapped me up. I chose not to move a muscle, still frozen with terror despite the creature's curious behavior.

As I stood there transfixed by the dragon's awkward position, I began to distinguish a sort of rhythmic pattern emerging from its throaty tones, almost as if it was trying to communicate with me. Stranger still, there was something familiar in the tone of its speech that made me think I could understand it. Then, all at once, though I don't know how, its voice began to make sense.

"Greetings, oh chosen one. The master has sent me to bring you to him in safety." The dragon's voice was soothing, much like a low whisper. I stepped to the side and ventured a look into the beast's eyes—they no longer blazed red, but instead glinted of soft silver. *"He bids I*

bring you to him without delay. You are in danger. Approach, oh favored one, and ride to freedom." It lowered one of its wings for me to climb aboard.

I found my voice at last. "A-Aviad sent you?" I asked weakly.

Its large eyes shifted as it answered, *"I will take you to the one who has the power you seek."*

The way Sam and Petrov had spoken to me the night before, I had expected to be traveling by foot for a couple of days—flying on a dragon sure seemed to be a nice alternative. Obviously it was not here to eat me or it would have already. Having settled my concerns, I picked myself up from the ground and gathered my things. This was going to make an even better "one-up" story than finding a meteor.

As I stepped forward, a lone warrior appeared out of the mist and pushed his way between me and the dragon, his Veritas Sword drawn. He was ready to do battle.

"Return from whence you came, beast. The boy remains with us!" Though his voice was uncharacteristically forceful, I still recognized it easily.

"Gerwyn? What are you…?"

"Leave, Hunter!" he commanded, keeping his eyes focused on the dragon.

"No, no, you don't understand. The dragon's good, he was sent here to…"

"Do not believe a word it has said! It serves the enemy."

As he spoke, I noticed a change in the dragon's demeanor; it no longer bowed before me, but had raised its powerful frame to face the new challenger. Its eyes switched to red as the dragon roared, *"You lie, old fool! You want the boy for yourselves but you cannot have him. He is a free man."*

Lunging forward, the dragon snapped its jaws at Gerwyn's stomach but the "old fool" was quicker than he looked. An arc of light from his Veritas Sword sped down, cutting a gash below its eye. Seething from the cut, the dragon pulled back and shot a stream of fire from its mouth. I scampered out of the way as Gerwyn deflected the flame with his sword—protected by an unseen shield. Apparently, there was more to this gentle man than I had ever given him credit for. Dumbfounded at Gerwyn's battle-savvy abilities I watched as he quickly avoided another attack and buried a blow deep into the dragon's leg. Yanking back the wounded leg the dragon jolted Gerwyn slightly off-balance.

Sensing Gerwyn's instability the dragon lashed its tail around to knock him flat.

"Gerwyn! Watch out!" I yelled. Once again, the white arc of his blade slashed out, severing the tip of the tail clear off, but the remainder still hit hard with deadly force, sending Gerwyn's frail body to the earth with a crash.

"No!" I wailed, hoping by some miracle he was still alive. I started running toward my fallen friend, but the dragon stepped in my way—its eyes instantly softening to the silvery light once more.

"Chosen one, I am sorry. Your friend was a traitor—poisoned with lies. Like the others here, he wants to keep you away from your true fate. Come with me! Your freedom is waiting." Looking over at Gerwyn's limp form through tearful eyes, I wasn't sure what to do.

"Do not mourn one who would have seen you bound as a servant. Come with me to find true freedom and power. You will understand everything soon." The dragon bowed once more and offered its wing.

My head was spinning—I was confused. A flood of emotions burned in my mind. *Was Gerwyn a liar? Were the Codebearers really trying to keep me from becoming free?* If what the dragon said was true, everything I had learned so far was a lie. Something was not quite right here; the dragon's words seemed compelling and good but I couldn't bring myself to believe them.

"Come quickly, young prince—your destiny awaits." The black fog seemed to be thickening, tightening its grip on the forest and on me.

Familiar, strong voices echoed through the crisp morning air. The Codebearers were coming; they were close, and getting closer. Out of the corner of my eye I could see the oncoming lights of the search party, their Veritas Swords ignited, armor glowing in various hues as they approached through the trees. I longed to run back to them, but something held me there.

"You must make a choice, dear prince. I cannot protect you from all of them. The master can give you the answers you seek and much more. There will be no more secrets."

No more secrets, huh? That sounded nice. I was becoming burdened by the book's confusing riddles and longed for some straight answers. I was about to mount the dragon's wing when a voice called out through the dawn.

"Hunter, don't do it!" Sam commanded.

"Ignore him, Hunter. Do what feels right to you," the dragon replied.

Unsure, I backed away from the dragon that was still bowed low. Sensing my retreat, the dragon lifted itself to full height and blew a ring of fire around us both. The walls of fire leaped ten feet high, completely sealing off the would-be rescue party from view.

"My protection will not last." I sensed desperation in the dragon's voice. *"This is your final chance. They do not care for you; they only want to steal what is rightfully yours. You were meant for great things, Hunter."*

The dragon was convincing but my heart told me he was wrong. Something was missing in his words, something that made all the difference in the world.

"Who sent you?" I asked boldly.

"One who knows your deepest desires," the dragon replied. It was not good enough.

"Do you come from Aviad?" I pressed.

The dragon did not reply, instead it shifted uncomfortably at the question. Its silence was answer enough. There was no time to delay; I had to get out and now.

Scanning the flames, I could see no break in the raging fire. Instead, I would have to leap through it. I ran for the wall, but pulled back in pain at the last minute. The flames were too hot—I was trapped. I had to face my fears, the final exam had found me, and I was on my own. The only escape now was to defeat my dragon.

"If you will not come willingly, then I must take you by force! It is for your own good!" The dragon sprung forward grabbing at my waist.

"By fear, a man appoints his master!" I shouted, swinging my sword skillfully down on its paw, removing one of its claws. The wounded beast pulled away in surprise. Looking down at the severed claw, I was almost as surprised as it was. Spinning around as Sam had taught me, I swung the sword again and again at the massive enemy. He continued to back away to avoid further injury and sent a stream of fire out of his mouth to drive me back. I was so focused on dodging the flame I forgot to pay attention to the creature's tail, which knocked my legs out from beneath me before I even knew it was there.

Falling hard to the ground, my head hit with a thump. There was a bright flash followed by a thousand dancing stars twinkling in my eyes. Shocked and slightly stunned I lay motionless on my back, staring up into the sky. *Way to go, Hunter, you let your guard down.*

The dragon's good paw pinned me tightly to the ground—its claws clinching my waist in a death grip. The creature roared victoriously and crouched low to the ground, beating its wings wildly as it prepared to take to the sky and me with it.

CHAPTER 13

FAREWELL TO THE FALLEN

Crack! Something snapped just outside the ring of fire and a thunderous groan echoed in the sky. Looking up I saw what the dragon never had a chance to see—a massive tree tumbling down with lethal force. The earth trembled as it struck. The collision was deafening. The hideous claws that clutched me stiffened for a moment and then went completely limp. All was silent. I blinked back the sting of dust from my eyes to find the tree had landed only a foot above my head, directly on the dragon's neck.

"Hunter!" Sam called. "Where are ya? Speak up, lad. Are ya okay?"

I could hear the sound of feet crunching through the undergrowth. The dust began to settle. Only a few dispersed fires remained of the encompassing blaze.

I called back, "I'm here, under the dragon!" With difficulty I managed to pry myself from the lifeless fist. Sam's strong hand reached down to find mine and lifted me up. I looked back at the limp body of the dragon in relief.

"Lucky shot with the tree, eh? I'm glad I had enough wits ta give it a go with my sword before that thing took off with you," Sam said.

"You mean, you cut the tree down on purpose? It nearly crushed me!"

"It was the best I could come up with at the time. No harm done. Looks like you're okay."

"Yeah, thanks!" I said half-heartedly. Having come within a foot of death was not something I was excited about even if it had saved me from wherever the beast was taking me.

The body of the dragon began to smolder and smoke. For a moment, I thought it would come back to life. Then, without warning, it disappeared into a puff of smoke and retreated back into the pit from which it came. In a flash, the meteorite shot back into the sky, leaving a glowing trail of green light behind it.

"Oh no," Sam said with a worried expression.

"What is it?" I asked.

"They found us. I don't know how, but they found us."

Before we had a chance to discuss it further one of the other Codebearers called for Sam's attention.

"Captain, we have a man down," a voice called from the far side of the crater.

"Gerwyn!" I shouted, rushing to where he had valiantly fallen. Two men knelt beside him holding his hands. He lay completely still, but I could see the labored rise and fall of his chest—he was breathing!

Dropping to a knee, I looked into his fading eyes.

"Is he…?" I couldn't bring myself to ask the question. I already knew the answer—Gerwyn was dying. The violent fall had most likely broken every bone in his aged body. Tears began to stream down my face, "Why did you fight…for me?"

The old gray eyes locked onto mine. His lips quivered as a faint whisper escaped his lips, "It was…my joy." Then, with a shudder, his body fell limp. He was gone.

I watched tearfully as the spirit of this quiet warrior faded silently away. I hadn't meant for this to happen, but I still couldn't escape the thought that I was somehow responsible for his death. If only I hadn't set out on my own so early, or if only I had run when Gerwyn first told me to, perhaps the result would have been different.

A gentle touch on my shoulder caused me to turn. There, through my own tears, I found the tear-streaked face of Sam. He held out shaking arms and I ran into the offered embrace.

"It was my fault! I didn't run when he told me."

Sam gently pushed me back to look me in the eyes, "Nonsense, Hunter. Gerwyn had prepared for this moment his whole life. The Codebearer's way is ta lay down his life for a friend."

"But he didn't really know me; I mean, I only spoke to him once." I wiped the tears away, trying to control my emotions.

"When you see those around ya as the Author intended them ta be seen, every man is your friend," Sam explained. "Gerwyn gave his life so ya would have a chance to meet Aviad. He couldn't have died for a greater cause."

As he talked, I noticed Gabby approaching through the mist, hobbling as fast as her aged body allowed her, unaware of what had happened.

"What's going on?" she asked, "I heard a terrible crash and... Hunter, are you okay?"

Tears pooled in my eyes again. Poor thing, she would be devastated; Gerwyn was all she had. Sam took her aside and broke the news. She shrieked in anguish.

"Gerwyn? No, not Gerwyn…" She rushed to his side and held his lifeless hand in her own, sobbing great tears. The scene was overwhelming. I could not bring myself to accept so great a gift. Not at the price it had cost Gabby and Gerwyn. There was nothing I could do to make it right, to reverse time and change the past, but I wanted desperately to try.

"Hunter," Sam said softly, "we should leave now. We must warn the others of the attack. I'm afraid it won't be long before more will come. Let's go."

I took another look at Gabby before walking away. The morning sun had finally broken, sending gentle rays of dust-speckled light down through the trees and wrapping the horrible scene in a peaceful glow.

As Sam led me around the fallen tree, I heard the unexpected sound of singing over my shoulder. Though her voice quavered, Gabby's song was not one of mourning but of celebration.

Be not sad, oh heart of mine.
Find the joy that's hid behind.
Through darkness light will find its way,
While we await the dawn of day.

The chorus trailed off as our steps took us farther away, but the song did not leave my thoughts.

"Sam, why is Gabby singing like this right now?" I asked. "She just lost her husband."

Sam slowed, allowing me to come alongside him before answering, "There is still much ya would have learned under me trainin', but I believe ya know the answer already. All things happen fer a reason," he replied.

"So, the Author had a hand in this too?" Sam didn't need to answer, but still a bigger question remained. "What good comes from dying?"

This time he did answer. "Death is not somethin' to fear; it's only the beginnin' of a new chapter in the Author's story. Gerwyn's spirit will leave this world to find his place in the next chapter of life."

"How do you know?" I asked

"Because there's more to the song Gabby was singin'. It's from the Author's Writ:

A greater story is being told,
Beyond the things you see and hold.
The pages turn in perfect time,
Leaving what we know behind.
Death is not the end, dear one,
Another chapter has begun.
So be not sad, oh heart of mine.
Find the joy that's hid behind.
Through darkness light will find its way,
While we await the dawn of day.

"No matter the circumstance, we can find joy in knowin' that he has a greater purpose in all things. There is power in that truth, Hunter—a great, freeing power."

Hope met up with us on our way to the temple to relay the news of what had happened. Faldyn was the only one of the captains not in attendance, as he had taken leave from the gathering the day before to tend to pressing matters on another shard of Solandria. After the shock and sadness of Gerwyn's death sank in, the discussion turned to the task at hand.

"The hour we have long dreaded is finally here," Petrov began. "We have been discovered. It is only a matter of time before they come. Every hour counts. They may be here before the day is over." A heavy silence hung in the air—a battle was coming and Sanctuary would never again be the same.

"Leo. Tyra," Petrov barked, "evacuate the women and children to the underground bunkers. Make sure nobody uses the portals, it is too risky." The captains saluted and marched off to carry out his orders.

"Ephriam and Saris," he continued, "gather every soldier and get ready for battle. If it's a fight the Shadow want, then we'll be ready to give it to them when they arrive." They nodded in agreement and left as well.

Now only Sam, Evan, Petrov, Hope and I remained in the temple.

Petrov turned to face me. "Hunter, we can't let them find you. I think it is no coincidence that Aviad has called you away today. You must get as far away from Sanctuary as possible."

"When do we leave?" I asked, suddenly anxious to get out of the fortress and head for safety.

There was an awkward pause. Evan and Petrov exchanged glances. Evan responded first. "We..." he paused, "we won't be going with you, Hunter."

"What! Why?"

"We have trained you in the ways of the Codebearer, and we can show you the way to Aviad, but the journey is one you will have to make alone, I'm afraid."

"You're kidding, right?" I gasped.

He shook his head.

"But...but...what if the Shadow find me?"

Petrov answered, "They already have. The dragon-probe was not sent by mistake. Our location has been compromised and they are coming for you in greater numbers. We'll need every man to fend off the attack. The people of Sanctuary will need our help."

The vision I had seen of Venator came suddenly to mind. I knew it was time to come clean about what I had seen, so I told them everything. I explained how the visions had started on the very first day I arrived, and how more recently Venator knew about our plans to meet Aviad.

"How is that possible?" Evan asked.

"It's obvious, isn't it? Someone must have tipped him off!" Hope replied.

"But who would do a thing like that? Other than the captains, we were the only ones who knew about the letter from Aviad."

Truth be told, I had my suspicions about the culprit. Faldyn's interaction with Venator in my dream had been more than mysterious, and his disappearance yesterday was a bit too convenient for my liking. I was about to offer my suggestion when Petrov cut in.

"It doesn't matter now. The damage is done, and it doesn't change a thing. Hunter must go. They will come looking for him here first, and when they don't find him they will continue their search. Either way, his journey must begin today."

"Why didn't ya share this with us before, Hunter?" Sam asked, visibly hurt that I hadn't been open with him.

"I don't know I was scared I guess. I didn't know what to make of it at first. I was on my way to tell you about my dream from last night when the dragon landed and I...I got sidetracked."

Petrov frowned as he looked at me. "The Shadow's connection to you is stronger than I thought. Still, as much as I would like it to be different, we cannot go with you. We can only hope they won't expect you to be traveling alone."

Evan walked to my side and set a hand on my shoulder, his concern for me written in his eyes.

"I know it's a lot to ask of you and I'm not going to lie and say it will be easy. But you also must know that the Author has reasons we cannot understand. Listen to what your heart is asking you to do."

My heart? It was racing under the pressure of having to make a decision. There was no way around it—I would have to go alone.

"Okay, I'll do it," I said with hesitation.

Petrov smiled with relief. "It's decided then, there is no time to waste." He ran his finger over a map of the Shard of Inire as he spoke, "Once you are safely back on Inire you will head north to find Aviad. You'll travel over the Black Desert, through Blood Canyon, to the Woods of Indifference where you must find the Lost Refuge of Aviad. He will meet you here, at the top of the stone stairs, behind the doorway."

Glancing over the map gave me an unsettling feeling about the trip. It looked like a long journey and as much as I wanted to leave and find Aviad, I had to face the facts—this was no joy hike through the woods. I was heading out alone on a journey that would most likely take days to complete.

"Sam, gather some provisions for the boy and ready his transfer," Petrov commanded.

Sam nodded in agreement and left without a word.

Evan gripped me firmly in an arm lock. "I'm proud of you, Hunter. Your father would be proud too, I imagine."

"You think?"

"Certainly, it takes a great deal of courage to face the unknown. You are doing the right thing and I have great faith in you."

"Thanks," I said, trying to tame the lump in my throat, "that means a lot."

"Well then. May the Author guide your every step until we meet again—Hunter Brown of the Dumpster!"

We shared a laugh as he stepped away. I turned to say good-bye to Hope, but she was already by my side.

"You won't really be alone out there. You know that, right?" she asked.

I nodded, not as comforted by the thought as she had intended for me to be. After all, I was heading out alone and the Shadow would be looking for me.

"Here, I want you to have this." She removed a slender gold chain from her neck and pressed it into my hands. The chain held a small medallion of the interlocking *V* symbol that glimmered in the sunlight, casting a golden light onto her face as she handed it to me. "It will remind you of your purpose when the journey gets tough."

"Thanks, it's great. You've been great," I said lamely looking down into her eyes. Suddenly, I became aware that we were standing closer than ever before and my heart began to race.

Over the past several days, Hope had saved me from drowning, had become my friend, and even though she had laughed at me a time or two she had been one of my biggest supporters. In that moment I promised myself that if we ever met again, I would find a way to do something nice in return. I was really starting to like her.

"Don't get too attached," she raised an eyebrow and broke the silence. At first I thought she was reading my mind; then she added, "I'm taking it back when you meet up with us again."

"Fair enough," I smiled back, gripping the chain tighter still. Then it hit me—the terrible thought that we might never see each other again. The reality was the Shadow were coming here, and she was staying behind to fight. I knew if I stayed I wouldn't be much use to anyone, but the thought of possibly losing Sam, Evan or Hope—the only friends I had made here in Solandria—was frightening.

"What is it?" Hope asked, noticing my sudden change in demeanor.

"I'm just not sure I'm up to it. Leaving everyone behind and heading out alone."

"But you have to go. You could be the one to end this war. The sooner you meet with Aviad, the sooner we find out why he has called you here. You're not abandoning us, Hunter. You're giving us hope."

"But I don't know what I'm doing—it seems like such a long journey." My fear of the unknown was getting the better of me and it wasn't doing anything for my confidence either.

"Seven and a half days by foot…" she confirmed, pausing briefly to let the duration set in before finishing her sentence. "But you won't be traveling by foot."

"What do you mean?" I asked, my eyes lighting up with the news that I wouldn't have to walk.

"You'll see." She smiled coyly, feeding my curiosity even more. "Come on, I'll show you. Sam will probably be at the landing already."

CHAPTER 14

THUNDERBIRD

The landing was a giant dome-shaped building near the outskirts of the city, one of the many places I had not yet been able to explore during my stay. Inside, the smell of hay and feed filled the air of an enormous room, surrounded by seven stories of animal pens. The pens were accessible by a series of ramps and balconies that extended all the way up to the partial ceiling high overhead.

"She's a beauty, isn't she?" Sam boasted proudly from the center of the room. The *she* he was referring to was a frighteningly gigantic hawk-like bird crouched beside him on its haunches and tethered to the floor with a leash. The creature was absolutely enormous, like a bird taken right out of the age of the dinosaurs. As we approached, she stood up and exposed the fearsome talons that were hidden beneath her belly.

Now, at this point, there is something you should probably know about me. Birds have always made me nervous. My sister had gotten a grumpy parakeet named Chirpy when she was ten, and even though he was only four inches tall, he intimidated me. Back then Emily wasn't nearly as annoyingly perfect as she is now. In fact, we got along pretty well—for siblings. In all honesty, the bird was supposed to be for both of us, but Emily was the one who really took care of him. Mom and Dad had been promising to buy us a pet for months and Chirpy was apparently our reward.

Anyway, Emily had decided that his cage needed cleaning one day and carefully brought him out to pet him. I begged to hold him and she carefully lowered her hand in front of my outstretched finger, allowing him to hop up and perch on it. Chuckling as the bird stepped up onto my finger I quickly lifted him to my face with an enthusiastic smile. That was the last fond memory I have of the foul beast.

For some unknown reason, he went berserk, flapping his wings in utter terror and sinking his beak deep into the soft flesh of my nose with ferocious strength. I screamed in pain and ran for the door, trying desperately to shake and pry his beak from my nose, but he wouldn't let go. Finally, he released his grip and flew out of the bedroom. I was in tears and ran to Mom with a bleeding nose. Chirpy hid behind a bookshelf where Emily spent the better part of the day trying to coax him out.

Of course, my sister blamed me for scaring him, but I knew I had done nothing to deserve it. From that day on I kept my distance from the cage. If I ever came within ten feet of him, Chirpy would stare me down with his "you want a piece of me?" look and I'd back away. We had an unspoken understanding between us—I left him alone, and my flesh would remain unscarred. Yes, I admit it. Chirpy owned me.

But, as much as I was scared of that parakeet, this bird was even more terrifying. Its massive form took my breath away. The bird ruffled its crown as we approached, cocking its blue head with a crooked twist of curiosity. Glossy black pupils glared back at us with unblinking focus. I didn't want to admit it, but the sight of the creature gave me chills.

"Her name's Faith," Sam continued, oblivious to my insecurity.

"What kind of bird is she?" I gasped.

"A Thunderbird," Hope answered calmly. "We use them to travel between the shards of Solandria when the portals are not safe."

As intimidating as the bird was, I had to admit she was beautiful. Her markings were simple enough; multiple shades of blue shimmering feathers ran down her back in stark contrast to her white underbelly. The feathers carried a hint of iridescent color throughout, almost as if they had been coated in a bubble solution or soap of some kind. The tips of her wings darkened in color, ending in near black tones, and there was a deep blue band across her chest that continued up to the neck. A saddle of some kind was harnessed on her back.

"Is she friendly?" I asked, still keenly aware that I was being watched by a bird who could easily tear me to pieces with its sharp beak.

"Sure!" Sam exclaimed. "Faith here has been with us since she was a hatchlin'—isn't that right, sweetie?" He raised his arm to rub her neck and she lowered her head in response, letting out a screeching chirp of satisfaction. "Just don't make any sudden movements, or you're liable ta frighten her."

"Good to know," I replied, freezing in place.

"She's the fastest beast with two wings and she's all yours, Hunter," he smiled, tossing me a pair of goggles and a leather helmet. "Here, put these on. You'll want them for the flight."

I swallowed hard, looking up at my ride, and put the slightly oversized helmet on my head. I wasn't particularly afraid of heights, but it didn't take a professional counselor to know that flying on the back of a giant bird would stretch anyone's limits, especially if you're still afraid of a parakeet.

"So…uh…how do I ride her?"

"Oh, that's easy!" Sam smiled. "For the most part you just hold tight to the harness up there and let her do the rest! She knows where she's goin'. But she'll respond ta some basic commands too if ya want. Squeeze with your left knee and she'll go left, squeeze with the right and she'll go right. Squeeze with both knees to fly higher and with your feet when ya want her ta come down easy. Of course, ta take off or dive, just hang on for dear life and give her a swift kick with your heels."

Just the thought of diving made my stomach queasy. No, I wouldn't be trying anything that fancy. With any luck, I planned to take her up gently and down gently—that was as far as I'd go.

Sam had already loaded a satchel of food, a map and my supplies onto the giant bird before showing me how to climb aboard. It was an awkward feeling, climbing up to perch atop a bird. Faith squawked at my first attempt, annoyed with my clumsy approach. When she turned her head suddenly to look at me with her great yellow eyes I nearly jumped out of my seat.

That must have been how Chirpy felt, I thought to myself.

"Well, I guess this is good-bye then!" Sam hollered up at me once I had settled into the saddle. I could tell he was holding back tears as he spoke. "Take care of yourself, ya hear!"

"You too," I replied, choking up a bit myself as I remembered the Shadow were on their way to lay siege to the city.

"If you run into trouble out there, remember what I taught ya," he advised. "Trust the Author, and look ta the book for the answers."

"I will. I promise." I looked over at Hope as she took Sam by the arm. She nodded at me and I knew that everything had been said that needed saying. I committed the scene to memory in case it was our last meeting. *Okay, Hunter, you can do this,* I assured myself. Then, I took a deep breath and gave Faith a solid kick with my heels; she opened her wings and leaped up into the sky, flapping with ferocious speed.

My knuckles whitened and I gripped the harness with all my might as we jolted upward in a near vertical climb. We cleared the roofline in seconds and Faith began to gain momentum.

Looking back over my shoulder, I could see a magnificent view of the entire city of Sanctuary spread out beneath me, lit in the yellow hue of the morning sun. I squeezed with my left knee and circled over the city a few times, testing my ability to control Faith's movements.

She moved her wings in strong steady strokes designed to take us much higher than I had expected to go. As we reached the apex of our flight just below the cloud line, Faith settled her wings and evened out in a long smooth glide. The air was crisp and cold and I was thankful for the helmet and goggles that protected my head.

The shock of take-off soon wore off and I found it exhilarating to be flying in the open air. As my comfort level grew, so did my courage. The cloud line overhead seemed low enough to touch, and I wondered if it was actually possible. I let go of the reigns with one hand, then two, testing my balance. Courage gave way to careless-ness and I raised my arms high in the air, dipping my hands into the ceiling of clouds overhead and leaving a trail of swirling mist in my wake.

"Woooohoo!" I shouted, laughing to myself at the sheer splendor of the moment. Then, unexpectedly a gust of wind blew me off balance and I shifted in my seat, slipping halfway off. I reached out frantically for the reigns to keep myself from falling off completely.

"Whoa! Steady girl," I pleaded, as Faith banked to the right, adjusting to my awkward position. I pulled myself back up into place and breathed a sigh of relief.

That was close, too close. My stomach turned at the thought of falling from such a height and I tightened my grip, promising never to try that again.

We covered the distance quickly and before I knew it we had reached the edge of the land-mass. The Shard of Sanctuary dropped off abruptly like a cliff into the emptiness of a cloudy void below. It was unnerving to see a giant mass of land hovering in a seemingly endless expanse of empty sky and colorful clouds. I watched the remainder of the island disappear into the mist, a sense of loss growing in my chest as we flew out into the void. I wondered if I would ever return to that wonderful place.

From what I could tell the flight would take us the better part of a day to complete, with nowhere to land between here and our destination.

We passed over several other islands along the way, but Faith paid no attention. She knew where she was going, and I was just along for the ride. The flight grew long and monotonous, with very little scenery to help pass the time. Still, all in all the hours seemed to pass faster than I expected.

Before I knew it, we had found it—the Shard of Inire. It was much larger from this vantage point, more like a floating continent than an island. Scanning the landscape, I recognized the lake where Hope and Sam had first found me. Over time the forest thinned out and the Black Desert emerged into view. The Crimson Mountains were off in the distance, their red glow lighting up the horizon.

It had been a long day of flying and I was getting hungry. When we finally reached the mountains I decided it was time to land. I needed a chance to eat and get my bearings.

"What do you think, Faith? Should we stop for some supper?" I asked.

"Craaaaa!" she squawked happily in reply as if she understood me. For all I knew, maybe she did. After traveling all day, my stomach was more than ready and I imagined hers was too.

I scanned the landscape for a clearing of some kind that would make an easy place to land. After several minutes of searching, I spotted a wide meadow leading up to the giant crater-lake tucked in amidst the mountain range, and decided it was the right place. All I had to do now was get her to go down.

Unfortunately, by this time I had forgotten the commands. *Was it squeeze with my knees or squeeze with my feet to go down?* I knew that kicking would make her dive, so I decided to avoid using my feet if possible. I gave a tight squeeze with my knees and we started to climb upward. *Okay, knees are up, feet are down,* I recalled. *You can do this, Hunter. Just don't kick her too hard.*

I gave a soft squeeze with my feet, but she didn't go down. Time after time I tried squeezing with my feet, using various degrees of strength but nothing seemed to work. Finally, I gave up and took another approach.

Leaning over on Faith's neck I pointed toward the lake below and said, "Go down! Eat!" At first, she gave me a bewildered look and only blinked in response. I tried again. "Eat. Food. Down there," I said pointing down to the lake.

This time she turned her gaze downward, like a dog looking for the stick you threw, but she didn't seem to comprehend. Then in a sudden burst of understanding, she cocked her wings back and plunged down toward the lake in a freefall. The speed of our fall left my stomach behind. It was all I could do to hang on for dear life.

We approached the lake with such force that the breath drained from my lungs. I expected the impact of our fall to kill us both and I squeezed with my knees as hard as I could in an attempt to get her to pull up. At the last second imaginable Faith pulled up from her dive, dunking her bottom half into the lake and skimming over the surface of the water. I gasped for breath, thankful to be alive. A shiver ran down my back from the cool water that found its way down into my clothes. Faith seemed to shiver a bit as well, her body jerking slightly every so often. I glanced down at her feet and saw the reason. An enormous fish was quivering in her talons. Faith had caught her supper.

No sooner had we landed on the shoreline than Faith began to tear into the fish, pulling the meat from its bones. I emptied my satchel and viewed the contents—a slab of cheese, dried meat of some kind and a hunk of bread. I was starved and munched happily on the snack, watching Faith finish off her meal in no time.

I looked over the map of Inire Sam had given me and located the lake. From the looks of things we were only a half-hour away from the Lost Refuge. With any luck, we'd be there before nightfall. We were ahead of schedule, so I placed the map back in the satchel and took a few minutes to read more of the Author's Writ. This time the book led me to a new passage I imagined was meant to prepare me for my meeting with Aviad.

Beyond the ancient door doth hide
The way to one whom you must find.
Knock and it will open wide.

I repeated the passage over and over. I hoped to commit as many of the passages to memory as the other Codebearers had. It would be so much easier to travel without lugging the book around all the time. I recited the passage under my breath and looked out over the lake in a blank stare. A storm was building on the far side of the mountain, dark clouds threatening to completely ruin my already difficult day.

A flicker of movement caught my eye in the distant sky. From where I stood it looked like another bird was making its way across the lake. As it approached, my focus cleared and I realized that what I was seeing was not a bird at all. A big, ugly, bat-like creature, dressed in battle armor and carrying a jagged club in one hand, was making its way to where we stood. I recognized it immediately as a Gorewing, one of the creatures I had seen in the forest patrol before we entered Sanctuary.

"We've got company!" I shouted, gathering my things together and darting quickly to where Faith picked over what was left of the fish. Crouching low she tucked her head back to cover the saddle and angled her wings slightly out, providing barely enough room to dodge beneath them. I huddled close into the down of her underbelly like a baby chick. The smell of fish guts invaded my nostrils. I held my breath, both to avoid the smell, and in fear of being found.

The Gorewing lowered its flight pattern to examine the scene more closely. The erratic flapping of his leathery wings sounded like a tarp blowing in the wind. Faith's cover provided some protection but not nearly enough to hide me completely. Glancing out from beneath the shadow of her wing I watched as the Gorewing passed overhead with a sinister glare in our direction. For a moment I was sure he spotted me, the gleaming yellow of his eyes connecting with mine. But to my surprise, he continued across the meadow and out of sight. *How had he missed us?* We were only 30 feet away at most from where he flew by! Maybe Thunderbirds are common around this area.

"Whew," I sighed in relief. "That was close. I thought we were in for it."

Stepping out from the safety of Faith's wing I turned around, expecting to hop up into the saddle. To my surprise, she had disappeared altogether. The only thing that remained behind me was the dead carcass of the fish she had eaten. *Had she flown away without me?* I looked skyward to spot any sign of my only ride but she was nowhere to be seen.

"Faith!" I called out. A beak and yellow eye popped out of nowhere, hovering in midair only a few feet from where I stood.

"Craaaa," came the floating beak's response. I toppled backward and fell to the ground in shock. The floating beak, eye and saddle were all that remained of Faith.

"What happened to you?" I said, sensing the slight presence of her movement in front of me. On second glance I realized what had happened. Faith had changed her coloring to match the surrounding terrain. Her feathers had become a haphazard pattern of colors that perfectly matched the ground around us. Amazingly, the detail was so accurate from every angle it was impossible to see her even from only a few feet away.

Fading back into blue, she took form once more and made herself seen.

"Whoa, that's cool!"

"Creee," she answered proudly.

"What I wouldn't give to be like you right now." I looked at my friend with newfound respect. She was truly an amazing creature.

"Screeech!" she replied turning her head to the meadow. I followed her gaze. Something was coming.

The Gorewing was coming back, but this time he wasn't alone. From the looks of it there were now two of them. No, make that three.

There was no doubt they knew exactly what they were coming back for. Leaping up into the saddle I gave a sharp kick of my heels and Faith took to the sky with the three Gorewings in pursuit. We climbed upward as fast as Faith could take us, but the bat creatures were not far behind.

The first one caught up with us before Faith could gain momentum, swinging his club at her with all his might, trying to disable my ride with brute strength. She evaded his blows with the skill of a bird familiar with the tactics of aerial warfare. This obviously was not her first time in battle.

Changing his approach, the Gorewing latched his club to his back and reached out, trying to grab me off the saddle before we got away. His thick-clawed hands whizzed overhead, and I ducked and dodged, narrowly escaping his grip. Faith saw her chance and made a move. With an unexpected lurch, she looped backward and twisted around so that she was suddenly positioned behind the Gorewing. Without missing a beat, she buried her strong talons into the guard's wing, tearing the flesh loose and snapping the bones. The whole thing was done in three seconds flat and the wounded warrior fell, plummeting to his rocky grave below.

"Yes!" I whispered under my breath. Us-1; Them-0!

The other two continued their pursuit. Faith dove downward to change directions, momentarily providing a greater distance between our attackers and us. She was heading for the mountains—hoping to use them as cover.

"C'mon girl, you can make it!" I shouted, encouraging Faith as she sped forward toward the mountain pass. Her speed was truly amazing, but our pursuers were not far behind.

I glanced back over my shoulder in time to see the remaining two Gorewings were only a short distance behind, already heading this way with weapons drawn. The one with a sword and the other with…

Thwwwwosh!

A harpoon sliced through the air, stabbing Faith's shoulder. She screeched in pain and stopped flapping midair from the shock. The archer slowed his pace to reel in his quarry, while the swordsman came quickly to finish the hunt.

"Hang on, I'll get it!" I shouted, pulling as hard as I could on the harpoon, with one hand still tightly clutching the reigns. The harpoon was embedded deep in her shoulder; this was not going to be a light wound. If I didn't pry it loose soon, the swordsman would be here to finish her off anyway. The least I could do was give her a fighting chance.

Throwing all caution aside I let go of the reigns once more and stood up on her back, yanking on the harpoon with all my might. The Gorewing swordsman neared, lifting his weapon overhead in expectation of landing the fatal blow. With one last tug I managed to pull the harpoon from her shoulder and Faith sped away with the sudden release of weight. I slipped and found myself plummeting through the air, clutching tightly to the rope and harpoon that now bound me to the enemy.

With a sudden jerk, the rope tightened. I swung back and forth, feeling a bit like a trapeze artist in a circus show. It probably would have been fun under different circumstances, but when you're a thousand feet in the air tethered to a Gorewing, you kind of forget to enjoy the moment.

The archer was now two hundred feet above me on the other end of the cord that held my life. Once he realized he had hooked "the boy" he quickly turned and began flying in the opposite direction.

"Faith, help!" I called out in desperation, knowing full well she was probably out of earshot and preoccupied with trying to escape a swordsman who was bent on evening the score.

So there I was, dangling in the sky like the tail of a kite. The way I figured, I had three options. Option One: give up, let them capture me and take me to Venator. Option Two: try to escape and find another way to Aviad. Option Three: die trying. While I didn't particularly like the third option, I figured the chances of them killing me at this point were slim, seeing as they probably wanted me alive. So I decided option two was at least worth a shot. I mean, even if I failed I couldn't think of a worse situation than the one I was in now. So, with nothing to lose I put my plan into action.

"I can't hold on!" I yelled up to my captor who glanced down with an almost humorous look of confusion on his face. "I think I'm going to fall!" I shouted again. This time his expression was priceless—complete panic. Yep, my hunch was right; whatever business this Venator guy had with me, his instructions had obviously been very clear. I was to be brought back alive, which gave me an advantage, at least for now. If things went as planned he'd be lowering me to the ground and I could try to run away.

My plan backfired, as usual. Instead of flying toward the ground the Gorewing frantically pulled me toward him, quickly hoisting me up within reach. The Gorewing was even more frightening up close,

his jagged
teeth jutting
out from his mouth like a
cobra ready to bite, and his hot,
yellow eyes burning with the knowledge of pure evil.
It was like looking into the face of death itself. Suddenly, dangling
from two hundred feet of rope seemed like the better option.

It was too late now; the warrior reached down with his giant
forearm and flipped me up onto his back in one calculated motion.

Well, that didn't go as planned.

Yep, things seemed pretty grim for the moment, but as I looked
out over the landscape, I caught a flicker of something speeding
behind us. It was only a glistening movement at first, but as the approaching figure drew closer, I recognized the form. Faith was alive
and she was flying this way, hidden by her camouflaged feathers.
The Gorewing swordsman was nowhere in sight, which meant she
either lost him or defeated him. Either way, the odds were two-to-
one against the remaining guard below me, and we had the element
of surprise.

Faith eased up behind us, still undetected by the Gorewing. I
knew what I had to do; it was my turn to put one on the board for
the good guys. Slipping my Veritas Sword silently from beneath my

outer layer of clothing, I took a deep breath and remembered my training. I had one shot to get this right, and it was now or never.

Jumping to my feet, I held the sword high and shouted, "For the Way of Truth and Life!"

I arched the blade downward in a flash of light, severing the creature's left wing from its body before it even knew what was happening. The archer howled in pain and I leaped off his back into the open air behind it. The Gorewing spun helplessly out of control toward the earth far below. It would be his last flight, and I had delivered the fatal blow.

I fell only a moment before Faith swooped past and caught me on her back midair. We had done it—defeated the Gorewings, and looked good in the process.

"That was close!" I laughed nervously from the excitement. "We make quite a team, don't you think?"

Faith chirped at me, as if to agree.

"For a minute there I thought you were gone for good!"

She remained silent this time, and I sensed in her flight that something was bothering her.

Together we crossed the Crimson Mountains, following Blood Canyon to the far side where the forest began. We passed through the canyon, flying low to the ground. I could tell Faith was weakening every minute; the wound had begun to take its toll on her strength. The dark storm that once threatened from a distance now hung overhead, lighting the sky with angry flashes of lightning.

We reached the end of the canyon and Faith collapsed to the ground in a desperate crash landing. We skidded across the rocky ground and smacked hard into an oversized stone. The sudden stop hurled me off her back into the bushes. I jumped to my feet, mostly unharmed, and ran to see if Faith was okay. She was lying on her side in excruciating pain, one side of her body painted in blood, most of which had come from the wound where the harpoon pierced her.

"Easy girl, let me take a look at that," I offered.

The wound was deep, and in many ways I was surprised she had been able to make it this far. I pulled my Veritas Sword from my side and went to work right away.

I held the sword against the wound as Sam had done for me and watched as the skin repaired itself. The healing properties of the sword never ceased to amaze me.

"There you go," I said when we finished. "You'll be good as new in no time."

Within ten minutes she was on her feet again and was beginning to regain her strength. She lowered her head to my level, allowing me to rub her neck with my hand. When I finished, she motioned toward a narrow, red rock path that led into the forest. The look in her eyes told me it was the path I should take. I pulled my things off her saddle and readied myself for what lay ahead. With a final screech that seemed to say "good-bye," Faith launched up to the sky and flew away into the last remaining traces of sunlight, leaving me alone with the task of navigating the woods in the dark.

If the map was correct, I didn't have far to walk to the Lost Refuge. I pulled my Veritas Sword out from my side and held it aloft in front of me, igniting it with a passage from the book. The soft blue flame glowed brightly enough to light my path.

An angry crack of thunder in the distance reminded me the storm was preparing to hit me with its worst. Then, like tiny missiles from the sky the rain began to fall. It pelted the ground around me, sporadic at first, a drop here and there, but it was coming more quickly by the second. A few raindrops connected with the supernatural flame of my sword, sizzling and steaming from the heat. There was no use staying put; the only shelter would be within the forest ahead of me. So, gathering my courage and hoisting my pack onto my shoulders, I headed into the woods alone, carrying the book in one hand while my Veritas Sword glowed brightly in the other.

I followed the path for over an hour, much longer than I had anticipated it would take. The storm intensified and I found it harder to press on. Tired, wet and feeling lost, I began to look for a place to sit out the storm and wait for morning. A boulder just slightly to the right of the pathway seemed perfect for the job. The near side was cut back at a sharp enough angle that it could provide some protection from the rain. Scooting back as far as I could, I huddled beneath the shadow of the stone shelter and waited for morning to come.

I wasn't exactly what you would call comfortable, but the rhythm of the rain and my exhaustion from the day soon took their toll and I fell asleep, dreaming of the Codebearers and the battle of Sanctuary.

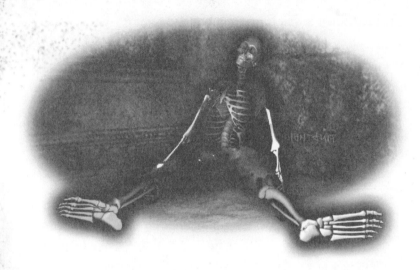

Chapter 15

FRIENDS IN LOW PLACES

The dream revealed the city of Sanctuary ablaze with the fires of war. The white walls that had long protected the city from invasion had been breached and the streets were now flooded with all kinds of dark creatures united under the Order of the Shadow: Dispirits, Gorewings, Scrills, ogres, trolls, dragons, phantoms and more. Sceleris' armies outnumbered the Resistance six-to-one but the Codebearers continued fighting to protect their homes and way of life.

Flames were scattered throughout the city, burning buildings to the ground and belching dark plumes of smoke into the sky, which was also alive with combat. Winged warriors from both armies battled in an amazing display of aerial warfare, though it was difficult to tell who was winning.

Venator stood outside the walls of the city with a satisfied smile. Things were going well for the Shadow; Sceleris would be pleased. The Resistance was falling and he felt closer to victory than ever before. He watched the battle unfold from a grassy hill overlooking the scene.

A winged Gorewing bearing a black steel sword approached Venator, landing beside him and kneeling in deference. I recognized him immediately as the swordsman who had tried to capture me earlier that day. Faith had escaped, but apparently the creature was not killed.

"Rise, Kane," Venator said with an almost cheery disposition. He was in a good mood, the battle was going well. "What news do you bring?"

"It is the boy," the Gorewing reported. "We found him on Inire, as you said. He was attempting to cross the Crimson Mountains."

"Predictable. He was captured, I assume?"

At this, the bat-faced warrior looked down in disappointment.

"Strangler was killed by the bird, and Rathclaw had the boy in his grasp while I chased after the Thunderbird, but…"

"But what?" Venator's mood turned sour. He knew the rest of the report would not be acceptable.

The Gorewing continued, choosing his words carefully. "The bird disappeared and when I returned to accompany Rathclaw, he was missing as well. I searched the area and found his body. His wing had been severed by a Veritas Sword, and…"

"And the boy?" Venator interrupted.

"The boy was not with him. I fear he escaped."

"Escaped!" Venator screamed. "I send three highly trained warriors on a simple recovery mission to capture a boy and you come back empty handed. Explain to me how that is possible!"

"Sir, I…"

"Hold your tongue, Kane, or it may be the last word you ever speak." Venator's staff glowed with his anger. The guard stood speechless under the threat of death.

"You are fortunate I don't kill you now for your carelessness. Instead, I am giving you a chance to redeem yourself. The boy couldn't have gone far. Take as many warriors as you need and comb the forests. When you find him, bring him back alive."

"I will not disappoint you," the guard said, thankful to be given a second chance.

"I expect not," Venator said, eyeing Kane as he knelt once more before leaving. The Gorewing stood to go, then Venator continued, "And Kane…"

"Yes, my liege?" came the reply.

"If you do fail, you might consider doing yourself a favor. Don't let me see you again alive," Venator said, turning his back to the winged one.

"Yes, my liege," the Gorewing snarled, leaping for the skies once more.

Fwoop, fwoop, fwoop! The flapping of wings nearby jolted me awake with a start. I sat up and hit my head on the stone overhead, only to fall back in pain. *Ouch! That was going to leave a mark.* I covered my mouth to muffle the groan as best I could and rubbed my forehead.

Glancing through the forest around me I searched the foliage, expecting to see a Gorewing appear from behind a tree at any moment. Needless to say, I was relieved when a jet-black raven flew up from the forest floor to a tree nearby with a loud *fwoop, fwoop, fwoop!* Apparently morning was on its way and even though the sun had not yet risen, the early birds were already hard at work looking for breakfast.

The rain had finally stopped and the sky was clear. If my sleeping arrangements had been more comfortable I might have considered rolling over to catch a little more shut-eye. But until I was safe inside Aviad's stronghold there was no use trying to get more sleep.

Rolling out from my hiding place beneath the stone, I discovered my left arm had fallen asleep and was completely numb and useless. Rubbing my arm as it slowly tingled to life I surveyed the area, looking for the path that had led me this far into the forest. The ground was wet and muddy, but the path should have been just a few paces away. Sure enough, there it was—the red dirt from the Crimson Mountains continued to the lowlands, making it easy to spot.

I gathered my things, ignited my sword again for a little extra light and began winding my way through the forest. Unfortunately, I hadn't gone far when the path ended at the edge of a swampy marshland, stopping me in my tracks. The surface of the water was coated in green slime, providing the perfect hiding place for the things living below. The smell was awful, like hard-boiled eggs. The stagnant bog spanned as far as my eyes could see, speckled with small scrubby plants, tall grass and trees nearly buried in stringy moss.

"Okay, now what?" I wondered aloud, holding my sword out in front of me, straining to see another way around. There was none; I had reached a dead end. The trail I was following disappeared into the murky water, leaving a blind path in front of me.

I lowered my sword in disappointment, then something caught my eye—a reflection in the water. The red path beneath the bog was responding to the glow of my sword. As long as I held it near the surface of the water, the red pathway beneath shone brightly up through the mire, marking my way with a crimson glow.

"Well, it looks like you're going to get wet again!" I sulked to myself.

With nowhere else to go, I rolled up my pant legs and stepped out into the murky bog, following the red glow of the path beneath it. One slow step at a time I sloshed my way through the swamp. It started only ankle deep, but before long I was up to my knees in the putrid mire. Still, as long as the reflection of the pathway responded to the sword I intended to trudge through it, hoping with each new step that I would soon come to a clearing and see the stone steps leading up to the Refuge. The morning sun broke over the horizon and made my travel much easier. The red road glistened in the sunlight and I tucked my sword away, no longer needing it to find the path.

A few steps later, a giant arm shot out from behind a tree and grabbed my leg, lifting me upside down several feet in the air.

"I caught you, thief!" a gruff voice growled, as I met my attacker face to face.

At first glance I might have said it was a giant man that had caught me. His skin was fair and human-like in appearance, his head completely bald. But that is where the similarities ended—he had no nose to speak of—just a couple of holes nestled directly between two slits of eyes. A pair of fangs protruded upward from his lower jaw, which was shifted slightly forward from the rest of his face and surrounded by a goatee.

"Thought you could steal from my swamp, did ya, boy?" he spat as he spoke.

"What? No! I'm just passing through, I swear. I didn't take any-thing," I begged.

"Hmmmm. We'll see 'bout that. Hold still," he said as he gripped my waist with his free hand and flipped me over to examine closer. I looked him over in disgust. If I had to guess, I'd say he was some kind of swamp troll. He wore no clothes except a loincloth; his chest was hairy and bare. He held me tightly in one hand while his other hand hung down near his knees, holding a giant club that he set down to examine me. He pulled at my pants, tearing the legs up the seams a little.

"Hey, watch it. Those are my good jeans!" I threatened, knowing full well I didn't scare him at all.

"Ah ha!" he exclaimed, pulling a knife from his side and bringing it up to my leg.

"Whoa! What are you going to do with that?" I demanded.

"Hold still, I said!"

There was nothing I wanted to do less than to hold still while he tore at my leg with a knife, but when you're held tight in a death grip, you don't have much choice. He seemed to be poking at my legs but I didn't feel anything. Then with a quick jab near my calf, I heard a faint squeal and he pulled his knife up to reveal what I hadn't felt. There, squirming on the end of his knife was an eight-inch leech.

"See! I knew you was a thief! You been stealin' my leeches, haven't ya, boy? Thought you could come down here and get yourself some food from my swamp, did ya?"

He bit off one end of the screaming leech, silencing it for good. I nearly gagged at the sight.

"No, I…I didn't even know it was there!"

"You know what I thinks?"

I shook my head. I couldn't possibly imagine what was going through the head of this simple brute.

"I thinks you're lying!"

The way he said it reminded me of a school bully who was about to dish out a whomping. I could tell there was no reasoning with the man…or troll…or whatever he was. "What are you going to do with me?" I asked, hoping he'd realize I was of no use to him and let me go.

"The same thing I do with every thief what steals from my swamp," he grinned. I swallowed hard, not wanting to hear. He pulled the remainder of the leech off the knife with his teeth, chomping happily on his snack, and picked up his club. Slinging me over his shoulder, he carried me off, tromping through the swamp with little effort, in the general direction I was heading to begin with.

The troll's home was only ten minutes away and was much more elaborate than I would have given him credit for. It was almost a small castle, nestled alongside a hill surrounded by the bog. Anyone else would probably consider the location unlivable, but for the swamp man it was probably prime real estate.

Once inside, he stripped me of my belongings and removed three more leeches from my legs before tossing me into a darkened cell.

"Welcome to your new home, slave!" he said, slamming the door behind me. I couldn't believe my misfortune. Here I was so close to the end of my journey, trapped by a…well…whatever he was. Never in my life had I wanted to be home more than I did now.

"Hunter?" I heard a voice call from over my shoulder. The voice was familiar but I couldn't place it. I turned around to see a boy approaching out of the shadows. As he passed into the light, my mouth dropped open in shock.

"Stretch! You're alive…!"

Smack!

My greeting was cut short when Stretch landed a swift punch to my face, catching me completely off guard. I fell backward from the blow and he lunged on top of me, wrestling me to the ground in a fit of rage.

"Stretch, what are you doing?" I said, trying to defend myself from another well-aimed blow.

"Giving you what you deserve!" he growled.

I had never seen Stretch act like this before. He had never been able to assert himself well back home.

"This is all your fault," he continued. "You brought us into this, Hunter! Because of you I'm never going to get home again!"

I grabbed his fists and pushed him away. Stretch fell, tripping over a wooden stool on the way down, and didn't try to get back up. Instead he scooted away into the corner, sobbing. I approached him slowly this time, palms open in front of me to make sure he knew I wasn't upset, and put a hand on his shoulder.

"You don't know what it's been like, being here alone," he finally said, sniffing and wiping his eyes with his sleeves.

"I'm sorry, Stretch," was all I could manage to say. "I didn't know it would end up like this."

"Well it did!"

I paused a moment, trying to find a way to reach out to my friend. I was sure he had been through a lot, and I couldn't blame him for being angry with me.

"For what it's worth I'm glad to see you," I offered.

He wiped his eyes again and looked up at me.

"Sorry about your lip," he said.

I felt my lip; it had swollen to the size of a small balloon.

"That's alright; you should have seen the other guy!" I laughed, trying to make light of the whole thing. It worked. Stretch started laughing, a sight that made me feel at home again.

"So what happened? You know, how did you get here?" I finally asked.

"Well, there isn't much to tell really," he started. "When we came through the book I ended up in a lake full of chained-up bodies and I knew you couldn't swim, so I spent the better part of the afternoon trying to find you in the water."

"Afternoon? You mean night, right?"

"No!"

"But it was night when I arrived at the lake," I told him.

"It was afternoon for me," he insisted.

"Weird, so we must have arrived at different times. That's why you weren't there when Hope rescued me."

"I guess so. Who's Hope?" he asked.

"Oh I'll tell you later. Go ahead and finish your story first. What happened next?" As he continued, I realized our experiences in Solandria had been very different. I had been granted a pretty easy transition compared to my friend. And to think I had actually been complaining about my experience so far.

"Well, when I couldn't find you in the water I swam for shore, hoping you had somehow managed to make it. I waited there for another day, but when you didn't show up I thought you were dead so I headed into the woods in search of help."

Stretch explained how he had seen the Shadow Patrol and hid in the bushes. After wandering for another day or so he was captured in a trap by Belac, the swamp-troll that owned this castle. Belac was on a hunting trip and brought Stretch home to the bog, where he was forced to work as Belac's slave.

"So that's how it happened," he finished. "And I haven't seen the light of day since."

"You mean he just keeps you locked up in here?"

"No. He prefers to sleep during the day. Says the hunting is better at night. That's when he takes me out."

"Out where?"

"To the swamps mostly; he uses me as leech bait." Stretch lifted his shirt to show the markings of leech bites all over his chest. I shivered at the thought of it. He was covered with them.

"Ouch!"

"Not really," he replied, "it doesn't hurt. That's the only good part. Leeches release an anesthetic when they sink their teeth into your skin. But it does bleed—a lot."

"Gross! How do you know that?"

"I took AP Science last year, remember? We got to study leeches for medical use. I guess it's making a comeback. Did you know doctors are still using leeches to drain blood from swollen faces, limbs and fingers after reconstructive surgery? It's really pretty fascinating stuff."

That was more than I wanted to know; just the thought of letting a leech drain my blood made me shudder. They were like little blood-sucking vampires.

"What does Belac do with all of those leeches?" I asked. Before Stretch could answer, the door flew open and Belac tossed two bowls of slop onto a small wooden table pushed up against the wall.

"Eat up, ya two," he grumbled. Then he slammed the door and lumbered away to get some sleep.

Heading over to the bowls I peeked inside. It looked like some kind of mush mixed with squirming leeches for good measure. One whiff of the slop told me all I needed to know, I wasn't touching it. Stretch, on the other hand, wasted no time digging into his bowl.

"You're actually eating it?" I asked.

"It's not bad, really—once you get over the gross factor. Besides, if you want to eat while you're here, you're going to have to learn to like it."

I forced myself to try a bite from my bowl but I couldn't keep it down. Stretch went to town, finishing both of our bowls in no time at all.

I couldn't help but feel sorry for all that Stretch had been through. While I was being stuffed full every night with Gabby's home cooking, Stretch had been here, learning to love the taste of leech meat. I only hoped he wouldn't hate me when I told him my story.

After lunch I did my best to catch him up to speed on my training, the mission and what was going on outside of these walls. He didn't speak through my whole story, though his expressions betrayed his thoughts once or twice. I could tell he was realizing I had gotten the better end of the deal. I finished by handing him his lucky knight. He was genuinely glad to have it again and for a moment we both were silent. Then, at last he verbalized what I knew he had been thinking all along.

"So you mean to tell me that all this time while I thought you were dead, you were really making new friends and having a great time learning how to use one of those cool swords?"

His voice was bitter. The worst part was that it was true, though it didn't seem nearly as convenient at the time.

"Sort of," was all I could manage to say.

"Nice," he said in jest, shaking his head with disbelief.

"Hey, it's not like I had a choice. I tried looking for you but we were being hunted and I didn't know where you were either."

Stretch didn't reply. I knew anything I said at this point was going to fall on deaf ears anyway. Still I had to try.

"Look. I can't change what happened," I offered. "I wish it was different, I really do. But we're together again, that's all that matters now. And we're going to find a way to get out together."

"How?"

"I don't know but there's got to be a way."

"Do you think I'm stupid or something?" his tone surprised me. "Don't you think I've been trying to find a way out ever since I got here?"

"Yeah, I guess."

"Well, I can tell you now, there isn't. I've tried everything already and it's hopeless," he replied. "It's impossible to run in the swamp, and Belac keeps me locked up when I'm not out there anyway. So unless you have a death wish, you'll never make it out alive."

I looked blankly at my friend. He didn't sound like the same guy I had known back home. Stretch was always the one who would go along with anything, even a hare-brained idea. Solandria had changed him; he had given up and resigned himself to being a prisoner for life. Couldn't he see there were good things happening at the same time? We were together again; didn't that count for anything?

"You want to know how to get out of this place? Ask Frank over there," he said, pointing across the room to a skeleton collapsed in the corner and covered in dust. The poor soul had evidently been unfortunate enough to "trespass" on Belac's land long before us.

"Unless you want to end up like him, you better start learning to like the food and playing by Belac's rules. You got it?"

I nodded half-heartedly.

"I'm going to get some sleep," Stretch finished, moving to his corner of the room where he'd gathered a pile of straw together into a make-shift pillow. He was out in no time, obviously already well-adjusted to the nocturnal lifestyle the troll kept. I sat against the stone wall of our prison and contemplated what the night was going to hold for us. Being leech bait was not something I was looking forward to at all.

Chapter 16

My Life as Leech Bait

Sleep was the last thing on my mind. Instead, I spent the remainder of the day searching in desperation for a way out of our cell. Stretch was right, there wasn't any. As the day came to a close Belac returned, throwing open the door.

"It's time," he sneered. "Hurry up! I'm gettin' hungry!"

Stretch knew the drill. He pulled off his shirt and I followed his lead. Belac bound us together with iron shackles, linking our wrists three feet apart. We followed him out of the cell, around the corner, out the front door and down into the swamp. The sun was just setting as we headed out. The troll followed closely behind, his large club clasped tightly in one hand. I was surprised at first that he didn't tether us to him, but I soon realized it would have been pointless. Just as Stretch had said, the mire slowed our steps to a crawl. We couldn't run, no matter how badly we wanted to.

"Get ta work!" he shouted, biting down on a pipe held between his teeth. A full moon lit the scene, making it easier to see my surroundings. I followed Stretch, lying down on my back and waiting for the inevitable to happen.

"How long do we lie here?" I whispered.

"Not long, they can smell and hear us. If you watch closely, you can sometimes see them dropping from the underbrush into the water." We lay there in silence for a moment before…

Plop, plop! Sure enough, the leeches started coming, inching their way across the pond like big black worms. All we could do was wait, while the thought of it nearly drove me crazy. I couldn't believe Stretch could just lie here like that. Surprisingly enough, I didn't feel a thing and before I knew it we were covered in over a dozen leeches each. Belac scraped them off with his knife, tossing their squealing bodies into a wooden bucket of swamp water. Then he sent us back out to collect more. We must have caught over a hundred leeches apiece before Belac was satisfied with the count and called off the hunt.

As we trudged back to the castle I took a moment to survey the landscape. Glancing up, I caught a glimpse of something along the ridge of the hill tucked behind Belac's place. It looked like the top of a stone tower, almost as if another castle was hidden by the crest of the hill. *Could it be the Lost Refuge, the place I was supposed to meet Aviad?*

I scanned the side of the hilltop, looking for the staircase. Sure enough, within a few moments I was able to make it out, a stone stairway curved up the hill. The base of the stairs started only a few hundred yards from where we stood. *Had we really been that close to Aviad this whole time?* This was good news.

"Stretch!" I whispered. "Look, I think that's the stairway I saw on the map. I think Aviad's refuge is right up there."

He paused for a moment, scanning the crest of the hill where I had pointed. A glimmer of hope sparked in his eyes when he spotted the tower, but the hope quickly faded.

"What good is it? We're still trapped."

"It's not that far; we could make a run for it," I suggested, realizing as I said it how stupid it sounded.

"Have you gone completely insane? Even if we could run we'd never make it before Belac smashed us with his club."

"Then we'll just have to find another way to escape when he isn't looking."

"Yeah, right. Good luck with that!" Stretch stewed.

What was his problem? Couldn't he see how close we were to safety?

Belac groaned impatiently behind us, "You there, move along." He kicked up some of the bog in our direction to emphasize his point.

I for one was not going to let Belac douse my spirit. As long as that tower stood at the top of the hill, I was determined to keep my hopes up. With newfound purpose, I began trying to think of ways we could escape.

Each night I watched for any opportunity to make a break for it, but nothing presented itself. Belac was always nearby, watching us like a hawk when we weren't in our cell. Eventually, my enthusiasm began to fade. Between being chained to Stretch and his negative perspective on things during the day, and the humiliating experience of being used as leech bait during the night, I started to give up trying. The sight of the tower that used to give me purpose just stood there taunting me as a vacant reminder that we were still as far away as ever. It was no use.

As thoughts of escape faded away, my only hope now was that the Codebearers would somehow come to our rescue—if any of them were left after Venator's raid. Three days of captivity had passed already and I began to fall deeper and deeper into despair. Being used as human leech bait took a toll on my mind and it seemed unlikely we would ever be free.

Just when we thought things couldn't get any worse, something out of the ordinary happened that took all three of us by surprise. Belac shot through the door and barged into the middle of the cell when he ordinarily should have been sleeping. He was holding a paper in his hand and he was angry.

"Why are ya here?" he shouted at me.

Shocked at the confrontation, I hardly knew how to answer him. The question seemed obvious enough, but his tone of voice made me worry that I was missing something.

"Well, I was walking through the swamp when you caught me, and…"

"Don't play games, boy, I know how ya got here; what I wanna know is what you were lookin' for in the first place."

"I came to meet a friend," I answered.

"You're one of them, aren't ya? One of the Resistance—lookin' fer Aviad! I bet they sent ya here tryin' to find him, didn't they? Am I right?"

I was surprised to hear him talk so boldly. *How on earth could he have known? Was he working for the Shadow too?*

"Well, am I right?" he yelled, interrupting my thoughts.

"Yes sir," I said, cowering under his ferocity.

Belac lowered his voice in a mocking demeanor. He was no longer yelling but relishing his role as the bearer of bad news just the same.

"Well he ain't here. Never was, never will be. I doubt he even exists—just a fairy tale the so-called Codebearers made up ta get boys like you to help 'em fight."

Now I was really confused. This troll knew more than I thought possible. He'd hardly spoken over the last several days except to bark a command at us now and then. But here we were, engaging in conversation about the Codebearers and Aviad.

"How do you know about all that?" I finally gathered the courage to ask.

"I'll ask the questions. A patrol of guards came by today, woke me up. Said they was looking for a boy like you."

For a moment, my heart skipped a beat. *Could it be that the Codebearers were in fact looking for me? Or was it the Shadow, following their orders from Venator as I had seen in my vision?*

He slammed the notice onto the wooden table in front of us. I recognized the symbol at the top of the paper immediately; the Shadow's mark of the double *S* was as clear as day.

"Says here, they're offerin' a handsome reward ta anyone who turns the boy in. See for yourself."

I read over the notice.

§

BY THE ORDER OF THE SHADOW:

BOY FROM THE VEIL WANTED IN CONNECTION WITH MURDER OF TWO SHADOW GUARDS

He was last seen heading toward the Crimson Mountains and is expected to be wandering these woods. Be it known that any man, beast or creature found to be harboring or aiding such a boy will be tortured and punished for his betrayal to the Shadow.

Should anyone find the boy and wish to avoid such penalty, capture him and return him immediately to the captain of your region for questioning.

Any subject who heeds this command will be rewarded for his obedience.

"What are you going to do?" I asked.

Belac just stood there, stroking his goatee, enjoying the suspense as I awaited his decision.

"Never helped out the Shadow before, but I fancy they'll think pretty highly of me if I do—might even make me rich."

"Please don't," I pleaded. "It would be a mistake to…"

"You listen here. I'll do what I want," he barked. "I don't take orders from no one. Not them, not you, not the Author, not anyone, see? I'm free to do as I please." He grumbled under his breath something I couldn't understand, then added, "Wretched Shadow think they own everythin' 'round here; a curse to us all. They can't just barge in here and take my slaves from me. I gots a right to keep whoever I finds stealin' from my land, don't I?"

I wasn't sure if he expected me to actually answer that question. I wouldn't know what to say even if he did, so I kept my mouth shut and just stared back.

"The Shadow do pay well, so I'm told. Maybe if I turns both of you in, they'll reward me double." A stupid-looking smile spread across his face, but it faded just as fast. "But that's just what they'd want me to do, the slime-faced rats. That's how they'd be stealin' my slaves. I'm gonna have to sleep on it."

Thundering back to the door in a foul mood, he slammed it shut and pounded down the hallway, mumbling all the way.

"Ugh, I'm so tired of this!" I screamed out loud. "What purpose does our being here serve? If the Author is so close, why doesn't he step in and help? I can't take this anymore; it's so pointless."

The whole journey seemed to be coming to a meaningless end. In an ironic twist of fate, we were most likely about to be sold back to the very enemy we had come here to escape—the dreaded Shadow.

Stretch fueled the fire of my rage. "There's never any purpose, Hunter. Face it—we're all just one step away from here to Frank over there." He pointed back to the skeleton slumped in the corner. "And there's nothing we can do about it."

The sight of Frank made me furious and I kicked a wooden stool at the dusty old skeleton in frustration. The collision of the stool shattered his brittle bones and sent his skull rattling across the floor to Stretch's feet. The only things left in place were a few ribs and a pair of boney legs. Stretch gawked in awkward silence.

I had completely lost it, never before had I been so controlled by my own anger. I rubbed my sleeve under my nose and breathed heavy, steady breaths.

"What did Frank ever do to you?" Stretch finally managed to say, picking up the spinning skull from the floor. All I could do was laugh a little hysterically at the destroyed remains of our roommate. Stretch joined in as well.

"Sorry, I don't know what got into me. This place is just so…so… depressing, I can't stand it anymore."

"I know what you mean," he replied, picking up bits and pieces of what was left of poor old Frank. We were still chained to each other, so I leaned over and helped him gather the remainder of the bones. Together we carried our piles back to the corner where he had rested in peace. As we knelt down to place Frank's parts back in his lap, I noticed something I hadn't before. Scrawled into the rock wall behind his ribs was a hidden message.

I pushed the remainder of Frank's body aside to get a better look at the inscription.

"Hey, have some respect will you?" Stretch griped. "You've done enough already, don't you think?"

"Look," I said, pointing at a mysterious script etched on the wall.

ꟼNIꟼƎꓭꓷIꚺꓕ'ꓕAꓕꟼꓕꓴꓳꟼƎꓕꚺꓷꟼꓴꟼ

"Whoa! Frank's last words," Stretch stared in reverent awe. "Too bad they aren't in English."

The two of us stood there dumbly, staring at the cryptic message for no more than a minute when the writing began to look familiar.

"Hang on, Stretch, I think they're letters!"

"What do you mean?"

"It's our old DaVinci trick. The letters are backwards, just like we used in the clubhouse." I was excited at the challenge of solving a puzzle.

"Frank knows DaVinci?" Stretch asked. I just shrugged it off and we both went to work interpreting the hidden message. After several days as Belac's prisoners the opportunity to entertain our brains was a welcome treat.

Before long we had deciphered the message by scratching each letter into a pile of dust as we went. In the end, the words were written in reverse and strung together in a single line, but a single phrase became clear:

FINDTHEJOYTHAT'SHIDBEHIND

"What a lousy thing to write in code," Stretch complained. "Frank must have been off his rocker when he wrote that."

"Maybe it's a code for something. Maybe he hid something behind a rock that brought him joy," I speculated.

We searched the area surrounding Frank's remains for the better part of ten minutes before the answer hit me like a ton of bricks.

"Wait! I know those words," I suddenly recalled. "They're from a song Gabby sang when her husband died trying to save me from the dragon."

"What does it mean?" Stretch asked, suddenly interested in the story behind the ancient text.

"It means the Author is at work even in the darkest of times, we just have to trust him."

We both sat there in silence, lost in our own thoughts. The timing of the words couldn't have been more perfect and I knew deep down it wasn't an accident at all.

"Do you remember the song?" Stretch asked.

"Part of it, I think," I replied.

"Can you sing it?"

I couldn't believe what I had just heard. Until now Stretch had seemed more or less uninterested in what I'd experienced in my travels, yet here he was asking me to sing. Clearing my throat I tried my best to sing the tune that had haunted me ever since Gerwyn's valiant last stand.

Be not sad, oh heart of mine.
Find the joy that's hid behind.
Through darkness light will find its way
While we await the dawn of day.

As I sang the words my chest filled with new hope. Somehow the Author had entered this place and changed my perspective. For me the proof was undeniable. There was more at work here than I could possibly understand. Belac and his leeches had nearly drained me of the will to survive, but now in our darkest hour yet, an unnatural peace came over me and I knew without a doubt that the Author was still in control.

Click! Creaaaaak!

Our thoughts were cut short by the sound of our cell door moaning softly open. We turned our heads, expecting to see Belac's shadowy figure in the doorway, but to our surprise nobody was there.

"What's going on…?" Stretch whispered.

"It looks like somebody opened the door," I replied softly.

"I can see that, but who? And why?"

"I don't know, maybe we should…" I was going to add, *check it out* but Stretch interrupted in a commanding voice.

"Who's there!" he said to the doorway. There was no response. Either the Shadow were hiding around the corner about to raid our cell and take us hostage, or something else was going on.

"Let's check it out!" I said at last.

"Yeah, you go first," Stretch replied.

"Why me?"

"Because you're older."

"Only by a month."

Stretch shrugged his shoulders as if to say *oh well* and I could tell arguing was pointless.

"Okay, fine, I'll go first; like it's going to matter, we're both chained together anyway."

"Well then, I'll be right behind you!" he said.

The two of us tiptoed across the cold stone floor, one in front of the other, carefully making our way toward the abandoned doorway. We reached the threshold and I turned to make sure Stretch was ready. With a nod from Stretch, I swallowed my fears and peeked out. The hall was empty.

"There's nobody here," I said in shock.

"You mean we're free?" Stretch was confused.

"I think so."

Free. The word never sounded as sweet.

"Well, what are we waiting for, c'mon let's go! The front door is right around the corner." Stretch leaped out the door and dragged me down the hall by our shackles.

"Wait," I said, digging in my heels and putting a stop to our flight. "Before we leave, we have to find my things."

"Are you kidding?" Stretch asked. "We need to get out of here as fast as we can."

"Listen, Belac still has my sword and the Author's Writ. We can't survive out there without them. We need to go to his room and get them back."

Stretch threw an *I can't believe we're doing this* look my way and I caught it. But before he could argue the point I set off down the hall, dragging him along behind me.

The main foyer was an empty room with high ceilings and a few ragged tapestries on the walls. To our right, two large double doors offered an easy escape, but on our left the stairway led up to Belac's bedroom. His snoring echoed through the foyer from his room at the top of the stairs. I remembered Dad used to snore just like that when he fell asleep on the couch watching a baseball game—only ten times worse.

"You sure you want to do this?" Stretch pleaded, looking over at the exit on our right. "I mean, isn't there a saying about letting sleeping trolls lie?"

"That sword is special. We're going to need it if the Shadow are looking for us and I can't use it without the book, at least not yet."

With cautious steps we made our way to the top of the stairs and opened the door to Belac's room. It squeaked slightly but he didn't seem to notice. The troll was sprawled out on an oversized bed in the center of the room, surrounded by piles and piles of stuff. Needless to say, Belac's decorating style was what you might call "eclectic." A collection of meaningless junk he had acquired over time was heaped in piles throughout the room and tucked into corners gathering dust. Some of the piles were so precariously stacked it was a wonder they were still standing at all. Finding my things in this mess was going to take a miracle, but we had to try.

We stepped into the room, searching for my missing backpack. After only a few minutes, I spotted it near the window on the far side of the room. The last rays of sunlight were shining; the afternoon had gone by far too fast. Belac would be waking up any time, we had to move quickly.

I held a finger to my lips and pointed to the window so Stretch could see where we were heading. One step at a time we inched our way over and around piles of junk to where my pack was. Belac had taken the liberty of rummaging through my stuff, emptying my pack, throwing things around on the floor. Stretch kept a sharp eye on Belac as I gathered everything. My Veritas Sword was only a few feet away, but the book was nowhere to be seen.

Turning to Stretch I pressed my palms together and opened them in a motion that was meant to mimic a book. He understood and shrugged, looking around the room. Just then, Belac snorted loudly and turned over in his bed to face us. My heart stopped, and then I noticed it—my book was under the bed, right below Belac's snoring head.

I pointed Stretch toward the book. His eyes widened as he shook his head, making a slicing motion across his neck as if to say *abort mission*, but I couldn't leave now, not when I was so close to getting what I had come for. I was determined to get the book back.

Inch by inch we crept closer to Belac's bed. When at last the book was within reach, I knelt down and took hold of it with my unchained hand. I slid the book toward me, across the stone floor, making far too much noise for Stretch's comfort. Belac didn't even move, his snores drowning out any noise that might have disturbed him.

I picked up the book with a sigh of relief but before I could turn away, a familiar sight caught my eye. There, shoved beneath the bed amidst a pile of junk, was the unmistakable form of a wristwatch. It's glass face was cracked and lifeless and it shouldn't have been worth a second look, except for the fact that I recognized it. This wasn't an ordinary watch; it was a binary one. Unlike traditional watches, binary pieces don't have hour and minute hands, but instead have a sequence of seemingly random LED lights. The unusual pattern is like a code that to a trained eye tells the time.

I knew this because Stretch and I used the binary code system when we wrote secret messages to each other. My dad had taught me how to read it several years ago, using a binary watch much like this one that he always wore—in all my life I'd never seen another person wear one like it.

Ignoring Stretch's silent protest to my extended delay, I moved to the side and reached for the platinum wristband, pulling the the discarded item from under the bed. As I held it in my hand I pondered the meaning of this discovery. *What were the odds that someone else had lost a watch like this in Belac's castle? Could this be my father's? Was it possible my father had actually been here before me?*

I stared at my reflection in the cracked face, not sure what to believe, knowing full well there was one way to find out. I swallowed nervously and turned the watch over, then gazed in disbelief at the back of it. The letters C.B. were etched in the metal—my father's initials.

A loud snort from Belac snapped me back to attention. There was not time to process what I'd just found, so I jammed the watch into a pocket and headed back to Stretch. Together we followed the path to the door, being careful to step over the piles of junk as we left. We had nearly made it out, when disaster struck. Stretch's foot caught the edge of a rug and he stumbled to the ground, pulling on the rug just enough to cause a leaning tower of junk to topple to the ground in a loud crash.

Belac sat up in shock. His eyes shot a look of terror down my spine as they met mine.

"You! How did you get out?" he growled, reaching to the side of his bed and pulling up his club.

Stretch bounced to his feet and pushed me out the door. "Let's get out of here!"

We tore down the stairs as quickly as our legs could carry us. Belac emerged from his room in a rage, threatening to crush us with his club. "You won't get away from me that easy," he shouted, jumping down the first three stairs in a hurry. As we struggled to open the front door, Belac missed a step and slipped, falling back and hitting his head hard. The clumsy oaf rolled down the remainder of the stairs in a painful sequence of bumps, finally coming to rest at the base of the steps in a moaning, motionless heap.

Stretch threw open the door, "Now's our chance! Let's go!"

CHAPTER 17

AN UNEXPECTED REUNION

The foul odor belching from the bog was still as repulsive as ever but no longer had the same stifling effect on me. I took in a deep breath, filling my lungs with the freshness of our newfound freedom. Immediately I felt some of my lost strength return, strength that had been sucked dry from our recent stint as human leech-bait. The revelation that my father had actually been here before us inspired me to press on, but there was no time to dwell on that right now; we were running for our lives. At least we were giving it our best effort, but it was hard trying to reach a true running speed when fighting against the downward suction of a bog with each step.

"Could you have taken any more time back there?" Stretch complained. "What were you thinking?"

"I found my father's watch, Stretch," I replied.

"What?"

"Yeah, I have it in my pocket. It means he was here before us. He was in Belac's castle." I started to say…*he probably escaped just like we did,* but then a terrible thought crossed my mind. *Maybe he didn't escape at all.* My thoughts returned to the pile of bones we had named Frank, the ones thrown across the prison floor. I shuddered at the thought.

"Maybe Belac found it while he was out hunting," Stretch offered.

"Yeah," I agreed, dismissing my concerns in the heat of the moment. "Hurry, Stretch! We've got to get to the gate before Belac recovers."

"Do you really think we've been that close all along?" he grunted as we both worked to slough our way through the thick brown ooze.

"Only one way to be sure, but I remember being told to meet Aviad at the top of the stone stairs, and the map had a towered fortress drawn for the Lost Refuge. It fits with what I saw yesterday." I tried not to slow our pace as I scanned the bleak scenery for familiar landmarks. It was difficult enough to differentiate one set of vine-tangled trees from the next in the daytime, let alone under the cover of night. A swirling ground fog added to the challenge, but my instincts were finally proven right when a familiar cluster of rocks emerged from the dark.

"There! We were near these rocks when I saw it. The stairs will be somewhere over there." I pointed through the darkness to where I remembered the bog ending and the stairs beginning up the steep hill. Under present conditions, it would be impossible to catch sight of the tower from here, but I felt a great surge of energy just knowing we were almost there.

"Come on, Stretch! It's got to be just at the top of this hill!"

Fighting our way out of the thick slop was harder than I expected. The swamp was as greedy a captor as its master, Belac. It clearly didn't want to let us escape, becoming thicker and heavier the closer we got to its edge.

That's when we heard the terrible voice again, shouting angrily into the night.

"Thieves! When I find you, your bones will be looking for another body!"

From the crashing sounds behind us Belac wasn't letting anything get in the way of chasing us down. His large feet and super-human strength would not be slowed by the bog as we had been.

We had no time to lose. We began to grab desperately at what trees and foliage survived in and around the swamp, but they offered no help, bending and snapping under our weight. Falling forward into more of a crawl, I was finally able to drag myself out of the muck and, using the chain that tethered us, pulled Stretch out behind me.

On firm ground once again, we hurried to sprint up the stone stairway inlaid into the hill, but being covered in swamp-slime definitely worked against us. Our feet slipped with every hurried step, but the resulting cuts and bruises were not going to stop our mad dash. Behind us, the wild thrashing and enraged shouts provided plenty of motivation to reach the top, and quickly. It was only a matter of time before Belac found us. Even now, looking over my shoulder as we scrambled up the steps, I could make out the glow of a torchlight waving erratically in the fog spread out below us. So far our pursuer appeared to be heading the wrong way.

"Hunter!" Stretch huffed as I crested the top. "Slow dow...ow!"

Whatever caused Stretch to fall, brought me down with him as the chain jerked violently from his sudden stop. Our landing was punctuated by a clattering of stones crashing down. My heart racing, I jumped up to check below us, hoping against all odds that Belac hadn't just heard that. He had.

"Aha! Got ya!" The flickering flame below started moving in a straight path toward the hill.

"Stretch, he knows where we are! Get up!" I pleaded, pulling on the chain.

Stretch wasn't budging, "Oh man, my ankle! I can't....Ah!" He pulled hard against the chain, trying to stand. "You gotta go on without me..."

Had he hit his head too? "What are you talking about? I can't leave you. We're chained!"

"Oh yeah," he grimaced, finally standing on his good leg while gingerly dangling his injured foot. "Uh, Hunter? Where's the door?"

Only now had I been able to stop and survey the hilltop. My eyes were drawn to the tower that stood just off to our left. It was the same one that had, like a lighthouse, signaled hope to me the other day. But its beam of hope was quickly snuffed out as my eyes moved down the tower to its foundation.

What should have been the surrounding walls of a fortress, lay strewn about like a choppy sea of displaced stone blocks. Surveying the ruins of the once proud fortress, I realized all hope of finding Aviad had vanished beneath the pile of rubble.

"No. No. No. No. No! This can't be right. His letter said he'd be here!"

The door had to be up here. I just knew it. Only, right now, the few things still standing were the two of us, the tower, and a few crumbling remains of a fortress wall.

I fought to keep myself from panicking. "It's here. It has to be here! We just haven't seen it yet..."

Stretch's unexpected death-grip on my arm caused me to fall silent. From somewhere below us came Belac's labored breathing and pacing footsteps, telling me that he was very near.

"Show yourselves, slaves! Ya can't hide from Belac forever," he snorted.

Stretch gripped me even tighter. "Hunter! Forget the door, we've got to hide! Get us out of here! He'll kill us if he catches us!"

My feet were all of a sudden jumpy, telling me to run, but I didn't know where to go. That's when I saw it in the shadows.

"There! Do you see it? The door!"

There, among the ruins, was the unmistakable shape of an arched doorway. It couldn't be more than forty yards away to our right. The only problem was, it wasn't standing upright anymore. Instead, it looked as if it had been tipped backwards, laying face up against the rubble-strewn ground. Even so, in the moonlight I could see its intricate stone framework and sturdy wooden door were still intact—that was enough to keep my hope intact too.

Making a run for it would normally have been the first choice, but with Belac so near and Stretch's sprained ankle, we couldn't risk hobbling out in the open. There was no clear path to the door. We would have to pick our way through the piles of crumbling stone before we could reach it. I had to put some more space between us and Belac.

"I have a plan."

Stretch grabbed my shirt. "You aren't seriously considering going over to the door now, are you?"

"No." I could see temporary relief in Stretch's eyes. "Not until we slow down Belac."

"What! Hunter, in case you didn't notice, the door is busted down. And from the looks of it this place has been in ruins for a long time."

"That's just it. Aviad knew the condition the Lost Refuge was in when he sent me the invitation, just four days ago," I reasoned. "There's got to be more to the door than meets the eye...and I intend to find out!"

"Are you nuts? Busted doors don't go anywhere. What you see is what you get. There's nothing for us here!"

I listened to my own voice refuse to back down. "I know. But the instructions never told me what kind of door I'd find—only that Aviad would be waiting behind it." I marveled at how Sam-like that sounded. *Was that really me talking?* Somehow, I knew I had to trust the Author's word.

I blocked out the rest of Stretch's logical rebuttal. Instead, I was intently inching my way back toward the portion of half-wall we had originally tripped over. Carefully peering over the top, I held my breath when I saw just how close Belac was to us. At the moment, he was nearly half-way up the stairs, swiping his torch low to the ground, apparently looking for any tracks we had left. Soon he'd find what he was looking for and then it'd only take him a couple of strides to march up the hill and finish us off.

"Stretch!" I hissed, interrupting his whispered comments on the ratio of how likely we were to die of bludgeoning versus impalement. "Get over here and help me push!" I didn't give Stretch a choice; he fell helplessly towards me when I yanked on the chain.

The weight of his fall, combined with my own push, sent a miniature avalanche of wall rubble down the steps directly toward where Belac was now bent low, examining some evidence of our tracks. The yell, followed by a thud and a hefty splat told me all I needed to know. Our avalanche had found its mark and sent Belac back down the hill a little.

"Now run!" I yelled, picking us both up from the ground.

Sprain, or no sprain, Stretch was hurtled into a painful dash across the rocky terrain with me. He could either suffer in pain now or die painfully in a minute. I knew he would thank me later.

"Aaaahh!" Belac bellowed his rage behind us. "You'll pay fer that!"

We had barely made it ten yards when something flew over our heads, exploding into a remnant of wall a short distance from us. Belac was madly hurling the very rubble we had toppled on him back at the stairs.

"Take that, ya brats!" I could hear him scream as he blindly launched another projectile that narrowly missed me. Stretch fought to keep up with me.

"Hunter,...ow!...are you...ow!...crazy? There's no...ow!...time for this!"

"Trust me, Stretch. We just have to get to the door!"

We were closing in on the door now. Just a few more yards. From this distance I could even make out the Author's triple *V* insignia carved into the wood. This had to be it! As soon as we were close enough, I threw myself onto the door.

"You won't get away that easy!" The sound of Belac's booming voice, followed by tumbling stones, alerted me that he had finally managed to make it back up the hill and was bulldozing his way through the ruins. I didn't bother to watch what he would do next, but instead shouted, "Quick! Find the handle!" Stretch couldn't peel his terrified eyes away from the approaching Belac while I frantically ran my hands along the door face, searching in vain for some trigger to open the door.

"Come on...come on...what am I missing?"

Immediately, like a compass needle snapping into polar alignment, my mind honed back in on the single passage from the Writ I had memorized just days ago:

Beyond the ancient door doth hide
The way to one whom you must find.
Knock and it will open wide.

"Hunter! Watch out!"

There was no time to second guess the instructions from the passage. I pounded my fist against the fallen door as hard as I could before turning, just in time to see the car-sized boulder Belac had heaved, slam into the ground about twenty feet behind us. The momentum of the stone carried it toward us with deadly speed.

It was too late to run to either side. There was nowhere to go. With a crushing death barreling down on us, we instinctively threw ourselves at the door. Landing on its sturdy wooden surface I felt my body lurch forward, but not from the crushing impact of the boulder. The door had somehow fallen open, and we found ourselves tumbling face-first onto a hardwood floor.

We hit the ground and the door slammed shut against the boulder behind us. The only evidence of the violent end we had just narrowly escaped was the soft, muffled *thud* of the boulder, mostly drowned out by a short, jingling bell somewhere overhead.

I rolled onto my back to take in our new surroundings. We were flanked by rows of shelves, stuffed full of books and surrounded by cats. I'll admit it took me a second longer than it should have, but I finally recognized where we were, and so had Stretch.

"Uh, Hunter...are we...?"

I nodded slowly as I took it all in.

Somehow we were now back in the mysterious bookshop where Evan had sent us days earlier to retrieve the book—the very book that had transported us into Solandria to begin with.

"Welcome, weary travelers!"

I spun around to locate the unidentified voice. There, standing at the closed door, was the one to whom we apparently owed our rescue from the boulder. It was the old book keeper himself.

His face showed a satisfied smile and his magnified eyes blinked, eagerly bouncing from Stretch to me and back again. Neither of us could find words to return his friendly greeting, but only managed to exchange dumbfounded expressions with each other.

"That was cutting it a bit close, don't you think? I'd been expecting you to knock. If I didn't know better," he winked mysteriously, "I might have doubted you were ever going to knock at all."

Shuffling over to Stretch he offered one of his wrinkled hands, "But here I am jib-jabbering away while you're still covered in mud and in chains on my floor. Let me help you."

"Uh, that's okay. I got it." Stretch politely refused the hand and strained to pull himself up on his own, swollen ankle and all. I sprang up off the floor to help him finish standing.

Shifting his extended hand towards the main aisle, the book keeper motioned us forward. "Don't worry about the dirt. You'll be just fine. Do come in! Come in! I can assist you better with removing those shackles back here."

Following his cue, I offered my shoulder to Stretch for support before directing our steps toward the sales counter. The old man ducked into a closet nearby before popping back out with a toolbox of some kind and a couple of towels. He let us use the towels to wipe off the excess mud before sitting us down on a couple of stools behind the register.

On the counter, I spotted a plastic container filled with some kind of dessert bars. Following my gaze, our host offered them to us, "Would either of you care for a snack while I work? Peanut butter pecan fudge. They're my favorite!"

At this point, I think we would have eaten a plate of cooked eggplant if it was offered to us. Compared to the filth we'd lived on at Belac's, anything was welcome. We both stuffed ourselves on the sweets while the kindly book keeper worked at picking the locks on our cuffs. Before long he had expertly worked the restraints free, joining us in polishing off the last of the fudge bars.

He wiped the crumbs from his mouth with a well-worn handkerchief before finally breaking the ice, "Now then, why don't you tell me what it was you came to see me for."

Stretch looked to me while he licked the last of the fudge from his fingers. I stared back blankly. Somehow in the shock of finding the bookstore, we had both managed to temporarily forget the significance of why we were even at the door to begin with.

"We were told to knock on this door," I finally blurted out, "and we would find Aviad. But…" I glanced around the store again, "from the looks of it, we must have gotten something wrong."

"Ah. But if you are seeking Aviad, then you are indeed in the right place." He clasped his hands together and leaned in toward us. A sparkle in his faded green eyes tipped me off that he knew a secret we had yet to realize.

Of course! The book came from this bookshop—a supernatural book-shop at that.

I jumped to what I thought was the obvious conclusion, "You mean, you work for Aviad?"

The old man burst into a cackling, but kindly chuckle before nodding, "You could say I do his work, yes."

Stretch nudged me. "Ask him if he's one of the Code guys too."

The book keeper intercepted Stretch's question, choosing to answer him directly, "Well, yes, I do have a strong bond with the Codebearers."

"Then, can you take us to meet Aviad?" I asked eagerly.

He paused to smile at us both. "As a matter of fact, if you would follow me, I will gladly make the introductions."

"What? Now? Here?"

He simply smiled as he unceremoniously headed off in the di-rection of an office at the back of the store. We followed at a slower pace. Personally, I was wrestling with the idea of meeting Aviad dressed like I was. I only needed to look at Stretch to get a general picture of how bad I was looking right now too. Trust me. It was bad.

Once the book keeper entered the office, Stretch took the op-portunity to spill his thoughts, whispering, "For a moment there, I was worried that he was going to end up being Aviad. After all the talk of him being this great and powerful leader... Man! Talk about a let-down!" We shared a quiet laugh over that thought before the book keeper popped his head back out the door.

"You were coming, right?" He held the door open with one hand, courteously making way for us to enter.

I took a deep breath. After all I had been through exiting the Veil, training with the Codebearers, risking life and limb to evade the Shadow, I had finally arrived at this key moment. I couldn't help but feel my pulse quicken at the prospect of finally meeting this mysterious man who was believed to hold the answers for us.

The office was simple, appropriate for the type of work you would expect a bookshop manager to do. A modest desk supported stacks of books and papers, lit by the soft glow of a green-shaded desk lamp. An old, burgundy leather high-back chair sat with its back turned to us, obscuring our view of whoever sat in it. The book keeper remained behind us at the doorway. I looked back at him for some clue as to what protocol our meeting should follow next. He simply gave me a friendly nod to focus my attention back on the turned chair and cleared his throat.

I heard the soft sound of a book shutting before the chair swiveled around.

"Welcome! I am Aviad. Please, do have a seat!"

It couldn't be! Sitting in front of us was the same old man who had just stood behind us a second before. Wheeling around, I found he was missing from his former post at the doorway. No, there he was, sitting in the chair.

An angry swarm of thoughts buzzed through my brain. *What kind of trick was he pulling? And did I just hear him right? His name is Aviad?*

Our combined mud-encrusted hair and bewildered looks must have made quite a picture. Aviad could not hold back another of his signature laughs. "I'm sorry! It's just that your expressions are so priceless. Please, please take your seats..." Chuckling, he wiped some tears from his eyes and adjusted his glasses.

I looked over to Stretch. He still wore the same slack-jawed expression I did and didn't even flinch as one of the bookstore cats padded its way into the office and leaped boldly onto his lap.

"Yes, you heard right. I am Aviad." The old man searched our faces with piercing, but compassionate eyes. "Not what you were looking for?" He paused for any response from us. "Perhaps I am not the great and powerful leader you envisioned—a let-down, even?"

Oh man, he had heard us! I shifted uncomfortably in my chair as an even more terrifying thought came to me. *Maybe he's capable of reading our minds!* To say that I was embarrassed at this moment would be a gross understatement. Here I was, finally in the presence of the powerful Aviad, the one who had called me here, to whom the whole Resistance looked for leadership as a famed warrior, sage...and me? Well, I had just thoroughly insulted him.

I could feel myself shrinking by the second at the prospect of having performed the single, worst, bad impression of my life. Stretch, on the other hand, was apparently far less convicted than I was, blurting out, "Are you kidding me?"

He turned to me, his passionate outburst having scared the cat from his lap. "No way is he Aviad! Hunter, you've been telling me how he'd be the son of the Author, a great leader with power, not a..." his better judgment finally managed to get a hold of his tongue.

"Not a feeble old man?" Aviad finished for him.

"Well, yeah. No offense, but we were expecting someone a little more...I mean, we've got a real problem here with the Shadow, and you were supposed to be the one with answers, who could solve it and get us back home. But here we are," he waved around us, "just sitting in a musty bookshop with a bunch of smelly cats."

"I see," Aviad conceded gravely with a nod. "And you do not believe I have the answers?"

This time I spoke up before Stretch could respond, "No...I mean, yes. We..." I paused, taking note of Stretch's annoyed look before continuing. "Well, I believe that if you are Aviad then you do have answers. Petrov and Sam, the Author's book, they all point to you as the one who holds the key to defeating the Shadow."

Leaning back in the chair he answered confidently, "Indeed. I do have answers for those who seek them."

A wave of hope washed over me. "Then please," I leaned forward, "tell me what it is I need to do."

Aviad seemed to take special delight in my request.

"You must give your complete allegiance to the Author and to the Resistance."

I didn't have to think about that too long. Become a Codebearer? "Of course I will. Yes! I want to. I will swear allegiance..."

"No," Aviad interrupted. "I'm sorry, Hunter, but your time has not yet come. First, the prophecy must be fulfilled."

As a teenager, I was well acquainted with rejection. Depending on the situation, the turndown was usually followed by the typical explanations of *too short*, *not cool enough*, and my mother's favorite *because I said so*. When did *the prophecy must be fulfilled* one get added to the list?

"Prophecy? What prophecy? What do you mean?"

He motioned with his hands for me to calm down. "Take out your Author's Writ and I will show you." I hastily picked up my bag and pulled out the book.

Aviad stretched his wrinkled hand across the desk. "Here, let me see it."

He took the book from me and with the knowledge of one who is intimately familiar with a book's content, opened it right to the precise page he was looking for.

"Aha! Here we are. Read this."

I took back the book, careful not to lose its place and began to read it silently.

Aviad cleared his throat. "Aloud, if you will please."

My face turned red. "Oh right. Sorry."

The Bloodstone Prophecy

Good and evil both confined
Within the sacred stone.
The stone will break and thieves will take
A knowledge not their own.
The Serpent is released to rule;
The broken halves will bind them.
The Author's curse cannot reverse,
For certain death must find them.
So I, the Author, have written.

Half you hold, as if your own,
The power in it given;
But in a body dark and cold
The other half is hidden.
No eye can see for by his will
Now veiled it resides
Until the Author chooses one
To plunge the depths of death and find.
So I, the Author, have written.

The curse of death is not complete—
The final choice awaits
Until the two at last shall meet
And the sacred pause abates.
The chosen one will hunt you down
To take your scepter and your crown.
So I, the Author, have written.

I looked back at Aviad. He was busy scratching the head of a new cat who had decided to explore his already crowded desk. Without looking up he asked me, "Do you have any questions concerning the prophecy?"

"Well, to start with...what does this prophecy have to do with me and fixing my problem?"

"Indeed, what *does* any of this have to do with you?" Aviad ran his hand slowly down the back of the cat in a final stroke before returning his attention to me.

"That's always the first question I am asked, in no uncertain terms, of course. My answer is always the same too..." He paused to make sure he had my full attention before adding in a hushed tone, "More than you know." The mystery behind that answer seemed to swell until it filled the room in silence.

"Let me show you something, Hunter." Aviad reached across the desk and turned to a new page in my Author's Writ. A red holographic image of a gemstone sprang to life from its text, much like the hologram I'd seen in Sam's book back at Sanctuary. The effect was captivating—the slow spin of the glowing image mesmerizing to watch. I could tell by the way Stretch shifted in his chair that it had commanded his attention too.

"Do you recognize this stone?"

Of course I did. How could I not? It was unmistakably the same stone I had seen taken from the tree in my vision.

"Yes...is that the Bloodstone?"

He nodded approvingly, "The very same. This stone is the key to freeing you from the Shadow's curse. While the Bloodstone remains shattered you are under their power, and the curse continues."

By now, Stretch had succumbed to his urge to reach out and touch the projected image, his fingertips passing through the light with no disturbance at all. This kind of thing was right up his alley. Whatever science was involved behind it would keep him occupied for hours. I, however, was more concerned with the implications of what Aviad was saying.

"So what do we do?"

"Find the two halves of the stone and return them to me, then the curse can be completed and I will free you."

The way he said it so matter-of-factly made it sound deceptively simple. Judging by the way he waited for me to respond, I wonder now if he would have been content to send me off on my way right then and there.

"But I don't have a clue where to start looking for them," I protested.

"Let me walk you through the text." He turned back the page to where the prophecy was written, dousing the hologram, much to Stretch's dismay. "Look with me at the last three lines of the prophecy. Who is it talking about here?"

The chosen one will hunt you down
To take your scepter and your crown.
So I, the Author, have written.

I read off the two names I saw. "The 'chosen one' and…the 'Author.'"

"Correct on both accounts, though you missed one." He pointed to the second to last line and had me read it again. "What do we know about the 'you' the text refers to?"

Oh man. This was exactly what Ms. White would do at school when she taught—make you work to find the answer for yourself. Personally, I would have preferred just to have the answer given to me straight out. It would save a lot of time and make the whole learning process a lot easier.

Seeing that Aviad wasn't about to feed me the answer, I reread the paragraph more closely before formulating my answer. "Um…they have a scepter and a crown?" It was less of an answer, more of a question, but hopefully passable.

"Again, correct." I could tell that Aviad was enjoying his role as teacher right now. "And someone who had a scepter and crown would be?" he prompted.

"A king, I guess."

"Indeed, someone in charge who rules. Now, put that in context of present-day Solandria and who would that person be?"

At first I wanted to answer *the Author* or even *Aviad*, as both of them were in high positions with the Codebearers, but then I figured that wouldn't make much sense since the prophecy had been written by the Author and Aviad worked for him. Now that I thought about it, the Codebearers were just a minority resistance in the land. The real control belonged to the Shadow—in the hands of a certain boy.

"Venator," I answered. "The 'you' is Venator, isn't it?" This time it was actually more of an answer, less of a question.

Aviad enthusiastically nodded his approval of my conclusion. "Since Venator does not actually wear a crown or carry a scepter, we have to consider them as symbolic imagery. The crown represents his authority, and the scepter represents..."

"His staff!" The thought had hit me so suddenly I couldn't avoid blurting it out. "The stone on his staff is the Bloodstone, isn't it?"

Aviad beamed proudly at my star-pupil performance. "You are quick at this! Yes. And that is where your mission will take you first."

Clearly some miscommunication was happening here. "Whoa! Wait a minute! *My* mission?"

"Why yes." Aviad didn't miss a beat. "You are the one the prophecy indicates will hunt down Venator." This was getting out of hand now. I was the one coming here for help, not a hero waiting for his next assignment.

"But how can I help? I barely know anything about being a Codebearer. I'm not a warrior." So far none of this seemed to concern Aviad. I launched into another round of defense strategies, claiming everything from "my left eye is going fuzzy" to "I'm afraid of killer demon-insect-thingies." If any of this was making a difference with Aviad, he didn't show it. He only smiled, hands folded on his lap, content to sit back while I finished my tirade. "I just don't have what it takes to defeat Venator."

Seeing my protest had finally come to an end, Aviad leaned forward, tapping his finger on the passage. "Yet, that's precisely what you were called here to do. That is your purpose."

It didn't make any sense. Why me of all people? If I had a vote in this matter, and it seemed more and more like I didn't, I would have picked out the most skilled warrior. Better yet, send a whole army of Codebearers—mount a full attack. Aviad was clearly too old to go, so I didn't even bother to ask him why he wasn't going. Whatever he had once been in his youth, he no longer had strength for it now. Maybe he was still a great strategist? Though seeing how committed he was to the idea of sending me on this insane mission was proof to me against that option.

Aviad reeled me back in with his steady, calming voice, "Hunter, if there was another way, wouldn't I have already taken care of it?"

I knew I couldn't argue that point with him if I still believed what Sam and Petrov had taught me about Aviad. To them, he was the final authority on all things. And he was speaking to me now, "You are the one the prophecy calls out, Hunter. There can be no other way."

There was nothing more I could say. I had to accept this charge to go fight the greatest evil known to this world and retrieve a lost part of the Bloodstone. A thousand questions begged to be asked next, but one pushed its way to the front. "Assuming that I'm miraculously going to be able to get the staff, the prophecy says that it's just one-half of the stone. What good is it going to be to have one-half without the other?"

"Good question. But…" he held up a hand in caution, "don't get ahead of yourself. Your first task must be to confront Venator. Once you have done this, you'll return to me and we will finish the quest together." With that he slowly closed the book in front of me, indicating our lesson was finished.

Stretch eagerly snatched up the book to try and find the hologram page again. "And then you'll help us get back home?" I was surprised to hear Stretch asking that question. As put-off as he'd originally been, I hadn't realized how carefully he'd been paying attention to all that Aviad said.

"When the prophecy is fulfilled, yes, I will be able to help you," Aviad answered.

That was apparently all Stretch needed to hear. He sat back with a satisfied grin, poking at the hologram he had finally reopened. I was reminded that as miserable as Stretch had been, lost on his own and trapped by Belac, he had not seen the darkest parts of Solandria like I had. He didn't know what Venator and his army of Shadow Warriors looked like or were capable of. I, on the other hand, knew exactly what we were going up against in this impossible mission.

Aviad had only to look at me to know what I was thinking. I was sure of that now. "Something still troubles you, Hunter." I lowered my eyes to avoid the searching gaze I felt on me.

"Back in Belac's castle I..." I swallowed hard to finish my statement. "I found something. Something that belonged to my father." Aviad didn't respond as I pulled the watch from my pocket and placed it on the desktop. "It was his," I explained. "I was wondering if you know where he might be, or if you know how I could find him." There was a brief pause as Aviad searched his memory. He lifted the watch from the table and smiled.

"Caleb Brown," Aviad said lovingly. "He was quite the star pupil for a while there, I can tell you that much. A fine swordsman and very adept in his knowledge of the Code. In fact, I believe your friend, Sam, shared several adventures with him."

My eyes lit up at his words. Just hearing that my father had actually been to Solandria and shared my experiences brought me closer to him than I had ever felt before.

"He progressed quickly and was even entrusted with the leadership of a small cadre of warriors. They were sent on a reconnaissance mission into enemy territory." Aviad's voice saddened, "Things went terribly wrong and his men were all taken captive. Your father alone escaped that day. He was never the same again. He blamed himself for the failure of the mission and the loss of his men. He left the Resistance shortly thereafter."

"Where is he now?" I ventured to ask.

"I'm afraid that is something I can't say." My eyes dropped to the floor in disappointment. "As hard as it is to hear, finding your father is not the answer to the problem you face right now, Hunter. You must put that behind you. Hold on to the hope that he may still be alive, but don't let it distract you from the task at hand. Your mission is to recover the Bloodstone. It is the only thing that matters right now."

Aviad handed me the watch across the table. I took it and examined the shattered face once more. Emptiness filled my heart as I wrestled with the thought of being left, yet again, with only the memory of my father.

"But, what if I fail too? I'm not a warrior like Sam or my father. It's just me and Stretch. How can we do it alone?"

I watched as Aviad slowly rose from his chair. Walking over to where I sat, he lifted the pendant Hope had loaned me and examined it through the bifocal half of his spectacles.

"Ah, but I never said you'd be alone, did I?" His eyes held that mysterious twinkle again. Letting the necklace fall to my chest, he started walking toward the door. "Follow me."

Grabbing my pack from the floor, I hurriedly snatched my book out of Stretch's lap to the sound of loud protesting. We had to hurry to catch up to Aviad. He'd already made his way down the back hall. We ended at a push door labeled "Emergency Exit." Stopping short of the door, Aviad turned to face us.

"This door will lead you back into Solandria where you'll begin your mission to recover the Bloodstone. When you're ready just give it a good shove." He demonstrated a push, then patted us on the shoulders before turning to leave. I watched him until he disappeared around the corner. *That was it, then? And now we were just supposed to strike out on our own through another door that would take us who knew where?*

Placing my hand against the push-bar, I instinctively paused to consider my action. The door looked like any other emergency exit I'd often mischievously ventured through over the course of my childhood. Even now I could hear the high-pitched squeal of the alarm system that would invariably go off, alerting my parents or principal that I wasn't where I was supposed to be. Ironically, right now the only voice telling me not to go out this door was my own. Fear was taking over where worry had left off. Fear of the unknown. Fear of what I knew was waiting for us.

I took a deep breath, trying to remember the lessons Sam taught me, "Through fear a man appoints his master."

Stretch's impatient voice interrupted my thoughts, "Come on! Let's go!"

The irony continued. In a reversal of roles, I was now the one dragging his feet to follow Aviad's directions. Tired of my dawdling, Stretch finally gave me a good shove, sending us both stumbling out the wide-swung door and into a forest of giant redwoods.

Morning light was sparkling down through the branches of the trees, casting its radiance on the thick underbrush of the forest floor. We were in the middle of nowhere. The scene was peaceful, especially after our experience with Belac. Time seemed to have flown by faster than I had expected. Night was approaching when we had entered Aviad's bookshop, and now it appeared another day was just beginning.

"I thought he said we wouldn't be alone," Stretch pointed out.

"He did."

"Then where is everyone?"

Whooosh!

Before I had time to answer, a net from the forest floor sprung up around us, plucking us skyward toward the tree canopy a hundred feet above. The world was spinning out of control and I was getting dizzy as we dangled in the trap. A lone figure stepped out of the darkened shade of the tree limbs, carrying a bow drawn tight, with an arrow ready to release at the first sign of trouble. I spun my head in a matching motion, trying to catch a glimpse of our assailant's face.

"Hunter?" The archer spoke at last. "Is that really you?"

CHAPTER 18

THE QUEST BEGINS

The voice on the other side of the arrow was sweet, soft and full of concern. I recognized it immediately.

"Hope!"

Dropping the weapon she pulled the net closer and flashed a beautiful smile at me that faded far too quickly into a look of disgust.

"Ew, you smell like swamp water." She released the net to cover her nose, letting us swing freely out over the forest floor once more.

"Nice to see you too," I replied, as we swung back toward her again. Apparently I would never make a good impression. "Are you just going to let us hang here forever?"

"I should. You guys reek," she said, still holding her nose. Eventually, she gathered her courage and pulled the net aside, dumping us onto a wooden platform.

"What happened?" she asked. "You look awful."

"Long story," I replied. "This is my friend Stretch, the one I was telling you about."

Stretch bobbed his head in acknowledgement of my introduction, trying to look cool in the process. It didn't work of course. When you're plastered in mud and smelling as bad as we were, there was no way you could really pull off *cool*.

"Good to finally meet you," she said to him.

"The pleasure is mine," he grinned stupidly, still trying to hold on to whatever suave persona he had in mind. *Please tell me he didn't just say that* I thought to myself. Hope returned a look of confusion, obviously thinking my friend was an idiot—which at the moment, he was.

"So…" she said, lingering on the first word with watering eyes and fanning her face. "How did you guys get here?" She was playing this *you stink* card way too much, but I was glad to see her and let it go without saying anything.

"Aviad sent us back," I started.

"We're on a secret mission!" Stretch blurted, looking to gain some credibility with Hope in the process.

"A mission, huh!" she replied, now somewhat interested.

"Yeah, we're supposed to find some bad guy and take back a magic stone or something." If he could only hear how stupid he sounded, I was sure he'd have toned down the dork factor about ten notches.

"So, where are the others? Is everyone okay?" I asked, anxious to catch up on every detail of what happened while I was away. From the look on her face the news was not good.

"Not really. Follow me, there's a lot to catch up on and this isn't the place for it," she said.

The suspense was killing me; I needed to know how everyone was doing. I tried not to let anxiety get the best of me, but I couldn't help but wonder who had survived the battle of Sanctuary. I forced myself to push my worries aside as we followed Hope across a series of rope bridges and zip lines to a hidden cluster of forts up in the trees nearby.

"This is one of our outposts," she explained as we approached the first fort. "We're using it as a rendezvous point for those who survived the attack."

As we entered the tree-village Ephriam stepped out to greet me, along with a few other familiar faces from the Resistance—too few.

After exchanging greetings and drawing more than our fair share of plugged-nosed comments about our smell, we thought it best to clean up before catching up. One of Ephriam's men led us down a rope elevator to a fresh-water stream that ran nearby. Stretch and I scrubbed the muck and grime off our bodies as best we could. While our clothes probably should have been burned, we had nothing else to wear, so we washed them as well. The men had loaned each of us one of their cloaks to wear while we waited for our clothes to dry, so we headed back up the elevator to the outpost in the trees, ready for lunch.

Finally, it was time to hear the news.

"So, what happened?" I asked, as we sat around the table in our borrowed cloaks.

"Sanctuary was destroyed," Hope replied bluntly, staring down at the ground. "We fought off the Shadow as long as we could but there were just too many and we didn't have nearly enough time to prepare. The first wave of the attack came only minutes after you left."

A wave of guilt swept over me, as if somehow I was to blame for the loss of so much; in a way, I suppose I was. After all, I was the one Venator wanted.

"We held back their first attack fairly easily, but as more and more started to arrive, their numbers eventually won out."

"What about Sam?"

"Sam…" she tried to answer but couldn't finish. There was a long pause as she tried to gather the words, but they never came. She didn't have to say anything; my stomach tightened, and I thought I was going to be sick. It was Ephriam, at last, who stepped forward to share the news.

"Good old Sam. There was no holding him back. He took more than fifty of the Shadow down before they overpowered him."

I couldn't believe what I was hearing! Sam, the strongest man I had ever met was gone. I couldn't have imagined a better instructor. Until that moment, I didn't realize how much he had meant to me. Tears welled up in my eyes and I couldn't keep them from falling. I couldn't bear to think about not seeing him again.

"What about the others?" I asked weakly, wiping the tears away and feeling as if my heart had been ripped from my chest.

"We don't know," Ephriam continued, "the Resistance scattered once it was evident we couldn't recover the city. To be honest, I expected to find more of them here, but so far we're the only ones. There will be more in time, I know there will."

A long silence followed that no one dared break. The memories of friends and loved ones that captivated our thoughts were too precious to rush. Stretch had no idea who or what we were talking about, but to his credit, he respected the moment and kept quiet as well.

"So, how about you, Hunter?" Ephriam finally asked. "How did your part in the struggle against the Shadow fair?"

The way he said it made me feel like an equal, as if my journey to find answers was as important as the protection of Sanctuary had been for them—maybe even more so. I told them everything, from my aerial battle with the Gorewings to my capture by Belac and our daring escape. Of course, Stretch interjected his own version as we went along, making sure to paint himself in the best light possible. Then at last, I came to our meeting with Aviad and how I was going on a mission to recover the Bloodstone from Venator.

"So it's true," Ephriam said. "You *are* the chosen one the prophecy has revealed."

"I guess so," I said. "All I know is that Venator has the Bloodstone and I'm supposed to take it back somehow. Other than that I have no clue where to begin."

"Perhaps we can help," Ephriam said. "Venator's stronghold is but a full-day's ride from here. I would like nothing more than to join you and help you bring an end to Venator's rule, especially after what has happened to Sam."

I sensed a hint of revenge in Ephriam's voice, a trait that was not considered honorable for Codebearers. Even so, Aviad himself had made it clear that we would not be going alone; obviously, we had been brought together for a purpose.

"So what do you say, Hunter?" he asked. "Will you allow us join in your quest?"

"Yes, of course," I agreed without needing to think twice. I had no desire to go alone into the enemy's fortress if I could help it. Having the support of experienced fighters could only help our chances of success.

"Excellent," he replied. "I'll gather some provisions and we can leave first thing in the morning. In the meantime, you boys better spend the afternoon learning how to ride."

Our clothes had dried by now, so after we dressed we followed Hope down a wooden elevator to the forest floor below. She led us to a rustic stable, nearly buried in underbrush.

As we approached, a foul stench invaded my nostrils, one that could not be ignored. It seemed to be coming from an unusually large pile of green dung that had been scattered across the pathway in front of us. The pile was crawling with flies and would easily have been knee deep if you were dumb enough to stand in it. I pulled my shirt up over my nose in an attempt to dull the smell but it didn't help.

"Gross! I'd hate to meet whatever made that!" I said, nodding toward the pile as we passed.

"As a matter of fact, you'll be riding it," Hope replied with a smile. "And if I remember correctly, you didn't smell much better when I found you this morning."

I ignored the snide remark. Stretch didn't seem to even hear it at all; he was too busy trying to determine what kind of creature would make a pile that big.

"You mean, your horses left that?" Stretch asked in amazement.

"Horses? Who said anything about horses? We'll be riding Uguas," she corrected him.

"Uguas?"

A low groan echoed through the air before he could finish his thought. To my surprise a gigantic iguana-like lizard rounded the corner of the stable with quick graceful strides. My jaw dropped in astonishment.

"Uguas," Hope clarified, pointing up at the saddle perched on the creature's back, fifteen feet above the ground. The creature's thickly muscled legs and slender body allowed it to move quickly. From tip to tail it must have measured at least fifty feet, and its head swayed back and forth in anticipation of the journey.

"They're relatively easy to ride if you can learn how to hang on. Ready to give it a try?" Hope asked, ducking into the stable without waiting for a response. She returned a moment later, leading a couple more of the creatures into the open.

"Here, put these on," she said, tossing a couple of leather belts at us. Each belt had a pair of metal clips in the front and back. I wondered what they were for, but before I could ask, the question was answered. "I'll help you up so you can latch your belts to the harness."

Our first several attempts to mount the beasts were a comedy of errors. The problem was, they were fidgety creatures and didn't stand still long enough to let you keep your balance. Hope found the whole thing amusing, laughing at our clumsiness. Finally, after several minutes of chaos, we managed to steady ourselves long enough to clip our belts to their saddles, cinching the straps tightly for safety. We wouldn't be falling off now even if we wanted to, a thought that made me anxious as to why it was necessary to clip ourselves to the Uguas in the first place.

Hope joined us on a third Ugua, and after a brief training in simple commands I finally was able to direct the creature around the stable grounds on my own.

"Well," she said at last, "neither of you are naturals, but I suppose we'll have to call it good enough." Her words inspired little confidence in our abilities. "Now, for the real fun."

Uh oh, I didn't like the sound of that.

With a sharp slap of the reigns Hope's Ugua sprung into action, scaling the nearest tree in a flash. Stretch and I dropped our jaws in amazement. I could tell we were both thinking the same thing.

Stretch gawked, "Did she just…?"

"Uh huh!"

"But how did…?"

"I don't know."

"You don't think we're…?"

"Yep," I concluded.

"Are you guys coming up or what?" Hope yelled down from her perch high above the forest floor.

"Man, I'm going to regret this," I said, closing my eyes and slapping the reigns. The creature lurched up the tree with a jerk, and before you could say, "What am I getting myself into?" it scampered up and came to a sudden stop. My head was aching, and when at last I opened my eyes, I found out why. I was hanging precariously upside down on the underside of a tree limb—the very same limb that Hope was currently occupying above me, or was that below me? *How is this even possible,* I wondered looking down, which was up, at the Ugua's grip on the branch. It reminded me of the little gecko I'd found climbing the walls and ceilings of my grandparents' condo in Hawaii three years ago. I never did figure out what kept the gecko up there.

I looked up, which was down, at Stretch who was still uncommitted, staring up in disbelief.

"Come on, Stretch," I called down. "It's not as bad as it looks." *Who was I kidding? I was terrified.*

Stretch shook his head, "You shouldn't be able to do that!"

"Oh, cut it out, already," I said. "It works, see? You're just afraid."

"No, I'm not," he said nervously.

"Then prove it!"

At first I thought he would chicken out, but then I saw him check his belt clips and tighten the straps once more. His Ugua began to moan, and after a few moments of anticipation Stretch slapped the reigns and the lizard rushed up the tree to join us. We were all together again.

"Not bad," Hope encouraged. "Now let's see if you two can keep up."

With no explanation of what she meant, Hope and her Ugua took off like a shot, racing across the long tree branch in front of us and diving from one tree limb to the next. It was a death-defying jump that even the most daring of stuntmen wouldn't attempt.

"Are we supposed to...?"

"I'm afraid so," I said, slapping the reigns and racing off after her in a burst of speed.

The sudden rush of wind took my breath away as we darted through the treetops, hundreds of feet above the forest floor below.

The Ugua navigated its way through a complex highway of inter-secting tree branches in the sky.

My peripheral vision became a blur of color, forcing me to look straight ahead to focus. The Ugua twisted, spun and dodged its way through a maze of branches with ease. It was like riding a cork-screw roller coaster, only a little less predictable. Every time we leaped from limb to limb my body cringed in anticipation of a rough landing, though in actuality the ride was much smoother than I expected.

Eventually we arrived back at the outpost and Hope tethered the Uguas near a small inlet off the river for the remainder of the evening. It was the perfect place for the Uguas to catch a quick supper.

Shlapp! Shlapp! A swarm of oversized mosquitoes hovered and buzzed beside the shady pond. The Ugua's tongues shot out wildly, like party blowers at a child's birthday, snatching several bugs at a time out of the air.

Back at the outpost, we gathered to discuss our travel arrange-ments for the following day. The outpost was near the black lake that had been my entrance into Solandria. The plan was to leave early the next morning and arrive at the lake before midday. Apparently, the lake was fed from a river we would follow up to Venator's stronghold on the crest of Forever Falls. Ephriam and Hope would accompany Stretch and me, but the rest would remain behind, in hopes of meeting up with more survivors.

There was no supper to be had. Hunting had proved unsuccess-ful, and the rations stocked in the outpost needed to be saved. As the day came to its end, I stole away and found a few moments to myself. There was something in the prophecy that bothered me, and I wanted a chance to study it again in solitude. Pulling the Author's Writ from my backpack I searched for the page that Aviad had shown us earlier that day. The second section of the prophecy intrigued me most, the part about the other half of the hidden stone.

Half you hold, as if your own,
The power in it given.
But in a body dark and cold
The other half is hidden.
No eye can see for by his will
Now veiled it resides
Until the Author chooses one
To plunge the depths of death and find.
So I, the Author, have written.

The location of the other half seemed to be described in this passage, hiding somewhere just beneath the surface of the text— almost within reach.

"In a body dark and cold, the other half is hidden," I repeated out loud to myself.

"A body dark and cold…dark and cold…a body…"

But no matter how many different ways I tried to say it, I could not decipher the riddle. So I moved on to the next phrase.

"No eye can see for by his will, now veiled it resides…"

One word in particular stood out to me like a sore thumb. I'd heard it used many times since I'd come here. It was the word the Codebearers used to describe the world we had left behind. Destiny was hidden in the Veil. Perhaps the other half was hidden in Destiny. It was definitely a possibility, but there was still more to the riddle. I read on with newfound excitement.

"Until the Author's chosen one will plunge the depths of death and find…plunge the depths of death…"

I was getting close, I could feel it; the answer was right there for me to grasp. What was I missing? The rustling of a tree branch startled me and I slammed the book shut, turning around to find what had made the sound.

"Hey there, you okay?"

I was relieved to find it was only Hope.

"Yeah, just catching up on a little reading that's all."

"Sorry, I didn't mean to interrupt…"

She turned to go, and I hurried to stop her.

"No, no! I was just finishing."

"You sure?"

"Positive."

She hopped over and sat down beside me, pressing her back against the tree trunk and staring up at the evening sky.

"Beautiful, isn't it?" she nodded toward the sunset.

"Yeah."

"I love it when he does that," she said mysteriously.

"What do you mean?"

"The Author. He never paints the sunset in the same exact light. It's nice to know he takes pleasure in the little things, isn't it?"

I simply nodded, thinking how Sam would have had a lecture for us on how everything happens for a purpose. If it was true, then there must have been a reason for the sunset tonight. Emboldened by the thought, I took Hope's hand in my own.

She shot a worried look at me and pulled away.

"What are you doing?" she asked pointedly, as if I had hurt her in some way. My ears glowed red with embarrassment and a twinge of anger at myself for having ruined the moment.

"Uh, I just thought, maybe you and I were…"

"No, we're not," she answered.

Her words cut into my chest like a dagger. I had been rejected by a girl before, but never with such repulsion as this.

"Oh I see," was all I could manage. She was treating me like I was diseased or something, and my anger started to grow toward her now. I scooted an inch away from her, the tension rising.

"No, it's not like that. I didn't mean it that way. I like you, Hunter, I really do. But it's just that we can't…I can't…it's complicated."

Complicated. The only thing complicated here was the way she was acting. After all, she was the one who came out to find me and this wasn't the first time she had flirted with me either. *Isn't the sunset beautiful,* she had said. *Here, take this necklace.* Ugh, why can't girls just say what they mean? What really bothered me was that she didn't want to give a reason. I mean, if she had a boyfriend already she could have been up front about it a long time ago and saved me the grief.

"Care to explain?" I pressed.

"It's just…I'm not like you, Hunter. We're different."

"Different? What, just because I was born in the Veil means I can't touch your hand?"

"No…I mean yes. We can be friends, but…but that's it. We can't be any other way."

"Okay, fine." I held up my hands in frustration, placing them firmly on my lap to emphasize the point. "It won't happen again."

We sat in awkward silence for several moments. She didn't leave, but I wished she would. Then at least I could stew in my newfound pain alone.

"Look, I don't expect you to understand. But I…I promise that if things weren't so…so…"

"Complicated?" I finished.

"Right, if it wasn't complicated, I'd think you were a pretty cool guy."

Talk about mixed messages, she was full of them. I removed the necklace she had given me from around my neck and handed it back to her. With a look of regret, she took it back and pulled it over her neck once more without saying a word.

"You going to be okay?" she asked at last.

"Yeah, I'm fine."

"Good, because there is something I have to tell you."

Oh boy, here it comes. The whole, I've got another guy spiel, and let's just be friends.

"When you told us about your visions…you know, the ones about Venator…" she lingered on the last word, waiting for a response.

"Yeah," I replied, trying my best not to look interested.

"Well, ever since you've arrived, I've been having them too."

"You mean, you saw the same visions I did?"

"No, just one. But I've seen it almost a half-dozen times now. It's the same vision, over and over."

She looked away, obviously hiding something very painful.

"What is it? What did you see?" I was anxious to hear, but incredibly worried at the same time.

"When we get to Venator's castle, I'm…going to die."

"What? No," I couldn't believe what I was hearing. "You can't die. How do you know?"

"In the vision, you and I face Venator, but I don't survive."

"But it could be wrong? I mean it hasn't actually happened yet, right? You don't have to go with us."

"Maybe not, but even if I didn't go, do you really think it would stop the vision from coming true if that's what the Author wanted?"

I was mad; only this time, I was angry with the whole idea of the Author being in control of everything. Who did he think he was, deciding the fate of others for them? If he really cared about his story, he'd stop bad things from happening. I'd heard enough about the Author, and losing another friend was not sitting well with me.

"How could he let this happen?"

"I don't know. But the Author has a purpose in all things, re-member. If I'm going to die, then it must be for a greater good. Sam believed it, and so do I."

My mind was reeling from the news. First Sam, and now Hope. Everyone I loved was being taken from me, it was all so pointless.

"Well, I don't," I said at last, somewhat surprised by my confes-sion. "Not if it means believing in someone who enjoys watching others suffer."

"Hunter," Hope said, tears welling up in her eyes. "You don't mean that."

"Yes, I do," I said with finality. "Tell me one good thing that has come from Gerwyn's or Sam's deaths—just one."

"I can't," she sobbed, "but there must be a reason."

"Well, I don't see it, and I'm not going to let anyone kill you either—not if I can help it. Not Venator. Not the Author. Not anyone."

Hope looked at me through swollen eyelids. Her brown eyes were full of emotions that were hard to read. Pain. Disappointment. Denial.

"You can't promise that Hunter."

She patted me on the shoulder and headed back over to the outpost to join the others. I stayed for a moment, watching the last rays of the sun set, pondering what she'd just said.

In the solitude of that moment, I secretly desired to go back home and forget everything. Having an adventure sounds like fun until you find yourself neck deep in it, struggling for a way out. One by one, the stars began to appear in the night sky. Tonight, they offered no comfort, I felt alone and small. I closed my eyes, hoping to drown out my thoughts.

"Why Hope?" I shouted out loud to the sky.

As expected, there was no response.

I wish she had never saved me from that stupid lake, I thought to myself. *Sure, I'd be gone, but Sam, Gerwyn and Hope would be alive, and I wouldn't have to carry the guilt of their deaths on my shoulders.*

My thoughts suddenly turned more morbid. *Maybe I should throw myself back in the lake. At least then I wouldn't be at Venator's castle, and Hope couldn't die, her vision couldn't come true if I wasn't there. No, who was I kidding?* Just the thought of plunging into the lake again to face the dead bodies floating around, made me sick to my stomach. I started to remember what the lake had been like. Cold. Dark. Bodies. Death.

Wait, those words sounded strangely familiar.

263

"The prophecy!" I shouted out loud to myself. "Of course, the prophecy was about the Lake of the Lost."

I flipped through the book's pages once more with excitement and read the prophecy out loud to confirm it to myself.

"Half you hold, as if your own, the power in it given. But in a body dark and cold the other half is hidden. No eye can see for by his will now veiled it resides. Until the Author chooses one to plunge the depths of death and find."

That was it! It had to be! Everything fit.

Racing back to the outpost as quickly as I could without falling from the tree, I found Ephriam and explained my discovery.

"So you see," I finished, "the other half of the Bloodstone is hidden in the Lake of the Lost."

Ephriam read the prophecy once more to be sure. "So it would seem," he finally said. "Excellent work, Hunter."

I was getting more and more excited by the minute.

"We're close to the lake right?" I asked. He nodded in return. "Then tomorrow while we are there, we can search for the other half of the Bloodstone."

"No!" Ephriam said bluntly. "We can't."

"What!" I nearly shouted. "But the other half of the stone is within our grasp. We could have both halves and finish Venator's reign once and for all."

"That may be, but Aviad's orders are clear. First, he has sent you on a quest to recover the half of the stone that Venator holds," Ephriam said in an even voice. He was no Petrov, but he was trying his best to sound like the commander. "We must go to Venator and take the stone, that's all there is to it."

I couldn't believe what I was hearing.

"Who are you to decide?" I scoffed. My voice was shaking with anger. "The last time I checked, I was the chosen one, not you, Ephriam. This is my quest, remember?"

"It is the Author's quest," he reminded me. "You could never succeed trying to accomplish this on your own. Aviad knew what needed to be done first, and we should follow his orders."

"Whatever," I replied.

I couldn't understand why everyone was being so closed minded they couldn't think for themselves and actually try and do some good on their own.

"I suppose being the chosen one makes you better than us, does it, Hunter?" he challenged.

I threw up my hands in disgust, and stormed off.

"Hunter, wait!" Stretch called out, worried that I was leaving him behind.

"No, let him go. He needs some time to think," Ephriam replied loud enough that I could hear as I found my way to the wooden elevator. I needed more than time, I needed space. I wanted to get as far away from them as I could.

Walking the forest floor alone at night, would have normally given me the chills but not tonight. Rushing through the under-brush like a rhino on a rampage, I stomped loudly, with no thought of what was lurking in the night shadows. It didn't matter anyway. If I got caught I might even be doing everyone a favor. I couldn't care less who or what heard me tromping through the woods. I pushed my way forward, grumbling with every step.

"Who do they think they are," I simmered under the heat of my anger, "*I'm* the chosen one, not them. I'm tired of everyone telling me what to do."

As I entered a small clearing, a tree root caught my toes and dropped me to the ground with a hard thud. My anger had taken me as far as I could go, and I lay there unwilling to get up, wallowing in my pain. I might have stayed there all night too if it wasn't for a most curious phenomenon overhead. Something in the air had captured my attention—a quick flash of light, then another, and another. Suddenly, the forest had come alive with tiny sparkling lights dancing all around me. The neon glow of the sparks reminded me of the fireflies we had back home, but these were far too small. They were tiny specks of dust twinkling in the air, perhaps even minuscule creatures of some kind.

I stood and reached my hand up to try and catch some of the enchanted dust, but the lights evaded my touch, spinning and twirling around my arm in a spiral. Then a voice like a thousand tiny whispers all speaking in unison broke the silence.

"Greetings, fair one," the whisper-voice said. I turned around to see who had spoken, but there was nothing there but the glowing dust that surrounded me on all sides.

"Who said that? Show yourself," I demanded, reaching for my Veritas Sword only to find I had left it back at the outpost with all of my belongings. *Smart, Hunter, very smart.*

"Here we are," the voice responded to my request. The tiny specks swarmed together to form a sphere of light, flowing with movement in a continuously swirling pattern. The view was mesmerizing and a sudden calm came over me, soothing my angered spirit.

"Who are you?"

"We are the Illuminaries." Now the voice in the sphere was louder and more defined. "And *you* are one of the boys from the Veil, are you not?"

"How did you know that?"

"We have lived in the forest for thousands of years, unseen and unnoticed by all who travel this way. We were there when you were rescued by the girl," the sphere moved slightly closer, but I didn't flinch. "What is it that is bothering you?" they asked.

I was so fascinated by the tiny creatures I didn't think twice about what I said next. Better judgment would have told me to hold my tongue, but I found myself divulging the details of my situation without hesitation. I told them how the Bloodstone prophecy seemed to suggest that the Lake of the Lost was the final resting place of the other half of the Bloodstone.

"We know of this prophecy, of course," they said. "You are very wise in your interpretation of the Author's words."

"I'm glad someone thinks so, nobody else seems to see it like I do," I fumed.

The sphere moved around behind my left shoulder.

"But if you are the chosen one, you can't expect them to understand what it is you have seen, can you?" As I spun around to see the sphere, it moved upward to the right like a fidgety hummingbird that couldn't hold still. "You have a gift. This may be your moment to shine."

The words of the Illuminaries seemed to be the truth. After all, the prophesy said, "No eye can see." Perhaps it was only meant for me to accomplish after all.

"I never thought of it that way," I said.

"At the very least it is reason enough to consider looking where your heart is leading. Perhaps you are called to the find the stone alone."

"You're right, I don't need them. The prophesy is clearly only meant for me to understand."

"Then follow us and we will show you the way to the lake."

CHAPTER 19

LAKE OF THE LOST

As I broke through the tree line and onto the outer shore, I was met by the familiar sight of the smooth, black lake where I had first entered Solandria. The fresh smell of pine awakened memories of my first night, when I was rescued from certain drowning. I remembered how frightened I was, waking on this shore to a blazing campfire where I met Hope and Sam. Their kindness had wrapped me in a warm blanket of comfort.

The warmth of that memory was quickly chased off, however, when a biting breeze whipped up off the water, reminding me there was no warm fire tonight and no companions except for the pulsing glow of the Illuminaries. Still, they seemed a knowledgeable guide, leading me by their collective light up the shoreline to a small, tethered rowboat.

At this point, I couldn't help but notice the discrepancy between the vast expanse of black water and the tiny vessel at my disposal.

"The lost Bloodstone half could be anywhere in this lake," I mused, "at any depth. Will I really be able to find anything out there?"

The Illuminaries once again offered their wise council, "You know the promise the prophecy gives to the chosen one. He is the one who will 'bring the hidden half to light.' Do not doubt yourself now when you are so close to realizing your call."

They were right. I was the chosen one. The prophecy spoke of my unique ability to see the stone when no one else could. If I just trusted in my inherent abilities they would surely lead me to the Bloodstone out there...in the middle of a black lake...where I nearly drowned because I can't swim...with a bunch of horrifying chained corpses.... Fears were rushing in from all sides now. I knew I was losing my edge. *Come on, Hunter! Don't chicken out now. You were born for this. You were chosen. If you don't do this now...*

Grabbing hold of the rowboat, I boldly shoved off into the foreboding waters, leaving my fears behind in the wake. My pep-talk seemed to have worked, I was feeling more courageous. But I went ahead and left the boat tethered to shore...just in case of an emergency.

Had I not known I was on a lake, I could easily have mistaken the black void in front of me for an empty, dark sky. Even the mist, slowly curling across the surface, could have played a convincing role as clouds. The rowboat and glowing orb of the Illuminaries only added to the surreal quality of the scene. I could imagine myself navigating through space, chasing a shooting star like those three boys in the old nursery rhyme Grandma used to read me. Only the quiet slap of the oars against the water kept me grounded to reality.

"How far out should we be going?" I asked the Illuminaries.

No answer.

The shining sphere kept moving steadily ahead of the boat. By now, the shoreline was no longer visible through the layers of mist. I could feel my insecurities about being in open water rise the further I drifted from shore.

"Are you sure you know where the Bloodstone is?" My voice was starting to hint at desperation. This time they answered.

"Look for yourself."

Before I had time to consider what they meant, the mist began to thicken, causing my glowing guides to dim from sight. I tried rowing faster to catch up to them, but the boat came to a sudden halt, the tether taut behind me. I had reached the end of the line.

"No, wait!" *Ugh, why did I leave that stupid rope tied?* I frantically fumbled at untying the knot. Fortunately, my better judgment and lack of knot-tying skills kicked in before I could actually remove my only lifeline. Still, I had to do something. Careful not to capsize the boat, I stood up slowly, straining to catch a glimmer of something over the mist. Not a hint of the Illuminaries in sight. I had lost them.

Now what? I wondered, as I looked around me at the endless sea of darkness. Daring to let my gaze venture toward the depths, I shuddered as the memories of what I'd seen down there resurfaced. Blank faces trapped beneath the inky waters, chained like prisoners with no hope for escape. *How deep down were they?*

Though I stared at the water I didn't really want to see anything. That's why I jumped when I saw a face looking back at me from the murky waters; the boat barely caught me before I fell out. Strangely enough the face appeared to be as startled as I was. I waited for my pulse to slow, and the boat to resettle before risking another look over the edge. Inching my head slowly over the top, I quickly found the face again. *What a dork!* Of all the things to be frightened by out here, I had been scared by my own reflection.

Standing back up to my full height, I looked down to address my rippling image. "So this is what the great chosen one looks like," I teased. My heart stopped at what I saw below me this time. Directly beneath my reflection was a faint red glow. *Was I seeing things?* I watched in rapt attention as the glow gradually increased until it was the clear image of the Bloodstone itself.

I had found it!

Had I really found it?

Of course I had found it!

I was the chosen one. I was the one who was able to figure out the clues in the prophecy, and now by some second-nature, I was able to navigate the lake to the precise location of the lost stone. Oh, I couldn't wait to see the look on the others' faces when I returned with the Bloodstone half, after they doubted my intuition. *Humble pie for everyone tonight!* But, I was getting ahead of myself. First, I needed to get the stone from the water.

Taking another long look at the glimmering red stone, I let myself get caught up with the power I knew I would gain from it. My pulse quickened as I imagined marching up to Venator's fortress, stone in hand. No longer did I fear the confrontation, but instead, almost relished it. The feeling was intoxicating, numbing me from thoughts of fear or reason. I couldn't wait any longer. I dove headfirst into the icy blackness.

As soon as I hit the water, all that changed. Instantly I was overwhelmed by an excruciating pain like that of ten thousand splintered icicles stabbing into every pore of my body. The painful shock sank deep into my skull. I opened my eyes, desperate to grab the stone and get out of there. Surrounding me were blurry silhouettes of chained bodies. I screamed. Bubbles raced from my mouth, stealing away precious breath. All I could do was scramble after them.

I broke the surface, gulping in a mouthful of air. My thrashing arms quickly led me to the boat's side, allowing a chance to regain control in spite of my chattering teeth. *Where was the stone?* I could swear I had seen it down there just moments ago. Clear. Bright. Now, as I bobbed in the lake, I saw nothing but shadowy, lifeless figures below me, fading quickly away into the depths where they were anchored.

Something must have shifted—moved in front of it, I thought. Perhaps my dive disturbed the bodies enough to block my original line of sight. Though I was still freezing, my heart began to burn once more with my mission, hungry to recover the stone. I had to recover that stone! Refilling my lungs, I reluctantly plunged my head back under the frigid water.

My arm and leg strokes were uncoordinated and awkward, but they worked well enough to get me down closer to the human "seaweed." Now that I was a little more accustomed to seeing the limp people drifting around me, I didn't hesitate approaching them. It didn't take me long to graduate from just looking, to actually pushing through the floating men, women and children. I was even annoyed when I finally had to resurface for more air, empty-handed. Convinced the stone was down there, I continued diving though I could no longer feel my fingers or toes. I was obsessed with finding that stone, ignoring my pain to take deeper and deeper dives. *Perhaps my decreasing inhibitions were a sign of the stone's power already strengthening me from a distance?* Hanging from the boat, I managed to crack a shivering grin as I warmed myself with that thought. It was true—the black lake, the swimming, even the submerged zombies—none of it scared me anymore. I was struck by the irony of how comforting it was to know that everything below me was dead. I didn't have to worry about anything getting me.

No sooner had I reached that conclusion than the sound of a distant splash reached my ear. I hugged the boat tightly, partly for comfort, but mostly to stop the violent shaking of my body, still dipped in the icy water. Clinching my chattering teeth, I strained to hear any other signs of danger. All was silent.

Then I felt it.

Something long and sinuous brushed against my numb feet, passing beneath the boat. Whatever was down there was large enough to cause a swell in the water, rocking the vessel with its disturbance. I had to get out of the water fast, but my frozen hands and severe shivering slowed my escape, keeping me in the water far beyond what my nerves could handle. Frantic, I tumbled into the hull, staying low beneath the side rails as the boat's rocky ride gently returned to stillness. All was calm again except for my racing heart. *What kind of creature was that? Had it seen me?*

Not wanting to stick around to answer those questions, I reached for the tether to pull myself back to shore. But what I grabbed was not a rope, and it wasn't connected to shore. I held in my hand a thick, leathery tendril attached like a whisker to a hideous, serpentine head that flashed a pair of glowing green eyes at me. I let go immediately, falling backwards in fright, but there was nowhere to run.

Offended by my movement, the creature flared the wing-like membranes bearding its neck and let out a piercing cry.

"Nyeaaaaa!"

There were too many teeth protruding from its open jaws to count. The lake serpent reared back its head on its long neck and towered fifteen feet above me for a strike. I reached for my Veritas Sword in defense, but it was not at my side. I had foolishly left it with my backpack at the outpost. With eyes wide, I looked up into the cruel face and seized the only option I had left, throwing myself overboard as it lunged after me. The boat flipped, deflecting the serpent's intended attack.

"Nyea…!"

The monster's scream muted as I went under.

Unmoved by the horrific scene unfolding above them, the lake-captives silently allowed me back in their prison. I kicked frantically to propel myself down toward a cluster of bodies whose chains had become entangled from the serpent's intrusion. This was no time for manners. I forcefully shoved my way into the middle of the pack and latched onto a chain…just in time.

Sploosh! The serpent's head plunged into the water above me, hungrily looking for the "morsel" that had just jumped off its plate. From below, I could finally see the full body of the creature. Its long neck, slim body and winding tail would have put it well past forty feet. Four flipper-shaped legs paddled softly, turning the sea monster slowly in place—thankfully moving it away from my hideout. I could tell from the deliberate movement of its head that it was carefully searching for me.

Please don't let it find me! I was so deathly cold. My body was on the brink of giving way to its involuntary shaking again. *Don't move!* I commanded myself. *Think dead thoughts!*

I knew thinking dead thoughts would soon give way to my actual death if the serpent didn't give up the hunt soon. My lungs were nearly bursting—I couldn't hold on much longer. My body shuddered under the stress, causing the chain I held to rattle. The monster snapped its attention immediately toward my hiding place, eyes narrowed in a devilish stare. Then, in a calculated motion the beast thrust itself towards me.

Aviad! Help! My grip gave out, surrendering my body to its approaching fate.

Then the sea serpent came to a stop, reset its focus somewhere far off as if being summoned from beyond, and swam swiftly away, its body undulating in wide arcs, leaving a trail of bubbles behind.

Weakened arms and feeble kicks were all I had left to reach the surface in time. I tried to coach my body upward. *Only a few more feet! Only...*

The ache in my lungs signaled it was too late already. Powerless to hold back the urge, I gasped, sending a mouthful of water into my lungs. I broke the surface sputtering and coughing up water between violent breaths. I was alive, but starting to sink quickly. Seeing the overturned boat floating a short distance away, I flailed to reach it, weakly latching onto its side before I went under.

Hold on, Hunter. Hold on. If I could hold on long enough, I'd be safe here until my strength returned...

or until the sea serpent returned...or until I... My mind began to drift.

A tug on the boat jostled me back to consciousness. I vaguely felt the sensation of water moving around me as the half-sunk boat began to carry me away. Something was pulling on the rope tether. The possibilities clashed in my mind. Maybe Stretch and Hope had discovered me missing, tracked me to the missing boat and were now pulling me back to safety. Or, I could be on my way into the eager hands of the Shadow's recruited bounty hunters. Maybe the sea serpent had come back after all, grabbed the rope in its jaws, and was dragging me off to its nest where I'd be a midnight snack for all the hungry baby serpents.

Regardless of what it was, I wasn't going to fight it—I couldn't. My body had stopped responding to my commands. All I could do now was drift on and let come what may.

"Hello!" A man's voice called to me from the approaching shore. "Are you alive?"

I weakly lifted my head to see who it was that spoke, friend or foe? What little I could see through my blurred vision didn't help answer that. The voice carried on indiscernibly in a low, excited tone. The sound of feet splashing in the water told me I must have reached the shallows. Hands drug me the rest of the way to dry land.

"Hunter!" a bearded face called to me. "What happened? You're like ice!" The rescuer got busy peeling away the soaked outer layer of clothing that clung to me, before taking off his own heavy cloak, revealing a gold and green breastplate. As he bent low to cover me with his cloak, I recognized his face.

"F-f-f-Faldyn," I managed to whisper, "is th-th-that you?"

He offered a half-smile, though his concerned look didn't fade. "Yes, it's me."

He was not one of my favorite Codebearers, but I was glad to have him here now. "H-h-how did y-you...?"

"That's not important. Tell me, were you out there alone?"

I nodded my answer. Knowing I was safely ashore, all I wanted to do now was sleep. My eyelids shut, only to be forcefully pried back open. Faldyn was in my face, demanding answers.

"What were you doing out there?" His eyes searched mine anxiously, like he was looking for something hidden. "I need you to tell me what is going on. What did you see? Why were you alone? Where are the others?"

Did he think I was going to answer those questions with him rudely pressing me? What kind of treatment was this? Didn't he appreciate that I had just narrowly escaped death? If I was able, I'd have liked to shove him away right then.

"G-g-et o-off me," was my only response.

He released his hold on my eyelids. The tone of his voice told me he wasn't happy with my resistance.

"No, Hunter! Not like this. I need you alive!"

What was he talking about? I just wanted a bit of shut-eye. He was acting like I was...

"You're suffering from severe hypothermia," Faldyn spoke urgently. "If we don't get your temperature up quickly, you'll likely die."

This new "you're going to die" tactic got a much better response from me. My eyes didn't have nearly as much trouble staying open now, and I became keenly attuned to my slowing pulse.

Faldyn grasped my shoulders and looked me in the eye. "I need you to stay awake long enough for me to make a fire. Can you do that?"

Assured of my participation, Faldyn jumped quickly to his feet and took a couple exploratory steps in several directions. Not finding what he was looking for, he spun back around. "There's not enough time," he concluded. Casting a worried look toward me, he retrieved a black pouch from his belt and looked at it hesitantly, as if unsure at first what to do with it. Then, turning resolutely back to me, he instructed, "You'll need to trust me, Hunter. This is the fastest way to give your body back the warmth it needs. It won't hurt, other than the usual tingling you'd expect when re-warming."

I had no idea where he was going with this, but I nodded my approval. It wasn't like I had many options at this point. Pulling the cloak over my nose he added, "And you'll need to keep from inhaling the smoke until it's died out."

Reaching into the pouch, he pulled out a small amount of black, granular dust, his hand trembling. I gasped. It was the same powder I'd seen Venator use when he attacked Faldyn and his men in the canyon ambush. Before I could react, Faldyn covered his own face and threw the dust directly onto me. On impact, fire instantly sprang up all over me.

"Aaaaah!" I screamed helplessly from where I lay—not from any real pain, but simply from the sheer shock of watching myself light up like a human torch.

Just as Faldyn predicted, the flames infused warmth steadily into my limbs without consuming me, as a real fire would have. I winced as the prickling sensation chased away the numbness that had paralyzed me, but other than that I was fine. In the span of a few short minutes, I had regained control of my fingers. Holding the cloak firmly over my mouth and nose as instructed, I was able to sit up. As I did, the remaining powder on my chest fell into my lap, where more flames shot up before slowly dying.

While I had been thawing under the fire, Faldyn had spread out my other wet clothing and started a fire on them too, safely away from my recovery area. I watched as the clothes burned, unscathed by the flames dancing over them. The effect was spectacular, although not as cool as seeing someone running around covered in it. This no-burn fire-dust would make for some great pranks. Faldyn left the clothes to dry and made his way over to check on me.

"How are you feeling?" he asked.

The smoke had finally dissipated, so it was safe to lower the cloak and answer him. "Fine...I guess." That was the best answer I could give considering my mind had just started wrestling with darker thoughts about all that had just happened. *What was Faldyn doing carrying around a bag of Venator's fire-dust? How did he manage to find me here at the Lake of the Lost? Why was he alone?*

"You know, you're lucky to be alive." Faldyn's words pulled me out of my hidden thoughts. "It was foolish of you to go out on the lake at night alone, without a proper weapon." His voice had taken on a lecturing tone that I didn't quite appreciate. He wasn't Sam, and there was still something about him that bothered me.

Faldyn lowered his head to look me straight in the eyes. "Now would be a good time to tell me *exactly* what you were doing out on the lake." His stern look told me he expected an answer.

Though I didn't fully understand why, I wasn't ready to tell him about the prophecy and my Bloodstone mission from Aviad. I decided instead to give him only certain parts of the story, starting with how Aviad sent Stretch and me to meet up with the other Codebearers at the outpost. I told Faldyn how I'd decided to take a walk, alone. His raised eyebrows warned me that I'd be hearing another lecture on that topic later.

Continuing my story, I told of how I met the Illuminaries, expertly leaving out the details about our conversation surrounding the Bloodstone and how they encouraged me to go out in the boat. Then there was getting lost, followed by the serpent's attack and ending with my narrow escape. I made sure to highlight the part about how clever I was to have evaded the serpent by hiding in the bodies. That caught us up to where Faldyn entered the picture. I took a deep breath and sat back to appreciate the masterful work I had done in keeping the story completely truthful, while not offering up sensitive information. *Maybe I had a future in politics?*

Faldyn was clearly not impressed with my report and all it told him about my series of screw-ups, though he was not angry either. Instead, his voice sounded more fatherly when he spoke next, rather than the lecturing, "If I've told you once, I've told you a thousand times..." drill. At least he was trying to sound as much like that as his snappish personality would allow.

Faldyn began by consoling, "Your encounter with the Illuminaries must have scared you."

Was he joking? How much of a kid did he think I was? Believe me, the little fairy-ball had been the only non-threatening part of my night. For Faldyn's sake I hoped he only said this because he had never met any actual Illuminaries before. The alternative was that he thought the little talking fireflies were truly scary. Embarrassing to say the least.

"They weren't that bad, actually. I think they were really only trying to help."

"Help?" Faldyn sneered, his brief attempt at tactfulness abandoned. "Obviously, no one taught you about the Illuminaries. I'm not surprised! Sam never cared much for this kind of subject matter."

My fist clenched when he mentioned Sam as if I had somehow been given a second-rate education under him. I decided it was better to hold my tongue...for now.

Faldyn continued, noting the scowl on my face, "The Illuminaries are one of our most powerful enemies."

Yeah right, like I was supposed to believe that. Those little guys were puny. Actually, what I really couldn't believe was how perfectly this conversation was steering us away from the questions I didn't want him to ask. My plan to keep Faldyn from discovering the critical details appeared to be working. So I played along with my responses, aiming to keep it that way.

"But they're so small. How bad can they be?" I asked in the most innocent voice I could.

His crooked smile told me he had taken the bait. "The Illuminary, singular, by itself is a fairly harmless being. Their strength lies in their numbers—Illuminaries." Faldyn had been illustrating his point using his one finger, and then wiggling the others as the "fingernaries" grew in number. "Let them gather together and," he clapped his hands together forcefully, "you will witness the full effect of their might."

I had to pinch myself to keep from laughing at his absurd melodramatics. Fortunately, he was too engrossed in his lecture to notice my reaction.

"The greater their number, the louder their voice and the more deadly is their ability to mislead you. Once they have your ear, they can march you straight into the jaws of death." He paused to let me organize all this information.

"Wait. So you're saying they wanted to kill me?" In all that had happened tonight, I'd never once thought the Illuminaries might be responsible for my near-death experience. Now here was Faldyn, singling them out as mercenaries. "How is that even possible? Do they brainwash?" I wasn't playing along anymore. I was genuinely intrigued.

He scoffed, "They don't have to. They take you where you already want to go."

"Huh?" So now he was saying that it *wasn't* the Illuminaries, but really that I was the one to blame?

"It's fascinating, isn't it?" I could see from a rare sparkle in his eyes that he was pretty excited about what he was sharing, like when a teacher shares something from his favorite subject. "They're masterful creatures. They know how to exploit your greatest weakness—you." Was it just me or did Faldyn have some kind of sick fascination with these things? He definitely had been more animated in this conversation than I had ever seen him before.

Faldyn expounded further, "Think of it this way. Would you rather listen to the voice that opposed your view or the voice that promoted it?" It was a rhetorical question with an obvious answer. "The Illuminaries give us what we want to hear. When they find a listening ear, they swarm to work their deadly wiles and only the most discerning man can resist." Faldyn thrust a finger into my face to make sure I didn't miss his point. "And *that* is what makes them one of the most powerful enemies in the Shadow ranks."

A lump formed in my throat. I couldn't believe what I had just learned. If all that Faldyn told me was true, the whole time the Illuminaries were going on about how I was chosen and affirming my interpretation of the prophecy, they were just luring me out onto the lake for the serpent to eat. It had all been a setup from the beginning.

Still, that couldn't fully explain how I was able to see the Bloodstone in the water. The Illuminaries couldn't have been behind that—Faldyn himself said they didn't brainwash and they had already left me by then.

So, that would mean I wasn't completely wrong. Maybe they had tricked me into going along with them, but I couldn't deny I had stumbled onto some truth—truth I could cling to. A renewed resolve was born. I knew I couldn't settle it tonight, but I was convinced now, more than ever, that I *was* the chosen one to find the stone and that the stone was still somewhere, lost in the body of darkness.

Faldyn had been silent until now, content to let me reflect on his impromptu Illuminaries lesson. When he spoke again, he used the earlier father-like tone. "For all the incredibly poor decisions you made tonight, I do not fault you for believing the Illuminaries when they told you that you were special."

I was stunned. *How did he know that?* I hadn't revealed any details of what I talked about with the Illuminaries. This conversation was starting to drift dangerously close to the information I was trying to protect. I quickly looked away, hoping he would interpret it as anything but nervousness.

"Don't act so modest," he scolded. "It's basic Deception Tactics: Tell the victim how special they are. Establish trust with them by insisting they are better than all the rest. In most cases, they are forced to lie. But you are different, Hunter." He eyed me curiously, scrutinizing me like I was a science project.

"In all my years studying the Shadow, I've never seen them focus as much attention on one person as they have on you." His eyes narrowed as he came to his conclusion, "The Shadow *fear* you." Seeing how uncomfortable I was with this topic, he reassured me, "Yes. It's true. You are special, Hunter."

I was at a loss for words. Faldyn could not have shocked me more. *Was he trying to butter me up? Trying to use basic Deception*

Tactics on me himself? Well, at least this time I wasn't going to be naive enough to go along with that.

Faldyn spoke more urgently now, "Listen, Hunter. Whatever the Illuminaries were telling you could be key to figuring out why the Shadow are targeting you. Tell me everything they talked about. I know how they work. I can help."

He was getting too close now. I had to say something, anything. "Does Petrov know you're using the fire-dust from Venator?"

Faldyn was shocked by my unexpected change of subject. His eyes were as wide as a kid caught with his hand in a cookie jar. Then in an act of retaliation, he snatched his cloak right off of me. Standing, he glared forcefully at me as he put on the cloak, clearly offended by my veiled accusation. "Your clothes are done and so is this conversation," he snapped. Turning to walk away he called back to me, "I'm going to the outpost. If you can catch up, you can follow me—that is, *if* you think you need my help." And with that he stormed off.

Fortunately, I had some experience in getting dressed while running. It was common practice for me back home, when I raced to button my pants and pull on my shirt before the bus left. Even so, my expert speed-dressing skills barely got me into half my clothes before Faldyn was disappearing into the forest. I would have to carry the rest and finish dressing in camp.

Faldyn made no attempt to soften his footsteps, making it easy to relocate him. He was in an extremely sour mood, which is pretty bad when you consider he is not too pleasant to begin with. If it wasn't for the fact that I would have been completely lost without him, I wouldn't have wanted to be anywhere near him.

I followed a good fifty feet behind. The silence gave me time to think about all that had happened. While I'd never intended the response to be so hostile, I had to admit the change of subject sure worked to divert Faldyn—he wasn't asking sensitive questions anymore. Obviously, I had hit a very touchy subject with him. It explained why he was the "black sheep" among the other captains. Still, I worried there was something darker to him than just black wool. I'd have to be careful. I slowed to allow an extra ten feet between us—just for good measure.

Before we could even see camp, I could tell something was wrong. Faldyn had slowed his steps, the stomping giving way to silent, stealthy maneuvers. *What did he sense?* The heightened suspense of the moment persuaded me to close the gap between us. I must have looked ridiculous tiptoeing half-dressed through the underbrush, carrying an armload of laundry, but I didn't care.

Without warning, Faldyn froze. He reached slowly for his Veritas Sword. *Oh man! I don't have my weapon.* I hurried to reach Faldyn for protection before whatever danger he saw got to me first.

A flashing white arc of light circled around to greet me. I caught myself inches short of the blade that pointed at my chest.

"Whoa! It's me. Put the sword down!" I pleaded, dropping my laundry and holding up my hands.

To my shock, Faldyn didn't lower his weapon, but advanced demanding, "Who do you think you are?"

"I'm Hunter. You know that. Come on, Faldyn, stop joking."

"What are you doing here?" He was nearly yelling now.

"What are you talking about? I was just coming back to camp with you to meet the others."

"You mean the camp you raided and the others you killed?"

"What do you mean raided? What's going on, Faldyn?"

"I'll ask the questions, boy. Convenient that you were the only one away from camp when it happened, is that what I'm supposed to believe?"

"Please, Faldyn. I have no clue what you mean."

"No? Then let me refresh your memory." He lifted the sword from my neck and held it high above his head like a lantern. The sword's light grew until I could see the disastrous scene in front of us. Chairs, blankets, papers and other miscellaneous supplies were thrown across tree branches, underbrush and the forest floor. Someone had raided the outpost and tossed it all over the forest below like confetti.

Faldyn threw me an angry look and then marched over to a nearby tree that once served as the outpost elevator; the cable vine hung limp from where it had been cut. He stopped to stare at a paper that was nailed to the trunk.

"Faldyn. You have to believe me. I had nothing to do with this!" Tears were welling up as I realized my friends were no longer here. My only hope was that they had somehow escaped. Maybe they were out looking for me when the looters came?

"No, Hunter." Faldyn tore the paper from the tree. "You have *everything* to do with what happened here."

I took the paper from him when he shoved it into my face. The message was short and to the point.

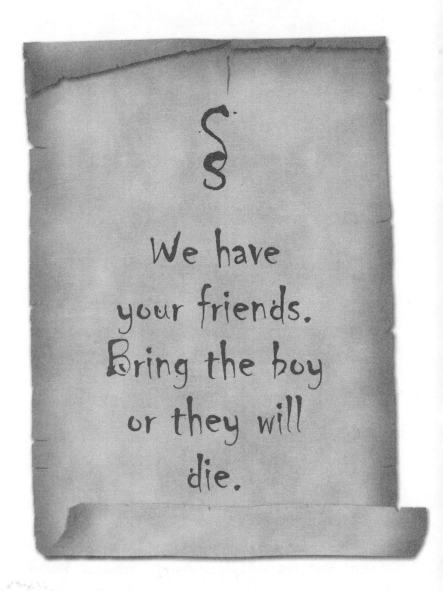

CHAPTER 20

BROKEN ALLIANCE

Faldyn was pacing back and forth, searching for clues to what might have happened during the attack on the outpost. "There are little to no tracks down here," he muttered to himself, kicking at the underbrush. "They must have attacked from above."

"Gorewings most likely," I offered. My observation was met with a scowl. I got the hint. Clearly he knew more about the Shadow than I would ever know and trying to help would only annoy him further.

Since I was not wanted there, I tried to find something useful to do. After I pulled on the rest of my clothes, I started searching the wreckage for any sign of my things, all the while keeping an eye on Faldyn. With Venator's capture of Hope, Stretch and Ephriam, the few remaining trusted friends who were going to help me were now gone. Instead, the only person left that I could look to for help was neither friendly nor trustworthy. I knew so little about Faldyn, but at the same time, I almost knew too much. Hadn't I seen him in my first vision?

He was the only one of his battalion to walk away from Venator's ambush; then Venator entrusted him to deliver a message. He was the only captain missing when Sanctuary was raided; now I knew that Faldyn was using a pouch of Venator's fire-dust. I still didn't have an answer as to how Faldyn discovered me in the lake, but that seemed suspect as well.

All my thoughts finally led me to a horrible realization: Faldyn could be working for Venator! He was a double agent, or at least, he was cooperating with them. It was the only explanation that made any sense. He hadn't just *happened* to be passing by the lake, he must have followed me there. He *rescued* me from the lake while sending his men back to the outpost to perform the raid. Now Faldyn was playing it all up to convince me the Shadow had destroyed the outpost and taken the others captive.

Considering how well he seemed to track with the Shadow, I was almost sure he knew about the bounty on my head. The price must be pretty high to have enticed a Codebearer captain to turn me in; either that or Faldyn just plain didn't like me. I definitely never entertained warm feelings toward him before, but now I downright despised the man. If my hunch was right Faldyn was probably the one who betrayed Sanctuary's location to Venator so the Shadow could attack.

My theorizing was interrupted when I caught sight of something familiar in the bushes. My backpack! I ran over to examine it and found everything but the book; the Shadow had taken the Author's Writ from my bag.

Reaching for my sword hilt, I glanced nervously toward Faldyn who was still combing for clues. Did I dare confront him now—it was only a matter of time before I'd have to—maybe this wasn't the right time. Even if I was able to overcome his superior skill, strength and size to defeat him, where would that leave me? The truth was that I had no knowledge of how to navigate this forest, let alone find Venator's fortress; I would need Faldyn to lead me... for now.

"We must leave immediately!" I could hear Faldyn bark over at me, his supposed investigation of the crime scene now complete. "Venator is not patient."

You would know, I thought silently as I put on my pack and started cautiously back toward him.

Faldyn continued, "If we fail to reach them fast enough, he will most likely kill them all, or worse yet, send them to Dolor."

"Dolor?" I asked cautiously.

"Yes, it's a horrible place, far away on the Shard of Suffering. Few have gone there and lived to tell about it." His eyes glazed over with the look of one who was lost in remembrance. "The Shadow reserve their most vicious torture for the souls of those who end up there. And if we don't hurry that is exactly where your friends will end up."

He says that like he cares. This pretense of his was making me sick. What were a few more lives to him, compared to the blood he already carried on his hands from Sanctuary?

"Normally it's a four-day hike upstream from here to Venator's fortress but I know a shortcut. We can be there in three if you can keep up with my pace."

Before he could lead us even one step, the familiar low moan of the Uguas reminded me of the beasts we had left tied up near the riverbed just outside of camp. I smiled. "Who said we'd be walking?"

I showed Faldyn where we had left the Uguas. We each had our own ride and I was relieved that I wouldn't have to talk with Faldyn for a while. I needed space to think. By the time we arrived at the fortress I would have a plan of my own.

Time flew by in a blur of branches as we raced through the tree-tops. If my mind hadn't been so distracted, I might have remembered more details from the trip, but it was needless trivia to me now compared to my one, all-consuming mission: save my friends. Save Hope.

When Faldyn finally decided to steer us back to ground level, I was surprised the quality of the trees had drastically changed. No longer were they straight and sturdy with lushly stocked limbs. Instead, they looked pale and sickly, their twisted trunks straining to hold up crooked branches burdened by the weight of their stringy foliage. The diseased appearance spread all the way through the ground cover as well; only the hardiest shrubs survived, barely clinging to life, completely drained of color. The sound of the near-by river offered a bit of cheer to this otherwise dreary landscape. Following Faldyn's lead, I unclipped and dismounted. He slapped his Ugua on its thigh and encouraged the creature to wander closer to the river and I did the same. Both were eager to wade into the shallow current and drink. I might have been too, if the water had not been a sickening, murky gray. Apparently Uguas didn't care.

"We go on foot from here," Faldyn announced abruptly, not wasting time to turn and walk upstream.

I looked back at the Uguas.

"Leave them!" Faldyn commanded, without looking. "The fortress is just beyond this riverbend. If they come any closer we blow our cover."

As if on cue, my Ugua let out one of its low signature moans. Faldyn had a point, the Uguas would stay.

I hurried to catch up to the long strides that carried Faldyn so urgently. He was already well out ahead of me and showed no interest in slowing or talking for that matter. I had to play my cards carefully with Faldyn and chose to be silent along the next mile of river. The river seemed willing to take over for our lack of conversation, growing steadily louder and louder as we approached the bend.

Before we reached the corner, Faldyn held out his hand to signal a stop, then motioned me to follow him into the trees. I cautiously followed through the forest. Soon, we edged near enough to the river again that we could see what was hiding around the bend. Towering some three hundred feet above us was an impressive waterfall. No doubt, if Stretch had been with us, he'd have spouted off an educated guess as to how many gallons of water per second it sent careening down the sheer rock face. I can only say it was a lot, and it was loud, but it was far from beautiful.

Camped menacingly atop the falls was an unnatural formation of black rocks that jutted up and over the fall's breadth, creating an illusion of the waterfall spewing from the mouth of an angry giant rock head. The stonework was rough; it took me a moment to recognize the formation as manmade. Yet the presence of windows and parapets were obvious once I knew how to look at it. Rough-hewn and raw, the whole structure screamed its evil intentions. There was no mistaking it, this was Venator's fortress.

Faldyn grabbed my arm to move me forcefully away from where I'd stopped, transfixed.

"Ow! Hey, let go!" I griped.

"Fool!" Faldyn hissed. "Get back before you give us both away." He directed my gaze skyward in time to see a small battalion of Gorewings soaring toward the fortress.

"Well, maybe you could fill me in on your plan now so I don't screw up something else," I retorted, earning a disapproving glare for my behavior.

"It will be complicated," Faldyn explained. "The main door is heavily guarded. Nothing gets in or out without the Shadow knowing." He pointed to the right side of the fortress where the newly arrived Gorewings were landing. "But my scouts have discovered a secret entrance behind the falls." Then, taking note of the sun's position, he concluded, "We must hurry. There is no time to explain."

Faldyn moved us quickly and silently from tree to tree until we were within two hundred feet of the cliff wall, crouched safely behind a boulder. Catching my breath, I reassessed my situation: I was deep in enemy territory with the enemy as my guide. *What on earth was I doing here?* The answer wasn't too hard to find. My friends needed me; their very lives depended on me making it into that fortress one way or another. For now, the "one way" involved following Faldyn as far as I safely could; the "other way" would come soon enough.

I couldn't see them now, but during our approach I had noticed a patrol of guards posted along the base, barring our progress. For some reason their presence didn't appear to concern Faldyn at all. He sat, wearing a confident smirk on his face, like one who knew what was coming next. Nervous that Faldyn might have chosen this place as his point of betrayal, I silently reached to put my hand on my Veritas Sword, readying myself for a fight. The gruff voice of a guard shouted an order, invoking the sounds of clanking armor and marching feet in response. *Are they coming this way?* I tightened my grip, but the footfalls never came close. They were leaving.

I nearly jumped when Faldyn touched my arm, motioning for me to stand and watch what happened next. Above the constant roar of the waterfall, a loud grating noise caught my attention, drawing my eyes to the fortress. The "mouth" of the fortress appeared to be closing; a massive stone slab was being lowered from where the fortress spanned the falls. Chains, gears, and the brutes powering the mechanism could all be heard groaning together as the gate slowly descended.

"The flood gate," Faldyn explained. "It is closed once every day to reroute the water into the lower dungeons. The diverted flow is used to torture the prisoners. I've timed the process—we must move quickly to get past the drain spouts before they block our way. The falls will only be completely stopped for less than one minute. That should be enough time to make it to the door."

Should? I didn't like how uncertain that sounded. My only comfort was the thought that Faldyn most likely had used this entrance before and was just pretending innocence to keep me from suspecting him of treason.

A spray of water shot out from the waterfall as the gate tightened the flow. It was our signal.

"Now!" Faldyn sprinted out, fully expecting me to follow. I raced after him, trying to watch my footing on the rocky ground while keeping my eye on what was happening above me. I could tell the waterfall was beginning to thin out. At the same time, a series of trickling streams began to flow out of the fortress, down the rock face high above us, like someone had just punched holes in it. What I had previously thought were lower windows now proved to be the drain spouts Faldyn had described. Reaching the cliff base, we were forced to splash through the raining drain water and fight our way over to the dying waterfall. We were wet, the rocks were wet. Footing was hard to maintain, especially when you added in the factor about me running for my life.

"Hurry, Hunter!" Faldyn yelled from ahead of me. "The falls will not stay closed for long."

There in front of us, cut inconspicuously into the side of the waterfall's rock backdrop, was a crude doorway. The metal door was perfectly camouflaged; its dark gray color and lumpy texture allowed it to blend right in with the rock face. *And Faldyn wants me to believe he discovered it on his own? Yeah right!*

"It's locked! It's not supposed to be locked!" Faldyn grunted as he tried ramming his shoulder into it.

Was this part of his show? Or had one of his accomplices forgotten to leave it unlocked?

Regaining his composure, Faldyn fished at a string around his neck. "No matter, this key should work." He pulled out a heavy iron key from his shirt, and seeing my reaction, added defensively, "My scouts recovered it off a fallen guard."

Already, the waterfall began to trickle down on us again. Faldyn fumbled with the key, trying to force it into the lock. It was not cooperating.

By now, Faldyn was beginning to show signs of panic. "I don't understand why it isn't working!" Water was pelting us in greater force. It would be only a matter of seconds before the full force of the waterfall resumed, battering us against the rocks, washing what was left of us down the river.

I suddenly felt compelled to act. "Stand back!" I hollered, pulling out my Veritas Sword. Faldyn ducked to avoid my unexpected attack. The Veritas blade blazed over his head in a powerful arc and found its mark, cleaving a gash across the door lock and deep into the stone frame. Having lost his balance, Faldyn stumbled awkwardly under the downpour of water. "Get in!" I screamed above the roar. Grabbing hold of his cloak I pulled him hard toward the door. His body rammed against it and the rusted hinges broke free, sending us both tumbling to the ground.

We had barely made it in time. The floodgate had finally released its hold on the flow and the waterfall now reclaimed the rock we had just occupied. Water swirled in around us from the open door. I struggled to my feet but Faldyn lay still, the water pooling around him. Was he dead? Unconscious? I could only hope as much. That would make it a whole lot easier to escape his company. I lit my sword, chasing away the shadows, and bent low to examine him closer. His left eye had a nasty swollen lump over it. *Ouch! That must have hurt.* It looked like his hard head did the work of ramming the door open.

"Ah!" Faldyn growled suddenly to life, blinking his eyes in pain. "Point that thing somewhere else." I dropped my sword from the surprise. As it clattered on the stone floor, the shadows flooded back in.

Blindly I tried to relocate my sword in the dark, booting it in the process. I could tell by the way the sliding sound stopped, that Faldyn had found it first. Moaning something about his head, his faint outline rose against the rushing waterfall behind him, filling the cramped doorway with his frame.

"If I didn't know better," he groaned sarcastically, while lifting my sword in front of him, "I'd think you were trying to kill me with this thing!"

My sword flashed to life, and behind the glow I could see a wry smile formed on his lips. He was too hard to read—was he amused that I might have tried getting rid of him, or at his dry attempt to be funny?

"I-I..." I stammered, unsure what action he would take next. "I was just trying to..."

"Calm yourself," Faldyn commanded coolly. "You saved us both with your quick thinking; however, I think I'll hang on to your blade for now. I find your technique a little too reckless."

Faldyn swapped my sword for his own off his belt. This was not good—without my weapon, making an escape from Faldyn would be much more difficult. His Veritas Sword held in front, Faldyn pushed roughly past me, taking the lead again. The light revealed that we were at the bottom of a steep, cramped flight of stairs carved deep into the mountainside. Whatever poor souls had spent their lifetime chiseling this hidden passageway hadn't spared any effort to make it larger than it had to be. The ceiling was barely tall enough for me to stand, but Faldyn's taller frame required him to duck to avoid adding another bump on his head. Faldyn led the way, cautiously taking the first few steps, brushing aside thick, dusty cobwebs hanging from the corners before setting a quicker pace up the steep darkened staircase. At least I had one good reason to still be following Faldyn—he got to clean out the majority of the cobwebs. The countless steps carried us upward on a winding route, much like a vein, coursing through the cold stone heart of the fortress.

With Faldyn filling most of the tunnel in front of me, my view ahead was severely limited. We hiked up the monotonous trail for what seemed to be an hour, but most likely was only twenty minutes. I knew we must be near the top when Faldyn slowed to a halt. I could see the faint glow of a doorway over his shoulder. He motioned me to stay back as he silently crept up to have a look around.

A tense moment passed before his whispered voice relayed what he saw. "The passageway leads directly to a chamber!" I could hear the excitement in his voice. *This is probably where he's planning to turn me in and collect his reward*, I thought. I tried desperately to think of some way to stop Faldyn before he could complete his plan, but there was no stopping him now. "Come with me, Hunter!" he called back greedily. "It's safe! The door is unguarded and the room is..."

Smack!

An unnatural flash of something invisible collided with Faldyn at the doorway, sending him tumbling back at me. I slid down as many steps as I could to avoid being crushed by his oncoming weight. His body ricocheted off the walls like a pinball before he fell still in a sprawled heap only a few steps above me. What had just happened? I pressed myself low against the stairs, trying to hide behind his motionless body. My heart was running wild with fear as I stared at the wide-open doorway. No sign of movement.

Waiting until I was confident no enemy was lurking in the room above me, I inched closer to the fallen captain. "Faldyn," I kept my voice to a whisper, just in case, "are you alright?" No answer. I quickly unhooked my Veritas Sword from his belt. Holding it as light over his contorted body, I felt his pulse. He wasn't dead, but the new bump on his head guaranteed he was going to have one nasty headache when he finally came to. Lucky for me, I would not be sticking around.

Ever since we set out together I was hoping to lose Faldyn after he snuck me safely into the fortress. While I had planned out numerous, more daring methods for getting him out of the picture, this accidental fall did the trick.

Actually, now that I was replaying it in my mind, Faldyn's unexpected collision made me laugh. It reminded me of Stubbs's dog, Goober, and how we used to trick him by standing outside on the deck, throwing a squeaky toy for him to chase—only we intentionally left the sliding glass door closed. He'd invariably dash off his bed on the couch and, well...you can imagine the rest. He was never the brightest of dogs although I did kind of regret hurting him like that.

Looking back at the unconscious Faldyn, the only thing I regretted for him was that I didn't have any rope or handcuffs to ensure he wouldn't escape the justice he deserved. If I had my way, Faldyn would be captured and punished for what he had done to harm so many Codebearers.

Quickly grabbing the stolen key and the pouch of fire-dust off Faldyn, I stepped carefully over his body to examine this mysterious door. Whatever force had blocked the doorway was completely invisible. I could see much of the torch-lit room and would have easily believed I could step right into it, if not for what I had just seen happen to Faldyn.

Holding my hand out in front of me, I carefully touched the unseen barrier. When my fingers reached the threshold I could feel a slight resistance meet them. Ringlets of silver light pulsated from where I touched, accompanied by a faint tingling sensation, like I was brushing against a pool of water. I tested the surface further, feeling it give under the pressure. Then suddenly it seemed to snap back, leaving my hand to protrude through to the other side. Instinctively, I yanked back my hand. What was going on? Why did the surface not remain solid as it had when it knocked Faldyn out cold? Maybe it only let you pass if you were slow? I tested my theory by punching at the invisible wall with light, then heavy jabs. Each time, my fist passed through with little resistance. Whatever was creating this phenomenon, it apparently liked me better than Faldyn. *Good. That means that Faldyn won't be going anywhere anytime soon.* Emboldened by my discovery, I leaned my whole body into the mysterious door and stepped out into the chamber.

My first impression of the room, while I was still in the passageway, was that it needed some serious help. Now that I stood inside, my opinion was even worse. Despite the adequate light that should have been provided by four pairs of wall-mounted torches flanking key furniture, and the randomly placed candle, the room felt dark and cold. Most everything was a somber gray. The only splash of color came from a couple of deep burgundy tapestries emblazoned with a black, backwards *S* and haphazardly thrown articles of clothing that added the finishing touches to the depressing decor.

Whoever made their home here was clearly not suffering from the "neat freak" syndrome my sister contracted as a child. Something on the desk piqued my interest, and as I turned to step toward it, I caught sight of movement in the passageway behind me. I pulled out my sword in defense and spun around to face the threat. I had expected to see Faldyn standing in the doorway; instead, there I was confronting a boy, his Veritas Sword drawn, wearing a frightened expression to match my own. What I faced was not a doorway or an attacker. I had been fooled by a mirror, scared by my own reflection.

My reflection may have scared me first, but it was what hung from the twisted black frame of the mirror that commanded my fear now. Four, white skull masks stared back at me. I knew those hollow-eyed faces could only mean one thing—this was not just any chamber I had entered. This was Venator's!

As soon as I realized where I was, I wanted out! Trouble was, the door I had stepped through only moments ago was nowhere to be seen. Only the menacing mirror provided a break to the otherwise solid stone wall. "I wonder," I thought aloud as I reached slowly for my reflection. The glass surface received my touch, then began to ripple until I pressed harder; the mirror gave way, swallowing my hand. *Fascinating!* Venator had hidden his secret escape behind an illusionary mirror.

Looking back up at the masks, I marveled at the power this boy possessed. He commanded an army and the elements, bending reality in ways I could only imagine. *What must it feel like?* I reached out to touch one of the skulls, half expecting it to zap me. I flinched, but it hung harmlessly by its band. Taking it down to examine it closer, I noted how cold it felt. Curious to know what it was made of I tapped it gently against the wall. *Ting, ting.* Metal. Fitting.

With the mirror standing in front of me, it seemed only natural to try on the mask. I slipped the ghoulish, form-fitting face onto mine, adjusting the band before looking up. The face of Venator peered back at me in the mirror. The effect was eerie. Disturbed by the result I quickly took it off. My hands were shaking as I lifted it back to its hook, which explained why it fell. I was horrified as I watched it slip right out of my fingers and spin end over end until it hit the stone floor. In case you didn't know, metal bowls falling off the kitchen counter can make a very loud noise. Metal masks falling on stone floors are even louder. *Clang-ilang-ilang!*

"Ah!" I gasped aloud. I fumbled around to stop it before someone heard the racket. Pounding on the chamber door told me someone had.

The low gurgly voice of a Shadow guard growled from the other side, "Master Venator? Is everything alright?"

My head raced with possible actions to take: hide, attack, beg for mercy, or..."Everything is fine!" I answered in a voice I hoped would sound like Venator. My heart beat loudly as I waited for his response, leaving me to wonder if my impersonation had worked.

"You do not sound well. I was told you were to be in the Lair," the guard pressed. He sounded suspicious. "Are you sure...?"

"It's none of your concern where I am. Leave me be if you value your head, fool!" This time I think I nailed it. After mumbling his apologies, the guard returned to his post. He had fallen for it!

Breathing a sigh of relief, I retrieved the dropped mask to hang it back up when a thought hit me; my ticket to moving about the fortress undiscovered was right here in my hand. All I needed were a few more items to complete my disguise. Kicking at the piles of dirty clothes on the floor, I found a suitable shirt and one of Venator's black hooded cloaks. They both smelled like sweaty gym socks, but I figured that would only help keep others at a distance. After I pulled them over my clothes, I took the mask and placed it on my head once more. I braved one last look in the mirror as I drew up the hood. The disturbing transformation caused me to shudder. This disguise was enough to fool me. I only hoped it would fool the guards as well.

Taking a deep breath to bolster my courage, I marched to the door and flung it open. "Out of my way, imbecile," I spat. I was really starting to get into character. The guard stumbled to one side as I pushed past him and headed down a flight of stairs. At the bottom, a long torch-lit hallway greeted me with the question: *where to now?* Seeing a group of guards gathered down a ways to the right, I opted for the path of least resistance and took a left.

The corridor led to another just like it. I took a right this time. Stairs. What I needed to find was stairs leading down. From every story I had ever read about castles, they always had a dungeon deep underground. Counting on the Shadow to have adopted these traditional floor plans, I figured this would be the first place I should look for my friends.

After another left turn I saw a heavy iron door at the end of the corridor, flanked by two of the larger Shadow guards. *That must be the dungeon*, I speculated. Even though I still wore my disguise, I didn't have the confidence to immediately engage with the massive guardians. I needed time to formulate my approach, so I casually turned to slip back to the hallway I had just come from.

Leaning against the wall, I started to rehearse what I might say to the Shadow brutes to get past them into the dungeon without raising suspicion.

"Open up! I wish to see the prisoners!"

No. Not mean enough.

"Step aside! I have business with the Codebearer vermin."

Now I was trying too hard. Maybe I would just keep it simple and demand them to...

"Open up!" a muffled voice rasped. I peeked around the corner to see one of the guards grab hold of a heavy steel bar that secured the door. The primitive lock complained noisily as he slid it back, allowing the door to creak open.

The pad-click, pad-click of irregular footsteps announced the approach of a hobbling goblin from the dungeon staircase. Hopping onto the top step, he revealed his handicap: a stubby wooden leg. This was unmistakably Venator's right hand guy, Zeeb.

"Step to it!" Zeeb barked down the staircase. "The master wants the new prisoners taken to their cells." He tapped his wooden toe impatiently. "Do *not* make him wait."

Three pale, abnormally thin Disprits, emerged slowly from the shadowed flight of stairs. Each of the creatures wore a scowl and a belt of keys that jangled noisily from their waists. One of them looked especially worse than the others, with scars covering his body, the most notable one being a thick, jagged scar that appeared to have sewn his left eye shut. They were the keepers of the prison. My thoughts focused on the new prisoners Zeeb had just mentioned. *He must be referring to Hope and the others!* If I wanted to find them, I figured my best option would be to follow the Dispirits.

As Zeeb rushed them into the corridor I tucked myself into one of the hallway's thickest shadows and let them pass by. Zeeb's distinctive footsteps made it easy for me to follow from a safe distance, always keeping to the shadows.

Up two flights of stairs and another two passage turns later, I found myself ducking for cover while a troop of goblins passed in the opposite direction of Zeeb and the guards. When at last it was safe to come out, I had lost sight of my unsuspecting guides. Racing down the hall I listened intently for the sound of Zeeb's pegged foot.

Nothing.

I began to worry I had lost them for good when I caught a faint echo of Zeeb's raspy voice dead ahead. Running to catch up, I discovered I was approaching a wider, vaulted hallway. Pinning myself against the wall I inched my way to the corner of the hallway and peeked around. Zeeb and the three pale Dispirits were disappearing behind an ominous set of black metal doors. I sprinted up to the slightly opened door, hoping to slip in before it shut.

Boom!

The hall resonated with the sound of an opportunity lost. In my frustration, I wanted to punch the door but thought better of it before I struck, partly because it would have given away my presence needlessly; but mostly because I was unnerved by the snakehead that glared at me from the face of the door. Actually, it was only one of many overlaid metal snakes that writhed their way across both doors in a single interlocking, knotted design. Breaking up this slithering game of Twister, in the center of the design, was the Shadow's signature *S* spanning the height of the doorway. Every snake had its mouth open, flaring its fangs at me as if to communicate the message "Keep Out."

Careful to stay away from any part of the door that looked like it was poised to strike at me I held my ear to the center crack, hoping to catch a hint of what was happening on the other side. I pressed my ear tightly against the small gap between the doors and was pleased to find I could hear every word.

"I'm through with these four. I tire of their stubborn resistance. Take them to the dungeon to await deportation to Dolor." That voice must have been Venator.

"As you wishhhh, Master," came the reply. It was clearly a Dispirit. "But what of the otherssss?"

"They will stay here with me. The boy intrigues me. He does not appear to be as foolish as the rest of them and the girl..." The voice changed to drip uncharacteristically sweet, "How could I let a flower of such rare beauty be locked away to wither?"

Slap!

"Save your illusions for someone else!" Hope's wit was still as sharp as ever under pressure.

"How dare you!" Venator raged at her defiance.

There was another slap and I heard Hope cry out.

"Take your hands off her!" Another voice shouted. It sounded like Ephriam, though I wasn't entirely sure.

A tussle ensued. Grunting. Chains rattling. Something fell—hard.

"Inssssolent foolsssss!"

Thwapp!

"Ah!" A Dispirit tongue had found a victim.

"Weak! Hopelessssss! Pathetic!"

Thwapp! Thwapp! Thwapp!

"Stop it! Leave them alone!" Hope begged.

"I give the commands around here!" Venator threatened. "Zeeb, bind her! She will be too much trouble left on her own."

"Let...go...errgh!" Hope was not going easily.

Whatever man's voice spoke next was too weak to understand, but I figured it must have been Ephriam, from Venator's response.

"Enough! Take the captain and his men down to the dungeon with the rest of the prisoners. I want them on the next transport to Dolor so they can learn the penalty for speaking when they should stay silent."

"Of coursssse," came the eager reply.

The sound of footsteps approached the door. Realizing my need to find cover, I pressed myself into the corner of the doorframe. The door swung outward and I sucked in my stomach in an effort to become as much a part of the wall as possible.

A train of four chained prisoners held captive by the Dispirits streamed out from the doorway into the hall. The prison guards were not sympathetic to the difficulty the Codebearers had walking with tied ankles.

"Move faster, ssssslave!"

Thwapp!

By now the scarred, one-eyed Dispirit bringing up the rear had exited and the door began to slowly close. The procession was still too close to make a run for it, but at the rate they were moving, the door would slam shut again before they were far enough away for me to make any move. I had to stop the door from shutting. Taking my Veritas Sword handle from under my cloak, I shoved it into the door jam. The hinges creaked slightly as it pinched against my temporary stopper. Now I just had to wait for the prison "train" to pull a little further away.

The distant sound of Ephriam's voice spoke softly to the others, "Do not lose heart, men."

Another responded in kind, "Yes. Remember who we serve…"

"Ssssilence!"

Thwapp!

It pained me to see the abuse these Codebearers were enduring, but now was my opportunity to slip inside unnoticed while the Dispirits were distracted with dishing out another round of tongue lashings. I tugged at the Veritas Sword handle so I would be able to let the door close after I entered, but the makeshift doorstop was stuck tight. As I attempted to work it free, Ephriam's voice called out over the torture, "The Author will make a way for us even here amidst..."

Thwapp!

"There will be no waaaay here but Venator'sssss." The tongue-lashings continued in greater numbers.

At that moment the sword wiggled free. The door began to close and with it my second chance to enter the room undetected. But something stopped me. I could not escape the feeling that I'd been given an undeniable opportunity to save these men. My choice was clear; I let the door slam shut.

"Okay, Hunter, it's now or never," I whispered to myself. Leaping out from my hiding place I shouted as loudly as I dared, "Hold your tongues!"

The Dispirits snapped to attention when they saw me appear as Venator before them.

"What do you think you're doing?" I demanded. The three Dispirits exchanged confused looks before one attempted to answer.

"We just assssumed..."

"Silence!" I interrupted. "You assumed wrong. These prisoners are special to me. Leave them unharmed until I come to deal with them myself."

"But, Massssster, their spiritssss are still strong," the thinnest one objected.

"Not once I'm finished with them," I retorted.

"But…thisss is so unfair…" whined one of the disappointed Dispirits.

"No! If I was being fair then I'd be ringing your little necks right now for challenging my authority." I squeezed a tightened fist in front of me for added effect.

The Dispirits only looked at each other blankly with their bulging eyes, unsure of how to respond to my threat. I got the impression that the "ringing your little necks" line was not quite in character for Venator. I should have gone with something a little more evil like "torturing your souls." *You're losing them, Hunter.*

"Go! *Now!*" I commanded with even more ferocity.

That seemed to do the trick. The three Dispirits jumped back in fright and began to scurry about to fulfill my demands. *Amazing. This disguise sure carried a lot of power.* I pressed my luck adding, "But I don't want to deprive you of exercising your poisonous skill, so…I order you to inflict thirty, no fifty tongue lashings on each other for your defiance."

The Dispirits looked back in shock, but none dared to challenge me this time. Instead, I watched as they pulled the fallen prisoners to their feet. As Ephriam stood back up, he turned his swollen face toward me. Something about the way his eyes met mine told me that he knew.

I watched long enough to make certain the Dispirits didn't harm the men further, and then stole my way quickly back to the door. How was I going to get in now without being noticed? As I pressed my ear back up against the door to listen, the ringing memory of

Ephriam's words was the only thing I could hear: *The Author will make a way for us...will make a way...a way...*

Pad-click, pad-click, pad-click.

The sound of approaching footsteps told me that a new way had already been made. I darted back into my corner hideout just seconds before the door opened and Zeeb hobbled out. Timing my entrance with the closing door, I slipped inside just before the door slammed shut.

CHAPTER 21

THE ILLUSIONIST'S LAIR

I found myself inside a long, cavernous throne room, supported by crooked columns of stone. The room was sparsely decorated, without the typical tapestries or banners usually found in a regal court. Actually, there was nothing regal about this place—it was grim, dark and suited its master well. On the far side of the room a dinner table was prepared at the foot of the stairs which led to Venator's throne. The only source of light in the space came from a wide fiery pit of green flames set in the center of the aisle in front of me.

My first objective after infiltrating the room was to find a place to hide. The pillars that rose on either side of the main aisle provided the perfect cover. I managed to slip behind one unnoticed, crouching low so as not to be discovered. I listened and watched from the shadows.

"Take as much as you like. I can always make more." Venator's voice echoed off the stone walls.

"Mm...tanks! Iz jus dat I habn't had da (Gulp!) proper nutrition since I got here." *Stretch!* I was glad to hear his voice, but why did he sound so funny? Was he eating Venator's food? What was he thinking?

"Did you know that the brain is made of more than 60% fat?" Stretch offered one of his usual "not-so-usual" facts.

Venator nodded politely and began to pour some drinks into golden goblets.

Stretch continued as he chewed his food, "This fish...trout is it?...chock-full of omega-3 fatty acids...which is important for a diet... Otherwise, your brain's fat level gets too low...and then you get depression...poor memory...low IQ..."

Venator concluded, "And to one of such a superior intellect as yours, that would be a tragedy. A toast then to Fat Brains!" The momentary pause was broken by the sound of two cups clinking together.

Venator took the opportunity to steer the conversation while Stretch guzzled down his drink. "You know, it surprises me, Stretch, that one as gifted as you would ever be content to follow others... especially Hunter."

Stretch slurped noisily, draining the last drop from his cup before asking, "What do you mean?"

"Well, not that Hunter is a bad kid, but let's face it; he's not you. You, my friend, can be reasonable in the face of adversity—unlike your feisty friend over there." Venator turned behind him to direct his question to someone else. "What do you say, beautiful, are you ready to behave yourself and join us at the table now?"

The muffled female voice communicated its anger and defiance clearly enough, even though it was obviously gagged. *Hope!*

I needed to move closer to get a better view. Keeping to the shadows I darted from pillar to pillar until I was as close as I could be without blowing my cover.

"Oooh! I think she still needs a little more time to cool off. Perhaps you would care for some more trout, my friend?"

I could not see what Venator did, but the effect of his trick could be witnessed in a rising puff of smoke and the faint smell of freshly seared fish.

Stretch was clearly impressed. "Whoa! That is so cool. How do you do that?"

"I have great powers."

"Because of the Bloodstone, right?"

Venator chuckled, "I'm impressed; you've done your homework." He leaned in eagerly toward Stretch, as if revealing a secret. "But, what is more important is what my power allows me to do. I control my fate. What I want, I get."

"Sounds nice."

What? Come on, Stretch! Stand up to this jerk. I couldn't believe he was falling for this garbage, but then he added, "But aren't you supposed to be…you know…evil?"

There you go, Stretch! Nice one!

"Evil?" Venator sounded amused at the accusation. "Come now, Stretch. Use that amazing brain of yours to think for yourself. I contend that you only believe I'm evil because the Codebearers told you to believe that. Surely you can come up with your own opinion. Tell me, how did you come to enter my domain of Solandria?"

Stretch did his best to relate our experience. "Well, there was this guy, I think his name was Evan, and he gave us this book.

Well, actually he just gave us a card to go get the book from a bookshop—only the book keeper actually turns out to be some big wig here in Solandria named Avi…"

"Yes, yes, yes…" Venator stopped Stretch before he could finish. "I know the old man you speak of. Let's leave out the details, shall we?" He cleared his throat. "The point I am making is that you should consider your sources. You entered Solandria through this book given to you by the Codebearers. Am I right?"

"Right."

"And the Codebearers are in complete opposition to my rule here."

"Right…" Stretch sounded wary.

"So, it is only natural they would tell you I was their enemy."

"Right…" Now Stretch was confused, "You mean you're *not* their enemy?"

"Of course I am," Venator quipped. "But the real question is, which side is the true enemy?"

Venator was working to make Stretch doubt the obvious truth, but Stretch was not biting. "Um…you're the one wearing the skull mask."

Go Stretch! Ha! His in-your-face remark almost made me laugh out loud.

Venator was not nearly as amused, but neither was he deterred. "Judging a book by its cover?" He clucked his tongue to reproach Stretch. "You discredit your intellect to be so shallow, my friend. Look deeper. Look at the facts. All you know of Solandria and the Shadow has come to you by way of the Codebearers. Does the word 'propaganda' mean anything to you?"

Ask Stretch a question like that and it's like opening a walking, talking dictionary. Stretch did not disappoint. "Sure, propaganda means: information, ideas, or rumors deliberately spread widely to help or harm a person, group, movement…"

"That's enough definition," Venator interrupted again. "Yes. Propaganda are ideas that are spread to 'help or harm,' as you so eloquently put it. So the question you owe it to yourself to ask is, are the Codebearers trying to help or harm?"

Let him have it again, Stretch!

Like he even needed to think about that…he had to have seen enough himself to know how much the Codebearers were trying to help us both fight against the Shadow.

Stretch began his argument, "Hunter believes they are trying to help…"

"Stop!" Venator sounded annoyed. "There you go again, insisting on following. Since when should a superior intellect follow the whims of a misguided friend?"

Misguided? If I had been facing Venator, I would have had a few choice words for his attack on me. *Defend my honor, Stretch!*

"You think Hunter is wrong?" Stretch asked in a surprised tone. That was not the show of confidence I was expecting from him.

"You answer that for yourself," Venator said slyly. I was sure he must have been smiling at that small victory before he burrowed deeper asking, "What have the Codebearers asked you to do?"

"First we were to come to Solandria and then, well actually, come here to your fortress to recover the Bloodstone."

Stretch! You just blurted out our mission! Great! There went any remaining element of surprise.

"Aha!" Venator was elated at his discovery of this information. It must have been what he was probing Stretch for all along. I expected now that he had gotten what he wanted, he would call his guards in and have Stretch and Hope hauled off to the dungeon with the rest. Instead, he continued the conversation further. "So, they capture you and then send you on their errands—clever. Did you ever wonder why?"

I was not sure what Venator's motives were for postponing the trip to the dungeon, but for Stretch's sake, I was glad for the delay. I needed more time to put a rescue plan into action.

"Well…" Stretch gave it some thought before answering. "Ultimately it was supposed to help me and Hunter get back home."

"That's what you want most of all, isn't it?" Venator pressed. "Oh, but did anyone really promise to let you go back immediately after you did their bidding?"

"Well, not exactly right away. But we would be closer to…"

"No!" Venator's interruption this time was his most impassioned yet. "There will always be another errand, another task, another job until you wake up one day to find that you have been reduced to nothing more than a slave." He let the full effect of that last word sink in before asking, "Does enslavement sound 'friendly' to you?"

Stretch gulped, "No. No, it doesn't."

Did he really believe what he just said? Or was he just intimidated by Venator's outburst?

Venator twisted the sharp blade of his false accusation deeper into Stretch's mind. "Maybe these Codebearers are a bit more harmful than you first were led to believe, hmm?"

Stretch shifted uncomfortably in his seat and looked down at the floor. I could tell this argument was having the wrong effect on him. *No Stretch! He's lying! Don't believe a word he's saying!* My friend's struggle to cling to the truth added urgency to my need for a plan. How was I going to stop Venator and save Hope and Stretch without dying in the process? I dared to lean out a little further, straining to catch a glimpse of Hope. She was tied to a pillar on the opposite side of the room.

Venator had no intention of halting his assault on Stretch's fragile beliefs. He had Stretch right were he wanted him and went for the kill, standing to give his next point more force. "Do you know why the Codebearers oppose my rule? Because I oppose theirs! They fear the power I have to rescue their recruited slaves, to set them free and send them home."

At the mention of this, Stretch snapped his head up to look at Venator. "What did you say?" he asked with rapt attention.

"That's right." A devilish smile bent its way onto Venator's face. "You can go home right now if you want to take my offer."

"On what conditions?" Stretch asked cautiously.

"No conditions. I am different from the Codebearers, remember?" Venator reinforced his point, "My way home is easy. In fact, it's as easy as walking through that door." Venator stretched his staff out toward the green-flamed fire and I watched as it flared up to reveal the shape of a ghostly door.

"All you have to do is walk through that door and you'll be home. You will forget this place and everything that has happened to you here. You can get on with your life…everything will be as it once was."

I quickly glanced back from the glowing green door to Stretch. He was standing now, his eyes wide with wonder, feet methodically moving toward the door. I knew this was too great a temptation for him to bear and I wasn't about to let my best friend walk into the enemy's trap without putting up a fight. I had to do something.

"Yes!" Venator encouraged Stretch. "Go on! You'll be home!"

Tearing the mask from my face, I stepped out from my hiding place and hurled the mask straight at Venator. My aim was true.

The make-shift Frisbee struck his staff hand, causing him to fall to the floor in surprise.

"Stretch, no!" I yelled as I raced to his side and grabbed him by the shoulders.

He shook his head as if just awakening from a trance, "Hunter?"

"Don't believe a word he's saying!" I urged him as I forcefully backed him away from where Venator was scrambling to retrieve his staff.

Venator was laughing as he sneered at my disruption, "At last, the ever elusive Hunter Brown. I'm glad you finally decided to join us, although I expected you to arrive with an escort."

Thinking back to Faldyn, I felt a bit of pride at my feats so far. "Yeah? Well, I gave him the day off. And you can consider this your last day too." I pulled out my Veritas Sword to back up my threat.

Stretch looked horrified and wrestled my sword arm down as he pleaded, "No, Hunter! You've got it all wrong. If you just listen to him for a second…"

"I've heard enough of his lies already," I snapped back, irritated at how far Stretch had let Venator lead him astray. Clearly, he could not be trusted to himself. "Get behind me, Stretch," I commanded, "I'm getting us out of here."

"No." The way his response hit me, Stretch may as well have punched me in the gut. He let go of my arm and took a step back from me.

"I-I'm not following you this time, Hunter. This time I'm making a decision for myself."

What was he talking about? We both came together and if I had anything to do with it, we would both leave together. "Don't be stupid, Stretch! It's a trap!"

I couldn't believe what was happening. My own friend was pulling away from me, even as I tried to save him. The look of betrayal and hurt on Stretch's face cut me to the core. I was speechless.

Venator, seizing the opportunity to drive the wedge in deeper, jumped in to coach his victim. "He thinks you're stupid, Stretch. He doesn't want you to make your own choice, even though you're smarter. This is your chance to shine! Take the lead, Stretch; show Hunter the way home."

I finally found words, but only to beg, "Stretch? Don't leave!"

He looked away, shaking his head. When he finally looked back at me, his eyes were black and his face had a look of determination.

"I'll see you back at home, Hunter," said Stretch.

Without waiting he walked straight into the flames and through the final exit.

"Nooooo!" I screamed, running after him, but it was too late. He was gone.

I whipped around to face my enemy, hatred buring in my heart. "What did you do to him?"

Venator held up his hands innocently, "I let him go home where he belongs."

"Bring him back!" I demanded angrily.

"What? And take away his free will? Never! He had a choice; this was what he wanted. Now he controls his own fate as is his right." I could tell that this could not have pleased Venator more. He was relishing this moment.

Pointing my Veritas Sword at him I shouted, "Bring him back, or I swear, I'll...I'll..."

"What?" Venator mocked, "Kill me? I'd like to see you try." He raised his staff to meet my challenge. "You do not realize who I am, what I'm capable of."

My eyes narrowed in pure contempt. "I know all I need to know about you, Venator," I seethed. Venator was the one who did not realize who *I* was. The prophecy was on my side. Vengeance would be mine. "It's time *you* realize what *I'm* capable of."

The time for talking had come to an end.

CHAPTER 22

THE DEADLY ESCAPE

With racing steps and a flying sword I lunged at Venator, striking out with a sharp-angled swipe of my blade. Unthreatened by my attack, Venator lowered his staff and an invisible shield spread out between us, thrusting me backward. I swung out in anger at the transparent wall between us, igniting red sparks where the blade connected with the protection of the Bloodstone's shield. It was no use; the Veritas Sword simply glanced off.

"Ha!" snarled Venator. "Your pitiful weapon is no use against the power of the Bloodstone."

Venator swung his staff in my direction and hurled a red fiery trail of light toward my chest. The Veritas Sword glowed to life, as if moving on its own, quickly deflecting the power of the Bloodstone back toward its master. It was all Venator could do to dive out of the way before the glowing force returned to singe the floor where he once stood. As he lunged to the side, I advanced to catch him off guard. His shield was gone and the arc of my Veritas Sword came down hard, missing him by a fraction of an inch. Before I knew what hit me, the end of his staff struck my chest. The force of the blow knocked the breath from my lungs and threw me to the far side of the fire pit where I collapsed to the ground.

"Pathetic," he snarled at my feeble attempt to fight. "You can't win, not as long as I hold half of the Bloodstone."

"You're wrong," I gasped, trying desperately to recover my breath. "I *will* strike you down, Venator, just as the Author has written," I exclaimed, stumbling to my feet. "Aviad has shown me the truth of who I am."

At the mere mention of the name, Venator became enraged.

"The Author has no power here, boy!"

Rolling over in pain, I raised the sword just in time to deflect three more light bursts. Venator ducked to avoid them as one flew over his shoulder cracking the pillar where Hope was tied. The impact of the blast rained dust onto her head and she shot a worried look my way. Obviously, the near miss was too close for comfort.

Jumping back to my feet I turned my attention to the enemy. We circled the simmering cauldron of fire with slow, purposeful steps—he on one side, and I on the other—neither of us committing to our next move. I studied his blackened eyes but they showed no emotion, making it impossible to read his thoughts.

"You fight well," Venator spoke at last. "It will be a pity to watch you die. With the proper training you could have been a great Shadow warrior. Sceleris could use another like you."

"I will never serve the Shadow," I said with determination.

"Oh, but you already have." His words surprised me; I'd heard them before. My mind wandered back to the vision of the canyon attack. Faldyn lay alone after the fire-dust paralyzed his men and the Scrill attack finished the others. It was the first time I had seen Venator in action, and he had used those very words then. As I replayed the scene in my mind I suddenly remembered the fire-dust I'd taken from Faldyn. A plan formulated in my head.

"Tell the truth, Hunter. Your friend Hope deserves to know how busy you have been."

"What are you talking about?" I didn't know where this was going, but I didn't like the sound of it.

"You've been working as an agent of the Shadow all along. It was your knowledge of Sanctuary that allowed us to finally destroy the Resistance."

"You're lying!" I shouted, slowly placing my free hand into my pocket to find the fire-dust.

"Of course Petrov knew you would betray him. He knew as soon as you told him about the visions, didn't he, Hunter? He understood the connection between us was strong. That's why he sent you away on this pointless mission. He wanted to be rid of you."

My chest tightened and my heart began pounding in a way I had never felt before, pumping blood through my veins in heavy steady beats. If what Venator said was true, he'd seen into my mind as easily as I'd seen into his.

"Think of it. Because of you the Resistance is finished. Because of you Hope will die." At this Venator lowered his staff and aimed it directly at Hope with blood-chilling purpose.

"Noooooo!" I yelled, pulling the pouch from my pocket in anger and throwing it into the fiery cauldron between us. The explosion that resulted was more spectacular than I'd expected. Apparently the amount of dust in the bag, combined with the already flaming pit, was more than enough to do the trick. The fire burst into one of the most surprising explosions imaginable, rattling the room with the strength of an earthquake.

"Ahhhhh!" Venator howled, caught completely off guard as the two of us were thrown from the center of the room by the force of the blast.

The flames rose high to the cavernous ceiling above, licking the pillars and spreading across the room. Rocks and debris flew as one of the pillars gave way and toppled to the ground near where Venator lay. Poisonous smoke billowed out of the cauldron in thick choking plumes that threatened to suffocate us.

"Hope!" I shouted, covering my face and running to save her. The smoke was already sliding its way toward where she was bound. There wasn't much time.

"What happened?" she asked as I approached. Her face was white with fear.

"Fire-dust," I answered, cutting the rope from her hands. "The smoke is dangerous. Cover your face. I'm getting you out of here, now."

The severity of the explosion alerted a handful of Dispirits who stormed into the room to see what had happened. Overcome by the sudden surge of lethal smoke, the guards were paralyzed on the spot and fell in the doorway. With the door now propped open by the bodies, the toxic vapors escaped into the corridors beyond. The pounding in my chest began again, this time sending a shock of pain through my body and stealing my breath. Moaning, I leaned over and clutched my chest.

"Are you okay?" Hope asked, holding the cloak over her mouth and nose to protect against the smoke. Her eyes were full of concern.

"Yes, I'm fine. We need to get out of here now!" I shouted, pulling her across the room.

"But what about the Bloodstone?" she asked.

"Not now, I'm getting you out first! I'm not going to let you die."

It was time to make our escape. Hope's bow lay on the table alongside the stolen book—the Author's Writ. We gathered our things and darted for the exit before the throne room collapsed.

The corridors of the fortress were littered with fallen guards. Toxic smoke from the fire-dust explosion had wafted through the passage and cleared the way for our escape.

"This way, hurry!" I called over my shoulder, heading for the front door.

"Where are we going?" Hope asked.

"I already told you, I'm getting you out of here."

"But the others," she answered, stopping dead in her tracks. "We can't leave them behind. We have to rescue them."

Keeping Hope away from Venator was my primary concern. But there was no way I could leave behind the brave men who had risked their lives for me—I owed them at least a chance at freedom.

"Okay, but we'll have to hurry. The sooner we get out of this place the better. Follow me; I know the way to the dungeon. It's in the lower chamber," I commanded.

Tracking my former path through the seemingly endless hallways that made up Venator's palace was like trying to get through a maze. After a few wrong turns I managed to find the barricaded dungeon door at last. The door was flanked by a pair of immobilized Shadow guards who had been foolish enough to inhale the poisonous fumes.

Cautiously, we stepped over the guards and unlatched the sliding lock. The primitive door opened with a groan, revealing the darkened stairwell that led to the dungeon below.

"Keep alert," I whispered, "we won't be alone. The smoke rises, it won't affect the guards on the lower level."

Silently we stepped down the switchback staircase. At the base of the stairs we huddled together behind a stone arch that ushered us into the dungeon hallways beyond.

From the safety of the archway we eyed the space, looking carefully for any sign of danger. The cobblestone floor that spread before us was damp and spotted with mudpuddles. The reflection of torchlight glistened on the wet surface and even continued up the walls, which looked as though they had been recently doused with water as well. If my suspicions were right, these were the lower chambers Faldyn had told me about—the ones Venator flooded with water to torture his captives. A shiver ran down my spine at the thought of being tortured with near drowning.

An unmetered chorus of drips echoed throughout the chamber, adding to the foreboding atmosphere. On either side of the room, a long row of prison doors lined the walls, directing our attention to the far end of the hall and a three-legged table surrounded by Dispirits.

The tabletop was piled with a heap of clothing and weapons that had been taken from the prisoners. The Dispirits bickered over which of them would get to choose the best of the prisoners' spoils. An assortment of Veritas Swords had been tossed to the side, considered useless in the enemy's hands. At the moment, a navy blue cape appeared to be the point of contention between the ghastly guards.

"I know that cape," I said softly. "It's Ephriam's. We must be close."

Hope nodded silently in agreement, so as not to alert the guards of our presence. My heart pounded with anxiety as I recalled Evan's encounter with the Dispirits the night I had crossed the Veil. He had his hands full fighting two Dispirits; what might three be able to do to against an inexperienced fighter such as myself? I stood my ground, unsure of what my first move might be. Not relishing the idea of hand-to-hand combat with the bug-like creatures, my eyes turned to Hope's bow.

"Think you can handle them?" I asked.

"Easy," Hope whispered back, "I can take them out from here." Keeping to the shadows, she pulled back the bowstring, letting an arrow of light appear out of nowhere to arm her weapon. As she readied herself, I stole one last glance around the corner to reassure myself of the enemy's position. Had I been more vigilant I might have noticed that another Dispirit was standing guard on the op-posite side of the archway. Instead, my sights were set only on the far end of the hall.

"All clear," I whispered, giving the thumbs-up.

At my word, Hope promptly stepped out from the archway and took aim at the first of the Dispirits.

"Intrudersssss!" the hidden guard snarled, catching Hope en-tirely by surprise. Before she could readjust her aim, the Dispirit lashed out with its gruesomely clawed fist and sent Hope sprawling at the base of the stairs. With a loud thump she hit the ground and fell limply. There was no time to think, I had to react quickly. Flashing my Veritas Sword into action, I broke cover and quickly sliced through the unarmed guard. The Dispirit dissolved with a hiss into an inky puff of smoke.

The remaining three guards that had previously been posted at the far end of the room were already on their way to engage in the scuffle. They approached slowly at first, one in front of the other.

"Codebearer you are NOT!" Venator's voice seemed to come out of nowhere.

I spun around, only to find there was no one there. Venator was whispering in my mind, playing with my fears just as he had done when I fought the stone guardians in the Revealing Room. When at last I turned my attention back to the approaching Dispirits, I found they had covered the distance between us faster than I'd expected.

Awkwardly, I attempted to steady my stance, preparing to fend off the threat of the Dispirits in front of me.

"Sssscared, aren't you?" the first one hissed.

"Yesssss, he isss," the second concurred, inhaling deeply. "Ssssmell the fear!"

"No, let's tasssste it!" the third one suggested licking its lips meaningfully.

My nerves abandoned me as the first Dispirit lunged forward with deadly intentions.

"By fear a man appoints his master," another voice echoed in my mind. But this time it was the words of Sam's training. The simple phrase inspired a burst of courage I didn't even know was in me.

"I am *NOT* afraid of you!" I screamed, hurling my sword in desperation toward the vicious Dispirit. Surprisingly, the sword sliced through him with supernatural force and continued to spin through the second and third as well. All three Dispirits vanished into flurries of black mist, their belts and keys clattering to the wet stone floor along with my sword. With one blow I had finished them all.

Crossing the room, I searched for my sword. *If only Stretch could've seen me in action, he would have been impressed,* I thought to myself. Not only had my approach proven effective, I had managed to dispatch all three of them without receiving even as much as a single sting from their tongues. Not even Evan had done that.

A glint of light caught my attention; the hilt of my sword was laying in a small puddle only a few steps from an open cell door. Reaching down, I leaned over to retrieve it but as my hand neared the handle, a slimy tongue lashed out from the darkened cell and struck it like a whip. The pain was unbearable; the poisonous sting seared into my skin like acid. Apparently, I had overlooked more than one guard in the room.

With my good hand I stretched out for the sword. "Not thisssss time!" The Dispirit tongue shot out of the darkness once more, grabbing the sword and throwing it across the room, out of reach. The Dispirit hobbled out from the empty cell and into the light. Its face was wretchedly maimed; a long gruesome scar ran up the side where its eye should have been. I recognized it as none other than the one-eyed Dispirit captain I had challenged in the hallway outside Venator's throne room.

"Ooopsssss, how clumsssssy of me," it said in jest.

Wasting no time I sprinted toward my sword, but the menacing fiend pounced overhead and blocked my path. In an attempt to change my direction, I slipped on the wet floor and collapsed at his feet. Grabbing fistfuls of my shirt collar with two of its six scarred hands, it lifted me from the ground to hover just inches from its hideous face.

"Your ssssssword won't sssssave you now," the disfigured guard teased, releasing a black fog of foul breath as he laughed.

"No, but mine will!" announced an unexpected voice from out of the darkness. A flash of light slashed through the surprised Dispirit, discharging it in an instant cloud of black. I dropped into a puddle and watched as the shadowy smoke that once was my foe wisped away, revealing the face of my rescuer.

"Faldyn?" I asked, recognizing his scowling face at once. "W-what are you doing here?"

"Saving your neck from the looks of it," he grumbled matter-of-factly, stepping over my legs to reach my forfeited sword.

"This yours?" he asked, scooping it up with his free hand and shaking the water from it.

"But, you fell…" I stammered, trying to figure out how he escaped, "How did you…?"

Faldyn raised an eyebrow to examine me. "Once I recovered from the fall, I hacked my way through the mirror and came here in search of the others." He feigned a chopping motion with his sword. "But, what I don't understand is how you managed to get in yourself? Only one who serves the Shadow can cross through the shield charm."

Uncomfortable with where this questioning might be heading, I scrambled to pick myself up from the floor, but winced in pain when I absent-mindedly pressed down on my injured hand.

Reacting quickly, Faldyn hurried to prevent me from standing. "Stay where you are," he commanded, pointing his sword at me. I instinctively threw my arm up in defense. Faldyn grabbed my arm before I could withdraw it. Then, much to my surprise, he kneeled next to me and placed his Veritas blade across the wound.

"You'll only slow us down with an injury like that," he explained. But that was as far as his tenderness extended. "It was foolish to have ever let go of your sword," he scolded in his typical brusque manner. Then, handing me back my Veritas Sword he added, "Next time, keep it close."

Though I disliked him and was suspicious of him, there was no getting around the fact that he had now saved my life twice. If he had intended to turn me over to Venator, he had just passed up his golden opportunity. Clearly I had misjudged this man with the conclusions I'd drawn. Before I could say anything, we heard a soft moan coming from the stairwell.

"Hope," I remembered, jumping to my feet and rushing to her side. "Are you okay?"

She nodded, rubbed the back of her head and replied smugly, "Next time, you go first!"

"Are you going to help," Faldyn interrupted, "or am I the only one ready to get us all out of here?"

"Captain Faldyn!" Hope exclaimed, giving the stoic leader a quick embrace, much to his discomfort. "How did you find us here?" Hope asked, unaware of the part he had played in the rescue mission that had brought me to the fortress.

"All of that is not important right now," he said abruptly, side-stepping the question. "Our objective should be to get everyone out of here as quickly as possible." Holding out keyrings he'd just collected from where the prison keepers had dropped them, he continued, "Here, take these; unlock the prisoners and follow me. I know the way out."

Hope didn't hesitate to grab her set and rush off to the far end of the cell block. Reaching for my own, I dared to look up into Faldyn's eyes. Sensing the reason for my pause he held up his hand. "You can thank me later. We're not out of danger yet."

It didn't take long for the three of us to locate and open all of the occupied cells. Ephriam and his men were not the only Codebearers locked up down here. In total, we were able to free nearly fifty other prisoners who had been captured at the battle of Sanctuary and imprisoned by Venator. Reunited with their swords, Ephriam and his men tended to each other's wounds and suited up for battle. Then, following Faldyn's lead, we rushed up and out through the corridors toward the exit. Along the way the unarmed prisoners among us took the opportunity to gird themselves with any weapons they could scavenge off the many fallen Shadow warriors. Soon, we'd found our way to a wide, moonlit courtyard. Once outside we raced across the rough stone pavement toward the double wall that separated us from freedom. Remarkably, the front gate was open and unguarded. This was too easy, only ten more steps and we would be free.

Klam!

The massive doors of the black gate slammed shut and locked themselves by an unseen force, blocking our exit. We were stopped in our tracks.

The booming voice of Venator seemed to surround us, laughing wickedly at our feeble attempt to escape.

"Leaving so soon? Things were just getting interesting."

Our rag-tag band of warriors spun aimlessly around, weapons raised, unable to determine where the voice was coming from. Venator was enjoying this, clearly amused with our confusion. He continued his taunting, his voice echoing throughout the courtyard.

"The fire-dust was clever, I must admit. We are more alike than you know, boy. Surrender yourself, Hunter, and I will spare the lives of the others."

"If you want him, come and get him!" Hope replied, stepping in front of me, challenging him to test her skill with the bow.

"Have it your way," Venator said. "Kill them."

From every dark place along all four walls emerged groupings of fearsome Shadow warriors. My fire-dust had not affected the outer guards. We had been ambushed.

Captain Ephriam didn't miss a beat, shouting out orders to the Codebearers. "Faldyn, take the East front with ten men. Gendron, the West. Mord, the Southern front. Hope, stay to the middle and provide cover with your bow." Seeing my confusion as everyone scurried into position, Ephriam grabbed me by the arm. "Hunter, stay close to me."

The sound of swords, spears, and maces filled the court as warriors from both sides readied for the confrontation. Still, the enemy did not advance, but instead waited. *Waited for what?*

An iron groan drew our attention to the North wall. A large sliding gate was slowly lifting to reveal a darkened tunnel. The Shadow warriors in front parted formation to make way for what was to come. I prepared myself for the worst.

"Hold your ground, men," Ephriam commanded, taking charge of the situation. A lone figure emerged from the darkness, hobbling across the stone floor. It was Zeeb, the short, peg-legged aide of Venator. But he was not alone.

A pair of glowing green eyes flickered to life high above him in the shadows.

"Crawwwwww," the unbearable sound of a Scrill reverberated through the night air, piercing our ears with its high-pitched cry. The fearsome beast stepped out of the tunnel and into the moonlight. It seemed much taller in person than it had in my dreams. I shot a terrified look at Hope who shared my concern. This was not going to be easy.

The bloodthirsty creature did not wait for a command, but immediately lowered its head and charged forward with the strength of its mighty forearms. Just like that, the battle had begun.

Our forces scattered to avoid being toppled like bowling pins, but some were too slow. A handful of our men were sent flying into the oncoming Shadow ranks, easily hurled aside with one swipe of the Scrill's giant head.

Mayhem reigned supreme as the wild beast ran rampant through-out the courtyard intent on destroying the Codebearers, smashing any of the Shadow who happened to get underfoot as well. Still, the Shadow warriors didn't hold back, but ran in to attack our dispersed forces. The sound of sword-on-sword rang out.

Sticking close to Ephriam, I watched as he deftly unleashed a skilled combination of strikes to fell three enemy warriors. One of them tumbled armless to the ground next to me. I did my part and finished him off with my sword.

"Incoming!" yelled Ephriam as the Scrill came bowling in from our left. Everybody scrambled out of the way—all except one. He and the Shadow warrior he'd been fighting were crushed instantly under the foot of the monster.

Ephriam picked himself up from the ground and yelled, "Someone slow that beast down!"

Hope took the challenge, releasing a well-aimed arrow that found its mark—embedding in the creature's right eye.

The Scrill howled in agony. Some men from Gendron's unit seized the opportunity, hacking its hind legs with their borrowed weapons. The swords proved useless against the Scrill, deflecting off its thick skin with little effect, except to catch his attention.

"Forget the legs!" Faldyn shouted, having seen their futile attack. But it was too late. The Scrill kicked back in retaliation, slamming them into the far wall, just as it had Faldyn's men in the canyon.

Enraged, Faldyn raced wildly toward the beast, cutting through two Shadow warriors in his way. Timing his jump perfectly, he soared through the air, landing squarely on the creature's neck. The captain reversed his grip on the Veritas Sword, driving it down into the creature's skull with a vengeance. But, before he could deliver the deadly strike, the Scrill flung its head upwards, sending the brave warrior to the sky. Faldyn's falling scream was silenced before he ever reached the ground. The Scrill had swallowed him whole.

"Faldyn! No!" Hope screamed, firing a flurry of light-arrows at the merciless monster. Though most struck true, the tough skin did not allow them to sink deeply. Standing upright, the creature turned to stare down Hope with its one good eye, hungry for more flesh.

"Crawww!"

The ear-splitting shriek cut short when a sweeping blaze of light slashed through the belly of the beast. Neon green blood gushed from the cut. The still-standing Scrill wobbled weakly before its top half slid apart from its bottom half into a pool of its own blood. Standing between the two writhing halves was Captain Faldyn, sword in his hands, dripping in ooze.

"The Scrill has been defeated!" a Codebearer shouted. "Victory will be ours!"

In an instant the momentum of the battle swung to the Codebearers. With renewed hope we took the offense against the Shadow. Led by Captain Ephriam's tactical skill, the Codebearers forced the remaining enemies to one side of the courtyard. Minutes later, the battle was over, with Hope finishing off the last of the retreating guards with her bow.

"Hurray!" I found myself yelling victoriously along with the others' shouts and whoops. It was pure exhilaration.

Looking over the final results of the battle, I was amazed at what we had accomplished, the odds we had overcome. "I can't believe we defeated all of them!" I exclaimed to whoever could hear me.

"Neither can I," came Faldyn's sobering reply. He stepped forward, wiping his sword handle clean as he eyed the walls suspiciously. "I fear the worst is yet to come."

The haunting echoes of a solitary person clapping, choked out our short-lived victory.

"Bravo," spoke the unseen voice once more. "That was all so... entertaining." Far from sounding defeated, Venator continued in a mocking tone, "I'm really quite sad that it's all over. What do you say we do it all over again, hmmm? Only this time, let me 'liven' things up a little."

A sudden chill swept through the courtyard. Looking up, we watched as the sky came alive with a swarm of ghostly green snakes. The spectral forms amassed together into a writhing column that quickly wound its way down to the stone floor, dispersing in a rush across the courtyard. The men nearest the oncoming wave of serpents stumbled in retreat only to watch the snakes pass by harmlessly on their way to their true targets. One by one, the serpents entered the eyes of the dead Shadow guards and even the fallen from our own ranks. Each corpse convulsed upon the arrival of his new spirit and then, with eyes glowing green, began to rise in wooden movements to fight once more.

"Leave our dead and gather to me!" Ephriam shouted, rallying the troops around him as the new threat assembled. "We must defend together!"

Venator's sinister laughter rang out once more as he delighted in our plight.

Gripping her bow, Hope leaped up on top of the dead Scrill's shoulders and began methodically picking off as many of the assembling corpses as she could. As each light-arrow found its mark, green smoke released from the serpent-controlled body as it fell limply to the ground.

"Look!" I shouted, pointing to a handful of new snake spirits streaming down from the sky.

"You've got to be kidding me," Hope complained as they coursed their way through the resurrecting army to reclaim the bodies that Hope had just felled.

"Captain, this is not a fight we can win," one of the men put into words what we all knew to be true. "Though we slay them all, they will keep coming."

"Unless we can stop the source of the spirits," Ephriam reasoned, turning to look me straight in the eye. "Hunter, you…"

"I know," I answered before he could finish. I knew what he had been thinking even before he spoke. The source; it was the Bloodstone that Venator controlled, just as the prophecy had spoken of: "*Half you hold, as if your own, the power in it given.*" Recalling the rest of the prophecy as it related to me, I knew what would have to be done.

"I have to go take back the Bloodstone from Venator," I said with conviction.

"What?" Faldyn interrupted, unaware of my mission, of my place in the prophecy. "That would be suicide!" he objected.

"You don't understand, Faldyn. I never told you that I met with Aviad," I explained. "He spoke from the Bloodstone Prophecy and charged me with retrieving Venator's half of the sacred stone—the source of his power. That's the mission I was on when you found me at the lake."

Faldyn's eyes flashed in anger at my last words, offended that I'd held such important information from a commanding officer—that I had betrayed him.

"He speaks the truth, Faldyn," Ephriam intervened. "Listen."

The captain closed his eyes in an attempt to collect his thoughts. "If that is so, then we have been fighting more than just Venator till now. To leave here without the Bloodstone would be in direct opposition to the Author's will."

"I'm sorry. I should have told you before…" I offered up lamely.

"They're coming!" one of our men shouted out over my apology.

There would be no more time to decide. Faldyn turned back to me, "What do you need?"

"Get me back inside," I said, pointing back to the inner fortress we had fled. "Once I'm in, I have the feeling Venator will find me."

Faldyn nodded knowingly.

Gripping me in an arm lock, Ephriam assured me, "We will not fail you."

Stepping to the front of our battered but brave band, the two valiant captains raised their swords.

"Do not despair, men!" Ephriam admonished. "By fear a man appoints his master. If we perish, let it be in the Author's name!"

The men all raised their weapons in unison and shouted, "For the Way of Truth and Life!" Then, running full-speed toward the oncoming corpse horde, Faldyn and Ephriam led a charge into the heart of the enemy's ranks.

Corpses were laid low once more, with green smoke accompanying every fatal strike. The path our surge cut through the host of Venator's army was impressive indeed, but it was far from enough and came at great cost. For every man we lost, our enemy gained a new recruit. The ghostly green snakes were busy swarming through the battlefield, reviving the fallen to Venator's control. The effect was suffocating. Unless a miracle occurred, we were doomed to be swallowed up by a tide of darkness.

The full moon momentarily flickered as a series of winged forms passed overhead, casting large shadows over our battle. Any terror that had accompanied their arrival was immediately chased away by the welcome sound of feathered wings, and an all too familiar call.

"Creee!" "Creee!" "Craaaa!"

It was a squadron of Thunderbirds.

The new arrivals did not waste time, but immediately swooped down into the thick of the fight.

"Codebearers, drop low!" a young boy's voice commanded from atop the first bird that came rocketing low over the battle scene. I ducked as told, but not before recognizing Philan riding atop Faith, followed closely by his friends. One by one, the mighty birds clobbered the enemy warriors to the ground with their strong wings and fisted talons. Faith even snatched up a few mindless foes, carrying them high over the waterfall and dropping them to a rocky death below.

Not to be outdone, Venator sent the winged members of the Shadow army skyward in an effort to slow the attacks of the Thunderbird riders. Even so, with our new reinforcements the battle was looking to shift back in our favor.

Amidst all the commotion Hope and I easily broke away from the fight and made our way up the staircase and into the fortress unnoticed. Once inside we dashed through the deathly silent halls and corridors, heading for the throne room, searching for Venator.

CHAPTER 23

THE OTHER HALF

The throne room was buried in a coat of blackness, the air thick with dust from the crumbling structure. With no remaining light source in the room, I ignited my sword to illuminate our path through the dangerous rubble. The supernatural flame exposed a scene of utter destruction; the fire-dust had done more damage than I had expected. Ducking under a fallen column we ventured further into the unstable fortress.

"I like what you've done with the place," Hope joked.

"Keep alert," I said, my voice sounding more heroic than I had expected, "Venator could be hiding anywhere."

A flash of light near the head of the room drew our attention toward the platform where the throne once stood. We tiptoed carefully around the splintered table and up the stairs. Once cleverly obscured by the throne, a hidden door in the rock wall had swung open. The passageway behind it led down a winding staircase illuminated by a ghostly green light somewhere far below. Thick cobwebs hung low from the ceiling, and a cold breeze blew out of the doorway.

"I think it's your turn to go first," Hope insisted, reminding me of her promise to let me take the lead this time. The light from my Veritas Sword caused more than a few mice and spiders to shrink back into their holes as we ducked into the stairway and slipped silently down the secret passage.

The foot of the stairs opened onto a small rock platform overlooking a deep cavern. The space was tall and cylindrical, like a deep well carved out of stone. The ceiling, I assumed, was somewhere high above me, untraceable in the darkness. A rough-hewn stairway coiled its way steeply down around the edge of the room. The bottom of the well, far below, was scattered with jagged rock spires, and in the center of it all was a cauldron of fire. The narrow stairs presented a treacherous descent around the room. One misstep and I'd be skewered on one of the spires below. I held my breath until we were safely at the bottom.

"Well, well, well…" Venator's voice mocked, seeming to whisper in my ear at first, then floating away as he continued. "Nice to see you again, Hunter."

His voice traveled in the air like the wind, making it impossible to locate his exact location. The room appeared empty, but I knew he was near.

"I'm here for the Bloodstone," I shouted, surprised at how the cavern echoed and magnified my voice.

"Then by all means, come and get it," he challenged, his voice ringing with cruel intent.

"What now?" I wondered out loud. "It could be a trap."

"Probably, but we don't have another option. Let's spread out," Hope suggested. "He must be hiding behind one of these stone spires." She turned to go, raising her bow in defense.

"Wait," I called out to Hope. She tilted her head in anticipation of my reply, but I couldn't find the right words. The momentary pause caused her to lower her brow in concern.

"What is it?" she asked.

"Just…be careful!" I said, hoping I didn't sound too worried.

"Aren't I always?" she smiled back with understanding. We moved up the west half of the room slowly, engaging in a deadly game of cat and mouse with our unseen stalker. Spire by spire, we searched the room, making our way around the perimeter.

"How quaint…" Venator's voice mocked. "It appears I underestimated you, Hunter. But really, letting a girl do your dirty work, you could have done better."

"Show yourself, Venator!" I shouted bravely, tired of the hunt but not really wanting him to appear, "unless you're afraid."

"No," came the voice, "not afraid, just waiting…"

I wanted to ask, *Waiting for what?* but I wasn't interested in playing games with him. Maybe he was wounded in the fire-dust explosion and was waiting to recover. I stuck to that thought and let it embolden my approach.

"Do you really think you can beat me?" Venator's voice rang out once again.

"I know I can, just as the Author has prophesied."

Venator laughed at my claim. "The Author's words do not scare me, boy. I am a free man. He has no control over my fate any longer. The Bloodstone gives me the power to do whatever I want."

"You're wrong. The Bloodstone was cursed; it will kill you, Venator. As long as you hold it you'll never be free, you're a slave to it."

"A curse? Is that what the old fool told you? Yes, I can see why he would want you to believe there is a curse; he doesn't want you to know the truth. He didn't tell you *why* he wanted it, did he, Hunter?"

Come to think of it, he actually hadn't. All I knew was that I was supposed to take the stone and return it to Aviad. Once both halves had been recovered, he was going to rid me of the Shadow's hold on my life somehow.

"Your silence is answer enough," Venator continued. "The Bloodstone's power is envied by all who learn of it, even the old man. Don't you get it? He is using you, Hunter. He needs you to bring him the stone so he can control your life. He wants to make you the Author's slave."

Hope spoke for the first time. "Don't listen to him, Hunter. He's lying."

"Am I?" Venator's voice challenged. "Then how is it that you are here, and he isn't? He doesn't care if you live or die, he's *just…using…you.*"

"Enough!" I shouted, rounding another spire only to find the space behind it empty as well. Venator's voice was getting on my nerves. "Where are you?" I called in anger.

"Here I am," his voice came from a rocky formation on my right. I plastered my sword into the side of the stone, sending a spray of rubble across the floor, but no one was there.

"No, over here," he called again, from the shadows on the left. I caught a flash of movement in the darkness and made my way slowly to the place. The pain in my chest began again. He was close, very close. A shadow passed behind me, and he whispered in my ear, "I am here."

I spun around and plunged my sword into the midsection of my attacker. Only too late did I realize what I had done—I was staring into the pained and frightened face of Hope. She swayed for a moment and then gazed downward. I saw the Veritas Sword protruding from her stomach.

"Hunter?" she asked with a furrowed brow.

With trembling hands I let go of the sword, and she dropped to the ground.

"Hope—no—not like this!" I cried, falling beside her in a heap. "Hope, no, don't die, you can't die—I didn't mean to…"

Her eyes searched for mine, and she held up her weakly trembling hand. I clasped it tightly in both of mine.

"Hunter—I…" she gasped deeply for air.

I started sobbing at her weakened state. "I'm here."

"Never alone…" her lips quivered with the words. Her free hand reached for her neck as she strained to breath. With her last ounce of energy she pulled the medallion from her neck once more and held it up.

"Take it…" she whispered in a barely audible voice.

I grabbed the necklace and watched the last breath of life escape her lips. Her head fell to the side and her arms went limp. Hope was gone.

I couldn't move, just holding her brought the only comfort I had left in the world. I would have remained there forever if Venator hadn't intruded on the moment.

"Too bad, isn't it?" he said stepping out of the shadows at last. "The almighty Author didn't care to spare her life."

I didn't move, I closed my eyes and let the rage inside me intensify.

"It's a pity too," he continued, stepping within a few feet of me. "I was so looking forward to watching her suffer. Perhaps now you see what I mean when I say the Author doesn't care."

"You did this!" I groaned, my stomach sick with emotion.

"No, Hunter…you did!" he said.

I had heard enough. In one quick motion, I pulled my sword from Hope's body and swung at the boy. Surprisingly, he was not prepared for the attack. He raised his staff a little too late and my sword connected with its shaft, severing the Bloodstone from the top and sending it flying into the cauldron of fire. I sensed true fear in Venator's blackened eyes for the first time.

I no longer cared about the Bloodstone, all I wanted was revenge. Revenge for Gerwyn. Revenge for Sam. Revenge for Sanctuary, and most of all, revenge for Hope.

I lashed out with the sword in an onslaught of angry strikes. Staggering backward to avoid the blade, Venator retreated as quickly as he could. His only defense was the shattered staff of wood, which he swung helplessly in an attempt to slow my approach. I did not give up, pressing forward and forcing him back into a stone spire. Venator stumbled awkwardly to the side from the collision. Seizing the moment, I whipped the Veritas Sword in an angled attack and smashed the side of his mask, opening a gash in his cheek.

A sudden pain flashed across my own face, and I winced in surprise, raising my hand to my cheek. Venator wiped black blood from his face with his hand and I did the same.

What had I missed?

Venator turned to run away and I swept my blade at his legs, this time catching him on the calf. We both howled in pain and fell to the ground. I looked at my own leg, where an open wound showed black inky blood flowing from it.

"What magic is this?" I yelled in confusion.

"No magic," Venator seethed.

"Then what!" I demanded, trying desperately to heal the wound on my calf with the Veritas Sword, only to find it didn't work this time.

"You still haven't figured it out, have you?"

"Figured out what?"

"Who we really are," he said mysteriously.

I looked up blankly, unsure of what he meant.

"Maybe this will help," he suggested. With a slow hand, Venator removed his now broken skull-mask, revealing the face beneath. Nothing could have prepared me for the horror of what I saw—I was looking into the blackened eyes of my very own face. Only this time, it was not in a mirror. Venator looked exactly like me.

"You see, Hunter, we are one and the same. We are connected," he said at last.

It was too much to take in, too strange for words. The wounds seemed to prove it, but I just couldn't bring myself to believe that I was somehow one with Venator.

"How is this possible?" I choked on the words as they came out.

"Aviad never told you about your true past, did he?"

"He told me you took the stone and that I am the chosen one to take it back," I said, hobbling away from him. My left leg ached from the gash I had placed there and I fell to my knees.

Venator rose and hobbled toward me, favoring his right leg as he followed.

"Convenient. Trust me. He only wants to ruin your life and it serves him well to leave you in the dark. The Bloodstone is the very thing that binds us, Hunter."

"But I didn't take the stone—you did!"

"Did I?"

"Of course you did, I saw it myself. The Author's Writ took me there; I watched you take the stone," I recalled aloud.

"Yes, you were there, but it was your desire to take the stone that created me, Hunter. The book wasn't showing you what I did, it was showing you what *you did*...through me. As a matter of fact, without you, I wouldn't even exist."

His words penetrated my soul in a way no weapon could. I was at a loss for words. Thinking back to the garden, I found some truth in what he said. I *had* wanted the forbidden stone more than anything else I'd ever seen. Even now, as half of it lay nearby in the fire, I began to feel an uncontrollable desire to command its power for myself. Still, I was not going to allow him to blame this on me; *he* had taken the stone. As persuasive as his words were becoming, I willed myself to ignore them.

"I don't believe you," I said, pushing my thoughts aside. On hands and knees I moved feverishly through the darkness toward the cauldron and Venator's half of the Bloodstone. I could feel my chest tightening—a sign that I finally realized meant the Bloodstone was near.

"We are the same, Hunter—two halves of the same person. You made me who I am. You belong with the Shadow, there is no escaping it."

"You're wrong," I said, gazing at the Bloodstone in the center of the mysterious green flames. "Once I find the second half, Aviad will complete the curse and the Shadow's reign will be over."

"But you already have the other half," Venator said with a smile.

I couldn't believe what I was hearing. Did he actually think I was dumb enough to fall for that?

"The other half is hidden in the Lake of the Lost—I saw it myself."

"No it isn't. The other half is hidden *inside you.*"

My heart pounded at his final words. The stone in the fire began to pulse red with life. Somewhere deep within my chest, where my heart should have been, a soft red glow flashed in perfect rhythm with Venator's Bloodstone. I couldn't believe what I was seeing; it was the other half, hidden inside me that now shone through my skin. The Bloodstone wasn't hidden in the lake as I'd thought; it was hidden in me. What I had seen in the surface of the waters was merely a reflection of the stone, buried in my own body.

The words of the prophesy came to life in a new light. I was the "body, dark and cold."

"But…but…" I fumbled for words.

"Ironic, isn't it?" Venator interrupted. "The very thing you have been looking for has been inside you all along. I hid it there when we escaped from the garden, when *you* stole the Bloodstone."

As he continued to speak, I found myself staring down at my own glowing chest in disbelief.

"Now perhaps you understand," he continued, "why we are united by the curse. We are the same person. You are to blame as much as I, Hunter. We are one."

No longer could I dismiss his threats as the ranting of a lunatic. The evidence was too strong to deny. The black blood, my darkened reflection—all of it pointed to the truth that I was cursed by the Bloodstone and somehow connected to the Shadow, connected to Venator.

"I'm cursed?" I whispered, struggling to comprehend the weight of the situation.

"Oh, it's not so bad," Venator said in an almost sympathetic tone. He inched even closer to where I sat. "The Bloodstone offers much more than a curse," he said mysteriously. "It also brings power…true power. Think of it, Hunter. As long as the Bloodstone remains broken it is yours to command. Imagine what you could do with a power so great."

I thought about what it must be like to be as strong as Venator—to use the power he'd obtained to get even with those who had wronged me. I pictured myself confronting Cranton with newfound confidence and throwing him into the dumpster as he deserved. A satisfied smile crossed my lips.

Suddenly, a surge of energy blazed within me, racing through my body, down my arms, to the tips of my fingers. The sensation was almost electric and yet I felt no pain.

"You can sense it now, can't you?" Venator asked.

I looked up, surprised to find he was now standing directly above me. I had been so mesmerized by his words, so caught up in my own visions of grandeur, that I hadn't even noticed he had come so close.

"Stand back!" I shouted, thrusting my hand out toward him. To my shock a red surge of light flashed from my palm, hurling Venator backward with amazing force. His body slammed into a spire and fell to the floor just as I'd intended. I looked down at my own hand in amazement. The power of the Bloodstone was alive within me.

I expected Venator to be angry with my newfound power, but he stood up in sheer delight.

"Very good," he laughed. "Now you see who you truly are—a god like me!"

"Stay away!" I shouted once more, threatening to send him flying again if he chose to step closer. He raised his hands, palms out toward me as if in surrender, a sign he intended no harm.

"You don't want to fight me," Venator reasoned. "You would only be hurting yourself. Accept who you are and join the Shadow in our cause. We were meant to rule together. I can teach you how to use the Bloodstone's power to do even greater things."

"Like what?" I demanded.

"Like bringing the dead to life," he offered.

Immediately my eyes shot to where Hope lay motionless on the floor, her stomach ripped open from the wound I had inflicted. The guilt of what I'd done hung heavy on me; the thought of bringing her back and undoing my mistake was too much to resist.

"You can…I mean…*I* can do that?"

"Of course," Venator assured me, "the Shadow are very adept at keeping the dead alive."

I had never imagined wanting to work with the Shadow, but now there was nothing I wanted more than to fix what I had done to Hope. In that moment I felt no allegiance to any cause, no reason to resist. I was ready to commit myself to learning the power of the Bloodstone for Hope's sake, even if it meant listening to Venator for the time being.

"Show me how!" I replied at last.

Venator smiled with obvious pleasure at my chosen path. "There is something you must do first."

"What now," I groaned.

"The book," he replied. "I need you to destroy it."

"What do you mean?" I asked suspiciously.

"It's just a simple statement of your allegiance to the Shadow," he reasoned.

"Destroy the book..." I was vaguely reminded of the phrase I had once heard whispered in my room. "Why should I?"

Venator was annoyed by the question. He tightened his fists into balls and tried his best not to sound angry.

"If you don't the Codebearers will keep coming for you. Destroying the book will sever the Author's hold on your life once and for all."

"But the book was my link to this world. If I destroy it how will I ever go home?" I asked.

"You don't need the book; it is only one of many paths to and from Solandria. Trust me, with the Bloodstone you can make your own way between the worlds."

"But the Codebearers, my friends, they..."

"They are misguided fools who believe in an almighty Author who seems to delight in the suffering of good people. Have you ever thought about that? If he is so good and so powerful, why doesn't he show himself? Why should the Author of this book be the only one who decides who lives or dies?"

"I don't know..." I was about to say more, but Venator did not let me continue.

"Think of it, Hunter. With the Bloodstone you'll be able to write your own future. You can undo what has been done. Until you release the book's hold on you, the full power of the Bloodstone can never be yours. You'll never learn how to bring Hope back on your own."

I found the book and clutched it tightly in my hands.

"Go ahead, Hunter. Drop it in the flames and be done with this story once and for all," Venator urged. "Take control of your life."

His words inspired me to believe that maybe, just maybe I could indeed write my own future. Slowly, I moved toward the fire pit and held the book out over the flames. In that moment I thought back over all of the adventures I'd had since the book had found me. Amidst all the difficulties my journey had brought, I'd learned some pretty incredible things about myself. And I had made some amazing new friends along the way too.

The light from the fire reflected off the golden embossing on the back of the book, giving it the appearance of movement and life once more. I looked closer and noticed the arrow was moving steadily toward the eleventh symbol on the dial. I took a second look.

Suddenly, what I used to think were random scribbles took on new meaning. They were pictographs representing the stages of my journey, each one lining up with an event in the story of my life.

With a surge of excitement, I studied the outer dial in a clockwise manner.

The first symbol is easy, definitely a book. The second is a lake; could that be the Lake of the Lost? The third symbol is a door in the woods, the entry to Sanctuary, of course! The fourth looks like a T; no wait, there's more to it, the hilt of a sword—my Veritas Sword. The next two are easy; the fifth symbol is obviously a dragon and the sixth a bird, Faith. But the seventh…now this one is a little more difficult to decipher. As I thought back over my journey it became more obvious…*a prison perhaps? Yes, Belac's prison where I met Stretch.*

I could hardly contain myself now as I followed the rest of the symbols. *The eighth is a letter of some kind…an A…for Aviad. The ninth is a serpent. The tenth is a castle, Venator's stronghold; and the eleventh….*

My heart skipped a beat as I focused on identifying the symbol the arrow had just slid to a moment ago. It was the Bloodstone, the two halves being united. The twelfth and final symbol was unrecognizable; try as I might I could not decipher it, but it didn't matter. The message was clear; the Author had been in control of my fate the entire time. There was no second guessing; there were no surprises.

The story was moving forward in perfect time with his plan. The thought of it chilled me to the bone. The idea that somebody, somewhere knew exactly what I was going to go through even before I did scared me.

"Well, what are you waiting for?" Venator urged me. "Drop it! Do it now!"

I lowered the book and gazed into the fire. A gleam of red light caught my attention in the flames. The other half of the Bloodstone was calling to me, beckoning me to hold it, to fulfill my purpose. The book had predicted what I would do; the Author had wanted this all along. The only question that remained was…did I want to do what the Author had planned for me?

"I can't," I said at last. "I don't want to!"

"Don't be a fool!" Venator demanded, obviously enraged that I was having second thoughts. But his threats were powerless now; without the Bloodstone he was no more than a boy.

I resolutely put the book in my pack and set my sights on the fire once more. With the power of the Bloodstone surging through my veins, I was determined to retrieve the half that lay in the middle of the pit. As I reached my hand toward the stone it began to rise out of the flames, spinning slowly through the air as it hovered over the fire in response to my will.

"What do you think you're doing?" Venator asked nervously. "Leave the stone alone!"

I paid no attention to him; nobody was going to tell me what to do. I was calling the shots and my mind was already made up.

The stone floated over to my hand, stopping just short of my touch. Without a word I turned and began to walk toward the stairs to leave.

"Stop! You can't just walk away." I sensed desperation in Venator's voice for the first time. "What are you going to do with the stone?"

"I'm going to hide it," I replied, "somewhere it will never be found again, by you or anyone else. Your reign is over, Venator, and there's nothing you can do about it. The power of the stone will be mine, and mine alone. I don't need the Shadow, and I don't need the Author. I am my own master."

Before I could speak another word, the stone above my hand flashed with a brilliant angry light. It dropped into my hand, clinging to it like a magnet. At first it felt cool to the touch, then began to burn terribly hot, scorching itself into my palm.

"Aaaahhhh!" I cried out in pain, dropping my Veritas Sword to the ground. Instinctively, I reached with my free hand to pry the stone away. Instead, when I touched the glowing gem with my other hand, it bonded to the Bloodstone as well. There was no use fighting; the stone was having its way with me.

A pulse of energy shot through my arms, creating a conduit between the Bloodstone in my hands and the half in my chest. Suddenly, I was reminded of the vision I had seen of the thief in the garden. My confidence faded and I knew in an instant things were about to go terribly wrong.

CHAPTER 24

THE DEATH OF HUNTER BROWN

T ry as I might, I could not release the stone. I fell to my knees, screaming in pain as Venator watched in horror.

"You fool, look what you've done…death is coming for both of us!" Venator cried out in a terror-stricken voice.

I held my breath as the phantom serpent emerged from the stone in my hands, just as it had in my vision long ago. Wrapping its coils around my body the evil spirit wound toward my face, raising its ugly head inches from my own. Its blazing eyes seemed to sear into my soul, whispering words that were mine alone to hear.

"Foolish ssssslave."

I cringed in fear, expecting to feel its fangs in my neck at any moment, but when I shut my eyes I was looking back at my own terrified face, hued in red. I was seeing myself through the eyes of the serpent. Terrified by the out-of-body experience, I wrenched open my eyes again to find the scarlet phantom was still staring back at me, only inches from my face.

"Yesssss, your ssssoul is mine."

The serpent began to grow, reaching monstrous proportions.

"Hunter? What are you doing?" a voice interrupted from above. "What's happening to you?" The serpent's eyes fixed on the unwelcome guests. Faldyn and a few Codebearers had barged into the lair, swords at the ready, rushing down the stairs to my defense.

A painful surge of energy flowed through the Bloodstone, robbing me of breath. In a flash of light the scarlet serpent broke free from the Bloodstone and took to the air like a ghost. My eyes locked shut in sheer agony at the separation and I screamed.

With my eyes closed, I was forced to watch through the reddened vision of the serpent as it lunged at Faldyn. The captain slashed out bravely with his Veritas Sword, but the serpent was too powerful for him, hurtling him down the precarious staircase. The remaining men were quickly snapped up in the deadly jaws of the scarlet snake. I watched through the serpent's eyes as its ghostly form again took to the air and flew out of Venator's lair, coursing along the spiraled stairs, across the throne room, out to the battle raging beyond.

The fury of the Bloodstone curse had been released in me and I was powerless to stop it. The ghostly giant snake flew over the courtyard battle. For the moment, the Codebearer army had continued to successfully stave off the endless supply of corpse warriors. The night sky was full of Gorewings and Thunderbirds engaged in fierce aerial combat.

The battle slowed for a moment as all eyes fixed on the gigantic phantom serpent that had just emerged on the scene. A single Thunderbird passed in front of my view and in a quick snap of its jaws the snake swallowed it whole. Venator's warriors began to cheer with excitement at the arrival of what they thought to be their new ally. But their celebration was short-lived as the serpent struck with deadly speed and snapped up two Shadow warriors. Clearly, the monster held no loyalties.

Suddenly, the battle disintegrated into complete and utter chaos. It was every man, woman and beast for himself, in a desperate race to escape the deadly monster. The snake began to ravage the battle-grounds, consuming all that fell in its path.

With great effort I finally was able to open my eyes, shielding myself from the horror I had been forced to witness through the serpent's vision.

"Help me," I pleaded, looking to Venator, my voice weak and thin.

He offered no consolation, choosing instead to make a mad dash up the steps in a cowardly escape. I was left alone to face the Bloodstone's doom.

"Ahhhh!" I wailed as another shock of pain surged between the two halves of the Bloodstone. My eyes closed for a moment, revealing once more the serpent's vision of the terrible things unfolding outside. Another unlucky Shadow warrior was swallowed whole as the snake lurched headlong into the fleeing masses. Whipping around through the courtyard, the serpent quickly cornered a small gathering of Codebearers, their swords raised high in defense. As it rose to strike, a hailstorm of rocks and sticks began flying through the air just in front of the serpent's face.

Out of the corner of its eye, I spotted three valiant Codebearers along the wall of the stronghold, trying to attract the attention of the snake. I recognized Philan, Alice and Ollie at once. *What were they thinking?*

"Thith way, you overthuffed worm!" Alice shouted at the top of her lungs. In no time at all the snake's fiery eyes glared at the foolish children, giving the cornered Codebearers time to escape. The distracted serpent flew across the courtyard toward the wall where the retreating children ran.

Philan led the way with Alice close behind, pulling Ollie along with her and ducking into a doorway that was too small for the snake to enter. The snake hissed in fury at its illusive prey. But the beast was not put-off for long; it just coiled itself around the tower and squeezed with deadly force. The stonework crumbled beneath the strength of the snake, exposing the children inside and trapping them beneath a pile of rubble. As if on cue, a swarm of Thunderbirds swirled around the serpent's head like pesky flies, keeping it from the wounded warriors inside.

I knew the Codebearers' distractions could not last forever, and my heart plummeted at the thought of Philan and his friends paying for my crimes. I had to find a way to release the stone and break the deadly curse, but how? Try as I might I was powerless against its grip on me. There was only one thing I knew to do.

"Aviad," I whispered at first; then shouted the name that the Shadow feared. "Aviad, help me!" The name echoed through the air and the fortress rumbled at the sound.

"I am here," a voice called out beside me. My eyes shot open in response to Aviad's voice. "I'm here to end this." His sharp blue eyes showed a mixture of determination and sadness. There was so much more to this "feeble old man" now crouched beside me. His appearance in this place, at this exact moment, told me all I needed to know.

He *was* the Author's son and he knew what I had done. His eyes held so many secrets behind their gaze, I was almost afraid to look into them, afraid of what he might see in me. This was not, after all, one of my finest moments.

"Why didn't you tell me who I was?" I groaned through the pain, looking straight into his piercing eyes.

"Because you had to see for yourself. Until now you wouldn't have understood the evil that was hidden within you." He paused to let his point sink in and studied me with thick bushy eyebrows raised in concern.

I swallowed hard. "But I'm not evil. There is good in me too."

"Being good and doing good are two entirely different things. Now, give me the Bloodstone and let me finish your mission."

Suddenly and without reason my emotions shifted, turning angry at the man I'd called out to only a moment before. Even now, in the midst of my pain, the idea of letting someone else take control of the Bloodstone seemed unthinkable.

"You set me up!" I yelled angrily. "You want the Bloodstone so you can control its power for yourself."

My words pained him.

"You're wrong. I want to free you, Hunter," he calmly replied.

"No! You want to make me the Author's slave," I fought back. "You want me to follow whatever he says. I want to be free like Venator."

"Venator isn't free; he is Sceleris' slave and so are you! You know this, Hunter. Don't you see what is happening to you?"

Another jolt of pain shook my body, emphasizing his point. The Bloodstone was starting to take its toll on me. I knew I was losing control.

"Please, you have to trust me," Aviad offered. "There isn't much time, let me help you."

"It's too late," I whimpered. "I can't let go."

"It's never too late," Aviad smiled. "I can take the Bloodstone from you if you let me, but I need both halves to complete the curse. One you hold in your hand and the other is your heart!"

The thought of surrendering my heart seemed impossible. How would he take my heart without killing me in the process?

"Yes, you will die," he answered before I could ask. "But to be free from the Shadow, you will have to come to the end of yourself. That is the only way to finish the curse."

"But I'll be dead!" I said, trying to remind him of the obvious. I almost felt silly for mentioning it. "Isn't there another way?"

"I'm afraid not, but even if you chose to keep the stone it would kill you eventually, Hunter. Remember who we serve. If you give me your heart, the Author can write you into a new story—one in which you'll no longer be a captive to the Bloodstone's curse and the Shadow's hold on you."

I pondered the situation. What he was saying was true. Clearly the Bloodstone had no intention of letting go until I was dead. I could already feel my strength fading as another burst of pain shocked my heart, causing it to skip a beat.

"So, what is your choice?" Aviad asked at last.

"Do I really have a choice?" I questioned.

At this he simply smiled.

"Choice is a tricky thing," he admitted. "The question isn't whether or not the Author knows what you're going to choose. That is a mystery you were not meant to fully understand. What is important to remember is this. He didn't bring you through all of this to abandon you. The answer you are looking for doesn't lie in logic, Hunter; it lies in faith and trust. The truth is that the choice you make right now will affect what the next page of your story holds. You will live with the consequences of that choice forever."

I swallowed hard, aware of the finality of this decision. If the Author could create me, surely he could rewrite me as Aviad promised. But would he keep his word?

"So what will it be?" Aviad continued. "You've come this far in the story, do you want to see how it ends together? Will you trust me with your heart?"

The moment of truth had come. What would I decide? I could hardly bring myself to say the words.

"Finish it. Take my heart," I said at last, raising my hands toward him.

"Excellent choice," he said, smiling mysteriously. I detected the hint of a tear in the corner of his eye as he pulled the Bloodstone from my grasp.

Closing my eyes, I became one with the serpent once more. The snake turned its gaze back toward Venator's stronghold, sensing what was going on. The creature flew away from the crumbled tower and the three helpless morsels that remained inside. With a howling hiss it sped through the air and headed back for the throne room to face its new and final threat.

I opened my eyes once more just in time to watch as Aviad reached out toward my chest. My heart raced at the thought of what was coming next. With gentle skill Aviad plunged his ancient hand into my body. The sight of his hand in my chest was shocking, to say the least; but surprisingly, I felt no pain. Streams of light burst from around the corners of his wrist. As he pulled the other half of the bloodstone from my chest, my body began to fade away into a transparent state. It was as if the Bloodstone was the very thing that gave me form. Now that it was in the hands of another, I was only a hollow shell of what I was before.

I couldn't speak or act, allowed only to watch as the final moments of my life unfolded. Aviad now held both halves of the stone in his hands. What he did next amazed me.

Combining the stones he plunged them into his own chest, uniting them within himself to complete the curse at last. Just then, the phantom snake burst back into the room, squirming uncomfortably at the exchange.

Aviad clutched his chest in agony as the united Bloodstone burned to life. He threw his arms out and looked skyward, surrendering himself to the power of the curse inside him. A thousand scarlet rays of light exploded from within and Aviad was lifted from the floor, arms outstretched, held in a state of suspended animation, spinning slowly above the ground.

The snake reeled at the sight, towering high above Aviad. "Thisss isss not the end," the snake hissed. Then, in one final act, the creature lunged at Aviad, bearing its fangs in a fatal attack.

An explosion of light lit the space and the two vanished completely. The battle was over.

Aviad was gone.

With the curse fulfilled, the power of the Bloodstone died with it and I began to fade away. But before I could disappear completely, a lonely echo of footsteps crossed the room. Faldyn had regained consciousness and hobbled over to where Hope lay. The last thing I remember was watching him hoist Hope carefully onto his shoulders, carrying her back toward the staircase.

Then, everything went black.

CHAPTER 25

BETWEEN THE PAGES

Surrounded by a blanket of darkness I remained aware of life, but somehow separated from it. At first I couldn't see anything. I couldn't feel anything. All I knew was that I was alone, my consciousness suspended in a place of nothingness, like floating in a bottle of black ink.

How much time had passed was impossible to say; there was no way to measure it and I had no desire to do so. Gradually, I became aware of an interruption to my solitude. The solemn glow of a single candle illuminated a freshly bound leather book, spread open on a wooden desk. The desk was unoccupied, but alive with movement. A feather quill bobbed across the book's pages as if someone unseen was using it to write. With precise and perfect strokes the quill made its marks, leaving behind an inky text in a language completely foreign to any I'd ever seen. A moment later the quill stopped, seemingly midsentence, and hopped across the desk to dip itself in a container of red ink.

Mesmerized by the sight of the mysterious quill, I watched for an indeterminable amount of time before I finally found my voice.

"Hello? Is…someone there?" I ventured.

"Yes. Hello, Hunter; I'm glad you're here," replied a Voice.

"Who are you?"

"I am the Author." The mention of the name stirred my soul. His voice was deep and strong, surrounding me in his presence. Then it hit me. If I was dead, how could the Author be here? And where was here anyway?

I gathered my courage to ask. "What happened? Where am I?"

"We are in the space between pages, Hunter," he said matter-of-factly.

"Are we dead?" I asked as I watched the quill scribble another line of text on the page.

The Author's voice chuckled lovingly at the question, like one laughs at a child who asks something completely absurd.

"Me? Dead? Heaven's no. I can't die."

"But what about me? Didn't I die?"

"You did die."

"So why am I here?"

"It is sufficient to say the first volume of your life has come to an end, and the real adventure is about to begin. In a way," he answered curiously, "you were never truly alive to begin with."

I looked down at myself and suddenly realized I didn't exist. I was aware of everything around me, I could hear, sense, see, and think, but there was nothing to contain me, no body to call my own. It was all very disturbing. Even after the Bloodstone had been taken and my physical form faded into a ghostly glow, I'd felt some level of comfort from the phantom state I was in. This, however, was different. I wasn't there at all.

"Why can't I see myself?" I asked in shock.

"Because your life is being rewritten—watch and see!"

Slowly, bit by bit as the Author's quill wrote on the pages of the book, I saw myself being formed. My body appeared out of nothing and I was a being once more.

"That should do it. Yes, I think that is perfect."

When he was finished I was whole again. I felt new.

"Well, how does it feel to be really alive?" the Author's voice asked.

I was at a loss for words. An awkward moment passed as I stumbled over my thoughts.

"Alive…er…new…uh…what I mean is…thank you!"

Apparently my ability to make a bad first impression hadn't been removed with the rewriting.

The voice chuckled again. "It was my pleasure!"

I realized in that moment there was much more at work here than I could possibly imagine. Before, I had thought all was lost, but now I knew the Author could do anything—I had chosen to put my trust in the right person after all. My joy was cut short only by the sudden remembrance of what had happened to the others I'd left behind. Hope was dead and Sam too.

"What's wrong, Hunter?" he asked, though I was sure he knew already what was on my mind.

"I was just wondering; why didn't you save Hope, Sam or Gerwyn?"

"Sometimes the darkness helps us see the light."

"What do you mean?"

"Everything for a purpose, Hunter," the Author reminded me. As he said it, Sam's words came suddenly to my mind—the words he'd told me after Gerwyn died. It was as if Sam's voice was speaking to me from somewhere far away.

No matter the circumstance, we can find joy in knowin' that he has a greater purpose in all things. There is power in that truth, Hunter—a great, freeing power.

Sam's voice sounded so real and alive I almost wanted to look for him.

"You see, Hunter, while there will be some who no longer play a role in the pages you travel, I can assure you those who have been rewritten will never truly die. No, they are at the beginning of a new and wonderful story, one in which there will be no ending, and every page is better and more beautiful than the one before."

A moment of silence passed as the Author let the memory of my fallen friends and their suffering sink in. Their memory held no sadness anymore; it had been completely replaced with peace. Peace in knowing that Hope, Sam and even Gerwyn were in the hands of someone who knew their future and had a purpose for them.

I looked back to where the Author was seated, and even though I couldn't see him I sensed his face now held a broad smile, as if he saw something in me that made him proud.

"What?" I asked.

"You will bear my Code well," he said with assurance.

I smiled back.

I was part of a new family. I was a Codebearer.

The strange clock that had once sat in the corner of the bookshop interrupted the moment with a loud chime. The arrow hand was pointing to the twelfth symbol, which I recognized at last—a quill.

"It's time. Are you ready to go back now?"

"Back where?"

"I have a special job for you, Hunter. I need you to go back to the Veil. There are many who still do not know about the secret of the Shadow, and I want you to tell them."

"You want me to go back there?" I was actually somewhat disappointed at the prospect of going back home. The things I'd done, the adventures I'd been on, and the friends I'd made were far too exciting to leave behind.

"It's where your next adventure begins, the first of many—you can be sure of that. Your friends need you; the Veil is growing darker by the day. Sceleris is extending his power in that realm even as we speak."

"Will I ever go back to Solandria?"

"That is something you're going to have to find out for yourself. The door is always open when you have faith. Well, you better get going. There's a pretty amazing story waiting for you! A few surprises too."

With that the Author blew out the candle that lit the room and everything disappeared once more. In the emptiness of time and space, his last words echoed through the caverns of my mind.

"Remember, you are never alone!"

Dear Reader,

As everyone knows, the best part about going on an extraordinary adventure is being able to share it with family and friends later—in my case that was not to be.

As I regained consciousness I found myself lying in the very same grave Stretch and I had fallen into the night of the Dispirit attack. I was back in the Veil. Back in Destiny, my home. It was the dead of night and Stretch was nowhere to be found, but luckily neither were the Dispirits. I gathered the Author's Writ and my video camera and clambered out of the grave. As I emerged, I was happy to find Stretch only a few steps ahead of me.

As it turned out, hardly any time had passed since Stretch and I had left.

Sadly, the only thing Stretch remembered was running across the graveyard and falling into the hole. He had no memory of Solandria at all. As far as he was concerned, we had imagined the whole Dispirit thing and he quickly adopted the "book is cursed" attitude Stubbs had first suggested.

Of course, I had hoped the footage we'd taken of the Dispirits' fight would prove what I remembered was true. Unfortunately, the only thing it showed was Evan, an old man in a robe, swinging an imaginary sword wildly in the air, in the middle of a street. The Dispirits remained invisible to the camera. To anyone who hadn't been there, it simply looked like I had taped a drunken madman fighting off an invisible enemy. I was disappointed to say the least.

Thankfully, Dad's broken watch was still in my pocket, along with Hope's medallion. They were the only real evidence I had to remind me that what I had experienced was, in fact, real. Whenever I look at the watch, I wonder what became of my dad. Maybe someday the Author will let me find out.

When Mom found I'd left the house, I was grounded for a whole week. I'm not sure it was completely fair, but I served my time and eventually emerged from my room to enjoy what remained of the summer.

I read the Author's Writ as often as I could, learning new things about the history of Solandria, its connection to the Veil and a whole lot about me too.

I guess there are just some things in life, good and bad that the Author allows to happen for a reason—things that move the story of our lives forward in strange and unexpected ways. Just because we can't understand at the time, doesn't mean the story isn't ultimately good. In fact, I don't think the true worth of a story can be fully judged until the final chapter is written.

As for me and my adventures, well, let's just say they aren't over yet. In fact not too long after school started I received a mysterious letter from an unexpected friend.

I can't spell out the contents of the message here, for fear this book may fall into the wrong hands. But I have posted it online, where the Codebearers meet, in hopes you will discover it. Hidden in the book you have just read are the clues you'll need to decipher the cryptic message for yourself. Please keep it in the strictest of confidence and under no circumstances leave the message out in plain sight. The lives of others could be at stake.

We are never alone,

Hunter